'Fresh and compelling . . . The prose is sharp, the characterisation even sharper . . . Higgins looks at the difficult moment of becoming parents with an unflinching but powerful humanity . . . A top-shelf novel about contemporary Australian life.'

The Weekend Australian

'. . . an enthralling read. Be prepared to burn the midnight oil, as it is impossible to put down.'

Sunday Herald Sun

'. . . a compelling insight into the modern family . . . it's hard to put down because it's just so *real* . . . I almost felt part of the group, getting to know them and sharing their inner thoughts, feeling their pain, frustration and confusion.'

WriteNoteReviews.com

'An insightful and sensitively written novel that will resonate with many new (and less new) parents.'

The Age

'I'm completely blown away . . . Make yourself comfortable before you start reading this book because you won't be putting it down . . . *The Mothers' Group* is the kind of book that stays with you long after you've read the final pages. Buy it, share it, and fall in love with it like I did.'

The Bub Hub

'. . . a compelling insight to the modern family . . . Honest and perceptive . . . the kind of book that will make the reader forget that dinner needs to be cooked. It's hard to put down because it's just so real . . . I almost felt part of the group, getting to know them and sharing their inner thoughts, feeling their pain, frustration and confusion. For mothers of all ages, all experiences—read this . . . It's a book

I will read again and I'm looking forward to reading more from Higgins.'

Write Note Reviews

'. . . this is a story that immediately rings true when it comes to real-life motherhood . . . This book grabbed me immediately because I've been there . . . I've felt the pain and the joy and shared the experiences with my own eclectic group of first-time mums . . . I felt like I was on the same level as the character—sharing in their world. Then before you even realise it you get pulled into the storyline and you can't put it down. *Brilliant.*'

The Truth About Mummy

'I never just stop and read. But this book had me hook, line and sinker . . . I loved it . . . It is funny, sad, thought-provoking and has fantastic twists in the plot that make you keep on reading.'

Woog's World

'Six mothers brought together by their babies and almost driven apart by unforeseen developments and events. I joined their group for two days and got the inside scoop on all the stuff we don't always talk about as mothers. Taboo subjects, controversial debates, differences of opinion. I could not put the book down and mourned the loss of my new-found friends when I turned to the last page . . . This is a book that any mother can relate to, whether she has a mothers' group or not.'

Crash Test Mummy

'. . . an engrossing story which slowly reveals each character's multi-layered background before leading to an incident that shatters them all.'

The Weekend West

The Mothers' Group

The Mothers' Group

FIONA HIGGINS

ALLEN&UNWIN
SYDNEY • MELBOURNE • AUCKLAND • LONDON

Allen & Unwin

83 Alexander Street
Crows Nest NSW 2065
Australia
Phone: (61 2) 8425 0100
Fax: (61 2) 9906 2218
Email: info@allenandunwin.com
Web: www.allenandunwin.com

Cataloguing-in-Publication details are available from the National Library of Australia
www.trove.nla.gov.au

ISBN 978 1 925 575 118

Internal design by Lisa White
Set in 11/16 pt Minion Regular by Post Pre-press Group, Australia

10 9 8 7 6 5 4 3 2 1

For my mother, Lesley, who did a remarkable job of mothering the three of us under very difficult circumstances

The mothers agree that indeed the years do fly. It's the days that don't. The hours, minutes of a single day sometimes just stop. And a mother finds herself standing in the middle of a room wondering. Wondering. Years fly. Of course they do. But a mother can gag on a day.

JAIN SHERRARD

Ginie

She lay naked on the dune, the sand stuck wet against her skin. Seagulls circled, calling to their mates through the sea fog, curling low and languid across the beach.

The smell of rotting seaweed was distracting, even as his tongue and hands moved over her.

She looked down at him, beyond her bare stomach.

Let go, he said. *Let go.*

She arched her back, pulling thousands of grains of sand into tight fists . . .

Startled by a sharp rapping at the front door, Ginie opened her eyes. She blinked, registering where she was. On the couch. In the lounge room. Next to Rose. The dream sprinted away and disappointment plummeted through her. She felt cheated.

Sex had become a thing of the past. Alongside other common pleasures like Sunday morning sleep-ins and uninterrupted showers, Rose's arrival had signalled the abrupt departure of Ginie's sexual appetite. She closed her eyes again, wondering if she'd ever get it back. That delicious sexual abandon with Daniel, a level of intimacy she'd never known before.

The knocking at the door resumed, more insistent now.

For fuck's sake, she thought, I'm tired. Go away.

She glanced at Rose, a soft bundle of pink in an old-fashioned bassinette, a nostalgic gift from her grandmother. The knocking hadn't disturbed the baby at all. Once she was asleep, nothing much did.

Maybe if I just lie quietly, Ginie thought, whoever it is will leave.

She stared at the modern chandelier suspended above her, its crystal beads catching the morning light. What time was it? She couldn't have been asleep for very long. Her laptop was still perched on her knees, cursor flashing in an unfinished email.

She'd been out of hospital for five weeks and Rose was doing everything right. Feeding from a bottle, settling easily, sleeping as well as a newborn could. A textbook baby, so her mother said. As if she'd bloody know.

As usual, thoughts of her mother sent a wave of anger coursing through her. Ginie took a deep breath, attempting to calm herself.

Her Buddhist-leaning life coach had taught her 'mind-fulness', the technique of watching her anger as if she was a third party. It was all part of making peace with her mother's absence during her childhood, apparently. Had Ginie's mother been sick or died, it might have been easier to understand.

But instead, as a primary school principal, her mother had devoted her life to education. She'd worked slavishly during school terms and holidays, ensuring thousands of children reaped the benefit of her dedication. Other people's children, Ginie had sometimes reflected.

When her mother wasn't working, she'd always seemed more occupied with her siblings. Ginie could remember watching her older brother at endless weekend soccer matches, her mother bellowing encouragement until she was hoarse. Or sitting by her side in the rooms of countless specialists, from orthopaedic surgeons to occupational therapists, discussing her younger sister's medical condition. *Hip dysplasia at birth*, her mother had explained to anyone who'd listen. *One of her legs is longer than the other.* Ginie had always been the dutiful middle child, compliant and sensible, playing Best Supporting Actress to her siblings.

But none of that mattered anymore. When Ginie looked at her present life, one thing was sure: it was far superior to that of her siblings. It was *her* time now.

She exhaled, soothed by the thought.

The tapping at the door grew louder.

She glanced again at Rose, certain the noise would wake her.

Through the opaque leadlight panels of their front door, she could discern two figures. Her iPhone flashed an impatient alert: *Daniel (Mobile)*. Her husband again.

I've organised painters for the nursery. They're waiting outside.

She rolled her eyes. *Hopeless prick.*

From the moment they'd discovered she was pregnant, she'd repeatedly asked Daniel to repaint the room for the nursery. She'd been frantic at work, organising the complicated handover required before she went on maternity leave. As the most senior female lawyer at the firm, she earned a hefty salary that allowed Daniel to pursue his writing and photography ventures. Most of which came to nothing.

'I'm tired,' she'd complained to him, eight months into her pregnancy. 'I really need you to repaint the nursery. Please, Daniel.'

'I'll get to it,' came his stock-standard response. 'Trust me.'

And then the baby had arrived, a full month early, and Daniel had run out of time.

Ginie read the message again, then tossed the telephone onto the coffee table.

Angry? she thought. I'm fucking furious.

Rose stirred in her bassinette. A tiny arm reached out of the muslin wrap. Ginie's anger instantly receded. From the moment Rose had been pulled from her body, covered in vernix and squirming in the light, Ginie was smitten. The depths of her newfound tenderness for this tiny mysterious creature had taken her completely by surprise.

For a moment she watched, transfixed, as her daughter's delicate hand grasped at the air. Floating fingers, no bigger than her own fingernails. *My daughter.* She shook her head, marvelling. Just a few months ago, the concept had seemed so abstract. Yet now, here she was, a mother to this living, breathing, milky soft being.

The knocking persisted. Ginie couldn't ignore it any longer.

She glanced at her watch and hauled herself off the couch. The first session of the mothers' group was due to begin. A reminder had arrived from the local baby health centre a week ago but she'd chosen to ignore it. She couldn't imagine anything worse than sitting around with a bunch of women she didn't know, eating biscuits and talking babies. Now, with the painters banging down the door, attending a mothers' group seemed an attractive alternative to watching paint dry.

She opened the front door and directed the tradesmen to the nursery, on the lower floor of their split-level home. Then she placed Rose in the pram and gathered up the nappy bag, a bunny rug and several stuffed toys.

'Nicole, we're going out for an hour or two,' she called up the stairs.

There was no reply. The nanny had arrived from Ireland yesterday, but she still hadn't surfaced. Jetlagged, no doubt.

The baby health centre was at the top of a hill, only a short walk from the car park. Yet the all-terrain baby jogger, purchased by Daniel the week before, was heavier than she could manage. She was forced to stop along the way to catch her breath, her caesarean scar throbbing beneath her jeans. It was a crisp June day, the sky so blue it almost hurt her eyes. Cerulean, Daniel would call it, in his writer's way.

When she arrived at the centre, the mothers' group had already started. She hated running late, for anything. Flustered, she pushed open the glass door with a force that caused it to slam against the adjacent wall. A group of women turned in her direction.

'Sorry,' she mumbled. She turned her back on the group and attempted to pull Rose's pram up the step.

'Shit.' The door was heavy against her back, and the pram unwieldy. I've got a law degree, she thought, and I can't even get a baby jogger through the bloody door.

A woman with honey-coloured hair appeared at her side. 'Let me help,' she offered, holding the door open for Ginie.

'Thanks,' said Ginie, hauling the pram inside. 'I'm still getting the hang of this.'

'Heavy, aren't they? I got mine jammed at the supermarket checkout the other day and a security guard had to help me. I was *so* embarrassed.' The woman grinned at her. 'I'm Cara, by the way.'

'Ginie.'

'Well, hello! Come on in.' A bespectacled silver-haired woman sat at the front of the group, waving a clipboard in Ginie's direction. This must be Pat, the chatty midwife who'd telephoned several weeks earlier to check on her post-natal progress. Ginie had declined her offer of a home visit.

'Have a seat, Ginie,' the woman said, consulting the clipboard and ticking her name off. 'I'm Pat. You're just in time for introductions.'

A dozen chairs were arranged in a semi-circle, but fewer than half were occupied. Most of the seats closest to the door had already been taken. As if the women in them might run from the room at any moment, Ginie chuckled to herself.

Cara returned to her seat, in the middle of the row, and

leaned over a bassinette to check her baby. Ginie steered her pram towards an empty chair on the far side of Pat, sidestepping car capsules and nappy bags. She sat down next to a woman with wavy black hair and startling green eyes, who was attempting to comfort her baby. She smiled at Ginie in a distracted way, while pushing a dummy into the baby's mouth. This only seemed to enrage the infant, all red-faced and writhing in its pram.

'Shhh, Rory, shhh,' the woman soothed. As the baby's cries grew louder, she stood up from her chair and began to push the pram around the room.

'Well,' said Pat. 'Now that everyone's arrived, let's get underway. Welcome.' She smiled. 'You're all here because you've had a baby in the past six weeks *and* you live in the Freshwater or Curl Curl areas. So, let's get to know each other first. I'd like you to tell us your name, your baby's name, and something you'd like to share about your birthing experience. We'll start at the front.' She waved a hand at Ginie.

Ginie shifted in her seat. She was adept at public speaking in corporate settings, but this was different. She felt strangely nervous.

'Okay, I'm Ginie,' she started. 'This is Rose. She's asleep, obviously.' She glanced down at Rose and, for the first time, realised how much she resembled Daniel. They shared the same high cheekbones and sandy-coloured hair. She looked at Pat again; she couldn't remember what else she was supposed to say.

'Would you like to tell us something about your birthing experience?' prompted Pat.

'Oh yes, sorry.'

Birthing. She hadn't properly described the experience to anyone. It was something she'd rather forget.

'Um, I was in labour for fifteen hours, then I ended up having a caesarean.'

Pat nodded, the picture of concern. 'And how did you feel about that?'

Ginie shrugged. 'Relieved, actually. I was bloody glad to get her out.'

Someone giggled.

'Right. Next.' Pat nodded at a voluptuous blonde. Ginie sat back in her chair, grateful the focus had shifted elsewhere.

She hadn't been ready for Rose's arrival at thirty-six weeks. It was seven thirty-five am and she was steering her two-door black BMW across the Spit Bridge, notorious for its peak-hour bottlenecks. At any other time of day, it only took her thirty minutes to drive from her home in Curl Curl to the Sydney CBD, but on this particular morning she'd already spent an hour behind the wheel. She was speaking to a client, leaning towards the hands-free phone on the dashboard, when she felt a sudden warmth between her legs. She glanced down to see light red fluid oozing beneath her, creeping across the cream leather seat. For a moment she stared at it, as if it was a phenomenon disconnected from herself, then she swerved out of her lane and towards the kerb. Flicking on the hazard lights, she'd abruptly ended her call and telephoned Daniel.

'There's something wrong. I'm . . . bleeding all over the car.'

'Just take a breath, Gin,' he'd said. 'Do you think you can keep driving to the hospital?'

'Oh for fuck's sake, Daniel, what do *you* think?'

'Alright, I'll call an ambulance. Where are you exactly?'

The ambulance officers had determined quickly that neither she nor the baby was in danger.

'The baby's kicked a couple of times, so that's a good thing,' said one.

'What about all the blood?' she asked.

'Looks like your placenta has started bleeding,' he said. 'It's quite common at the end of pregnancy. Very soon, you'll be a mum.'

'So close to Mother's Day too,' said the other. 'You planned that well, didn't you?'

Oh yeah, very well, she thought. That's why I'm going to the hospital in an ambulance, propped up on a stretcher, wearing a business suit.

'Trying to give us all a scare, eh?' the obstetrician joked as he attached the CTG machine to her bulging abdomen. 'Let's see what's going on in there.'

The scan indicated that the baby was fine.

'You've had a placental bleed,' he confirmed. 'We'll give it twelve hours and see what happens. But you'll have to stay in hospital, I'm afraid.'

At least she'd brought her laptop.

Several hours later, she felt the first contraction. But after fifteen hours of labour, her cervix was only five centimetres dilated. She was slippery with sweat, exhausted. Daniel stood next to her, offering her water, a cool washer, lip balm. *And what should I do with that?* she wanted to scream at him. *Stuff it up your arse?* Instead, she ignored him, pacing the room and squeezing a cushion as the contractions peaked.

She wished she'd opted for an elective caesarean. At thirty-nine and with private health insurance, she could have demanded one. But a part of her wanted to *conquer* childbirth, as she had conquered all the other challenges in her life to date. An elective caesarean seemed like a cop-out, and Ginie wasn't a quitter.

'Ginie.' The voice came from afar.

She looked up from the cushion and watched the obstetrician mouth the words. 'I'm recommending a caesarean.'

'Okay.' She was beyond caring. She squeezed her eyes shut against another crushing contraction.

The operation was a haze of anaesthesia and bewildering sensations. She was conscious throughout the procedure, with Daniel standing beside her, stroking her hair. Two obstetricians hovered over her abdomen, talking between themselves like pilots landing a jumbo jet.

'I tend to go in here, less vascular,' said one.

'Do you?' replied the other. 'I prefer a more muscle-sparing route.'

She felt suddenly nauseous. 'I think I'm going to die,' she breathed.

The anaesthetist, an impassive man in his fifties, leaned towards her. 'It's just your blood pressure dropping,' he said, not unkindly. 'Let me fix that for you.' He injected a vial of clear liquid into her drip and, almost immediately, she began to feel better.

She clung to Daniel's hand and begged him to talk to her, to drown out the matter-of-fact commentary of the obstetricians.

Suddenly there was some forceful pushing and pulling, as if her insides were being wrenched apart.

She couldn't take any more. 'Daniel, I . . .'

'Here we are,' announced one of the obstetricians.

A bloodied baby floated above her eye line, not even crying. It was a little girl. She was perfect.

Back on the ward, Ginie's pain was intense. The wound itself—incision through skin and muscle—throbbed with even the slightest movement. The painkillers they had given her appeared to be having little effect. She watched with interest as the curtains began to billow of their own accord, swelling in front of the unopened window. It was a narcotic hallucination, she knew, yet the pain was getting worse.

She tried to explain this to an officious-looking midwife at three o'clock in the morning.

'Well,' came the stern reply, 'you're not due for any more pain relief. If you have an *intervention* like a caesarean, it *will* hurt more. Natural births are much easier on the body. Pain is very subjective, dear.' The midwife bustled away.

Ginie was too exhausted to object. Defeated, she lay back on her pillow. Rose was in the nursery; the midwives would bring her in when she woke. Ginie desperately wanted to hold her again, to bury her nose in her folds of soft flesh, but she couldn't even climb out of bed. The noise from the nursery was audible across the corridor. Every time the door opened, the sound of babies crying was like cats mewling in an alley.

Six hours later, Ginie's limbs trembled beneath the blanket, defying all control. Her wound was throbbing, weeping through the cotton pad stuck across her pelvis with surgical tape. Beneath her hospital gown, her nipples were chafed from repeated unsuccessful attempts to clamp Rose to her breast. So much for natural, she'd thought, as a midwife palpated her nipples like a farmhand milking a cow. Nothing much had happened, despite these exertions. A thin watery substance had oozed from her right nipple, which the midwife attempted to capture with a syringe.

'Hello there,' chirped a friendly voice. 'How are you this morning?'

She'd never seen this nurse before, a young woman with red hair. She strode over to the window and threw back the curtains. The sunlight was painful.

The nurse turned to her. 'You're shaking. Are you alright?'

Without warning, Ginie's eyes filled with tears.

'How's your pain?' asked the nurse.

Ginie's voice cracked. 'I've been telling your imbecile colleagues all night. But they're too interested in making sure my milk comes in, never mind my fucking pain.'

The nurse looked taken aback.

Instantly ashamed of her outburst, Ginie began to cry. 'I'm sorry . . .'

'We'll fix that straight away,' said the nurse. She patted Ginie's hand. 'You shouldn't be in that sort of pain, you poor thing. I'll call the anaesthetist and get something stronger written up for you.'

The nurse's kindness caused Ginie to cry harder. She wept into her hands with long, shaking sobs.

'You'll be alright,' said the nurse, passing her a tissue. 'Once you're pain-free, you'll feel so much better about everything.'

Ginie doubted it.

'Hello, everyone. My name's Suzie.'

Ginie started at the sound. The voluptuous blonde pushed a mass of ringlets behind her ears. Her pale blue eyes darted nervously around the room. She couldn't be much older than twenty-five, Ginie guessed.

Suzie glanced into the pram parked next to her. The baby was making loud suckling sounds. 'I think Freya needs a feed,' she said, apologetic. She fumbled with the top buttons of her camel-coloured cardigan, then lifted her baby to her chest.

Ginie looked away, a little embarrassed. Briefly she wondered if *her* chest might have looked like that had she persisted with breastfeeding. But she hadn't. After five futile days of hot packs and breast pumps in the hospital, she'd gone home with a tin of formula and a plastic bottle. 'You've got the lowest milk supply I've seen in years,' one of the nurses had said.

Ginie had been gutted. The benefits of breastfeeding were spruiked from every corner—her obstetrician, her mother, even Daniel was an advocate—and Ginie had just assumed it would all happen effortlessly. No one had considered that she might not be *able* to breastfeed, let alone prepared her for the crushing guilt when she couldn't. Now, watching Suzie feed her baby so naturally, Ginie felt responsible for depriving Rose of the best start in life.

It was hard to tell if the baby was a girl or a boy: it was pudgy and pink, with a white-blonde tuft of hair poking up from its crown.

Suzie cleared her throat. 'My daughter's name is Freya,' she began. 'After the Scandinavian goddess of love.'

Oh God, thought Ginie. Bring on the flower power.

'My partner has Swedish heritage,' she continued. 'My ex-partner, I should say. We separated when I was seven months pregnant. So my birthing experience . . .' Her blue eyes filled with sudden tears. 'I mean, I had the loveliest midwife at the hospital, but . . .' She brought a hand to her mouth and shook her head, unable to continue.

No one moved. Ginie looked at Pat, willing her to intervene. But Pat sat motionless, her head tilted to one side, a contemplative look on her face.

Eventually, someone spoke. 'That must've been hard.'

Ginie turned towards the voice. It was Cara, the woman who'd helped her at the door.

'Do you mind if I go ahead?' she asked.

Suzie nodded, clearly relieved.

'I'm Cara,' she continued. 'And this is Astrid.' She bent over her pram, flipping her thick ponytail over her shoulder. She was attractive in an understated way, with a classic hourglass figure and lively brown eyes. When she smiled, it was hard not to follow suit.

Cara beamed as she held up a chubby, strawberry-blonde baby. Daddy must be a redhead, Ginie mused.

'Astrid was overdue by ten days. So when she finally came along, she was in a bit of hurry.' She shifted Astrid into the crook of her arm and stroked her hair. 'I had my first contraction at six o'clock and she arrived two hours later. It wasn't too painful either, which was a bonus. I guess I was expecting the worst.'

Pat clapped her hands together. 'Wonderful. Was anyone else pleasantly surprised by the birthing experience?'

'Me.' It was the woman Ginie had sat next to earlier. She'd been pushing her pram around the room nonstop.

'I'm Miranda.' She pointed to a muslin cloth covering the pram. 'This is Rory. I don't think I can stop walking him *just yet*.' She peeped under the edge of the cloth, and Ginie caught a glimpse of dark hair. 'Well, at least he's closed his eyes.' She lifted a bottle of water to her lips and swallowed several mouthfuls.

Ginie admired her profile; she was tall and slender, with no trace of baby weight. Her green eyes stood out against translucent skin, peppered with attractive freckles. Her hair fell in black waves over slightly pointed ears, giving her a pixie-like look. Ginie guessed she was in her early thirties. The substantial diamond on her ring finger glinted as she screwed the lid back on to her water bottle.

'And what about your birthing experience, Miranda?' asked Pat.

'Well, I thought it would be horrible.' She shrugged. 'But I quite enjoyed it.'

Ginie wondered how anyone could associate the word *enjoy* with giving birth.

'But, then, I'd done a lot of prenatal yoga and breathing exercises beforehand,' Miranda added, 'which probably helped me move through the contractions.'

Well isn't your life perfect? thought Ginie.

Pat lit up like a Christmas tree. 'And I suppose they've helped with your recovery?'

Miranda shook her head. 'I don't have much time to do yoga anymore. I've got a three-year-old at home too. My husband's son from his first marriage.'

Ginie raised an eyebrow. Perhaps not so perfect after all.

'But do you get a bit of a break when the toddler visits his mum?' Pat asked hopefully.

'No,' said Miranda. 'Digby's mother died when he was six months old.'

God almighty, thought Ginie, rather guiltily.

'Oh.' Pat looked deflated. Then she rallied. 'Well, one of our topics in the coming weeks is "Making Time for You". When there's a demanding older sibling around, it's doubly important to schedule in me-time.'

Miranda didn't look terribly convinced.

Pat glanced around the group. 'So . . . who haven't we done yet?'

A pale, unsmiling woman raised her hand. 'I'm Pippa.'

Her mousy brown hair, pulled back in a tight bun, was oily at the crown. She was diminutive in stature and her high-pitched voice wavered like a child's, but the fine lines around her eyes suggested a woman in her thirties. Her clothes were drab; a shapeless grey skivvy teamed with an ankle-length black skirt.

'That's Heidi asleep in there.' Pippa nodded at an over-sized stroller shrouded in black windproof meshing, through which it was impossible to see the baby. 'My birth experience wasn't pleasant.'

Ginie leaned forward, straining to hear.

'Would you like to share some of it with us?' Pat asked.

'Not really.'

Pat faltered; she clearly wasn't used to such directness.

'Right,' she gushed. 'That's absolutely your prerogative.'

Pippa's hazel eyes were expressionless as she shifted in her seat, smoothing her skirt over her knees.

'Now, lucky last . . .' Pat scanned her clipboard. 'Made . . . and baby Wayne?'

An Asian woman raised her hand. She was petite, almost doll-like, with a heart-shaped face and warm brown eyes. Her shiny black hair was cut into a chin-length bob, which she pushed behind her ears with long, smooth fingers. She smiled shyly at the group, white teeth flashing against caramel skin. She looked barely old enough to have a baby.

'I am Made.' Pat had pronounced 'Made' as if it rhymed with 'paid', but Made herself pronounced her name as 'Ma-day'. 'And this is baby *Wayan*.'

'That's an unusual name,' said Pat.

'We from Bali.'

The baby gurgled from beneath a colourful sarong that covered the pram. Made reached in to lift out a toffee-skinned infant with a shock of black hair. She held the baby up to the group.

'My firstborn boy,' she said proudly.

Ginie stifled a gasp. The baby's mouth was open, disfigured by some kind of bulbous growth adhering to his lip and spreading up towards his nose.

Ginie glanced around the room. Everyone else was poker-faced. Made was nuzzling her son's ear, oblivious.

Pat was the first to speak. 'Is . . . Is there anything about your birthing experience that you would like to tell us, Made?'

Made paused, thinking for a moment. 'It was very paining,' she said. 'But he is . . . healthy boy. This is appreciating.'

Ginie smiled. Made's grasp of English was rudimentary, but her meaning was clear.

'Good, good,' said Pat. She shuffled her notes. 'Now that we've introduced ourselves, let's have a chat about how this group works. My role is to support you on the marvellous journey of motherhood, because being a mum is the most important job in the world.'

Ginie glanced at her watch.

'Today we'll talk about sleeping, which is something every new mum is interested in.' Pat chuckled. 'Sleep is extremely important for growth and development.' Her voice had assumed a rehearsed, singsong quality. Ginie wondered how many times Pat had subjected a group of new mothers to this exact spiel.

The session dragged on for another thirty minutes. Ginie spent much of this time checking work emails on her iPhone, concealed beneath the nappy bag balanced on her lap. Officially, she'd taken three months' maternity leave. But as the firm's only venture capital specialist, she couldn't trust Trevor, a private equity colleague, to manage her files properly. She checked her emails regularly, often sending two-line commands to Trevor which usually went unanswered. Her colleagues seemed reluctant to 'bother her', as they termed it, so soon after the birth. Ginie had never felt so disconnected from her working life.

'Oh, ladies, one more thing,' said Pat, turning to the whiteboard. 'We'll meet once a week until the end of July, then once a month to November. You'll be experts by then.' She wrote out the dates in a neat line on the board. Even her handwriting was irritating, Ginie thought, all curly and feminine. Instead of dots above the i's and j's, she drew tiny heart shapes.

'Around the four-month mark, we'll have a special "Fathers and Partners" session.' Pat circled the date for emphasis. 'It's important to get the dads involved.'

The bell on the back of the door jangled and Pat whirled around, a curt expression on her face.

'It's not eleven o'clock yet.' She scowled at a thin, white-haired man who stood in the doorway. 'There's a mothers' group in session here. Didn't you see the sign?'

The man looked contrite. 'I'll wait outside.'

Made stood up. 'I go,' she said. 'My husband. Thank you, Pat.'

She wheeled Wayan in his pram towards the exit. Cara, who was closest, rose to her feet and held open the door for her.

Husband? Ginie stared at the man beyond the door. He must be in his fifties, she thought. *Is Made a mail order bride?*

'Made, you might need some help with breastfeeding, considering Wayan's condition,' Pat called after her. 'I'll contact you next week to organise a meeting with one of our lactation consultants.'

Ginie repressed a snort. There could only be one thing worse than a midwife, as far as she was concerned: a *specialist* midwife.

Made nodded politely as she stepped onto the street. Ginie craned her neck to peer beyond the door. She caught a glimpse of the white-haired man stooping to kiss Wayan in his pram, before placing a protective hand on Made's hip.

The rest of the group began to assemble their things.

'Well, thank you, ladies,' said Pat. 'I'll see you next week. Everyone's contact details are here.' She waved a bundle of photocopies at them. 'I suggest you meet up informally before we reconvene. Being a new mum can be daunting, so it's good to support each other.'

Cara stood up and looked around the room. 'Well . . . would anyone like to meet up for coffee this Friday morning?' She seemed a little self-conscious.

No one said anything. Suzie and Pippa were fussing over their babies, while Miranda drained the last of her water. Ginie stared at her iPhone, pretending to read a message.

'We could go to the café across the road?' Cara ventured.

Ginie glanced around the group. She didn't have time for old friends, let alone new ones. All the same, she reasoned, her problems with breastfeeding had taught her that babies weren't always predictable. There was hardly anyone in her social network she could turn to for advice—most of her friends were childless professionals. And damned if she was going to ask her own mother.

'Okay,' said Ginie. 'I can make it unless something comes up at work.' It was a convenient excuse, should she need an exit strategy.

Some of the others nodded too.

'Great,' said Cara. 'Ten o'clock across the road, then?'

'Um . . . what about the beachfront park, instead?' Pippa's voice was hesitant. 'There's a little kiosk there, Beachcombers. It might be nicer for the babies, being outdoors.'

Do babies even *care* at this age? Ginie wondered.

'Yes, there's that little playground nearby,' said Miranda. 'I'll have Digby with me and he needs somewhere to run around.'

'Okay,' said Cara. 'Let's say ten o'clock this Friday at Beachcombers. I'll let Made know.'

Ginie plugged the date into her iPhone. The rest of the group began to disperse. Unlike the other babies, Rose was still asleep in her pram. She looked like a cherub, floating in layers of pink and white. A tiny pulse flickered at her temple. She was so fragile, so dependent upon Ginie for everything. And I'd do almost anything for her, Ginie said to herself. Even attend a mothers' group.

She gathered up her things and began to push the pram towards the door. Pat held it open for her.

'My husband bought the deluxe model, I'm afraid,' Ginie said ruefully, nodding at the pram. 'I can't even fit it in the boot of my car.' Her BMW coupé had been perfect pre-baby.

'I'm glad you decided to join the group, Ginie,' said Pat.

'Well, I'm going back to work next week,' Ginie told her. 'But I'll come along to as many sessions as I can.'

'Goodness, that's a rapid return to the workforce.'

Ginie forced a smile. 'Well, someone has to pay the mortgage, I'm afraid.'

She lowered the pram onto the street and started towards the car park.

Why did everyone have an opinion on her returning to work? She'd had a similar reaction from her mother, and Daniel hadn't been all that enthusiastic, either. If she'd been a man, no one would have questioned it. People expected fathers to go back to work as quickly as possible after their children were born. But mothers, she was learning, were judged differently. An alternative set of principles applied, even if the mother was the breadwinner of the family.

Ginie lifted her face to the warm winter sunshine, such a welcome relief from the dull hours she'd spent inside the house lately. The truth was, as much as she adored Rose, she'd been thinking about returning to work since her release from hospital. In the days after the birth, she'd been half expecting to have the sort of personal epiphany she'd heard about in other women: a loss of desire to work, and a sudden passion for the grander, higher calling of motherhood. But Ginie had worked too hard, become too specialised, to let go of it all lightly. One type of love, the maternal kind, had not usurped the other. Her love for the law remained.

She'd waited until Rose was one month old before raising the issue with Daniel.

'We need a nanny,' she told him, returning to the dinner table for the third time in thirty minutes. The quiet Friday night meal she'd planned had been hijacked by an unusually fractious Rose.

Daniel looked up from his plate, a chunk of lamb speared on his fork.

'What?' she asked, defensive.

'I'm listening,' he replied.

'Okay.' She took a deep breath. 'I've been thinking. Maybe I should go back to work sooner rather than later. I mean, I'm enjoying Rose and everything, but it's been a month now and the bills keep coming in.' Ginie's salary was quadruple that of Daniel's earnings. It had always been that way, from the moment they'd met on Curl Curl beach, just over a year ago. And now, with the global financial crisis worsening and Daniel's communications work dwindling, hers was the only income on which they could rely. Daniel kept insisting that the novel he'd started not long after their wedding would be finished within the next few months, but as far as Ginie was concerned, that was about as likely as winning the lottery.

'We've got a great life,' she continued. 'Why change it? Obviously I don't expect you to alter your own working arrangements because of Rose.' She paused, offering him the opportunity to say that *he* would be the primary carer until he started bringing in more work. Daniel remained silent.

'I've looked into au pairs,' she went on. 'They're quite inexpensive for what they do. They stay in your home, help with the housework, look after the baby. I could work four days a week in the office and one from home. You'd be free to do your own thing without having to worry about Rose. Maybe we could even get some quality time together. I mean, we haven't been ourselves lately . . .' The words were tumbling out of her mouth. She stopped herself short.

Things had changed between them almost as soon as she'd discovered she was pregnant. When the severe morning sickness had finally subsided, mind-numbing fatigue set in. In the final weeks of pregnancy, her stomach's swollen surface had resembled blue vein cheese, crisscrossed with newly formed blood supply lines to the baby. And while Daniel claimed her pregnant body was beautiful, she was appalled by it. He'd actually wanted to photograph it, for God's sake. It was a secret relief to Ginie when Rose came early, so it was no longer an option. But they hadn't been intimate since. Something had changed for her after the birth. Her body was different, that was clear, but it was more fundamental than that. Every time he reached for her, she almost flinched.

Daniel coughed. 'When do you think you might go back to work, then?'

'Three weeks,' she replied. 'I spoke to Alan today. He wants me back as soon as possible. Trevor's covering the Kentridge matter, but he's struggling.'

'Oh.' Daniel nodded, the movement slow and exaggerated. It was something he did, she'd learned, when attempting to contain his irritation. The ticking of the cedar clock on the sideboard punctuated the silence.

'Why don't you consider this a bit more?' he said finally. 'I mean, Rose is only a month old.'

Ginie shook her head. She'd spent hours trawling the internet in the weeks before the birth, researching and comparing agencies. She'd already spoken to the staff at Mother's

Little Helpers and confirmed the availability of a likely candidate, willing to start in a fortnight. Ginie had been impressed by her profile: a registered nurse from Ireland with qualifications in childcare. What else was there to consider?

'But this way, with an au pair, we can *both* keep working,' she said. 'We don't have to change our lifestyle, we don't have to worry about compromising Rose's care. And we can still get some time for us.'

Daniel stared at her.

'Right, well, mother knows best.' He pushed his chair back from the table. 'I'm going for a walk.'

As he reached the doorway, he turned to face her. 'Not everything in life can be controlled, you know. *Babies* can't be. But go on, Gin, try to map it all out before Rose is two months old.'

The front door slammed behind him.

Ginie dabbed at her mouth with a napkin, her lips trembling.

It's all very well for *you*, she thought. Taking the moral high ground with no work to speak of, except a bloody novel. We can't *eat* words.

An electronic chime announced receipt of a new message. She reached across the table for her iPhone.

I hate this fucking thing, she thought.

When Ginie got home from the mothers' group, the painters were crouched near the front door, cigarettes dangling from their lips.

'Smoko,' said one, stating the obvious.

She grunted an acknowledgement and steered the pram around them. Typical bloody tradesmen, she thought. They'd only been there an hour and were already having a break. Where had Daniel found them, anyway?

As she manoeuvred Rose's pram along the hallway, she detected clattering sounds from the kitchen. She rounded the corner to find Nicole standing at the sink, pink rubber gloves stretched up to her elbows, scrubbing the bottom of a baking tray. The flesh on her upper arms jiggled with exertion. Her brown hair was pulled up into a dishevelled ponytail and her skin was the typical milky pallor of the Irish.

Ginie cleared her throat.

'Oh, hello,' said Nicole, wheeling about. 'I didn't hear you come in. I hope you don't mind me getting started?'

'God no,' said Ginie. 'That's great, thanks. Have you settled in?'

Nicole couldn't possibly object to the guest quarters on the top floor, complete with king-size bed and ensuite.

'Honestly,' said Nicole, her eyes alight, 'it's the most beautiful room I've ever seen. With ocean views, too! It's the Sydney I've seen in the movies. I can't wait to tell the folks back home.'

Ginie smiled at her girlish enthusiasm. Nicole was only twenty-three, and it showed.

'Yes, Curly's a great spot,' she said. 'We love it here.'

Daniel had moved in not long after their engagement, selling his one-bedroom apartment near Mona Vale, ten kilometres north of Curl Curl. The price differential was significant; the proceeds of the apartment's sale paid off only twenty per cent of Ginie's mortgage. After her break-up with Frederic, her former partner of four years, she'd borrowed heavily to purchase her dream home on the North Curl Curl headland. And while money couldn't buy happiness, the hundred-and-eighty-degree view of the Pacific Ocean had certainly helped.

'Well, Rose has woken up and is due for a feed,' Ginie announced, lifting Rose out of the pram.

'I can do that,' said Nicole, peeling off the rubber gloves. 'I've seen where you keep the bottles.' She began spooning powdered formula into a bottle of cooled boiled water, before attaching a teat and shaking the mixture. 'Is Rose still having six feeds a day?'

'Five actually,' said Ginie. 'I think she might have dropped the midnight feed. She's been sleeping through to dawn over the past few days.'

'Oooh, lucky you,' said Nicole. 'They don't all do that at six weeks, you know. What a good girl you are!' She took Rose from Ginie's arms and lay her in the bassinette, clicking her tongue and waving her fingers. Rose looked at her with interest, hands and feet pummelling the air.

'Oh, you're excited are you?' Nicole laughed. 'We're going to have some fun, you and me.'

Ginie smiled. Nicole was a natural.

Daniel would surely see that too.

She'd met Daniel on Curl Curl beach just after sunrise on a winter's morning. The beach was deserted, as it often was at that hour, with the exception of a few surfers bobbing about like teabags on the swell. Ginie jogged along the soft sand near the dunes, her head down, focusing on her feet. She'd sprained her ankle six months before and didn't want to injure it again. The physiotherapist had recommended a program of hydrotherapy to aid recovery, but floating around with a group of retirees depressed her. Unless she was puffing and sweating, it didn't feel like real exercise. As soon as her ankle felt stable, she'd taken up beach jogging again.

Her iPod blared in her ears and she sang aloud to The Verve, unselfconscious in her solitude. She turned to see her footprints in the sand, a transient protest against the corrosive wind. This was one of the wildest beaches on the peninsula, with notorious undertows and collapsing sandbars. She loved its volatility. Starting the day on Curl Curl beach was an antidote to the long hours at Coombes Taylor Watson.

He was almost on top of her when she saw him, running up the beach carrying his surfboard. Given the beach's emptiness, he was ludicrously close. She stopped jogging to let him pass.

'Hi.' He smiled.

For a moment, she didn't know what to say. The ocean was upon him, tanned skin gleaming in the wet. A long sandy fringe flopped into bright blue eyes. His wetsuit was rolled down below the navel, a fine trail of blond hair disappearing beneath it.

She instantly wanted to touch him.

'Hi,' he said again.

She removed her earphones.

'Beautiful morning,' he said.

She sensed he might keep running.

'How are the waves?' she asked, trying to stall him.

'Awesome. The big green void puts everything in perspective.'

Who *was* this delicious creature?

'I'm Ginie,' she said, suddenly courageous.

'Glad you told me,' he said. 'I've seen you jogging every day for the past month.'

This surprised her: she'd never seen him once. But then again, she'd never really looked in the surfers' direction. They were as much a part of the landscape as the flocks of seagulls at the water's edge.

'I'm Daniel.' He stretched out his hand. She felt its cool, calloused palm against her own.

'Might see you tomorrow then?' he asked.

She felt her cheeks flush. Then he hoisted his board under his arm and disappeared over the dune.

They exchanged pleasantries on the beach for two months. In the beginning, their conversations were brief and oriented around the weather. Then, slowly, they began to disclose minor details about their lives.

One morning, Daniel hailed her with particular enthusiasm.

'Six-foot waves out there,' he said with a grin. 'Now *that* gets the creative juices flowing. I'll be productive today.'

Ginie seized upon the inference.

'You're an artist?'

'A writer.'

She remembered his calloused hand. The idea of writing for work was alien to her.

'What sorts of things do you write?'

'Well, all sorts of marketing junk at the moment.' He laughed. 'Keeps the wolves from the door. I run a communications company with a friend of mine.' He planted his board in the sand. 'But when I'm not doing mindless corporate work, I write poetry, plays, fiction. The sorts of things that don't pay. It's hard to be a full-time renaissance man, but that's my dream. To write the stuff I'm passionate about, and be paid for it.'

Ginie digested his words. He'd released more information in two minutes than in the past eight weeks. But poetry, plays and fiction? Was *anyone* successful at that?

'What about you?' he asked. 'What do you do?'

The sorts of things that *do* pay, she thought.

'I'm a commercial lawyer. In venture capital, mostly.'

She thought she saw his eyes widen a little. She was used to that sort of response. Most of the men she'd dated over the years had been intimidated by her intelligence, her success.

'Well, you keep pretty fit for a fuck-off lawyer,' he said, his eyes dancing. 'There can't be many like you.'

Her mouth dropped open. She didn't know whether to laugh or feel offended.

'See you tomorrow,' he said, winking at her.

Later that morning, she buzzed herself into the office. She was usually one of the first to arrive, but she'd been slow in getting ready. She'd stood for half an hour under the shower, water coursing over her shoulders, thinking about Daniel. How he'd dropped the word *fuck* into their conversation. There was something coarse about it, and something intimate.

'Nice skirt!' Arnold popped up from behind the reception desk. 'Got a hot date tonight?'

Arnold, the firm's business manager, was the only element of office culture that ever surprised her. He'd worked at Coombes Taylor Watson for almost as long as she had; in fact, she'd been instrumental in giving him the chance. Amid all the pinstriped suits and plaid bow ties, he was a breath of fresh air. And if he hadn't been so good at his job, the firm's conservative partners would have jettisoned him long ago. He was loud, he was camp, but he was far superior to any other business manager they'd ever had.

'Not in a good mood, hon?' He pouted theatrically. 'This will cheer you up. I've got a *great* piece of spam for you this morning.' He pointed to his computer screen. 'Subject line of email reads: *Your sex prong will grow like on yeasts.*'

She suppressed a smile.

'Body of text reads: *Lovers will hanker to observe your bulge and exhibit. Press button now.*' He removed the lid from his grande-sized skinny-cino. 'I tell you, I'm gonna press that button *big time*. I just love those spammers in the Ukraine. Now, can I get you a coffee, hon?'

She shook her head and started towards her office.

'You ignoring me?'

Ginie pulled a face.

'Well, what about this, then? *These* arrived for you.' Arnold lifted an enormous bunch of yellow roses from beneath his desk. 'A super-cute courier delivered them five minutes ago. Could've opened a bottle with his buttocks. I *almost* got his number.'

Ginie frowned. 'Who's trying to bribe me this time?'

'Dah . . . da-da-da-da dah . . .' Arnold held a hand over his heart, humming a vaguely familiar tune.

'Don't tell me you're too *young* for classic Elton John?' He grimaced in mock disgust. 'Who's *Daniel* then? Tell Uncle Arnold.' He pointed to a card taped to the bottom of the arrangement and smiled cheekily. 'There was no envelope, I'm afraid.'

Ginie stared at the words on the card: *Can we take things beyond the beach? Daniel.*

'Oh.' Her stomach somersaulted. 'It's just some guy I met jogging at Curl Curl. We've spoken for a total of, I don't know, two hours.' She read the card again. 'I can't imagine how he found me.'

'There aren't too many venture capital lawyers in Sydney, hon,' said Arnold. 'Not *lady* ones, anyway. And *certainly* not of your calibre. He probably just googled you.'

'Well, that's flattering, but he could be a stalker.'

'Oh, spoilsport! You need a night out. Go for it.'

'Maybe,' she replied. 'But take these home for Phil.' She dropped the flowers back onto his desk.

'Oooh, fabulous!' Arnold buried his nose in the bunch. 'Phil just *loves* roses.'

The next morning Ginie rose at five o'clock, as usual, for her mandatory six laps of Curl Curl beach. But today, she showered first. She pulled on her lycra leggings and a black sports singlet, sniffed at her armpits and applied two coats of deodorant. She shook her head even as she did this; she was behaving like an adolescent. Her reflection in the bathroom mirror taunted her. *Older, ever older, than yesterday.* At thirty-nine, she worked hard to stay fit. She kept her weight low, her muscles taut, her limbs supple. But time had marched across her body, bringing with it an army of age spots across her décolletage, a slight sagginess around the hips, and crow's-feet in the corners of her eyes. She leaned forward and strained to inspect the crown of her head, her face almost touching the mirror. No stray white hairs protruding, not today anyway. She brushed her blonde hair into a long plait before pushing it back through her sports visor. She rubbed her lips with cocoa balm and, for an instant, imagined Daniel's smooth mouth pressing against hers.

As she bolted along the sand at Curl Curl, her heart rate monitor sounded its alarm. The beach was uncharacteristically still, shrouded in a blanket of sea fog. The ferries would be cancelled on Sydney Harbour this morning, she thought, they couldn't run in a fog like this. Arnold would be late for work.

She was close to the northern end of the beach when she spotted Daniel, some twenty metres away. He held his board under his arm, turned in her direction and waved. She continued jogging towards him, increasing her pace. When she finally stopped in front of him, she leaned over, hands on her knees, and sucked in deep, ragged breaths.

'That's some effort, sporty,' he said.

She smiled. 'Thank you for the flowers. I'd like to . . . take it beyond the beach.'

She looked down at the sand. For a moment, she recalled the sober face of her ex-boyfriend, Frederic. His character-istically French self-assurance, his razor-sharp intellect and passion for the law, his unflinching conservatism. His desire to raise a family which, at the beginning, had seemed so endearing. They'd loved each other, no question. But while Ginie had continued to vacillate on the question of children, he'd been resolute. In the end, he'd delivered an ultimatum: *Marry me and start a family, or we go our separate ways.*

Her mother had wept when she'd conveyed the news of their break-up. It had been a long eighteen months of celibacy since.

Daniel's blue eyes moved over her, then met her gaze.

He took her hand and they scaled the dune, picking their way through a carpet of fleshy succulents on the other side. She followed him, almost bent double, pushing through spiny grass and twisted banksias, until they found a sheltered, sandy trough. It was the northernmost dune on the beach, above the scrubby undulations of a popular dog exercise area. But there was no distant barking this morning. The sun was only just beginning to rise, obscured by the thick sea fog.

'Here,' said Daniel. He brought her hand to his lips and kissed her palm, lingering at the underside of her wrist. She gasped at the sensation. He looked up at the sound and smiled.

I can trust you, she thought.

They slid into the sand. He peeled off her singlet, her sports bra, her leggings. Suddenly she was naked, vulnerable on the dune. He rolled down his wetsuit, its rubber squeaking against damp skin.

'We can't . . .' She didn't carry contraceptives around with her.

'I know,' he said.

His mouth roved downwards, his hands gripped her hips.

'Let go.' His breath was warm on her stomach. 'Let go.'

She closed her eyes, falling towards annihilation.

She wasn't sure if they were having a relationship, but she knew she was having the best sex of her life. She'd had so many stitched-up years of long hours and sensible choices. Daniel was like a wild vacation from her ordinary life. Three weeks after the encounter on the sand dune, Arnold popped his head into her office.

'You've got a lovely little inner glow going on,' he said with a fiendish smile. 'Dare I ask—Daniel?'

She nodded ever so slightly. 'Get me the Kentridge file, please, Arnold.'

But work was a farce; all she could think about was having sex with Daniel. On Curl Curl beach, in her car, against the wall in a public toilet, from behind on the roof of his apartment. He was insatiable, devouring her body and reconstituting it in written form. His poetry was sensuous, simple. She'd never felt so sexually liberated.

Six weeks later, she began to feel sick.

'It's not a disaster,' he said, reaching across the restaurant table to take her hand.

'I'm almost forty,' she snapped. 'Having a baby wasn't part of my life plan.' Daniel had been using condoms, boxes and boxes of them. But even so, here she was, pregnant at thirty-nine. A statistical anomaly.

'Life doesn't always go to plan.' Daniel smiled. 'It's only taken me about thirty years to learn that.'

She sat back in her chair and considered him.

A waiter approached, but she waved him away.

'How old *are* you, Daniel?'

They'd been having sex for two months and he'd dodged the issue with smart-alec quips like 'over the age of consent' and 'old enough to know better'. She'd assumed they were roughly the same age.

'Does it matter?' he replied.

'Not really,' she said. Thinking, *maybe it does now.*

'How old do you think I am?'

'No idea. I'm not good at guessing games.'

'Go on, have a swing at it.'

'Well . . .' She surveyed his tanned skin. 'Maybe thirty-seven?'

'I'm thirty-two,' he said. 'The surfing makes me look older. Way too much sun.'

'Oh.' She swallowed hard. *I'm pregnant to a man seven years my junior.*

She studied the menu. 'Are you eating?' she asked.

'Are you buying?' he replied.

She looked around for the restrooms. 'I think I'm going to vomit.'

She slammed the bathroom door behind her and leaned

heavily against a wash basin, her forearms resting on the cool marble. She turned on the tap and watched the water cascade down the plughole. Slowly the nausea receded.

She splashed her face and stared at her reflection in the mirror. An accidental pregnancy. So fucking adolescent.

She could abort it now, and no one would ever know. She'd already googled a clinic on Macquarie Street that could practically do the procedure in her lunch hour.

The thought made her retch. She pressed her hands across her stomach as she heaved into the basin. There's something growing inside of me, she thought. *Someone.*

The door swung open. It was Daniel.

'This is the ladies' room,' she snapped.

'Clearly,' he replied. 'Are you alright?'

'I don't know.'

He walked across the tiles and slid an arm around her waist.

'Marry me,' he whispered. His breath was warm on her face.

'What?'

'You heard me. How about it?'

She stared at him, stunned. 'And why would *that* be a good idea?'

'Because we're great together, Ginie. Okay, we haven't known each other for very long. But we laugh, we have fun. We have *fantastic* sex. And when we're apart, all I think about is you.' He pulled her closer. 'I could spend the rest of my life making you happy.'

No one had ever said anything like that to her. Frederic

had only managed 'I love you' two years into their relationship.

'But . . . I'm pregnant.'

'Icing on the cake.'

'You're crazy. It'd be the biggest risk of our lives.' She knew about risk. She spent her working day managing it.

'Living is risky business,' he said, smiling. 'We're two intelligent people. We'll make it work.'

She'd always been so measured in her life choices. Prudent, her mother called it, as if it was a good thing. But all this risk aversion had got her where, exactly? At the top of her game, having take-away Thai dinners on a Saturday night, alone.

She was ready for a change. Daniel's confidence was infectious.

A month later, she'd taken Daniel to dinner at her parents' home in Lane Cove and announced their engagement. Her mother, unable to conceal her alarm, was silent throughout the meal. Her father seemed much more relaxed; relieved, almost. He kept winking at the two of them, leaning back in his chair and saying, 'Well, well.'

As Ginie cleared the plates after dessert, her mother followed her to the kitchen and ushered her into the walk-in pantry. Ginie could remember scaling its broad shelves as a child, in pursuit of the biscuit barrel. It had seemed so spacious at the time, concealing all manner of tantalising treats. Now, face to face with her mother inside the pantry, she felt claustrophobic.

'Who *is* this man?' her mother hissed. 'And why are you in such a hurry to marry him?'

Ginie sighed. 'Mum, I don't expect you to understand. But Daniel's a good person. You just have to get to know him.' She considered blurting out the news of her pregnancy.

'Do I just?' Her mother's lips quivered. 'And how long have *you* known him?'

'Long enough to know he's worth marrying.'

Her mother frowned. 'But he doesn't seem . . . your type.'

'Opposites attract.'

'This is so unlike you, Ginie.' Her mother's voice was anxious. 'Be careful.'

Ginie shrugged.

'Mum, I appreciate your concern, I really do. But I hope you can be happy for us.' She pushed open the pantry door.

'Have you told Jonathan or Paula yet?' her mother called after her.

Ginie shook her head. Her mother would telephone her siblings, she knew, as soon as she and Daniel had left.

Her mother had never offered guidance when it mattered. Ginie had sought her opinion on countless occasions throughout adolescence, on issues that seemed so important at the time— the machinations of female friendships, the uncertainty of future career paths, the angst of unrequited love. Irrespective of the question, her mother's response had always been the same: 'You'll do the right thing, Ginie. *You'll* be fine.' *Compared to Paula*, was the inference. The daughter with special needs, the one who monopolised her mother's time and attention.

'Paula won't be as lucky in life as you,' her mother had often whispered. 'She'll have to choose her career carefully, she'll have trouble finding a husband. Nothing will be easy for her. *You'll* be fine, Ginie.'

But despite her mother's assurances, Ginie hadn't been fine. As the recipient of an equity scholarship at an elite Catholic girls' school, she'd never felt entirely accepted by her peers, most of whom were the daughters of doctors, solicitors and accountants. With a teacher for a mother and a plumber for a father, her lower socioeconomic status had been obvious to all. But she'd been blessed with natural intelligence and she'd worked hard to gain entry into law, a prestigious career path that carried the social cachet her family lacked.

It was in her first year at university that she'd met James, a handsome postgraduate with an internship at one of the Big Five law firms. She'd seen him around campus; he was outgoing vice-president of the Law Society, a member of the Student Representative Council, and a regular at student debates. She couldn't believe her luck when a friend introduced him at the end-of-year law revue. And she couldn't believe her ears when he asked her out for coffee the following evening, the last day of semester.

He'd arrived at her parents' house in a navy Alfa Romeo just after eight o'clock.

'It's my dad's, don't worry,' he said, grinning at her mother. 'He's a QC and he'll put me behind bars if I scratch it.' His laughing eyes turned serious. 'I won't have her home too late. We're just going for a coffee.'

'James, don't be silly,' her mother purred. 'You two just enjoy yourselves.'

Their conversation in the car was stilted. Ginie was nervous and desperate to please: she'd never had a boyfriend before. James seemed preoccupied and, unlike the night before at the law revue, a little reserved.

When he turned into a dark cul-de-sac that bordered parkland at the back of the university, she was confused.

'Come for a walk,' he said, flashing a disarming smile. 'Then we'll go for coffee.'

'Okay.'

The night was moonless and the terrain unfamiliar. They hadn't gone far before she was disoriented. Suddenly she found herself pinned against a tree, his mouth all over hers. She tried to follow his lead, but his tongue thrust so deeply she gagged. His hands moved up under her shirt and into her bra, tugging at her nipples.

'Ouch,' she said.

'What, first-year nerves?'

'No, it's just a bit . . .'

'Whatever.' He breathed into her ear, biting hard on the lobe.

'That hurt. James . . .'

His hand groped beneath her skirt.

'No,' she said, pressing her thighs together. 'Can we . . . go for coffee?' She tried to move away. But he was much bigger than her—a second-rower in the university rugby union team—and she found she couldn't.

In the darkness, the whites of his eyes hovered centimetres from hers.

'Please,' she begged, unable to believe this was happening. 'Let me go.'

James said nothing at all.

Afterwards, he drove her home in silence.

She turned the key in the lock, pale and shaking.

Her mother looked up from the newsletter she was reading. A pile of documents was stacked on the table next to her, work she'd brought home for the weekend.

'Oh dear,' she said, in a disapproving tone. 'You didn't have a very good night, then?'

Ginie shook her head, not trusting herself to speak.

'Well, that's a shame,' her mother said, before returning to her newsletter. Ginie stood for a moment, blinking back tears. Then she retreated to the bathroom, betrayed for the second time that evening.

And so Ginie had buried the experience deep inside herself, carrying the shame around like an invisible, oversized coat. But she'd sworn that she'd never be so vulnerable again. She'd avoided sexual relationships, focusing instead on her studies and, later, on advancing her career. Until Frederic came along, with his innate solidity that, at last, signalled some kind of safety.

It was only in her late thirties, prompted by the life coach she'd hired after breaking up with Frederic, that Ginie recognised how *angry* she was. The first time the life coach had articulated it—gently asking Ginie if she felt abandoned by her mother—she'd sat dumbfounded, tears streaming down her cheeks. It wasn't her mother's *fault* that James had assaulted her, Ginie realised. But like so many other times in Ginie's life, her mother hadn't been there for her. She'd either failed to see the signs of Ginie's distress, or simply ignored them. It was the common pattern of her childhood: *you'll be alright, Ginie.*

Weren't mothers supposed to have some sort of instinctive maternal alarm bell, Ginie had demanded of her life coach. Weren't *they* the ones who knew how to nurture and comfort their children best? And if your *mother* doesn't look out for you in this world, who will?

I can't answer these questions for you, Ginie, her life coach had said. *I can only help you answer them for yourself.*

But when Ginie met Daniel, she'd cancelled her life coaching sessions.

In a matter of months, she'd reinvented herself. Suddenly she had sex, love, a pregnancy and wedding plans. Even an invitation to apply for a partnership at Coombes Taylor Watson.

Life had never been better.

It was while compiling the guest list that Ginie learned that Daniel's parents had died in a car accident when he was fifteen years old. An only child, Daniel had gone to live with his aunt for the remaining three years of high school. After that, he'd lived independently and worked his way through university.

'That must've been terrible for you,' Ginie had remarked, shocked. She couldn't conceive of losing both parents, even now.

Daniel grunted. 'Growing up, it was always the three of us—Mum, Dad and me. Then suddenly it was just me. I'd never wanted a sibling until then.'

Ginie reached for his hand, unsure what to say.

'My aunt was great,' he continued. 'She didn't try to pretend it away. The night I moved in to her house, she said, "Dan, I'm never going to be your second mother, but I'll always be your friend." And she has been.' His eyes were watery.

'I understand,' said Ginie, although she wasn't sure she did. 'Were you lonely?'

'Not really,' he said. 'When I wasn't at my aunt's place, I hung out with my best mate, Chris. He's like a brother to me now. And I wrote pages and pages in my diary. Lots of bad poetry.'

Ginie smiled.

'And I got serious about surfing. It was my lifeline.'

Ginie nodded. Somehow she'd sensed that Daniel's connection to the ocean was more than just a hobby.

'I've asked Chris to be my best man.' He passed her a list of names. 'But I don't have too many people to invite, really. Aunt Emma and Uncle Dave are the only family I've got.'

Ginie scanned their two lists: sixty-four on her side, twenty-three on Daniel's. Why did he have such a limited circle of friends?

'What?' asked Daniel.

She gave him the benefit of the doubt.

'Nothing,' she said. 'I just can't imagine what you've been through.'

They were married on Curl Curl beach on a Sunday afternoon in early January. The day was stifling, a typical summer scorcher, but by mid-afternoon a bracing southerly had sprung up. The theme was 'Barefoot on the Beach' and, much to the bemusement of Ginie's mother, most of the guests were shoeless. Ginie wore a simple champagne-coloured slip with spaghetti straps and a beaded bodice. It was a floating, summery kind of dress, not particularly bridal. She knew she could wear it again.

Her whole family attended, apart from her brother, who couldn't extricate himself from his work in London. The market was skittish, Jonathan had explained, and trading across equities had slumped. A holiday to Australia was out of the question, even for his sister's wedding. Ginie hadn't been particularly disappointed. His absence was more than compensated for by a swarm of other friends and relatives.

'You've got dozens of cousins.' Daniel laughed as they stood side by side, greeting arrivals near the North Curl Curl Surf Club.

It was all over in thirty minutes. The celebrant, a woman in her fifties with wild red hair, had difficulty projecting her voice above the wind. But Ginie didn't care. She stood, goosebumps creeping across her arms and chest, looking into Daniel's eyes. Her world was changing right now, she realised, in this very moment. The predictability of her former existence was gone forever: this was day one of the rest of her life. It was terrifying and thrilling in equal measure.

They exchanged white-gold wedding bands and kissed as the crowd cheered. Ginie had never envisaged herself as a crying bride, but the tears came. She clung to Daniel, beaming and snivelling. This must be what true love feels like, she thought, wiping her cheeks with the back of her hands.

Afterwards, guests milled about at the top of the dunes, sipping champagne and nibbling canapés. Ginie felt positively buoyant as she watched them. She was a married woman now, a surprisingly satisfying thought. The guests appeared to be enjoying themselves, despite the persistent wind. She closed her eyes and inhaled the sea air. When she opened them, she found Daniel among the throng, talking to her sister. Ginie stared at Paula's transformation from dowdy housewife to flirty coquette, twittering like a canary in Daniel's presence. Ginie downed the rest of her champagne, before realising she'd just flouted the alcohol guidelines for pregnancy. She touched her belly reflexively. She'd have to be more careful in future. At eighteen weeks, her slightly rounded form was still concealed by the contours of her dress. No one knows what's inside me, she thought.

'You look beautiful,' said a voice behind her. She turned to see Chris, the best man, holding out a bottle of champagne. 'Can I get you another one?'

'No thanks,' she replied. 'That's enough for me.' She nodded towards the horizon. 'I don't think we'll be here much longer anyway, by the look of that.' Dark clouds were rolling in from the south, hanging low over the ocean.

'Great ceremony,' said Chris. 'Very Daniel. I'm glad you've made an honest man out of him. I didn't think it would happen.'

'Oh?' said Ginie. 'Why's that?'

'You know, with his parents and everything. Dan's always been a rolling stone.'

Ginie looked at Chris, wondering what else he knew about her husband that she didn't.

'It's a good thing we can all change, isn't it?' she said, feeling a little queasy.

Suddenly the clouds opened overhead and splinters of rain fell across the beach. Guests scrambled for cover, holding handbags, esky lids and overcoats above their heads.

'Time to go!' called Daniel. She ran towards him, giggling and kicking sand behind her.

She was thirty-two weeks pregnant when she fronted the interview panel, wearing black to minimise her bulge.

Ginie wanted the role of partner more than anything, but she knew she didn't stand a chance. Not now, anyway.

The week before, Arnold had printed out a confidential email and slipped it into her in-tray. He'd risked his job to do it, transgressing the firm's privacy protocols.

'Sorry, hon,' he'd whispered, raising a finger to his lips and backing out of her office.

As she'd read the email, from the firm's managing partner to the selection panel, the blood had drained from her face. It confirmed the candidates shortlisted for interview and singled out Ginie for comment:

While I have added Ginie's name to the shortlist, in my view she will struggle to be the preferred candidate. While her pregnancy should not, in itself, be an impediment to her appointment, we all know what kind of commitment a partnership requires. It is important, however, that due process be observed.

She reread the email countless times.

'Due process'? What the fuck is this, the Middle Ages?

The panellists had clearly made up their minds before the interview. Or, if they hadn't, the managing partner had set her up for failure. She scanned the list of other interview candidates and recognised them all. She was their junior by at least ten years.

In the days leading up to the interview, she considered her position. It was a patent contravention of the Sex Discrimination Act, a breach that the Equal Opportunity Commission would relish. She'd win the battle, she knew, with publicity and compensation. It was unthinkable that an established law firm such as hers, with overt diversity guidelines and an impeccable record of gender equality, couldn't ensure a fair recruitment process. She pictured the front-page headline: OLD BOYS NETWORK SHAFTS PREGNANT LAWYER. But she'd be practically unemployable afterwards.

She imagined confronting the firm internally. But what would she demand from them? An apology? Hush money? Unless she was prepared to leave her job, the prospect was untenable. Not to mention the position she'd put Arnold in, when forced to reveal her source. She contemplated withdrawing from the process altogether, citing ill-health or a change of circumstances. But the fundamental injustice of it all prevented her from pulling out, on principle. So she resolved to make them sit through an interview with her, despite the foregone conclusion.

Arseholes, she thought, smiling at the five panellists.

'Ginie, why do you want the role?' asked the managing partner.

It was an unoriginal opener.

'I have the leadership skills and technical experience to take our venture capital and private equity practice to the next level,' she replied. She rattled off several examples of her pivotal role in gaining, and servicing, several of the firm's existing clients.

'And in terms of the way the current partners run the firm as a whole, how would you do things differently?'

I'd sack a few swinging dicks around here. And I'd offer paid maternity leave.

'The current partners are well-respected,' she replied. 'It would be an honour to join them. I have a few ideas for innovation, of course. But my partnership style would be one of refinement, not revolution.'

'Now, Ginie,' said the only female panellist, the director of a recruitment firm. 'You're obviously pregnant. That has no bearing at all on our decision today. But tell us, how do you think you'll cope with a new baby *and* a partnership?'

Ginie swallowed. They're clever, she thought, getting a woman to ask that question.

'Look, I have female staff members with children on my team and, in my experience, they're actually *more* productive than most people in the office. But I have good support mechanisms in place, including a husband who's committed to shared parenting.' She could feel her face reddening. 'It shouldn't impact on my capacity at all.'

She eyeballed the managing partner. He jotted some notes on the edge of his paper. He was just going through the motions.

The managing partner called her late on a Monday evening from Beijing. The line was poor, but the message clear.

'I understand, thank you.'

She put down the telephone and began to cry. Daniel cradled her head against his chest.

'I'm sorry,' he said.

'Fuckers.'

'You knew it was coming.'

'Bloody sexist, ageist pigs.'

'I know,' he soothed. 'It's terrible.'

She wiped her eyes with the tissue he proffered. She didn't begrudge the successful candidate his partnership. He was an accomplished lawyer and a strategic thinker, a private equity specialist she'd worked with for several years. But she still felt betrayed. By the firm, and by her pregnant body. She had no doubt that if she hadn't been pregnant, she would have had a fighting chance.

'You never know, Gin,' said Daniel. 'Maybe it's for the best.'

She lifted her head from his chest. 'What's that supposed to mean?'

'Well, you know,' he said. 'With the baby and everything. You might end up glad you *didn't* get the role.'

'I doubt that.' She leaned against the kitchen bench. The baby had started to kick boisterously, particularly at night. She'd heard of other women who enjoyed watching their stomachs ripple as the foetus moved, but she found it disconcerting. It was like watching a science fiction movie.

'You okay?' he asked, rubbing her shoulders.

'I'm fine.'

She wanted to slap him. To scream that if she'd known the baby would cost her a partnership, she might have got rid of it.

What sort of person am I? She was horrified by herself.

She needed to book in with her life coach again, and quickly.

'Come to bed,' said Daniel.

She nodded.

As she turned off the kitchen light, her mobile rang. It was her mother, again. Ginie had only told her of the pregnancy two months earlier, when it had been impossible to obscure any longer. Since then, her mother had rung on a daily basis, offering some piece of unsolicited wisdom.

'For God's sake, Mum, it's late,' she muttered, pressing the 'ignore' button.

It takes a pregnancy to spark her interest in me, she thought. She'll probably make a really great *grandmother.*

'Come to bed,' insisted Daniel.

She watched him pad down the hall in boxer shorts, the muscles in his back moving beneath tanned skin. For the briefest of moments, she remembered the sweet delirium of their first few weeks together. The taste of sea salt and perspiration, languid words whispered on twisted sheets. That woman was a world away now. Her stomach was a lumbering impediment to intimacy. After one particularly awkward attempt when she was six months pregnant, they'd given up on sex altogether.

She followed him into the bedroom. Wearily, she changed into her maternity pyjamas and rolled the elasticised support band across her abdomen. Bedtime had become an elaborate exercise in the placement of cushions, propping her body at precise angles in an attempt to ease the heartburn that visited her at midnight.

They lay in bed, hands touching.

'Can you *please* repaint the nursery?' she pleaded into the darkness. 'It's a shit-hole in there.'

Daniel didn't reply.

'Did you hear me?'

'What, babe?' he slurred. She couldn't fathom how he fell asleep so quickly.

'Nothing.'

'I can't believe how fantastic Nicole is,' Ginie whispered. They lay in bed listening to her move about the kitchen, fixing Rose's bottle. It had just gone five thirty, the feed Ginie loathed. Anything between midnight and six am was insufferable.

'I know,' agreed Daniel. 'You were right, Gin. I was against the idea in the beginning, but she's really great.'

Two months after Nicole's arrival, they could hardly remember life without her. She made herself useful in ways even Ginie hadn't imagined. Planning and cooking their weekly meals, doing the shopping, collecting the dry-cleaning, going to the post office. One week, when something had come up for Ginie at work, Nicole had even attended a mothers' group meeting and written up notes on the topics discussed. *Handwritten notes!* And now she'd offered to do the dawn feed to allow Ginie to return to her jogging routine.

Ginie could hear Nicole in Rose's bedroom now, lifting her

from the cot to the change table. She rolled over and looked at Daniel's silhouette in the semi-darkness. He reached out and traced a finger down her cheek. She lay perfectly still. You're the father of my child, she mused. The reality of that fact still amazed her. How they'd moved from two to three, how Daniel had morphed from husband to father. She loved watching him with Rose, playful and tender. And yet for all of that, his sexual advances still left her cold. Why didn't she feel anything, anymore?

The kettle in the kitchen began to whistle.

'Better take that off the stove,' said Daniel, rolling out of bed. 'Don't want the house burning down.'

Ginie listened to him walk down the hall, muffled voices in the kitchen. Rose squawked, impatient for milk.

After several minutes, Daniel popped his head around the bedroom door.

'Hey, why don't you go down to the beach for a jog?' he said. 'Nicole's got it all under control here. Clear your head.'

Ginie smiled, grateful.

'Is anyone else getting up five times a night?' Pippa's tone was flat. Heidi lay sleeping beneath the sun-proof canopy in which her pram was permanently covered.

Ginie glanced sideways at Pippa. She often had an unwashed look about her, but today was worse than usual. Her oily hair was uncombed, and her chin was dotted with small red spots. In fact, Ginie swore she could detect an odd, stale smell about her. Ginie shifted in her seat, edging ever so slightly away from Pippa. Whenever she could, Ginie always tried to sit next to Cara or Miranda. But she'd arrived late today, and she'd had no choice. Now she was marooned between Pippa and Suzie, the women she liked least in the group.

'Heidi's more than three months old,' continued Pippa. 'All the books say she should be waking up no more than twice a night. But sometimes she wakes five, even six times. I just don't know what I'm doing wrong.' Her eyes darted in Cara's direction.

'Oh, don't be too hard on yourself,' said Cara, her tone sympathetic. She brushed her honey-coloured fringe out of her eyes and rocked Astrid's pram with the other hand. 'Astrid wakes *at least* three times a night and disturbs poor Richard, who has to go to work the next morning. So I just keep pulling my boobs out to *make* her quiet. I wonder what the books would say about *that*?'

Everyone laughed, even Pippa. But that was Cara, Ginie thought. Always putting the group at ease.

Apart from Cara, Ginie felt most drawn to Miranda. She'd had a successful career in arts management before Rory arrived, and her husband worked in finance. Ginie had seen their house, perched on the southern cliffs of Freshwater beach, and was struck by how similar it was to her own. Architecturally elegant, a simple rectangular prism with a slatted facade, oriented to a dramatic waterfront view. They were clearly aesthetes, moving in social circles similar to hers. And despite being permanently tired, Miranda always managed to look stunning. Her long limbs, pixie ears and intense green eyes gave her an otherworldly quality that drew the eye.

As for the others in the group, Ginie often struggled to make conversation. For starters, she could never tell if Made understood her properly, so she'd given up trying. And when Made had revealed her age—just twenty-two years old—Ginie couldn't quite believe it. Under no other circumstances, apart from this mothers' group, could she imagine socialising with an Indonesian woman almost twenty years her junior.

Suzie, on the other hand, was just plain irritating. She wore long earrings that jangled and figure-hugging clothes in psychedelic colours, inevitably overemphasising her curvaceous figure. If I had a bum like that, Ginie had thought on more than one occasion, I wouldn't be wrapping it in bright green batik. And she didn't know when to stop talking, often hijacking the group's conversation with inanities. Last week, it had been a ten-minute tirade on the benefits of pawpaw ointment: it was all Ginie could do not to yawn.

As for Pippa, Ginie couldn't work her out. She was educated, with a degree in psychology, but always seemed so prickly and uptight. She was thin-lipped, pale and never laughed out loud. Ginie had tried to engage her on several occasions, but Pippa had never kept the conversation going. It was like having an undertaker in the group, Ginie thought, solemn and lingering at the edges.

Cara looked at Pippa. 'If the night waking's getting to you, maybe you should take a break. Do you have any family nearby?' she asked. 'Someone who could take Heidi during the day, maybe?'

Pippa shook her head. 'My parents are frail, I couldn't leave Heidi with them. Robert's parents are pretty much unavailable. He's the youngest of seven kids, so they're always busy with everyone else's children.'

'Maybe you should consider a nanny?' Ginie suggested. 'It's made such a difference to me. If Rose cries in the middle of the night, the nanny handles it. When I'm at work, I know she's in safe hands. Don't get me wrong, Daniel's great. But you know what men are like. They're just not as thorough.'

Pippa didn't meet her gaze. 'We can't afford it.'

Ginie said nothing. It was hard not to feel superior. No one else in the group had been as proactive in getting hired help, and now they were all sleep-deprived. Except for Suzie, who claimed she was getting ten hours a night by co-sleeping with Freya. Which only served to confirm how crazy she was.

'So the nanny's working out for you then, Ginie?' asked Miranda, leaning forward to check on Digby, who was worming his way under a nearby table.

'Absolutely,' she replied. 'We're going away together next weekend. I couldn't bring myself to leave Rose behind, so we're taking Nicole along to babysit.' Ginie glanced about the table, trying to contain her glee. 'It was Daniel's idea, actually. It'll be the first time we've had a whole night to ourselves since Rose was born.'

'Oh, lucky you,' said Cara, her smile wistful.

Suzie pushed her blonde curls behind her ears. It was another grating habit of hers. 'Gosh, I wouldn't be *brave* enough to leave Freya alone with someone I didn't really *know*,' she said, all wide-eyed and earnest.

Ginie bristled. Over the past two months of mothers' group meetings, her initial lack of interest in Suzie had morphed into active dislike. She was always mouthing some platitude about positive parenting, or trying to save the world one eco-nappy at a time.

'Nicole's a professional with nursing qualifications,' said Ginie, her tone even. 'She's more equipped to look after babies than anyone else I know.'

Suzie pursed her lips. 'But Nicole hasn't had any children of her *own*, has she?'

Ginie could feel the anger rising, constricting her chest. *We're not all hand-holding hippies like you*, she wanted to say. Instead, she drained the last of her skinny latte. 'Well, she's done a great job of looking after Rose so far. She's worth her weight in gold.'

'Oh, that's good to hear.' Suzie's smile was beatific. 'Because I can't imagine how *awful* you must feel, leaving Rose every morning.'

Ginie blinked. The truth of Suzie's words stung. The first day she'd returned to the office, leaving Rose in Nicole's arms, she'd cried all the way to work. She'd been forced to redo her makeup in the car park and talk sternly to herself. *It's all for the best. I'm doing the right thing. Daniel's there for Rose too.* Later that night, she'd returned home and scooped up Rose, hugging the baby so tightly that she'd squealed her objection. Nicole had politely suggested that, in future, Ginie refrain from texting her quite *so* much in one day.

Ginie glared at Suzie, seething. Then she lowered her head and pretended to check her iPhone.

The awkward silence was broken by Astrid, who suddenly farted loudly on Cara's lap.

'Oh, lovely,' said Cara, rubbing Astrid's back. 'What a delicate little flower you are.'

Cara had a knack for defusing tension.

They went to the Central Coast for the weekend. Ginie organised everything online—two apartments, each with a laundry and kitchenette. The resort-style complex was set in rainforest hinterland, and had a heated pool, sauna and tennis court.

Nicole gave them all the privacy they needed, entertaining Rose in her room or by the pool. Precisely the conditions they needed for sex, Ginie thought. But when they'd arrived on the Friday night, they'd just collapsed on a couch and watched a DVD. Months ago, it would have worried her. But now she was secretly relieved.

'Nicole's amazing,' said Ginie as they lazed by the pool on the Saturday afternoon.

Nicole had purchased a pink polka-dotted swimming costume for Rose and was wading with her in the pool. Ginie only wished *she'd* thought of buying it.

Rose gurgled with delight as her feet skimmed the surface. 'Rose is becoming so much more interactive now, isn't she?' Ginie remarked.

'Mmm,' said Daniel. He was lying on a banana lounge in board shorts and black sunglasses, a sheaf of papers stacked next to him. He was supposed to be working on his novel, but he sounded half asleep. 'Makes me want to have another one.'

'Another weekend away?'

'Another baby, bozo.'

Ginie flinched. This was the second time in as many

months that Daniel had raised the prospect of having another child. They'd talked about it at length the first time, with Daniel admitting that his desire was based, mostly, on his experience of losing his parents.

'I just don't ever want to leave Rose alone in the world, without a sibling,' he'd argued. 'It's not fair to have just one child, if you can have more.'

It had taken all of Ginie's powers of persuasion to convince him to defer the discussion. But she resented having to revisit it again so soon, on their weekend away.

'You *know* we can't consider another baby yet,' she reminded him. 'Not in the current climate. We don't know when this financial crisis will end. Look at Jonathan.'

It was her trump card. Only last week, her brother had been forced into voluntary redundancy, along with thousands of other workers in the finance and investment industries globally. The flow-on effect was becoming evident across all professional services, especially legal and accounting firms, even in Australia. Coombes Taylor Watson was the quietest it had been in years. If *she* was made redundant, they would lose their home, their lifestyle.

'But I'm happy to consider it when the crisis is over,' she added. 'When we're on a firmer financial footing.'

'That's if you're still, you know . . .' Daniel trailed off.

She knew exactly what he was referring to: her age.

She flicked through the pages of her book, trying to suppress her irritation. She'd hoped to rekindle their sexual spark, but this conversation was an instant turn-off. It was all very well for *him* to hanker after another child so soon after the first. But *she* was the one who'd have to put her body through another pregnancy and deal with the career disruption. Not to mention the effect it might have on their relationship. Why did he want to complicate things so quickly after their first?

She'd had enough of this discussion.

'I'll go over and give Nicole a break.' She nodded towards the pool.

'No, I'll go,' said Daniel, sitting up and stretching. 'You've had a busy week.'

He picked up the pile of papers next to him. 'Maybe you could have a read of this? I've almost finished. Dominic reckons it's ready for submission. He's talking an advance of ten, maybe fifteen thousand. Publication in May or June of next year, if we're lucky.'

Ginie sighed. 'Can't Dominic do any better?'

Her only meeting with Dominic had left her wary of literary agents. Too much talk and not enough action, as far as she was concerned.

Daniel looked wounded. 'Dominic works hard. He knows a lot of people in publishing. He's the best chance I've got. No one makes any money out of writing, you know. Unless you're J.K. Rowling.' He stuffed the manuscript under the banana lounge.

'Look, I'll just finish this chapter.' She waved a copy of *Eat, Pray, Love* in his direction. 'I'm doing the hard yards here. For the mothers' group book club, remember? Then I'll start on your novel, I promise.'

Daniel shrugged.

She reached over and touched his face, a conciliatory gesture. 'It's good to get away with you.'

He stood up and tightened the drawstring of his board shorts. 'I'll go keep the nanny happy.'

He ran towards the pool.

'Rosie,' he yelled, spraying Nicole with water as he jumped in.

She laughed and splashed water back in his direction.

Nicole could lose some weight, Ginie thought.

Daniel held out his arms and Nicole passed Rose to him, fussing over her rash vest and hat. She clearly wasn't going to let Rose out of her sight, even in Daniel's presence. Ginie found this extremely reassuring.

We'll definitely do this again, Ginie decided. A few more trips like this and we'll be back on track.

She closed her eyes, resting her book on her lap. She felt as if she might sleep for days.

Ginie grimaced at the sign on the door, penned in Pat's girlish handwriting: *Fathers and Partners—Welcome!*

'This could be gauche,' she whispered as they pushed the glass door open.

'It's okay,' Daniel whispered back. 'I chose to be here, remember?'

For a moment, she saw what the others would see as Daniel walked into the room.

Tall and muscular, handsome in a dishevelled kind of way. He grinned at her, that mischievous smirk of his, and her stomach fluttered. He could still do that to her, even now.

Suddenly she felt so much better about the upcoming session, which she'd been dreading. She was sick of Pat and her solicitous advice, however well-intentioned it might be. She smiled to herself to admit it, but she much preferred the group's informal meetings at Beachcombers on Friday mornings.

'Hello!' called Pat, all teeth and clipboard as usual. 'Ginie and . . . ?'

'Daniel,' he replied, grinning as if she was a long-lost friend.

Pat cocked her head. 'I've seen you before, haven't I?'

Daniel winked. 'I hope not. I've only fathered one child, as far as I know.'

Pat exploded into laughter, clutching her ribs for support. Daniel's charm was irresistible, it seemed, to almost everyone.

'Hello,' Cara called from the change table. She was grappling with Astrid, holding her two ankles in one hand, changing a dirty nappy. A red-headed man hovered at her side, holding wipes and a tube of rash cream. 'This is Richard, my husband.' Cara nodded in his direction.

'Pleased to meet you,' said Richard. He made a 'no hands' gesture with the wipes and rash cream.

'I know how you feel, mate,' Daniel said with a laugh. 'This is Ginie, I'm Daniel and . . .' He picked up Rose from the pram. 'This is our little Rose, between two thorns.' Rose giggled as Daniel lifted her above his head. Ginie loved that little sound: a gurgling, airy guffaw that only Rose could make.

'Help yourselves to refreshments,' called Pat, gesturing towards a rickety table stacked with styrofoam cups and instant coffee. 'Ah, who do we have here?' She turned towards the door.

Ginie nudged Daniel. 'This is the couple I told you about,' she whispered.

'I'm Gordon,' said the white-haired man, holding the door open for Made, who pushed Wayan's stroller through the gap. 'Made's inferior half.'

Before he'd closed the door, Suzie arrived, all windswept and smiling, carrying Freya in a sling. 'Hi,' she said.

'Come in, come in,' Pat said, scanning her clipboard. 'Good to see you. Is anyone joining you today?'

Suzie looked embarrassed as she shook her head.

'Me neither,' said Miranda, stepping through the doorway too. 'Willem's interstate again.' With Rory balanced on her hip, Miranda attempted to shepherd three-year-old Digby over the threshold. Digby pouted his objection and pushed an elbow into her leg.

'Come on, Dig,' urged Miranda. She propelled him through the door and towards a crate of toys in the far corner of the room.

Pippa arrived next with her husband, who was carrying Heidi in a BabyBjörn.

'Hello, Pippa,' said Pat, crossing her name off. 'And you are . . . ?'

'Robert.' He was athletic, with the look of someone who spent a lot of time in the outdoors. The polar opposite of Pippa, Ginie thought. She couldn't imagine how *they* came to be together.

'Right, come and join the circle.' Pat pointed to a ring of

chairs. 'We've got limited time today and a lot of territory to cover while we've got these gentlemen here.' She smiled as they took their seats. 'But first, let's do introductions.'

Not again. Ginie glanced heavenward.

'These ladies already know each other quite well,' added Pat. 'They've been meeting outside our formal sessions, haven't you?'

Several of the others nodded.

'So, gentlemen, I'd like you to tell us your name, a little bit about yourself, and one thing that you *like* about fatherhood. And then perhaps one thing that you're finding *challenging* about being a dad.' Pat smiled at Daniel. 'How about we start here?'

Ginie glanced at Daniel, edgy on his behalf.

'Thanks, Pat,' he said, exuding his usual confidence. Daniel was good at ad-libbing.

'Hi, everyone. I'm Daniel, Ginie's toy boy.'

Several of the women giggled. Ginie stared at her hands. She didn't know these people well; why was Daniel being so casual?

'I'm a writer,' he said.

After a fashion, Ginie thought.

He bounced Rose on his knee. 'I'm really enjoying being a hands-on dad. My work's pretty flexible, and Rose is doing lots now. Smiling and laughing and all that. Aren't you, sweetie?' He nuzzled Rose, who responded with a squeal. 'As for what I'm *not* enjoying . . . Well, Ginie and I are both pretty strong-minded . . .' Ginie's eyes widened. 'And because we're first-timers, I guess it can be a bit hard to know who's right, you know?'

Ginie couldn't allow him to continue. 'That's why having a nanny's been great for us, hasn't it?' she interrupted. 'It's like having a parenting expert on tap.'

She turned to Daniel with a forced smile. *Back off now*, she said with her eyes.

'Yeah, Nicole's been great,' he agreed. 'But sometimes it's like having three chiefs and no Indians.'

Ginie tried to look nonchalant.

'Ah yes,' said Pat with a chuckle. 'The balance of power between a couple can shift after children. That's a very good point, Daniel, and one we'll return to later.'

Pat nodded at Richard, signalling it was his turn to speak. Ginie consciously focused on the man's pale lips moving, his ginger hair thinning at the crown, the square tortoise-shell glasses. But her irritation remained. *Three chiefs and no Indians?*

'I'm an accountant,' said Richard.

No prizes for guessing that one, Ginie thought.

He was obviously nervous and stumbled over his words. Cara leaned back in her chair and casually rested a hand on his.

It seemed to make all the difference. He relaxed and smiled at Pat. 'I'm enjoying watching Astrid grow,' he started. 'She's already much bigger and that makes bath time a bit easier.' He paused. 'What I don't like is . . . not really knowing what I'm doing a lot of the time. If she'd come with a manual, that would've been great.'

Pat laughed. 'Ah, but babies are do-it-yourself and that's what makes them *fun*! There are some good resources available, including this baby health centre. We're here to support you.'

Pat's eyes roved across the group and stopped at Made's husband. 'Next?'

'I'm Gordon.' He held Wayan in his arms and jiggled him from side to side. 'I'm an engineer by trade, so I understand why Richard wants a how-to manual for babies. But our Wayan's got his own little agenda.' He ruffled Wayan's hair affectionately. 'I think the *best* thing about being a father is discovering that my wife is a natural-born mother.' He smiled at Made. 'It's one of the most satisfying experiences of my life.

'As for what's challenging, well, keeping this little fellow off the floor for the past three months has been pretty tough at times.' He looked around the room. 'Made might have told you that the Balinese believe newborns are pure, closer to the gods. So you can't let their feet touch the ground, or they're vulnerable to black magic. But once they've had a special ceremony at three months, it's all sorted.' He laughed. 'We'll be heading back to Bali in the next month or so. But Wayan's getting heavier by the day and I'm an old man. I'm not sure my back can take it anymore . . .'

Made giggled and slapped him on the knee as if he'd just told a fabulous joke.

Pat looked from one to the other. 'Is that similar to a christening ceremony?'

Gordon shook his head. 'Not really. For Balinese parents, it's when you find out who your baby really is. A spirit medium tells you who's been incarnated in the baby. There's nothing like it in Australia. Fascinating stuff.'

It sounded completely foreign to Ginie. And to Pat, too, it seemed.

'Right, one more,' said Pat, moving on. 'Robert?'

'Yep,' said the rugged-looking man at Pippa's side. His faded blue work shirt was tucked into navy King Gee trousers, and his Blundstone boots were caked in dried mud. 'Um, I've got to go back to work soon, sorry.' He looked around at the group. 'I'm a builder.'

A man who actually works hard, thought Ginie.

'What do I like about being a dad? Um . . .' He rubbed his hands together, thinking. 'Um . . .' The silence began to drag. 'Well, I guess it's nice seeing her asleep.' A pinkness had spread across his cheeks. 'And what I don't like is . . . when she doesn't sleep very well.' He glanced nervously at his wife. 'I mean, it's really hard when she's waking up six or seven times a night.'

Pippa's gaze was fixed on the white wall opposite.

Pat nodded sagely. 'Yes, sleeping problems are by far the biggest cause of stress for parents in the first year of their baby's life. That's why it's so important to get babies into a good sleep routine from the outset.'

She stood up. 'Right, thank you very much for sharing, gentlemen. It's great to have you here. Today's topics are: effective co-parenting, communication skills and finding time for "us". Some of you have already touched on these issues. So, let's get started.'

Ginie's eyes began to glaze over. Her hand strayed to her iPhone.

*

'Yeah, I enjoyed it,' said Daniel, pushing Rose's pram as they made their way back to the car park. 'I mean, especially the informal chat afterwards. No one's got a clue about parenting, really. We're all just having a swing at it. And shit happens, literally, to everyone.'

'How very philosophical of you.'

'Robert's a nice guy, Richard's a bit quiet,' he continued. 'I'm not sure why you're so hung up about Made and Gordon. He seems pretty laidback. He's a surfer too, you know.'

Ah, thought Ginie. The surfing fraternity prevails.

'But don't you think she's a bit young for him?'

'Well, *you* married a younger guy.' He winked at her. 'No one's calling you a cradle-snatcher.'

Her irritation erupted to the surface. 'Yes, what the hell were you thinking, referring to yourself as my "toy boy" back there?'

Daniel stopped walking and turned to face her.

'What's wrong?' He seemed genuinely puzzled.

'I just didn't appreciate it, in front of people I hardly know. And as for "three chiefs and no Indians", you made me sound like a control freak.'

He looked at her for a moment then grinned. 'Well, you are. Don't tell me you're going to deny *that*?'

She relented a little. 'Well, maybe I am, sometimes. But not when it comes to Rose.'

'Oh, right.' His smile was teasing now. 'Well, all I can say is, I could do with a fathers' group to give *me* some support. Maybe I'll contact those guys back there and suggest a men's shed for the downtrodden and demoralised.'

'Oh come on,' she scoffed. 'What could you *possibly* need support for? You've got me *and* Nicole. Don't tell me *she's* not working for you?'

He couldn't refute it, she knew.

'Right you are, Counsel.'

Ginie stared at the gridlock, snaking across the Spit Bridge and up into Mosman. She sipped at her takeaway coffee. Some mornings were better than others, when she left Rose with Nicole. There were times she practically ran down the driveway, eager for the sanctuary of her car. But other days, and today was one of them, she felt a peculiar tightness creep across her chest as she slipped into her charcoal grey two-piece. She'd watched them in the rear-view mirror, a lump in her throat, as she drove away. Nicole standing in the drive-way, flapping Rose's hand madly before turning back towards the house to start on the breakfast clean-up.

She glanced at her watch. Right about now Nicole would be putting Rose down for her morning sleep and Daniel would be taking a shower before retreating to his home office. Sometimes he'd take Rose for a walk at midday while Nicole had lunch, sending a digital snap of Rose to Ginie's iPhone. Receiving such images in the middle of a meeting would instantly affect her: she'd flush red with pride or love or, sometimes, a wave of jealousy. She envied Daniel all the time he spent with Rose—unencumbered *fun* time, with Nicole at the ready to do the drudgery of changing nappies, bottle-feeding, or baths. All the things that Ginie automatically did on the weekends, by virtue of her role as mother.

Ginie sighed and stared out the car window. She hated thinking like this. All these petty resentments, percolating non-stop. I've turned into a bloody whingeing mother, she thought. Just like *my* mother, always bitching about something. Quit it, Ginie, she said to herself. You *chose* this path.

As if on cue, her iPhone chimed.

Where are you? Arnold wrote. *You have an eight o'clock. Kentridge and Co.*

'Oh, fuck.'

She'd arranged it the Friday before, she remembered, on her day off. But somehow she'd failed to put it in her calendar. Thank God she had an ally in Arnold. She hurriedly texted him back.

Cover me? Buy you lunch.

She shook her head, castigating herself. Her job wasn't working for her anymore, in so many ways. She'd been back at Coombes Taylor Watson for more than two months and, on the surface, she'd slipped seamlessly back into corporate life. Nothing had changed in the office, yet *she* was different somehow. Things she hadn't noticed before were becoming regular irritants in her day: the partners' expectations of acceptable working hours (arrival by eight, dinner at your desk); the extended networking lunches with boozy clients; the hours wasted on water-cooler trivia or non-essential meetings. All of it was precious time she could have been spending with Rose. She loved her work—the intellectual stimulation, the expertise she'd accrued, the relationships she'd developed in the office. But for all of that, she loved Rose more.

She remembered the exclusive Catholic girls' school

at which she'd been educated. The headmistress, Sister Ursula—a formidable woman of indeterminate age—had drilled her charges with the mantra 'girls can do anything'. As a teenager, Ginie had admired her energy and conviction in assembly, as she exhorted her students to study law, medicine, engineering. The world had been hard for women once, Sister Ursula had said, but not now. *These days, girls, biology isn't destiny. You're limited only by your imaginations. You can do it all.*

Only now, with Ginie back in the office and her four-month-old daughter at home, Sister Ursula's words rang hollow. The worlds of work and family weren't that easily reconcilable. Contrary to the propaganda, Ginie thought, women *can't* have it all.

Her iPhone beeped. Arnold again.

Quick sticks, sweetie, you're officially pushing it.

She threw her iPhone onto the passenger seat.

Something had to give.

Made

It was the last Friday of the month, a warm spring day in October. Although it was only ten o'clock, the sun already had a sting in it. They'd parked the babies' prams beneath the broad white umbrellas of Beachcombers, and pulled together two tables for their first book club session. The idea had been suggested by Cara a few weeks earlier.

'My brain's turning to mush,' she'd said, laughing. 'I used to be a journalist, and now I can't even read two pages at night without falling asleep. I need a book club to keep me motivated.'

They'd all submitted suggestions for books, then drawn titles out of a hat. Suzie's suggestion, *Eat, Pray, Love*, had been selected for the first session.

Made had been thoroughly intimidated by the prospect of reading an entire book in English and hadn't even tried.

'This has *got* to be my favourite book of all time,' Suzie gushed, thumbing a dog-eared volume. 'I just *loved* every single chapter, especially the India section. It was such a spiritual journey for the author.' Suzie's blonde curls bounced behind her ears. The way her hands fluttered as she spoke, her child-like eagerness, reminded Made of her younger sister, Komang. Suzie's face was open too, and her heart was good, Made was sure. When Suzie asked Made how she was, she actually *waited* to hear the answer.

Ginie coughed impatiently. Australians were always in a hurry, Made had come to understand, and none more so than Ginie. She was tall and athletic and rather old, with white hairs springing from her blonde plait. This was not unusual in Australia, she'd learned, women having babies at an age when they could be grandmothers. Ginie's face was lined across the forehead and slightly drawn, giving Made the impression of hunger or thirst. Her restless, dissatisfied energy seemed to unsettle the group.

'I found the India section the hardest, actually,' said Ginie. 'Italy was passable, but India was dull. In fact, I found the whole story a bit tedious. I just couldn't get past the fact that after the author split up with her husband, her publisher gave her an advance to go and have an overseas adventure and write about it.' She rolled her eyes. 'I mean, how many unhappy thirty-somethings get to do *that* after a messy divorce?'

As usual, Ginie spoke too quickly, making it difficult for Made to follow what she was saying. But her tone spoke volumes. Suzie looked chastened.

'I know what you mean,' agreed Pippa, sipping at her peppermint tea. 'That seemed a bit premeditated. But in the end, I thought the author was really courageous to write about such personal things. Sometimes I'd read a paragraph and think, "Gosh, did she really mean to tell us that?" I liked the way she described all the unexpected things that can happen to us in life.'

Made had never heard Pippa say so much.

'Oh God, I hated all that,' objected Ginie. 'Why put your own bullshit out there, unless you're someone of world importance? The author kept rabbiting on about how challenging her life was and I kept thinking, come on, this is so indulgent.'

Made's eyes widened; she'd heard at least one crude word. No one else in the group seemed troubled by it. A waiter arrived with a tray of coffees, their second round. These women drank milky coffee, with hardly any sugar in it. It was too creamy for Made, so she always ordered tea. At Suzie's suggestion, she'd tried a variety of herbals, but they tasted like warm flowers.

'I agree with Ginie,' said Miranda, bouncing Rory on her knee. 'I just wondered how hard the author's life really was.' She stood up from the table to check on Digby and, seeing him scaling the climbing frame, sat down again. 'I mean, she didn't have any children, did she? I loved her honesty and humour, but hated how much she didn't know about life. I kept thinking to myself, honey, if you think this is worth whining about, just wait until you have kids.'

Everyone laughed.

'What did you think of it, Cara?' Suzie's expression was hopeful.

'Well . . .' Cara looked thoughtful, fingering the end of her ponytail. She had hair the colour of teh panas, Made thought, the dark orange tea she missed so much. 'I felt like I got to know Elizabeth Gilbert quite well in the Italy section. Then I found the India section a bit odd, mostly because she spent all her time in an ashram full of expatriates.' Astrid gurgled and suddenly coughed; she hadn't long been fed. Cara dabbed at the baby's mouth with a wipe.

'But I guess more than anything, I felt sorry for the writer,' Cara continued. 'She spent most of the book trying to make sense of her pain. I was relieved when she found happiness in Indonesia. I found that part quite beautiful. And I'd love to hear what Made thought of it.'

All eyes fixed upon Made, who rummaged through her bag for her notebook. She'd prepared for this moment.

'I write down my thinking,' Made announced, glancing about nervously. 'I want not to say the wrong.' She didn't want to be on the receiving end of Ginie's scorn. She'd seen how she made the others wilt at times, Suzie in particular.

She folded back the pages of her notebook. Cara nodded at her encouragingly.

'Too hard for me to read book,' she said. 'But Gordon borrow DVD for me. I watch four times. I learn many new word in English. Like celibate, mozzarella and gelato.'

The others laughed. She wasn't exactly sure why.

With Gordon's help, Made had pored over her dictionary the night before, trying to piece together the right words. Even so, she knew her expression was imperfect. She'd wanted to tell the mothers' group that she'd been perplexed by Elizabeth Gilbert's journey. That the Bali portrayed in the film, the popular holiday town of Ubud, was a world away from the village life she knew. And that many of the Balinese characters looked and sounded like the opportunistic buaya—or 'crocodiles', according to her dictionary's translation—that hung around tourist precincts, waiting to prey on foreigners. Eat, Prey, Love, she'd jotted in her notebook, proud of her first English joke.

'This movie confusing for me,' she started. 'Elizabeth Gilbert take long journey to find happiness. She throw away old life, old husband, search for new things. But why she not like old life? I wonder. Sometimes life happy, sometimes life sad, but always life have meaning. In Bali, life not only about happiness.'

Ginie interjected. 'What is life about then, in Bali?'

Made shifted in her seat. 'I think ... ' She wished her grasp of English was better. 'In Bali, life is about ... accepting.' She glanced around the group. 'No person or place give the happy feeling more than few days, maybe few weeks.' She looked at Ginie. 'Author Elizabeth, she run from the sadness, but sadness natural. Happiness not always the normal thing for humans. This is the way, in Bali.'

Made stared at her hands, doubting she'd made herself clear.

Cara broke the silence. 'I think I know what you mean, Made.' Her smile was warm. Even when Made couldn't entirely understand what Cara was saying, her tone was always kind. 'I have an old friend from university who comes from a small village in rural India. Bali is mostly Hindu, like India, isn't it?'

Made nodded.

'Well, this friend taught me that the pursuit of happiness is a very Western concept.' Cara folded the canopy down over Astrid's pram, signalling it was sleep time. 'In most parts of the world, in places like Indonesia or India, people are busy just surviving. Trying to get enough food, clean drinking water, or education for their children.' Cara zipped up the canopy. 'Achieving happiness or enlightenment is a preoccupation of the privileged, for those of us in the first world. Only people like Elizabeth Gilbert can afford to worry about being happy. Billions of others can't. It's one of the reasons I chose a career in social justice journalism.'

'Well, good on you,' said Ginie. 'I must be quite decadent in the scheme of things, with a life coach I pay to keep me happy.' Her tone was jovial, but her smile didn't reach her eyes.

'You're dead right,' replied Cara, without hesitation. 'We're all part of the global elite.'

Ginie reached for Rose, who had started to whimper in her pram. Cara didn't seem to feel threatened by Ginie, Made reflected, unlike the rest of the group.

'If you ever come to Bali,' said Made, 'you see life very hard outside the tourist area. Difficult to get the food and the water. Happiness not always possible.'

Ginie pushed a bottle of formula milk into Rose's mouth. 'I've never been to Bali,' she said. 'Daniel's wanted us to go for a while now, for the surfing. I'd prefer Paris.'

'Me too,' said Miranda.

'Well maybe you come to Bali with me one day.' Made smiled. 'You all come. Then you see the Balinese way.

Accepting the good and bad together. You help other people, that is happiness.'

There was a brief silence.

'Well, I'd better bring my husband on that trip, Made,' said Miranda. 'He's hell-bent on working his way to happiness. Usually on Sundays—it's his version of church.'

Several of the others laughed, but Made couldn't grasp what was funny about Miranda's words. Humour was the hardest thing about learning a new language. You never could tell what these women would laugh at, or why. But she'd noticed, over the past four months, that it was really only Miranda who could make Ginie laugh.

She closed her notebook: the conversation had moved beyond her.

Even now, after attending every single mothers' group meeting, Made still felt her difference keenly. In the early weeks, it had been a challenge to familiarise herself with the women's incessant babbling. Their words ran into each other, like the cackling of a brood of chickens. There was Ginie, who was always receiving telephone calls; Cara, the one who smiled as if she knew her; Suzie, who bubbled like a cooking pot whenever she spoke; Miranda, who was always distracted by the difficult Digby; and Pippa, the subdued one. With babies inevitably crying or feeding, it was difficult to conduct a one-on-one conversation with any of them. So she usually took their cues and laughed when they did, or simply listened as the conversation coursed around her. But over time, despite the fact that she knew none of them very well, she began to find comfort in their company.

A sudden shriek from the playground jolted Made out of her seat. Digby lay face down at the base of the climbing frame, wailing. Made turned to Miranda and held out her arms to take baby Rory.

'Thanks,' said Miranda, bounding down the small set of stairs, across the grassy slope and into the playground.

Made watched as Miranda kneeled next to Digby, who raised a bloodied face towards her and pummelled the ground with his fists. Miranda rocked him in her arms, trying to pacify him. Digby lay limp in her lap for a moment, before suddenly rearing up. The crack of their foreheads connecting was audible, even at a distance. Miranda fell backwards, dazed, still holding Digby.

Made immediately started down the stairs, carrying Rory on her hip. 'Miranda alright?' she called.

Miranda shrugged. An angry red mark had appeared across the bridge of her nose.

'Come on, Digby, let's take you home.' Miranda's voice was low and controlled. 'We'll put some band-aids on your face.'

Digby continued to wail. The noise seemed to irritate Rory, who began to squirm in Made's arms.

'I help you to car,' offered Made.

Digby was upping the ante, writhing and kicking as Miranda carried him from the playground.

'Bye, everyone,' she called, apologetic. 'Sorry for cutting short book club.'

Everyone made sympathetic noises; they'd seen it all before.

Made returned to the table and, with Rory in her arms,

slung Miranda's nappy bag over her shoulder and scooped up the Evian bottle under her seat.

Then she joined Miranda on the street, watching as she wrestled Digby into his car seat. He arched his back and screamed in indignation, as if she was prodding him with a hot poker. Finally, Miranda was able to pin his arms and legs down and buckle his seatbelt.

'I hate you,' he screamed as she shut the car door.

Miranda turned to Made.

'There's only one thing worse than a screaming baby,' she said quietly, taking Rory and the nappy bag from Made. 'And that's a screaming toddler.'

Made smiled.

Miranda fixed Rory in his car seat, then opened the driver's door.

For a moment, they looked at each other.

'Miranda work very hard,' said Made, unsure what else to say. 'You do good job.'

It was true. For all the challenges of life in a foreign land, Made couldn't imagine dealing with a child like Digby every day. What's more, Digby wasn't even Miranda's own son.

'See you next week,' said Miranda, pulling the car door closed.

As Made walked away, a car horn sounded behind her.

She turned to see Miranda jogging back towards her, the car engine idling.

'Forgot that,' she said, pointing to the Evian bottle in Made's hand.

Made smiled and passed it to her. Australians drank far

more water than Indonesians, even though the climate was cooler.

Miranda waved as she drove away.

She was always calm, Made mused, even when Digby gave her every reason not to be. She was carefully groomed, lived in a beautiful house, and was married to a successful financier. And yet, for all of that, there was something about those piercing green eyes. Despite so much to be grateful for, Miranda wasn't happy.

Made could remember a happier time, before the Bali bombings, when her family never went hungry. But after the bombings in 2002, tourist numbers had plummeted. Suddenly there were fewer rich Westerners holidaying in expensive resorts. The price of basic goods rose, and employment fell. And like almost everyone else on the island, her family was affected.

Being of Sudra caste, they'd never been affluent. They worked hard, cultivating rice and soybeans on the small plot of land they leased from Ida Bagus, the head of the village. They ate what they grew and gave Ida Bagus his share. Her mother took great care of the money earned from the sweet cakes she sold outside the village temple, keeping the notes straight and smooth in a tattered leather pouch beneath her mattress.

That pouch was only ever produced in the most desperate circumstances. Like when her older brother Wayan had fallen ill with blood fever, before the second Bali bombings in 2005. In his typical entrepreneurial way, Wayan had been supplementing the family's income with a small tyre-repair service at the foot of the mountain. When he fell sick, lying motionless and glassy-eyed on his bed for three nights, her mother had walked half a day to fetch the doctor. Made's stomach had churned with anxiety as she watched her mother bow down and touch the doctor's feet with handfuls of her long black hair. Her silent plea: *save my son*. The doctor had stayed two days in their village, mixing up all manner of potions and poultices, leaving instructions with her mother on how to use them. Then he'd accepted all the notes from her mother's pouch, promising to return the following Tuesday. But Wayan had died before the week was out. And so her only brother had gone, along with her mother's savings.

Within two months of Wayan's death, they were eating only one meal a day. The whole of Bali was suffering, the second bombings having frightened the Westerners away again. Forever, some said. Her mother refused to beg and ran the household as though nothing was wrong. She dismissed Komang's complaints with a raised hand.

'Komang, we are very fortunate,' her mother would say. 'Your father works hard and so do I. Do not dishonour our efforts with your ungrateful words.' Then she would push most of her own meagre rice ration into Komang's bowl, reserving the rest for Made. When Made objected, she would raise her hand for silence again.

But Made would hear her mother at night, weeping quietly into the sarong she used as a pillow. As she listened to her mother's grief, she would imagine Wayan alive again. His cheeky smile, his husky voice accompanying a four-stringed guitar on moonlit evenings, his wily schemes to make money. At family gatherings, her father had always told the story of how Wayan, at seven, had picked wild lychees in the wet season and sold them at market. He'd hung a sign over his bicycle with the words *Magic Lychees—Make You Strong* and spent several hours spruiking their qualities to the market throng. He'd returned that night with six thousand rupiah in his pocket, much to his parents' amazement. 'There's no doubt about Wayan,' her father chuckled. 'He could sell eggs to a chicken.'

All of that was gone now. Since the day Wayan died, her father hadn't spoken much. He spent much of his time smoking under the papaya tree. Made would see her mother watching him from across the yard, a worried look on her face.

Three months after Wayan's death, Made came to a decision. With her brother gone, she was the eldest. She was eighteen years old: it was *her* responsibility to help the family. She needed to find work, one way or another.

Early one morning, before the rooster crowed, she slid out of bed and began to get dressed.

Komang stirred at her side. 'What are you doing?' she murmured.

'Little sister,' Made whispered, kneeling next to her, 'I am going to find work. Tell mother I will return soon with good news.'

'But . . .' Komang began. Her small hand gripped Made's.

'Shhh,' whispered Made. 'It is my destiny to go. It is your destiny to stay.' She stroked Komang's hair and kissed her forehead. 'Go back to sleep.'

She stole out into the cool dawn and took Wayan's bicycle, unridden since his death. With a knapsack of clothes strapped to her back, she set off for the coastal town of Sanur, where her cousin Ketut worked.

She hadn't been gone two hours when a nail punctured her rear tyre. Her legs were weary from the pedalling, and her arms ached from steering the heavy steel frame around potholes. When she saw the thin metallic spike protruding from the tyre, she almost cried.

What would Wayan do?

She picked her way along the road, wheeling the bicycle next to her.

'Where are you going to, missy?'

Made stopped and turned, scanning a nearby rice paddy for the source of the voice.

'I'm trying to get to Sanur,' she said.

'Down here.' A woman's head popped out from a water channel running alongside the field. She was hauling a large wicker basket on her back, loaded with wood. She straightened up with some difficulty, then clambered out of the channel. Made guessed she had just been drinking the water, or defecating in it. Her dark skin and dress immediately announced her lower caste. But she didn't look Balinese, Made thought. More Javanese, like her own mother.

'Good morning, Ibu,' said Made courteously.

'Sanur's a long way to go by bicycle,' said the woman, looking Made up and down. 'Especially for a scrawny girl like you.'

'Do you know where I can fix my tyre, Ibu?' asked Made. 'I've never visited this area before.'

'There's a petrol seller straight ahead, on the right.'

'Is it very far, Ibu?' Made glanced at the sun rising higher in the sky. Soon the heat would become uncomfortable.

'Not far. You tell him that Ibu Lia sent you. He will help.'

Made thanked the woman and continued on to the petrol seller's. There she sat in the shade of a coconut palm while the tyre was patched by a boy of no more than eight years.

'You have a strong son,' Made said, smiling at the petrol seller. 'Just like my brother.'

'Where did you say you were going?' asked the seller.

'Sanur, sir, to find my cousin.'

'Sanur? On a bicycle?' The seller threw back his head and laughed. 'Did you hear that?' He gestured to his son, then turned back to her. 'You *know* how far that is, don't you, buffalo brains?'

Made shook her head. She felt ridiculous. But if she didn't get to Sanur, what hope did her family have? Tears began to slide down her cheeks, dropping into the dust in front of her.

'Now you've made her cry, Dad,' the boy said in an accusing tone. He wheeled Made's bicycle towards her.

The petrol seller stood up from behind the stall and squatted next to Made.

'How old are you?' he asked, his tone kinder.

'Eighteen.'

'Then you're old enough to know that it's too far to cycle to Sanur. Do you know where you're going?'

Made shook her head. She knew nothing of distance or maps.

The man sighed. 'My brother drives the bus to Denpasar,' he said. 'He'll be coming through in an hour. Why don't you save your legs and catch the bus? Then you can cycle from Denpasar to Sanur. That's not so far.'

'That is very kind,' said Made. 'Ibu Lia said you would be kind to me. But . . .' She reddened. 'I have no money for the fare, sir.'

The man looked at her. 'Well, if Ibu Lia knows you, I'm sure my brother can give you a free ride.'

'Oh, thank you, sir.' Made stooped forward into a bow, touching her hand to her heart.

The seller stood up. 'Sanur's a big place, and shifty too,' he said. 'Be careful down there.'

The bus traversed winding mountain roads and, eventually, the heavy traffic of Denpasar's outskirts. Made sat at the rear of the vehicle, next to an elderly woman with three chickens and a goat tethered to her seat. The frequent lurching of the bus and the panicked bleating of the goat made her feel queasy. On several occasions she thought she might be sick, but she pinched her nose to control the urge. The petrol seller had been right, she reflected. She never would have made it by bicycle.

When they arrived in the centre of Denpasar, the driver unloaded her bicycle from the luggage rack on the roof of the bus.

'Thank you for your kindness, sir,' Made said.

'Sanur's to the south, that way,' replied the driver, pointing to a highway.

Made had never seen so many vehicles. Trucks carrying all manner of cargo careered down the carriageway, weaving between motorcycles and four-wheel drives. Buses competed with minivans for space in the narrow shoulder, where she would be cycling. Quietly, she prayed for safe passage before mounting her bicycle.

It took her more than two hours to reach Sanur, stopping for directions along the way. When she finally arrived at Pantai Raya Resort on Duyung Road, the sun was setting. Breathless with fatigue, she stopped on the footpath and stood astride her bicycle, staring at the ocean. It was bigger than she'd imagined. The waves made a peculiar sucking sound, like the rush of strong wind through a forest. The air was sharp and cool, carrying pungent aromas she'd never smelled before. She was as far from her mountain home as she'd ever been.

She approached the resort's security post and smoothed her hair with one hand. Pantai Raya was one of the best-known resorts on the island, favoured by diplomats, corporate travellers and government officials. Only the wealthiest tourists could afford to stay there.

A middle-aged man in a brown uniform looked up from his newspaper. Six security screens blinked black and white behind him. Beyond the security post, dozens of cottages with thatched roofs dotted tropical gardens. Pebbled paths sloped down to a golden sweep of sand.

'Yes?' the security guard asked, his tone uninterested.

'Sir, my name is Made. I have come to visit my cousin Ketut. She works here.'

The security guard folded his newspaper. 'We have eighty staff members. What is her job?'

'She's a cleaner, sir. I'm hoping to find work here too.'

The security guard yawned. 'You and half of Bali.'

'Please, sir.'

The security guard cleared his throat, rolled a glob of phlegm around his mouth, then spat it out the side window of his booth.

'I'll call housekeeping.' He picked up a telephone and dialled three digits. 'Security,' he announced. 'There's a girl here looking for a cleaner called Ketut. Her cousin, she says. Do you know her?'

Made waited.

'What time tomorrow? Right, thanks.' The security guard replaced the handset. 'It's your cousin's day off. She's on tomorrow morning at seven o'clock. Come back then.'

Made gripped the handlebars of her bicycle. 'Sir, I left my village early this morning. I am happy to come back tomorrow, but I have nowhere to stay tonight.'

'That's a shame.'

'Please, sir, may I stay in Ketut's room?'

'No.' The security guard was firm. 'You *say* you're her cousin, but can you prove it? Besides, only staff and paying guests are permitted on site.'

Made stared at him, helpless. The sound of the ocean was frightening.

'What will I do?' she asked, her voice shaking.

'Come back tomorrow.'

*

It was cold, colder than a mountain evening, lying on the beach. She attempted to shelter from the wind by curling up against the exposed roots of an enormous banyan tree and resting her head on her knapsack. Her limbs throbbed from the day's exertions, but sleep evaded her. She was too alert to the foreign sounds around her, too frightened of being discovered, too ashamed of her predicament, too homesick. She missed her mother's familiar smell, the smoothness of her skin, the warmth of her embrace. She imagined lying next to Komang in the bed they'd always shared, their toes touching, giggling at each other's jokes. She drew the flap of her knapsack around her ears, attempting to muffle the high-pitched whine of mosquitoes encircling her. All night she drifted in and out of an uneasy sleep.

In the stillness before dawn, she was jolted awake by a snuffling sound. Her heart raced as she tried to make out the creature in the sand nearby. She sighed with relief; it was only a stray dog scrounging for scraps. Her body was stiff and her clothes damp. The beach was shrouded in mist, but she could detect a faint arc of light creeping across the eastern horizon. She slung her knapsack over her shoulder and began to walk across the sand, her limbs warming with the movement.

She gazed out at the endless green expanse beyond, heaving with hidden currents. The ocean was alive, she could feel it. Her uneven breaths were barely audible above its rhythmic surge; she felt insignificant in its presence. This sea had delivered sustenance to the people of Bali since the beginning of time. A light breeze tugged at her clothes, like the invisible spirits of ancestors calling her on.

The mist swirled and suddenly parted. In the semi-darkness, not two metres ahead of her, an elderly woman stood facing the sea. Her skin was dark and her frame skeletal. Her long hair, streaked with silver, cascaded down her back. Made gasped and immediately crouched down on the wet sand.

'Dewi Sri,' she breathed.

The woman was a crone: she looked nothing like the goddess of rice venerated in the small shrine in her father's field. But the name had sprung instinctively to Made's lips. A tingling crept along her spine and down her arms.

The woman did not acknowledge Made's presence. Instead she stood, unmoving, her eyes fixed on the sea. Her clothes flapped in the breeze. A batik sarong was wrapped around her body, fixed in place by a bright yellow sash. A blue shawl of woven lace lay over her right shoulder. Her lips were moving, but Made couldn't make out the words. She stooped to place an offering on the sand. A lychee, rice, a sweet cake and several brightly coloured flowers were nestled within the basket. The woman staked the offering to the sand with a wand of burning incense, then turned towards Made and smiled. Her mouth was stained with the reddish-brown juice of betel leaf and several of her teeth were missing.

'The most important thing, child, is not what is in the basket, but that the offering is made with love.' Her voice crackled like dry wood on the forest floor. She was terrifying, yet strangely familiar. 'Even the fanciest offering, given without love, is worthless. True love is divine.'

Made stared at the woman, speechless.

The woman nodded once, then turned and disappeared into the billowing mist.

Made took several steps forward. She wanted to follow the woman, to sit at her feet. To tell her about Wayan, her parents, Komang and the responsibility that was now hers. To beg for the woman's help and protection against the many things of which she was ignorant.

The first rays of sun fell on her face and stretched across the deserted beach. As the mist began to clear, the jagged out-line of jetties, flagpoles and reclining chairs emerged, littered like flotsam and jetsam across the sand.

The old woman was nowhere to be seen.

Made turned back the way she had come.

It was time to find Ketut.

'Little cousin!' cried Ketut.

Made stood to one side of the security post, conscious of the guard's glare.

'You look awful. Are you alright?' Ketut dropped her bags and hugged Made to her chest.

'I'm fine.' Made lowered her voice to a whisper. 'But I slept on the beach last night.' She nodded in the direction of the guard. 'He wouldn't let me in.'

'That doesn't surprise me.' Ketut's bright eyes danced. 'What are you doing here? Let me look at you. You've grown so *big*.'

Made smiled. Ketut herself, at twenty, looked much older in her crisp brown uniform.

'Mother would never admit it,' said Made, 'but it's been

terrible since Wayan . . .' She bit her lip as tears spilled down her cheeks.

'Poor darling,' said Ketut, drawing Made to her chest again.

'I need to find work.' Made wiped her eyes with her sleeves. 'I thought you might help me, Tut. Is there any work going here?'

Ketut shrugged. 'I don't know. It is very hard now, after the bombings. Not so many tourists. But I can introduce you to Ibu Margono today. You'll need to get changed first. Come with me.'

Ketut marched over to the security booth and, holding Made's hand, smiled at the guard.

'Sir, this is my cousin. She is a village girl from the mountains, looking for work. She needs a bath before I can take her to see Ibu Margono. May I seek your approval to take her to my quarters?'

The guard smiled at Ketut. There was a leering quality to his gaze. 'Well, since you asked so nicely, Miss Ketut, certainly.'

He pushed a clipboard towards Made. 'Sign here. But make sure you report back to me by this time tomorrow,' he added. 'We don't want people overstaying their welcome.' His breath stank of cigarettes and coffee. Made recoiled, stepping away from the booth.

'Thank you, sir,' said Ketut, shepherding Made up the driveway.

'You're welcome,' the guard called, his eyes following them. 'Have a nice day, Miss Ketut.'

*

Made showered in Ketut's room, then borrowed a fresh change of clothes. While she was changing, Ketut telephoned ahead to organise a meeting with Ibu Margono, the manager of guest amenities.

'Don't get your hopes up, though,' said Ketut as they walked to Ibu Margono's office in the administration building. 'She's a bit of a dragon.'

Made bowed her head and said a silent prayer, preparing for the worst. Ketut knocked on the door.

'Come in,' commanded a voice.

'I'll wait outside,' whispered Ketut. She turned the handle and pushed Made into the room.

Ibu Margono's office was dominated by a large timber desk. Bangkiri wood, Made guessed. Papers, folders and clipboards were stacked in neat piles across its varnished surface.

'You're a village girl, then?' asked Ibu Margono, leaning back in her chair and studying her.

Made nodded.

'Did you complete your schooling?'

'I finished middle school,' Made replied.

'And what experience do you have working in this sort of environment? Where's your CV?'

'I don't have a CV,' said Made. In truth, she wasn't entirely sure what it was. 'I've never worked in a resort before.'

Ibu Margono put down her pen with a loud sigh. She looked irritable.

'But I've worked hard all my life, with my parents,' said Made quickly. 'I have experience cooking, cleaning, sewing, tending fields and animals. I'm a diligent worker. I'm willing to learn new skills.' She swallowed, desperate. 'And if you give me a chance, I'll be loyal to you always.'

Ibu Margono drummed her fingers on the desk.

'Loyalty is hard to come by in this day and age,' she said. 'Especially in this part of the island.'

Made hesitated. 'Whatever you ask, I will do your bidding, Ibu.'

Ibu Margono looked at her. 'We'll just see about that.' She opened the top drawer of her desk and removed a clipboard. 'One of our housekeeping staff resigned yesterday due to ill-health.'

Made began to smile. 'Oh, thank you, Ibu . . .'

'But this is a Western-style resort,' barked Ibu Margono. 'And these are difficult times. Do you understand what that means?'

Made shook her head.

'It means standards of cleanliness that *you* can't even imagine. It means being able to eat breakfast off the bathroom floor. Do you understand?'

Made nodded, uncertain if she did.

'And you'll also be responsible for placing offerings around the resort. Every morning, without fail. Can you do that?'

'Oh yes,' Made replied. It was an activity she was familiar with at home. 'I'm an early riser.'

Ibu Margono unclipped a form and passed it to Made. 'Fill this in and return it to me tomorrow. Report for duty at six am.'

Made nodded again. 'Yes, Ibu Margono.'

'You'll be working under Gusti Agung, head of housekeeping. If he's happy with you by Saturday, you can keep your job and a permanent room in the staff quarters. In the meantime, you can share with Ketut. The wage for cleaners is twenty thousand rupiah per week, including on-site accommodation. Are you satisfied with that?'

Made attempted to contain her excitement. An extra eighty thousand rupiah a month would mean her family could return to two meals a day, with a little left over for savings. She thought of her mother, so thin and anxious, and her empty leather pouch.

'Yes, Ibu Margono.'

The next day, Gusti Agung demonstrated the meticulous standard of cleaning required. They stood outside a newly vacated cottage on the ocean side of the resort. Gusti Agung gestured to a trolley crammed with mops, brushes, dusters and cleaning products.

'This is your trolley, no one else *ever* uses it,' he said, his tone stern. 'It's your responsibility to refill it every day from the store run by Pak Anto. If you start using too much of one thing, Pak Anto will know. And *he'll* tell *me*.'

Made was puzzled by the inference. She wasn't a thief.

'The first thing is, *you* need to be neat and tidy.' Gusti Agung looked her up and down. 'Our foreign guests expect the best. *Always* tie your hair back.' He passed Made an elastic band and she hurriedly pulled her hair into a ponytail.

Gusti Agung stared at Made's feet. 'And no open-toed sandals. Get yourself a proper pair of shoes.'

Made wondered how much this would cost. She would ask Ketut to show her the cheapest market stalls in Sanur.

'Now,' said Gusti Agung, pushing open the cottage door. 'Let's get started.'

Over the next hour, Made learned that bed sheets had to be changed on a daily basis, even if the guest had not slept on them. All towels had to be replaced, unless a guest hung them neatly back on the towel rack. This had something to do with the resort's environmental policy.

'And as for bathrooms, Westerners have standards way beyond our own,' Gusti Agung explained, brandishing a toothbrush. 'Use this for hard-to-reach crevices around faucets, shower screens, plugholes. And don't think you can just wipe over the top of them. Our guests pay top rates. They will report anything less than perfect. And if that happens, I'll deduct a penalty from your wage.'

All furniture had to be dusted and polished, the carpet vacuumed, bathroom and mini-bar replenished, mirrors and glassware buffed, ashtrays emptied and washed, cushions shaken and plumped, any missing items documented, curtains repositioned and tied with a sash, frangipani and hibiscus flowers tastefully arranged on the vanity and, finally, air freshener sprayed throughout the rooms. Made doubted she could remember it all.

Gusti Agung closed the door. 'Now, your turn,' he said. 'Do cottages four through to ten. Their guests have all checked out. Call me if you have any questions.'

By the end of her first day, Made's back was aching. By Saturday, she was exhausted.

'You're a good worker, I can see that,' said Gusti Agung,

passing her a pile of neatly pressed brown clothes. 'Here are your uniforms. And your first pay packet. Welcome to the team.'

Made smiled, grateful. She stuffed the white envelope, weighty with thousand-rupiah notes, into her pocket. She'd never felt so tired. She'd always worked hard for her parents, but at least there'd been a rest period between noon and three pm, the hottest part of the day. Not at Pantai Raya. She was expected to clean up to twenty cottages in ten hours, and thirty minutes per cottage was hardly enough. She didn't even have a lunch break. Instead, she snacked on guest leftovers—pastries from bread baskets, pieces of fruit, cheese and crackers. At night, dinner was provided in the staff quarters—large servings of rice or noodles, sometimes with pieces of fried chicken or fish.

Her rostered day off was Tuesday, the slowest day of the week. Travelling home to the village and back again in one day was going to be a challenge.

She waited until the following week, when she had been at Pantai Raya Resort for a fortnight, then caught the earliest bus back to where she had met the petrol seller and his son. She imagined telling them of her success in Sanur, assuring them that it wasn't all bad. But when she arrived, it was still too early and the stall was deserted. She cycled home without stopping, hoping to arrive before the daily chores started.

She stopped outside the high stone wall of her family compound. As she hoisted her bicycle through the narrow gateway and leaned it against the wall, she caught sight of her mother. Busy as ever, she was draping wet washing over the bushes in the yard.

'*Bu*,' Made called.

Instantly her mother dropped a sarong and rushed at her.

'Oh, you naughty girl,' she cried, throwing herself at Made. 'I thought I had lost you. Why didn't you tell me where you were going? I have been worried, sick to my heart.'

Her mother was thinner than ever.

'I am sorry, *Bu*. I didn't mean to worry you. I wanted to make you proud.'

'You do, my little Made. You do.' She hugged Made to her.

'*Bu*, I have found work.' Made removed the white envelope from her pocket and closed her mother's hand around it. 'Eighty thousand rupiah a month. It won't make us rich, but it's something.'

Her mother frowned. 'You don't have to do that, Made. What sort of work is it?'

'Cleaning,' Made replied. 'In a big resort for foreign tourists. The same place Ketut works.'

Her mother appeared to relax a little. 'And Ketut is there with you every day?'

'Yes, except her day off is Sunday. Mine is Tuesday. We live in the same staff quarters.'

Her mother hesitated. 'Well, as long as it is a proper job and you are only expected to clean. Come and talk to your father about it. I will make some tea. You've lost weight. Have you eaten today?'

Made shook her head. She was ravenous from the cycling.

They walked towards the bamboo pavilion in the centre of their compound, where her grandmother sat washing soybeans.

'Hello, *nenek*.' Made stooped to kiss the old woman.

'Where have you been?' she asked in her gentle, wispy voice.

'Working.' Made smiled, proud of herself.

Her grandmother gripped her hand. 'Good girl.'

There was no sign of her aunt, uncle or cousins. They must be in the field, Made thought.

'*Bapak!* Komang! Made is here,' her mother called. Komang emerged from the cooking area and ran to Made, throwing her arms around her waist.

'I missed you,' Komang cried. 'Please don't go away again.'

Made patted her sister's hair. 'I'm working now, little sister. I have to go back to Sanur today.'

Komang began to whimper.

'Now, who would think you are a big girl of fourteen? Only babies cry.' She stroked Komang's face and whispered, 'I missed you too.'

Her father appeared, scythe in hand. From the mud caked around his ankles she could see he had been working in the field.

'Made,' he said, his face grave.

'Good morning, *Pak*.'

He didn't return her smile. 'Why have you made your mother sick with worry?'

'I wanted to help. I have found some work.'

Her father stood silent, waiting.

'As a cleaner in Sanur, at a resort for foreigners. Ketut helped me to get the job.'

He cocked his head. 'How much?'

'Eighty thousand rupiah a month.'

Made could hear the hens scratching in the dust, squabbling over tiny scraps of rice thrown out with the dishwater. It was a familiar, comforting sound, one she had grown up with.

'Good,' said her father finally. Then he turned and walked towards the gate.

Made looked at the ground, resisting the urge to cry. But what had she hoped for?

Her mother took her hand. 'Your father still misses Wayan.'

Made nodded, the tears tumbling down her cheeks.

'I am very grateful, Made.' Her mother cupped her face in her palms. 'You are a good girl. Not every daughter would do what you have done. Are you sure they treat you well?'

'Yes,' said Made.

Her mother lowered her voice. 'Well, if that changes, promise me you won't stay there. I don't want you mixing with lowlife in Sanur. The city can be a dangerous place. Smiling faces can hide ugly hearts. And a pretty girl like you . . . just be careful. There are too many village girls working as prostitutes in Sanur, Kuta, Legian. Don't you ever, *ever*, do anything like that. It would break my heart.'

Made nodded, solemn. Her mother rarely spoke with such vehemence.

'I won't, *Bu*,' she promised.

The day passed all too quickly. Word spread around the village that Made had returned, bringing news of a job. Many of the villagers stopped by and her mother was kept busy serving endless glasses of tea. She even made a batch of her best sweet cakes, usually reserved for formal occasions.

After lunch, Made sat with her mother and sister on the cool white tiles of the central pavilion, fashioning an offering. Komang threaded the young banana leaves together to serve as the container, while Made wove the circle, triangle and square to represent the moon, the stars and the sun. Her mother then placed flowers in their cardinal points: red in the south corner of the offering, white in the east, blue in the north and yellow in the west. They added rice, betel vine and several sweet cakes.

'It is ready,' announced her mother.

They changed their clothes and walked to the ancestral temple. Her mother presided over the placement of the offering, while Komang lit incense sticks around the shrine. Then they stood, three as one, with Made in the middle. Holding a jasmine flower between her fingertips, she pressed her hands to her forehead and closed her eyes, whispering her thanks to the ancestors.

They walked home in silence, their arms linked. They all knew it was time for Made to leave, if she was to be safe in Sanur by sunset.

She changed out of her ceremonial clothes and bade farewell to her father, who had just returned from the field. He wiped his forehead and, for a moment, she thought he might embrace her.

'Made,' he said, with the briefest of smiles. He shifted his weight from one foot to the other and then turned away.

Her mother and Komang stood by the gate, waving. As she cycled, Made kept turning her head to glimpse them again, until they were blurred specks in the distance.

Weeks became months and Made began to see the effect of the extra income on her family. Her mother's face was fuller and brighter, her father seemed more talkative. Most importantly, Komang returned to school. Komang was naturally clever, adept at school in a way Made had never been. Every week when Made returned to the village, she would sit with Komang and quiz her on her studies. And every week she would return to Pantai Raya with renewed energy to continue her work. It gave her enormous satisfaction to see Komang complete her first year of middle school, and then her second.

Within a year of starting work at Pantai Raya, Made had been assigned the most important cottages to clean—those of the highest-paying corporate clients. After two years, Ibu Margono gave her a pay rise.

'You have done well for me, Made,' said Ibu Margono, an uncharacteristic softness in her voice. 'From now on, you will receive one hundred thousand rupiah per month. And if you work hard for another year, I will make you my assistant manager.'

Made was astonished.

'Thank you, Ibu Margono,' she said, pressing her lips to her hand.

The next morning, Made rose before dawn and, as she always did, carried the day's first offering to the sacred banyan tree growing at the edge of the beach. The tree was ancient and sprawling, a mystical guardian of the shore. The lower part of its bulbous trunk was draped in black and white checked *poleng* cloth. As she placed the offering on the stone altar in the semi-darkness, she noticed a Westerner walking along the beach towards her. It was hard to make out his features below a shock of white hair. He seemed oblivious to her presence as he sauntered, barefoot, across the sand. She stood up quickly and, in so doing, startled him.

'Oh!' he said. An indistinguishable string of words followed.

She opened her hands, palms up in an apology. Then she gestured towards the offering in the tree.

He pumped his arms quickly. 'Walking,' he said. It was, she realised, a reciprocal explanation.

'Ah, *jalan-jalan*,' she said. She lifted the edge of her sarong, which was trailing in the sand, and nodded at him. 'Goodbye, sir.'

'Goodbye,' he replied.

As she was walking away, he called something out to her which she couldn't understand.

She turned and smiled over her shoulder.

The man laughed, then continued along the beach.

Later that morning, she knocked on the door of Cottage 12.

'Hello, cleaner,' she called out.

In her two years at Pantai Raya she had memorised a number of useful English phrases—'How are you?', 'It's a nice day' and 'Come back later'. She'd also learned how to say 'good morning' and 'thank you' in Japanese, Mandarin and Dutch.

'Hello, cleaner,' she repeated, louder this time. She inserted the master key into the lock.

The door swung open, revealing a man in a white bathrobe. She immediately averted her eyes.

'Come back later,' she said, backing away.

'No, no,' said the man. She looked up at him. Was it the Westerner she'd met on the beach? She couldn't be sure; they all looked the same. But the white hair was similar.

The man smiled and said something, gesturing over his shoulder.

'No English,' said Made, shaking her head.

'Come in,' said the man.

She followed him inside. A laptop was perched on the coffee table, surrounded by large sheets of paper with elaborate diagrams on them.

'My work,' the man said, pointing to the table. 'Engineer.'

She nodded and looked away. She didn't want the man to think she was prying.

She began her cleaning routine in the kitchenette. One used coffee mug, one glass, one plate. She glanced into the bedroom; the bed was rumpled on one side only.

The man's mobile phone rang. He picked it up, slid open the glass doors and stepped out onto the tiled balcony overlooking the beach.

Made listened to his muffled words as she changed the sheets, dusted the furniture, adjusted the curtains and plumped the cushions. She wondered where he came from. America, she guessed.

Made pushed her trolley into the bathroom. She replaced the shampoo, disposed of a used razor and shaving cream, and changed the toilet roll. Then she commenced the painstaking process of cleaning the tiled walls and floor, and scrubbing the toilet bowl. No matter how repugnant the task, she thanked the gods every day for her work in Sanur.

The man's laughter floated in from the balcony. It was a deep, rich laugh and, for some reason, it reminded her of Wayan. He'd always been a prankster. Wherever he went, someone was always laughing. But humour had almost entirely disappeared from their house since his death.

Something moved behind her and she jumped, bumping her head against the cistern. It was the Westerner, standing in the bathroom doorway.

'I'm sorry,' he said. She'd seen enough Western movies to understand. She shook her head, indicating that she was fine.

'Are you alright?' the man asked.

She shook her head again and carried on scrubbing.

The man walked away. A moment later he returned, a large dictionary in his hands.

'*Anda sehat?*' he asked. *Are you well?*

Made sat back on her heels and laughed aloud. She immediately clapped her hands over her mouth, horrified by her impertinence. The man might report her for rudeness. But he'd said the words with such an odd accent, she couldn't help but giggle.

'*Saya baik-baik saja, terima kasih,*' she responded slowly. *I am just fine, thank you.*

The man looked delighted.

'No Indonesian,' he said.

For a moment they simply looked at each other, smiling.

'My name is Gordon,' he said. He stepped gingerly across the damp tiles and crouched down, his hand outstretched. She wiped her hand on a rag before she took his.

'Made.'

The man's phone rang again.

'Working,' he said. 'Always working.' He took the phone and walked out onto the balcony once more.

Made completed her tasks in the bathroom, then sprayed air freshener throughout the apartment. She wrinkled her nose as she did; she didn't like its artificial smell.

She closed the front door behind her.

The next day, she had only just arrived at Cottage 12 when Gordon opened the door with a flourish.

'*Selamat pagi, Made*,' he said. *Good morning, Made.* He was clearly proud of this achievement.

'Good morning, sir,' she replied in English.

'Gordon,' he said. 'Call me Gordon.'

She said nothing. It was resort policy to refer to guests as 'sir' or 'madam'.

'Come back later?'

'No, no, come in.'

She commenced her cleaning routine and watched him out of the corner of her eye. He was sitting at the table, referring to his dictionary and writing words on a piece of paper. It looked like a laborious exercise.

Twenty minutes later, just as she was preparing to leave, he beckoned to her.

'Made?'

She walked over to the table and looked at the words he had written: *Anda tidak di pantai tadi pagi? You were not at the beach this morning?*

She smiled. Gordon had obviously been out walking again, just as he had the previous day. It had been an unusual morning for her. The night before, despite her fatigue, she'd been unable to sleep. When she'd finally closed her eyes, she'd heard the distant crowing of a rooster. Then, what seemed a moment later, Ketut was banging on her door. It was six forty-five. Made had scrambled out of bed in a panic, donned her uniform and reported for duty.

'*Besok*,' she said.

Gordon shrugged and held out his pen.

She grasped the pen and, as neatly as she could, wrote: B-E-S-O-K.

Gordon thumbed through his dictionary, then smiled.

'Tomorrow? Good.'

He seemed satisfied.

'Finish,' she said.

She pushed her trolley out onto the path and closed the door behind her.

The next day she spotted him walking along the sand before dawn. He saw her, too, but waited at a respectful distance while she made her offering at the banyan tree. Completing the ritual, she turned in his direction.

'*Selamat pagi*, Gordon.'

'*Selamat pagi*, Made.'

He fell into step beside her and they walked along the beach in silence. It seemed like the most natural thing in the world to be doing, walking with a Westerner she barely knew. He was old, probably older than her father. But he had kind eyes, and a mouth that curved upwards even when he wasn't smiling. He wasn't as large and intimidating as the other Western men she'd seen at the resort.

They picked their way along the shoreline and once, when Made stumbled in the sand, Gordon caught her arm and steadied her.

'Thank you,' she said.

'You're welcome.'

When they reached the timber pier at the far end of the beach, they turned back towards the resort. The sun's rays were just starting to warm the sand.

Made wondered if Gordon would join her again the following morning. She pieced together the English words in her head as they stood at the junction of a pebbled path leading to staff quarters in one direction and guest cottages in the other.

'Gordon stay tomorrow?'

Gordon nodded. 'Yes, I'm staying four weeks. Working.'

Made couldn't be sure that she'd heard him correctly. *Four weeks?* She would check again later, when she cleaned his cottage.

'Made work now.' She gestured towards the staff quarters.

'Me too. Thank you for the . . . *jalan-jalan*.'

She smiled at his attempt. 'Yes, thank you for the walking.'

*

A fortnight later, she borrowed an Indonesian–English dictionary from Ketut. Her daily visit to Cottage 12 had become a pleasant distraction from the mundane aspects of her job. Gordon had started writing more and more Indonesian sentences on paper, reading them aloud so she could correct his pronunciation. She discovered that he was from Australia, not America; that he was a civil engineer contracted to work in Bali on a large retail development in Legian; that he enjoyed his job, but enjoyed surfing more. In turn, she'd begun listening to an English language CD on the small disc player he had given her. Every night she plugged in the headphones and lay back on her bed, mouthing the foreign words. She imagined Gordon doing the same with the *Indonesian for Beginners* CD he had purchased.

Their early morning walks became a fixture in Made's day. Gordon always waited by the banyan tree, watching quietly while she made her offering. They walked the same route, but never failed to discover something new along the way: a silvery shell glinting in the sun's first light, an ancient piece of timber washed up on the shoreline, a single shoe with a US dollar note curled inside it.

One Saturday morning, they almost fell over a Western couple, half naked in the sand. The pungent smell of alcohol hung in the air as the woman writhed on top of the man. A tattoo spiralled down her sunburned back, bold purple letters inscribing a word Made didn't recognise: P-U-R-I-T-Y.

Made blushed, embarrassed, as they veered around the couple. Suddenly she felt very conscious of Gordon.

Gordon shook his head. '*Bules*,' he said, as they continued walking. She stared at him. How did he know that colloquial, slightly derogatory term for Westerners? She certainly hadn't told him.

'*Bules* not polite,' he said.

She nodded, relieved he thought so too.

After his first stay of one month, Gordon came and went from Pantai Raya every few weeks. She was always disappointed to see him leave and relieved when he returned. She practised her English between his visits and noticed that he, too, had been practising his Indonesian. Their conversations became less staccato, more natural. One morning in July, eight months after they'd first met, Gordon passed her a piece of paper with the words on it: *Umur saya 47 tahun. Made berapa? I am 47 years old. How old are you?*

She considered the gap of almost thirty years between them and decided against writing a sentence. Instead, she simply wrote down the numerals: *2-0.*

'You're twenty?'

She nodded. Then she took up the pen.

Bapak saya berumur 47 tahun juga, she wrote. But he isn't as white-haired as you, she thought.

He studied the words, checked his dictionary, and then, slowly, penned a translation beneath them.

He laughed aloud. 'Your father is also forty-seven?'

His fingers flicked over the dictionary's pages, finding more words.

Finally he said, '*Saya tua. Rambut saya putih sekali.*' *I am old. My hair is very white.*

She laughed guiltily. Had he read her mind?

His face became serious and he said something in English that she couldn't understand. Then he reached into his back pocket and removed a black leather wallet, producing a dog-eared photograph from one of its compartments. It was a picture of a woman on a beach, holding up a toddler towards the camera. The toddler had the glorious pudginess of most Western babies. The woman was smiling proudly.

Made nodded politely.

'My wife,' said Gordon, 'and my daughter.'

She squinted, attempting to maintain a neutral expression as his mouth formed more words. She was only halfway through her cleaning routine, but she had to get away.

'Made go.' She backed out the door, pulling the trolley behind her.

She heard him call after her, but she didn't look back.

Now that she knew that Gordon had a family, Made didn't want to see him again. She felt foolish. He was old enough to be her father, a Westerner from another world. How had she become so attached to him in a matter of just eight months? They'd shared morning walks, no more than an hour a day together. That was all, she reminded herself. He'd given her no cause to hope. And yet she'd grown accustomed to his presence in her life. She'd looked forward to their conversations, his laughter, his steadying hand as they walked along the beach. When Gordon wasn't in Bali, her life felt empty. But I am just a cleaner, she reminded herself. My destiny is here, at Pantai Raya.

The next time she saw Ketut, she asked if they could swap cleaning zones for the remaining three weeks that Gordon was in Bali.

'Are you alright?' asked Ketut. She knew Made too well.

'I've been very stupid.'

'How stupid?'

Made shook her head. 'Not *that* stupid.' She knew the kind of trouble Ketut might have in mind. 'But I'm . . . interested in someone I can't have.'

Ketut lowered her voice. 'A guest?'

Made nodded.

'A *bule*?'

Made nodded again.

'That *is* stupid. They'll fire you for that, you know. Let's swap tomorrow.'

Ketut's cleaning route took Made to the opposite end of the resort, closer to the nightclub and restaurant areas. The guests here were younger and rowdier, leaving their rooms in disorder. Thirty minutes per cottage was a challenge, but at least it kept her mind off Gordon.

She didn't return to the beach in the mornings. Instead, she asked Ketut to take the offering to the banyan tree.

It wasn't the same.

One week later, she was sweeping the patio of Cottage 39, focusing on the rhythmic sound of straw on concrete, when a familiar voice called out to her.

'Made.'

She turned to see Gordon standing on the pebbled

pathway beyond the hedge. The sun was setting behind him.

'Made,' he repeated. 'May I speak with you?'

She gestured towards a bamboo pavilion beneath a palm tree, glancing about self-consciously. She hoped Ibu Margono wasn't conducting one of her spot-checks nearby.

Gordon touched her forearm and she flinched.

'*Made yang manis . . .*' he began. *Sweet Made.*

She blushed.

He pulled a piece of paper from his pocket and began to read aloud.

'*Saya minta ma'af karena mengejutkan Made minggu yang lalu.*'

I'm sorry I startled you last week.

She refused to meet his gaze. He continued reading.

'*Isteri dan anak perempuan saya mati dalam kecelakaan. Sudah lama kecelakaan itu. Saya masih membawa foto mereka dalam dompet saya.*'

She searched his face.

My wife is dead. So is my daughter. It was a terrible accident, a long time ago. I still carry a photograph of them in my wallet.

His eyes glistened.

'I'm sorry,' she said. She cupped her hands around his, brown on white.

They sat in the pavilion, their hands entwined, until darkness closed in around them.

A fortnight later, Gordon asked Made to marry him. The moment had a dreamlike quality to it. One moment she was cleaning the wash basin, the next she was out on the patio, watching him unfurl an enormous sheet of drafting paper inscribed with the words: '*Nikahlah aku, Made.*'

Marry me, Made.

He caught her hands in his and murmured, 'I love you.'

She looked into his face and thought of her family. Her hard-working mother. Her intelligent sister. Her dead brother. Her dispirited father. Her dear grandmother. It was as if they were all standing alongside her, observing this moment. She didn't feel for Gordon the kind of topsy-turvy flutterings she'd felt when walking past Kadek in the village, but eight months had shown her that Gordon was kind, honest and hard-working. Kadek was handsome, but his prospects were limited to the one-acre patch behind his family's compound. Gordon, she knew, offered much more.

'*Gordon perlu minta izin bapakku dulu.*' *You must ask my father first.*

Gordon nodded. 'When?'

'*Besok.*'

Tomorrow was Tuesday, her day off. They could travel to the village together.

The presence of a *bule* prompted half the village to find a reason to drop by. In the end, her sister Komang was assigned the task of standing at the compound's gate, turning them away.

'He has important business with my father,' explained Komang, not untruthfully. 'Please come back later.'

They sat on the tiles of the central pavilion, looking at each other. Her mother served glasses of hot tea, trembling

as she did. She'd never met a Westerner before. Her father
squatted on his heels, sizing up Gordon through columns
of smoke exhaled through his nostrils. After Gordon had
drunk half his tea, her father leaned over and offered him a
cigarette.

'No, thank you,' Gordon said, waving it away with his left
hand.

Made could see that her father was offended.

'*Orang asing tidak merokok*,' Made explained. *Foreigners
don't smoke.*

Her father grunted. 'What's this visit about, then?'

Made nodded at Gordon, just as they'd agreed. It was time.

'Mr Pulu,' said Gordon, his expression serious, 'I would
like to ask for your daughter's hand in marriage.'

Her father's eyes narrowed. Her mother looked from one
to the other.

'*Bilang apa, dia?*' asked her father. *What did he say?*

'He asked your permission to marry me,' Made replied.

Her mother's hands flew to her mouth. Her father's eyes
widened in surprise. Made knew from the telltale rustle of
her sarong that Komang was listening around the corner in
the cooking area.

Slowly, her father began to smile.

It was her mother who spoke first. 'You don't have to do
this, Made.'

Made glanced at Gordon, relieved that he couldn't
understand.

'He's not forcing me to,' she replied.

Her mother looked unconvinced.

'But he is an old man,' she said. '*Look* at him. You would do better to choose someone closer to your age.'

'Better?' snapped her father. 'You think it's better for Made to marry Kadek from up the road, just because he's young? No, that is not better.'

Her father dragged on the end of his cigarette, then flicked it out into the yard. 'I think Made is showing great wisdom with this choice. Indeed she is.'

Made shifted on her cushion. Her father's tone made her uneasy.

Gordon turned to her. 'Is everything alright?'

'You tell him that I grant my permission for him to marry you,' said her father. His lips curled into a fixed smile. 'But you tell him also, it will be a great sadness for us to lose our eldest child. He will want to take you away to his country, no? I hope he is prepared to . . . compensate us for our loss.'

Made swallowed. She didn't know how to translate his words into English, and she didn't want to.

'Well?' her father demanded. 'Tell him.'

Her mother stood up and began collecting glasses. Then she stopped, walked over to Gordon and sank to her knees in front of him.

'You tell him,' she said, looking up into Gordon's face, 'my only wish is for my daughter's happiness.' She glared at her husband, then rose to her feet and stepped into the yard.

Made turned to Gordon, who was looking from one to another.

'Mother say, she happy if Made happy.' She hesitated, struggling to find the right words in English. 'But father say . . . you take Made to Australia, family have the money problem.'

Gordon looked thoughtful. He nodded at her father.

'We'll return to Bali regularly,' he said, glancing around the compound. 'And we can help your family with money. I will make sure that we do. Please thank your father.'

Made smiled at him, relieved.

She turned to her father. 'Gordon thanks you for your permission, and promises to help our family by sending money from Australia.'

Marrying a *bule* seemed to open bureaucratic doors far more easily than if Gordon had been Indonesian. With the help of an immigration lawyer, a stern Javanese man named Jono Sugianto, the whole thing was arranged in less than three weeks. At their first meeting in his stuffy, windowless office in Denpasar, Jono described the raft of documentation required to legitimise their marriage.

'You'll both need to lodge a Notice of Intention to Marry with the Civil Registry Office in Sanur,' he said, twirling his pen between thumb and forefinger. 'Then for you, sir, a Letter of No Impediment signed by an Australian consular official and a Certificate of Police Registration.' Jono turned to Made. 'As for you, we need a Letter of No Prior Marriage signed by the head of your village and . . .' He coughed discreetly. 'I assume you're under the age of twenty-one?'

'I'm twenty-one next month,' she said.

'Then you'll still need a Letter of Parental Consent signed by your father.'

Made was baffled by the terminology, but impressed by Jono's capacity to switch seamlessly between Indonesian and English.

'I can arrange it all, of course, for an appropriate fee,' Jono added. He mopped his brow with a starched white handkerchief.

Gordon leaned forward. 'Yes, I wondered about the cost.'

Jono batted the air as if swatting a mosquito. 'No, no. We can discuss that later. First, according to the law, marriage in Indonesia is legitimate only if it has been performed according to the laws of the respective religious beliefs of the parties concerned.'

Made waited for an explanation.

Jono looked at them. 'You two will have to make a decision now about who's going to convert. Will you become a Christian, Made, or will Gordon become a Hindu?'

Made frowned. She hadn't considered matters of religion. As Jono translated his words into English for Gordon, she stared at her hands. She had no idea of Gordon's religious beliefs, but she was quite sure of one thing: he wasn't a Hindu.

Gordon sat back in his chair, digesting Jono's words.

Eventually, he leaned forward. 'Well,' he said, 'that's easy. I'll become a Hindu.' He turned to Made. 'I know how important your religion is to you, but I'm an agnostic.'

Made hadn't heard of that religion before.

'It means he's undecided,' Jono explained. 'He doesn't have a religion, so he'll convert to yours.'

In Indonesia, this was practically unheard of. *Everyone* had a religion.

She turned to Gordon. 'Why you have no god?'

Gordon sat silent for a moment. 'When my wife died, I stopped believing in God.' He shrugged. 'Life is too unfair. I can't pretend to believe, Made.'

She nodded, remembering the long days she had spent at the village temple during Wayan's illness, praying for his recovery. All to no avail.

'You be Hindu now?' she asked, under no illusion that his conversion was anything but nominal.

Gordon smiled. 'A Hindu for you, and for the Civil Registry Office.'

His lack of belief troubled her. She wanted to take his hand and tell him that faith in God wasn't baseless, that life wasn't random. That amid all the suffering and pain of life, every being that crept, crawled and strode across the earth actually sang its praises to the Creator.

But she didn't have the words, and now was not the time.

She had the rest of her life to show him.

'Thank you, Gordon,' she said simply.

They were married on a Monday afternoon deemed auspicious by Pak Tulu, a Hindu priest contracted by Jono to conduct the ceremony. Once Ibu Margono had recovered from the shock of a *bule* proposing to Made, she did everything she could to help. In fact, she became quite proprietary about it, as if *she* was personally responsible for the relationship. Much to Made's amazement, she offered them free use of the resort's largest function room and access to catering.

The floor-to-ceiling windows in the function room

overlooked the stretch of beach on which Made had met Gordon ten months earlier. The room was too spacious for the small number of guests gathered to witness the ceremony: her mother, father and Komang, her aunt, uncle and Ketut, her grandparents, Jono Sugianto, Ibu Margono and several cleaning staff rostered on that day.

The ceremony marked Gordon's conversion to Hinduism before progressing to the more complex marriage ritual. Pak Tulu recited blessings and made several offerings, before sprinkling them both with holy water. The tinkling of a silver bell signalled the completion of the ritual, and a dour official from the Civil Registry Office stood up to complete the required documentation. With the formalities concluded, they shared a modest meal of rice, satay chicken and sweet cakes.

Later that evening, Made and Gordon stood outside Cottage 12 and said goodbye to their guests. The first stars had begun to appear in the darkening sky.

Komang hugged Made. 'Be brave, sister,' she whispered. 'You have a good husband.'

Her mother stepped forward and kissed her on both cheeks.

'You are a good girl, Made.'

For a moment, Made's resolve wavered. Why was she forgoing the life and family she loved, to marry a man so much older than her? The opportunities of a distant land seemed far removed from the comforts of the world she knew. She clung to her mother and kissed her, breathing in her sweet, familiar smell. Then her father stepped between them.

'Leave them now,' he commanded, motioning her mother away.

Gordon shook her father's hand and then took hers, leading her over the threshold.

As Gordon closed the door behind them, Made caught a glimpse of her mother. She stood motionless, staring out over the ocean, like a stone sentinel on a seaside temple.

The first thing Made noticed about Australia was the light. It was March, the beginning of autumn, yet there was a sharp, crystalline quality to the light that made her squint. As they drove from Sydney airport to Gordon's home near the sea, her skin seemed to tighten in the cool, dry air. She stared out the taxi window, wondering where all the people were. It was mid-morning on a Wednesday—why were the roads so empty? Cars and trucks moved at high speed along the motorway, but she couldn't see a single motorcycle.

The baby shifted inside her and Made patted her stomach. It's alright, little one. This is the beginning of our new life together.

Gordon, who was seated in the front passenger seat, turned and smiled at her.

'What do you think of Sydney?' He gestured towards the cityscape streaking past her window, shiny silver buildings jutting into an impossibly blue sky.

'It very neat,' she replied. 'Air smelling new.'

He laughed. 'We don't have much pollution here.'

It had been eight months since their marriage. Gordon had returned to Australia not long after their wedding, flying back to Bali three times for work. Each time he returned to Australia, he left a mobile telephone with her and called every day. Although Jono Sugianto had lodged her permanent residency application the week after their marriage, the process had taken much longer than expected. She'd kept her cleaning job in the meantime, returning every week to the village to spend her day off with her family.

The baby had been growing inside her for seven months when, at last, Gordon flew into Bali and announced that Jono Sugianto had finalised her Australian visa.

Saying goodbye to her mother and Komang was the hardest thing she'd ever done.

'When will you return to Bali?' her mother had whispered as they embraced for the last time.

'I don't know, *Bu*.'

'You must come back for the one-hundred-and-five-day ceremony, for the baby's sake. Promise me, Made.'

Made had nodded.

And then her mother had waved them off, tight-lipped with the knowledge that her first grandchild was being spirited away to another world.

Made continued to stare out the window of the taxi. This landscape was so different, its people utterly foreign. She touched her stomach and remembered her mother's face, pale and careworn, as Made and Gordon had left the village.

Whatever the gods deliver to me in Australia, she thought, I must make this separation from my family worthwhile.

*

'It's called a haemangioma,' the paediatrician said, pointing to a mottled red swelling above the baby's lip. Wayan was only four hours old, but Made had never felt so deeply connected to anyone, anything. It was as if she'd suddenly discovered a part of herself she'd forgotten, revealed in the flesh of another. She instinctively understood the terrain of Wayan's body, from the chubby folds around his ankles and wrists, to the swollen red diamond obscuring his upper lip. The first time she'd seen it, lying on her back in the maternity ward, she'd kissed it fervently, reverently.

'It's a collection of abnormal blood vessels that form a lump under the skin. We don't really know why they occur, but in eighty per cent of cases, they resolve by school age.'

Made looked to Gordon for clarification. He shrugged, indicating his own ignorance of the matter. Made shifted her weight on the hospital bed. The delivery had been long, with Wayan's head almost too large for her pelvis. This was often the case for Asian women, the midwife had said, especially those married to Caucasians. In the end, the obstetrician had used forceps.

'In Wayan's case,' continued the paediatrician, 'with a haemangioma of the lip, it's more likely to become ulcerated due to the friction of wet surfaces rubbing together. You'll probably have trouble feeding him. We'll need to get you some extra support. Where do you live?' The paediatrician scanned her chart. 'Freshwater?'

Gordon nodded.

'They've got a good baby health centre up there, so make sure you use it for health checks, mothers' groups, that sort of thing.'

Made watched Gordon listening to the paediatrician. He would relay it all to her later, she knew, in a mixture of Indonesian and English. She lay back against the pillows and looked over at Wayan, asleep in his bassinette next to her bed. She knew what her family would say about his facial defect: that it was the karmic consequence of some wrongdoing in a previous life. She'd always been a devout Hindu, but watching Wayan now, she simply couldn't accept that he was anything but perfect.

'I'm also going to ask one of our paediatric surgeons to take a look at Wayan when he's six months old,' the doctor told them. 'At that point the haemangioma will be as big as it's likely to get, and he'll be able to make an assessment of treatment options, including whether surgery is required.'

The doctor turned to Made. 'Many women find it difficult to adjust to their child's appearance as the haemangioma grows larger, especially if people stare or make comments.' He pushed a leaflet into her hands. 'This should help.'

Made read the words at the top of the leaflet: *Bringing up a child whose face looks different.*

'Thank you, doctor.'

She looked at Wayan. *I think you're perfect.* She was grateful that he had been born in Australia, where the medical system was vastly superior. Had he been born in her village, a doctor would not have been present. And then what would have happened, given the trouble she'd had? No forceps, nothing. She shivered at the prospect. The disfigurement on Wayan's lip wasn't life-threatening. It could have been much, much worse.

The paediatrician stood up. 'I'll ask one of the nurses to get a lactation consultant to come and see you shortly.'

She nodded.

Gordon accompanied the paediatrician to the door and they stood outside the room, speaking in low voices.

Made swung her legs over the bed and stood up. She bent over Wayan, wrapped in a blue cotton blanket in his bassinette.

'You are the most handsome boy in the whole world,' she whispered.

Wayan's dark eyes moved in her direction and then, suddenly, he began to cry.

'Oh sweet one,' she soothed. 'Don't cry. Are you hungry?'

She lifted Wayan from the bassinette and brought him to her chest. She'd seen it done in the village a hundred times before. Her breasts had become full and taut in the past twenty-four hours. Now they oozed a thick yellow colostrum.

As she pressed him against her breast, Wayan began to suck noisily. She smiled at the sound, and the not-unpleasant sensation of his mouth tugging on her nipple.

'That's it, Wayan. Drink.'

She settled back onto the pillow and watched Wayan as he suckled. He was so vulnerable, yet so strong. Born of her body, yet destined for his own path in life. It was such a privilege to be charged with his care, and such a responsibility. She thought of her own mother, who had toiled so hard for their family, and the thousand small sacrifices she must have made along the way. Made resolved to send a letter to Komang just as soon as she was out of hospital, asking that she read it aloud to their mother. Sharing with her mother the one thing she'd learned, as she'd pushed Wayan out of her body: that having a baby was like falling into God.

On the afternoon they returned from hospital, the first thing Made did was make an offering at the small shrine she had fashioned in the northeast corner of the backyard. The shrine looked incongruous, a tower of red bricks stacked between the garage and the fence bordering the neighbour's property. It had been quite a feat to construct at eight months pregnant. One day while Gordon was at work, she'd moved the bricks one by one from an untidy pile near the barbecue. After selecting an auspicious corner of the garden, she laid the bricks across each other, creating four sturdy columns. Then she poked around Gordon's shed, and found a length of wire mesh and a stepladder. Finally, she took from her suitcase a black and white checked *poleng* cloth and a bamboo parasol. She wrapped the cloth around the base of the columns, before positioning the open parasol in the mesh at the very top of the shrine.

It had been a source of comfort while she was in hospital knowing that the shrine was there, awaiting her return.

'I thank the ancestors for baby Wayan now,' she announced to Gordon, then padded out into the backyard.

It was late afternoon and a sliver of crescent moon hung low in the sky. This same moon watched over her family in Bali, she knew, yet it looked different, somehow. She patted Wayan in the sling, his body snuggled against hers. Then she lay out the items she'd taken from the kitchen: a sweet biscuit, a handful of rice and several incense sticks. Using the broad leaves of a paperbark tree that stood on the southern side of the yard, she set about fashioning a basket. She placed the biscuit and the rice in it, sprinkling them with the soft white petals of a flowering plant that grew near the back door. Camellia, Gordon called it. She liked the softness of the word. If they were ever blessed with a daughter, it would make a lovely name.

She stood before the shrine and pressed her hands together at her forehead, quietly murmuring her prayers of thanks. Sweet incense wafted across her, the heady scent of her homeland. She imagined the earth pulsating beneath her, rich with worms and rotting leaves, the soil simultaneously decomposing and renewing itself. Like all of us, she thought. Living and dying at the same time.

She felt her body loosening, becoming lighter, until she was floating in the comfortable darkness behind her eyelids. Suddenly she saw the face of an old woman; the holy woman she had encountered on the beach in Sanur.

'Excuse me.' A sharp voice disturbed her prayers.

Made opened her eyes, disoriented. A head hovered above the wooden fence to her right. Then a neck appeared, and two arms over the fence. The face of a middle-aged woman peered at her. Her neighbour, Mrs Carter, in all likelihood. Gordon had mentioned her, but Made hadn't seen her in the three months since her arrival.

'Hello, I am Made.' She smiled at the woman, then looked down into the sling. 'This is my boy, Wayan. We come from hospital today.'

'And what exactly is *that*?' The woman pointed at the shrine.

'I . . . pray,' explained Made. She wasn't sure why the woman seemed irritated.

'Well,' said the woman, 'in Australia, we pray in *churches*.' The woman glared at Made.

Suddenly Gordon was at her side.

'Mrs Carter,' he said, his tone genial. 'I've been meaning to introduce you to my wife, but I haven't seen you lately. Have you been away?'

The question caught her off guard. 'I had a spell in the country with my sister. She hasn't been well.'

'I'm sorry to hear that,' said Gordon. He placed a hand on Made's shoulder. She instantly felt better.

Mrs Carter looked from Gordon to Made.

'Well, I was just telling your *wife* that this isn't the sort of neighbourhood that's . . . all that *used* to foreign ways.' Her eyes narrowed. 'Goodness, she looks *young*. She could almost be your daughter.' A smile played at her lips.

Gordon stared at the woman for a moment, as if he might say something. Then he put his arm around Made and ushered her back to the house.

He shut the door with unusual force.

Made sat on the sofa and put Wayan to her breast. Her heart was hammering. She hadn't fully comprehended Mrs Carter's words, but her expression had said it all. She wasn't welcome here, even in Gordon's backyard.

She looked at Gordon. His face was flushed. Was he embarrassed by her?

'Gordon, I sorry,' she began.

'Oh, Made, I'm the one who should be sorry.' He lowered himself onto the sofa next to her and wound an arm around her shoulders. 'You'd think we were living in a country town, not the northern beaches. Talk about the bloody insular peninsula.'

Made wasn't sure of his meaning.

'Small-minded people make me angry, that's all.' He pulled her towards him and kissed her on the cheek. 'Mrs Carter was very rude. I'm sorry about that.'

Made leaned into his chest.

Her sister Komang had been right. Gordon *was* a good husband.

Still, Made missed her family with such intensity, it made her heart ache. Every part of Wayan brought to mind another—the softness of her mother's hair as it dried in the morning sun, her father's shy smile, Komang's gentle hand on her arm, the cheeky flash of her brother's eyes. Despite the haemangioma, Wayan was a contented baby. Nothing seemed to provoke him. But Made grieved for the fact that her family couldn't witness his small daily triumphs.

She would often sit on the concrete stairs leading down to their backyard, cradling Wayan and imagining the scene in her family compound. Her mother, stooped at the waist, sweeping the yard with long strokes of her rattan broom. And there was her father, chewing betel leaf and sipping tea under the papaya tree. Komang washing clothes in the large silver basin in which the three of them had played as children. And then she would imagine Wayan into the scene: his grandparents swinging him across the yard in a sarong, or his Aunty Komang, still young enough to play older sister, fussing over him.

Gordon's parents were long dead and his only sibling, an older sister, lived in a cold country in the northern hemisphere. The thought of her own family, not so far away, brought tiny pinpricks to her eyes. She made sure Gordon never saw them.

But at night she was plagued by dreams of her mother. Sometimes she would sit up in bed, barely awake, searching for her mother's form beyond the reaches of the bed.

'*Bu? Bu?*' she would call into the darkness, certain of her presence.

'You're dreaming, Made,' Gordon would whisper, finding her hand with his.

Then she would lie down again, blinking back tears.

As an answer to homesickness, Made attended every single session of the mothers' group. Initially she'd been confused by the concept. Mothers' groups weren't necessary in Indonesia, as there were always enough women in a village to share the load of child-rearing. But in Australia, neighbourhoods were divided by high walls, security grilles and unfriendly dogs. New mothers had to be introduced through the baby health centre, or they might never find each other across the empty stretches of suburbia.

At first they met at the Beachcombers kiosk, drinking countless cups of coffee while discussing their babies. Then, when winter began to bite, they met in each other's homes, sharing homemade biscuits and steaming pots of tea.

One week in spring, Miranda offered her home as a venue. Made was the first to arrive, just after two o'clock. She'd caught the bus five stops from her house, down to Miranda's home in the Freshwater Basin. It reminded her of Pantai Raya, being so close to the beach.

'Come in,' said Miranda, greeting her at the door with a smile. 'Digby's asleep, finally. Rory's through here.'

As Made walked behind her carrying Wayan, she stared wide-eyed at the spacious corridors of Miranda's home. Austere white walls were decorated with enormous canvases of modern art and delicate objects of glass and stainless steel. Compared to the two-bedroom red-brick cottage in which Made lived, Miranda's home was palatial. What did Miranda *do* with all these rooms?

'There he is,' said Miranda, nodding to a plush grey rug that covered the slate tiles on the living room floor. Rory lay on his back in the centre, gurgling at a stuffed giraffe suspended above him in a play gym. 'Are Wayan's feet allowed to touch the ground yet?'

Made smiled. 'Yes, we had ceremony in Bali last week.' Made placed Wayan next to Rory and watched the pair eyeball each other. Rory suddenly rolled onto his stomach and Wayan giggled at the movement.

'Oh, of course,' said Miranda. 'I'd forgotten you'd gone back. How did it go? It must have been nice to see your family.'

Made nodded.

It would be too hard to explain to Miranda how she'd felt, meeting her family again for the first time since Wayan's birth. The joy of her reunion with her mother, countered by her family's shock and consternation at Wayan's haemangi-oma. The mystic who'd been called in to divine the karmic reason for his defect, and the lengthy rituals that followed. At Wayan's one-hundred-and-five-day ceremony, conducted several months later than it should have been, the medium had pronounced that Wayan was, in fact, the incarnation of her dead brother. How goosebumps had spread across her skin and stayed there for days. It was too hard to express all of this in English.

'Sit down,' said Miranda, gesturing towards a shiny leather couch positioned against a wall. But Made lingered close to Wayan; after carrying him around for so long, it felt strange to be physically disconnected from him. It was as though a second, unseen umbilical cord had been cut by the Balinese priest who'd blessed him.

A splash of colour on the mantelpiece attracted Made's attention; a gold-framed photograph on the otherwise empty expanse.

Miranda followed her gaze. 'That was taken in Paris,' she explained. 'Four months before Rory arrived.' In the photo, Miranda stood in front of the Arc de Triomphe, the colours of sunset brushed against the sky. Her cheeks were ruddy with cold or exertion. One hand held Digby's, the other rested on the curve of her belly.

'It was a happy holiday?'

'Very,' said Miranda. 'Life was a lot less complicated then.' Made nodded.

A knock on the door announced the arrival of others.

'Come in, come in,' called Miranda.

A moment later, Ginie entered the room at her usual pace, followed by Cara. 'Oh my *God*, Miranda,' said Ginie. 'That's an Arthur Boyd near the front door, isn't it?'

Miranda blushed with pleasure. 'Yes, Willem's latest acquisition. I can't stop him at Sotheby's, I'm afraid.'

Ginie lifted Rose out of her pram and placed the baby on her tummy next to Wayan and Rory. She rolled a soft ball in their direction. 'Well, you can tell Willem he's done well. Daniel would *love* it.'

'Oh, you arty types,' said Cara, parking her stroller on the other side of the room. 'I couldn't tell a Boyd from my bum.' She lifted Astrid out onto the rug. 'Hello, Made. And how are *you*, Wayan?'

Made loved the way Cara always acknowledged everyone in the room, even the babies.

Within twenty minutes Pippa and Suzie had arrived and Miranda's gallery-like lounge room had been transformed by the nursery hubbub of six babies. There was the usual flurry of activity, complicated by the fact that most of the babies were now sitting and rolling. Astrid had even started 'commando crawling', using both arms to haul herself across the floor on her stomach, dragging her feet behind her.

Despite the noise and activity, Made didn't spend a lot of time talking to the other women. It was always like that, she reflected, everyone too busy to talk. It wasn't like passing time in the village with her mother, sister, aunts and cousins. There were no comfortable silences, no wild laughter born of years of familiarity. Perhaps that would come with time, she mused.

She felt most comfortable with Cara, who always tried to include her in the group's discussions. And it was easy to talk to Suzie, who never seemed to draw breath. It was a challenge deciphering Pippa's words, as her voice was so soft and she rarely looked Made in the eye.

'Does anyone know a good children's photographer?' asked Ginie suddenly. She slid her iPhone back into her bag and looked around the group. 'We'd like to get some professional shots done of us as a family. We've got this big blank wall at home that's crying out for a canvas. But we don't know anyone who specialises in kids.'

'I do,' said Miranda. 'Stephanie Allen is a great local freelancer. She does some beautiful work down on Freshie beach. She's a little expensive, but she's worth it.'

Ginie found her iPhone again and began plugging in the details.

Made watched Miranda and Ginie as they talked. Their conversations often ranged across completely foreign territory—from art and restaurants to clothing and homewares. It was all Made could do to understand the general gist.

'Have you read the next book for book club, Made?' asked Pippa, crouching down and propping Heidi next to Wayan.

Made smiled and shook her head. She hadn't managed *Eat, Pray, Love*, and the next book—Ginie's suggestion, *We Need to Talk About Kevin*—was much thicker, with smaller print.

'Is it good reading?' she asked.

Pippa glanced in Ginie's direction.

'No,' she said, her voice low. 'I mean, it's well-written. But as a mother, I wish I'd never opened it. I wish I could erase all the images it's burned into my mind.'

'Oh.' Made was relieved she hadn't attempted it. She studied Pippa's face. 'This book, it make you . . . sad?'

Pippa pulled Heidi onto her knee. 'Well, it showed how little control we have over our children and how things can go horribly wrong.' She grimaced. 'It was frightening. Don't read it.'

Made shook her head. 'Too hard for me. Book club next week, yes?'

'Yes, at Cara's house,' said Pippa.

Suzie sidled up to them. 'Are you talking about *Kevin*?'

Pippa nodded.

'You didn't like it either?'

Pippa shook her head.

'Well,' said Suzie, as if emboldened, 'any chance we could postpone book club?' She glanced around at the others. '*Kevin* is so full on, I'm having trouble finishing it.'

Ginie looked bemused. 'Full on? It pretty much boils down to nature versus nurture, doesn't it? Do we wreck our children's lives for them, or do they wreck them for themselves?'

Suzie flushed. Made couldn't tell if she was embarrassed or angry. Ginie always seemed to fluster her.

'Maybe with more time, I read some too,' Made added, mostly for Suzie's benefit.

'I haven't read it yet either, I'm afraid,' said Cara. 'Maybe my book club idea was too ambitious. I can't believe I'm even saying that. I used to read a book a *week*.' She laughed. 'Well, how about I send a text around later with some new dates?'

'Okay,' said Miranda. 'But why don't we go out as a group next Friday night, anyway? Have a few drinks or something?'

'Now *there's* a woman after my own heart,' agreed Ginie. 'Daniel's always having bloody beers with his best mate, Chris. It's well and truly my turn.'

'Sounds nice,' said Cara. She turned to the others. 'What do you think, girls?'

'Okay.' Pippa didn't seem terribly enthused.

'Can we go somewhere close by?' asked Suzie. 'I'll have to organise a babysitter.'

'We can go to that new wine bar in Manly,' said Ginie.

'Isn't it a bit pricey?' said Suzie.

Ginie shrugged. 'Not terribly. Come on, live a little, Suzie.'

Suzie stared at Ginie for a moment, then seemed to draw herself up several inches. 'I'm a single mother,' she said, her voice wavering a little. 'I'm on a tight budget. You probably don't understand that, Ginie, but I am.'

Ginie opened her mouth, then closed it again. 'Okay,' she said. 'The first two rounds are on me.'

Suzie paused, as if waiting for Ginie to say something else. Then she nodded, a hint of triumph in her smile, before turning to Freya. 'Pooh, you stink, madam. Can I use your change table, Miranda?'

Miranda showed her through to Rory's bedroom.

'What about you, Made?' Cara asked quietly, turning to her. 'Will you be able to come next Friday night?'

'I think so,' she said. 'But if Wayan wake for feed, Gordon have to pick me up. I no drive.'

Gordon had encouraged her to apply for a driver's licence,

but the idea of taking to the Australian roads was intimidating. So many rules.

Made dabbed absently at Wayan's mouth with a wipe, absorbing the spittle that drooled from the permanent cavity above his lip.

'Sure,' said Cara. 'How is Wayan's . . . condition going?'

Made was grateful that Cara didn't shy away from the issue. The others rarely asked; it obviously made them uncomfortable.

'He start to take the solids now,' said Made. 'He very good eater.'

'That's great,' said Cara. 'Is your doctor pleased?'

'We see him on Thursday, when Gordon flying overseas.'

'You mean, you're going by yourself?' Cara looked concerned. 'I can go with you, if you'd like. I've got nothing else planned for Thursday.'

Made had been anxious about the upcoming appointment with the paediatrician. With Gordon away on business, she feared she might miss crucial information about Wayan's health. She looked down at him, lying on his stomach on the grey rug, legs and arms flapping about like a sea turtle in the shallows. He was so defenceless, her little man, yet so brave.

Made beamed at Cara. 'Thank you, Cara,' she said. 'You very kind.'

'Just let me know the details, and I'll be . . . *we'll* be there.' Cara glanced in Astrid's direction. 'Uh-oh, Little Miss Trouble is up to no good again.' She stood up to retrieve Astrid, who had somehow dragged herself to the other side of the room, half-rolling, half-crawling. She was now spreading sticky handprints across a glass cabinet.

The wine bar was busy, with throngs of people weaving to and from the bar carrying trays of expensive drinks. Men in business shirts stood around in packs, ties loosened and sleeves rolled up, accompanied by women in thick makeup and flimsy black dresses.

Made wondered what they did of a day, all these loud, laughing people. Her own life revolved around Wayan's quiet rhythms, interspersed with long stretches of daytime television and informal English language lessons on CD. She was proud to have completed level three, with another seven levels to go.

Made spotted the mothers' group at a table in the far corner. Everyone looked so different, she thought, wearing their going-out clothes. Ginie was every bit the corporate lawyer in a slick charcoal suit. Her bright red lipstick made her look younger, somehow, than on their casual Friday gatherings. Cara was wearing a summery white dress, brown leather sandals and dangly hoop earrings. Her hair, usually pulled back in a loose ponytail, fell to her shoulders in waves. She was laughing, and her teeth flashed white against sun-kissed skin. Miranda was wearing her trademark skinny-leg jeans, but with an emerald-coloured blouse that highlighted her intense green eyes. Pippa appeared to be wearing black, as usual, but she'd made an obvious effort with her hair and makeup. Her brown hair had been blow-waved, with the fringe swept back and fixed behind her ear with a glittering green hairclip. Her hazel eyes seemed brighter too. As for Suzie, Made hardly recognised her at all. She looked like Marilyn Monroe.

Ginie hailed her. 'What are you having, Made?' She lifted her hands to her lips to make the point.

'Ah . . .' She found a seat next to Pippa; there was always a vacant seat next to her. Made looked around at what the others were drinking. She'd arrived more than an hour late, delayed by Wayan, who'd been unsettled for most of the afternoon. Cara was having a glass of red wine, and so was Suzie. Pippa was sipping an elaborate green cocktail, the type she'd seen at Pantai Raya—but it looked odd in Pippa's hands. Ginie and Miranda were sharing a bottle of champagne.

'Ah   ' Made spotted an almost empty glass of sparkling mineral water near Miranda. 'I have like Miranda, mineral water.'

Miranda laughed. 'That's not mineral water, Made. It's vodka and soda. Ginie and I got here early, so we had an aperitif. Now we're onto the champagne chasers, aren't we, Gin?' She giggled as she raised her champagne flute. 'Cheers.'

'Oh.' Made was astonished by how much alcohol Australians drank. It was rare for Balinese men to drink, even rarer for women. She'd only ever tried alcohol once, at one of the five bars at Pantai Raya Resort. At Ketut's urging, she'd taken a swig from a half-used bottle of guest champagne. She'd spat it out onto the sand in disgust.

'What about a Jalapeño Margarita?' Ginie nodded in Pippa's direction. 'They're fabulous. I ordered one for Pippa earlier, to match her hairclip.'

Made turned to look at Pippa; Ginie's comment had

sounded rather sarcastic. But she could never be certain of sarcasm in English.

'It's a bit spicy for me.' Pippa looked embarrassed. 'I probably should have stuck to the mineral water.'

'Oh, *come on*,' objected Ginie. 'This is our one night off.'

'Not for me.' Pippa's voice was low. 'I'll be getting up to Heidi for the rest of the night, if Robert's managed to get her down at all.'

Cara made a sympathetic sound. 'Is Heidi still difficult to settle?'

Pippa nodded. 'I'm up five times a night. Robert doesn't hear her crying anymore.' There was a resentful tone in her voice.

Ginie rolled her eyes. 'I swear to God, men are inept.' She glanced at Pippa. 'No offence, Pippa. It's just such a bloody common story. Men and their friggin' selective deafness. Daniel does it too. They're oh-so-keen at conception, but they lose interest afterwards.' Ginie quaffed a mouthful of champagne. 'Okay, so . . . two mineral waters for Pippa and Made. Anyone else need a drink?' She glanced around the table. 'Suzie, you're almost finished. Another red?'

Suzie shook her head. Her mane of curls was uncharacteristically neat and glossy tonight. She wore a red wraparound dress with a plunging neckline. She'd clearly spent a lot of time getting ready. 'No, I shouldn't, really,' she said. 'I'm still breastfeeding.'

'Suit yourself,' said Ginie, striding off in the direction of the bar.

'Actually . . .' Suzie leaned towards the rest of the group

in a conspiratorial way. 'I can't drink too much because I'm meeting someone after this. For *dinner.*'

'What, a *man*?' Cara nudged her theatrically with an elbow.

Suzie nodded. Her smile was euphoric.

'Oooh, you're a sly one,' said Miranda, downing the rest of her champagne. 'How long has this been going on, then?'

'Not long. I only met him a few weeks ago.' Suzie giggled. 'But when he asked me out to dinner tonight, I couldn't say no. I'd lined up a babysitter anyway, so it's kind of worked out. But I'll have to go and meet him soon.'

'What, you're going to pass up more drinks with us for a *man*?' Miranda joked.

'Good luck to you,' said Cara. 'What's his name?'

'Bill.'

'Who's Bill?' Ginie returned to the table. 'The mineral waters are on their way, ladies.'

'Suzie's got a boyfriend,' volunteered Miranda.

'He's not my . . .'

'Well, ring-a-ding-ding.' Again, Made couldn't tell if Ginie was being sarcastic.

'You're a better woman than I am, Suze,' said Miranda. 'I couldn't go back out on the dating scene.' She topped up her own glass, then poured the remainder of the bottle into Ginie's. 'All that waxing and preening and God knows what. I'm too damned tired for any of it.'

'Well, it's been a while for me,' said Suzie quietly. 'It was nice getting dressed up tonight.'

'God, it's been a while for *me* and I'm *married*. Look

at me.' She pointed at her black jeans. 'This is the most dressed up I've been lately. I actually cleaned the vomit off my jeans.'

Everyone laughed.

'Miranda, you *always* look great,' said Cara. It was true, Made thought.

'Well, it's a big illusion,' said Miranda. 'Because I feel like *crap* most of the time.' She shook her head. 'I'm just not getting enough sleep. And now Willem's moved back into our bedroom. He's been in the guest room since Rory was born. He probably thinks he'll get some *action* now.' Miranda fidgeted with her wedding ring, twisting it on her finger. 'But really, it's the *last* thing on my mind.'

Ginie laughed. 'So I'm not the only one who doesn't feel up to it anymore? Thank God for that.'

'I think it's pretty common, actually,' said Cara. Her gold hoop earrings swung as she spoke. 'I'm not really back in the saddle myself yet. So to speak.'

There was laughter around the table, but Pippa's smile seemed strained. She fiddled with the straw in her cocktail. Made assumed a slightly mystified expression, as if she didn't quite understand. She knew they were talking about sex, but she didn't want to divulge the details of her private life. Gordon was tender and considerate in the bedroom, as he was in every other domain. Having Wayan hadn't changed that. But she'd never experienced the sort of sublime sexual ecstasy her village girlfriends had gossiped about.

Made glanced sideways at Pippa. She'd barely drunk anything alcoholic, and the mineral water stood on its coaster untouched. It was six months since their babies had been born, and over four months since they'd started attending mothers' group. And yet Pippa was still on the periphery, rarely smiling or laughing. Why did she persist, Made wondered, week after week? She squinted at Pippa's profile, partially obscured by the dim lighting in the bar and, for a moment, thought she saw the face of another. A wise, gnarled face, floating in the mist on Sanur beach. Made could still remember how the mist had parted and there she was, the old woman with an offering, radiating light from her wiry frame. And her message about the primacy of love, beyond outward appearances.

Maybe Pippa's like me, Made thought suddenly. Missing another world.

She blinked.

'In Bali, we think like this,' Made started, a little hesitantly. 'Sex is the human way, but true love comes from the gods. Anyone can do the sex. It easy thing. But real love is hard work.' She leaned forward; it was difficult to make herself heard above the clamour all around them. 'We are mothers now . . . maybe less sex for husband, yes? But we work hard, for love. Sometimes it make the pain for us. We sacrifice many things. We give more love to husband, more to baby, sometimes we lose ourselves.' She paused. 'But Balinese say, this effort not wasted. The gods *see* the hard work of mothers. They help us continue. They give us their blessing.'

No one said anything for a moment. Made stole a sidelong glance at Pippa. Her eyes were shiny in the shadows.

'Made, you have a way with words,' said Ginie suddenly, lifting her champagne flute. 'I salute you.'

'Here, here!' said Cara.

The others raised their glasses and they clinked them together.

'To more love, less sex!' Miranda laughed. 'With the exception of Suzie, who's got it all going on right now.'

Suzie giggled and looked at her watch. 'And I've *really* got to go and meet Bill.' She swung her handbag over her shoulder. 'He's taking me to Saltfish.'

'Oooh, lovely,' said Miranda. 'Willem took me there before Rory was born. The food is *very* nice.' Miranda's elbow slipped off the edge of the table and champagne splashed across it. 'Oops!' She cackled loudly.

'See you next Friday then, girls,' said Suzie. 'And thanks for suggesting tonight, Miranda. You too, Ginie. It was nice to catch up without the babies.'

Ginie waved her off. Miranda was too busy mopping up the spilt champagne with a wad of serviettes to notice her departure.

Made watched Suzie pick her way to the door, through the pack of humanity sweating and heaving and bawling at each other across the crowded bar. It was a world away from her mountain home in Bali.

She sipped at her mineral water. No, this mothers' group was *not* her family. They could never replace Komang or Ketut or her own beloved mother, or the comfort and camaraderie of village life. But these women weren't so different from her, after all. And apart from Gordon and little

Wayan, they were the best thing about her life in Australia right now.

She was a foreigner far from home, and these women were her *friends*.

Suzie

Suzie dug around in the khaki hemp basket she carried everywhere, groping among the organic rusks, spare cloth nappies and aloe vera gel. Finally, she found her purse. She opened the coin compartment and retrieved the pastel blue business card she'd been searching for.

'There,' she said, passing it to Pippa. 'He's the best naturopath I've ever been to. I started going to him not long after Nils left.' Suzie grimaced, remembering the break-up. She'd been twenty-seven, more than seven months pregnant, and financially dependent on Nils. 'I was so stressed out. He really helped me.'

Pippa inspected the card, turning it over in her hands. She didn't look well: her eyes were bloodshot, her skin sallow, her cheeks sunken.

Suzie glanced around the table. Everyone else seemed subdued today too. It was the last week of spring, but rain was pelting down beyond the white umbrellas of Beachcombers.

'It's amazing what he can do,' Suzie continued. 'He just looks in my eyes and tells me what I need. The first time I went, I was zinc and iron deficient. He mixed up some herbs on the spot, and within three weeks I was . . .'

'Thanks,' Pippa said abruptly, cutting her off.

'It's called iridology,' Suzie added. 'He can tell what's wrong with you just by looking in your eyes. You should try it.'

Pippa looked mildly irritated. 'I'm not sure that natural therapies can help me.'

Suzie shrugged. What *was* Pippa's problem? Whenever Suzie made a friendly overture, she bristled like a porcupine. God knows, she'd tried to draw her out. Others had, too. But Pippa was *such* hard work. Even Cara didn't get very far with her—and Cara was *everyone's* friend. And now she'd rejected Suzie's advice, all snippy and ungrateful. Well, I can't be bothered anymore, Suzie thought. I've got too much to smile about.

Freya squawked loudly, pulling against the straps of her stroller.

'Shhh, miss,' said Suzie, passing her a rusk.

At six months old, their formerly compliant babies were now exerting their personalities. Astrid squirmed on Cara's lap and lunged towards the ground, squealing with indignation at being restrained. Rose sat in a portable highchair alongside Ginie, gumming a pink marshmallow. Outside in the playground, puddles were forming beneath the climbing equipment. Digby was hunched on a stool next to Miranda, miserable, poking a drinking straw at Rory in his pram. Made was attempting to spoon mashed vegetables into Wayan's mouth, most of which simply fell out of the twisted gap above his lip.

Suzie couldn't recall the medical name for Wayan's condition, but Made had recently seen a specialist about it. Apparently he'd told her that surgery would be inevitable by the time Wayan was three years old. The swelling on his lip had grown with each passing month; Suzie couldn't help but look at it. She'd given Made her naturopath's card, too, but Made had never followed up, as far as she knew. If only people would give alternative medicine a *chance*, Suzie mused, they might actually learn something.

Her bag vibrated under the table. She reached down and retrieved her phone, its message alert flashing.

I'm back from Tokyo. Are we still on for that massage tonight?

She smirked.

'Bill?' asked Cara.

She nodded. 'He's just back from overseas.'

'So it's working out for you two, then?'

Suzie tried to contain her smile. 'Well, it's early days.'

Her first date with Bill had proven that he was everything Nils had never been—attentive, generous, strong. She'd struggled for the first months of Freya's life, alone. It was something that no one else in the mothers' group could really understand. But now Bill had appeared in her life, like a white knight charging out of the grey fog, reminding her of life's goodness. She couldn't wait to see him again tonight.

She'd bumped into him, literally, at the laundromat-cum-café she stopped at every morning while walking Freya. She'd arrived thirty minutes earlier than usual, just after six thirty. Pausing around the corner from the café, she stooped to pull a stuffed bear from the compartment beneath the stroller. As she passed it to Freya, she smoothed her hair and surreptitiously pinched her cheeks, hoping to inject some colour into their pallor. For weeks, she'd been trying to extend her conversations with the barista behind the coffee machine. He was mostly aloof. But once, in late winter, he'd actually asked about Freya. Ever since, she'd been hoping he might ask again.

'Hi,' she said, pushing the stroller up to the counter.

'The usual?' he asked.

She nodded.

He began to froth the milk for her skinny cappuccino. 'How far do you walk each day?' he asked.

She smiled, delighted by his interest.

'It's an eight-kilometre round trip from my place. Gets me out of the house, starts my day off well.' She looked at him, pouring the milk into the cardboard cup. Any moment now, their interaction would be over. 'All up, it takes me about an hour.'

'Three dollars fifty, thanks.' He pushed the coffee towards her.

She fished the coins from her purse and passed him the exact change. 'Thanks.' She tried to think of something else to say.

She took a step backwards and bumped into a tall, dark-haired man in a pinstriped suit. Hot coffee slopped out of the small hole in the cup's lid across her right hand.

'I'm sorry.' She hadn't realised anyone was behind her.

But, then, her attention had been focused solely on the handsome barista.

'Are you alright?' asked the man.

'Yes,' she said. 'I didn't see you.'

'What would you like this morning, sir?' asked the barista, ignoring her. It wasn't a casual use of the term; the man commanded respect. Apart from his expensive-looking suit, he held himself with an air of authority.

'A short macchiato,' he said. 'It's that type of morning.' He fingered his BlackBerry, scrolling through messages.

Suzie took several serviettes from the bench top and began to dab at her hand.

The man looked up from his BlackBerry. 'Let me buy you another one, you've lost half of that.'

She looked at him, surprised. 'That's very nice of you.'

'What are you having?'

On a whim, she replied, 'I'll have what you're having. I've never had a . . . what is it, a short something-or-other?'

His face relaxed into a smile. His teeth were white and straight, like a dentist's in a toothpaste commercial.

'A short macchiato,' he repeated.

'Yes, please. I like trying new things.' She flicked her blonde curls over her shoulder.

The barista set to work.

The man slid his BlackBerry into his pocket and turned to look at her. 'Eight kilometres a day is a long way. That's forty kilometres a week, not including weekends. You're walking a marathon every week. How do you do it?'

Suzie flushed. He'd heard her conversation with the

barista. What's more, he'd actually remembered what she'd said.

'Walking an hour a day is easy compared to . . .' She glanced at Freya, who was banging her teddy bear against the side of the stroller. 'Compared to full-time mothering.' She looked down. 'I don't have a partner, you see.'

Even now, eight months after her separation from Nils, she felt embarrassed by this confession. Almost as soon as Nils had left, she'd come to understand the stigma of being a single mother. The disapproving silences, the thoughtless assumptions, the pointed comments made by people she hardly knew. She prepared herself for his censure, in one form or another.

'I can only imagine how hard that must be.'

She looked up, surprised.

'My sister has two boys under three,' he continued. 'She has a husband and I *still* don't know how she does it.'

Suzie beamed at him.

'Here we are,' said the barista, pushing two miniature latte glasses in their direction.

'Oh,' said Suzie. 'It's not takeaway?'

'No.' The man smiled. 'Short macchiatos are designed to be drunk the way the Italians do it. Standing at the bar, while enjoying scintillating conversation.'

He raised his glass to hers.

'Cheers,' he said, then downed the liquid in a single mouthful. He didn't take his eyes off her. 'Now that's what they call a heart-starter.'

Suzie giggled as she raised the glass to her lips. *The way the Italians do it.* There'd been something in the way he'd said those words that hinted at an invitation.

'Go on,' he urged. 'Drink it all at once.'

She threw back her head and swallowed the coffee, wincing as she did. She was used to milky varieties.

'There you are,' she said, placing the glass on the counter. 'I've done something new today.'

The man smiled. 'Come back tomorrow and we'll try a doppio. Now *that's* for coffee connoisseurs.'

She looked at him, incredulous. That *was* an invitation.

Freya whimpered and threw her teddy bear to the ground.

'I'd better go,' she said, scooping up the toy. 'Thank you for the coffee.'

'The pleasure was all mine.'

The next morning, she woke Freya early to ensure she left the house at six, just as she had the day before. She tried to quell her anxiety as she followed her usual route to the café. Would the handsome stranger actually return?

She paused around the corner from the café and checked her watch: six thirty exactly. She refrained from looking around to see where he might be. Inside the café, in a parked car, or approaching on foot? *Or not there at all*, chimed a voice in her head. She was used to disappointment.

She bent down and rummaged beneath the stroller for the brand-new Fisher Price crocodile with rotating claws and extendable tail. She'd bought it the previous afternoon, knowing that its novelty value would keep Freya occupied for at least fifteen minutes, possibly longer. She desperately wanted to meet the stranger again. And not to be disturbed, if she did.

She approached the counter with an air of studied nonchalance.

'Hi,' she said, nodding at the barista.

'I thought you mightn't be coming this morning.'

There he was, perched on a stool next to a washing machine, reading the business section of *The Australian.*

'I thought I might have frightened you off,' he added.

She smiled at him. 'I came back for my doppio.'

'Good decision,' he said. 'Best coffee on the northern beaches.' He signalled to the barista. 'Two doppios, please.'

'Coming up, boss,' the barista replied.

Yes, she thought, he *is* the boss. He looked the quintessential high-flyer this morning. A silver and navy-striped tie set off an immaculately ironed white shirt.

He gestured to a stool next to him. 'Don't think for a moment you can take away a doppio. Do you have ten minutes?' He didn't wait for her answer. 'Let's bring your daughter in here.' He stepped out onto the street and began to manoeuvre the stroller into the laundromat section, behind the coffee machine.

'You've done that before,' she remarked, as he parked the stroller and flicked on the brake with the tip of his shoe.

'My nephews.'

'Do you spend a lot of time with them?'

'Not as much as I'd like. I travel a lot for my work.'

He pulled the stool out for her. 'Allow me,' he said. His tone was confident, persuasive. He's probably in marketing, she thought.

'I'm Bill.' He extended his hand towards her. 'It's nice to meet you.'

'Suzie,' she replied, suddenly awkward.

His face was symmetrical, chiselled like a Renaissance sculpture. He was older than her, by ten years or so. His black hair was peppered with streaks of silver, his only visible flaw. Other than that, all she could see was divine perfection. Soft brown eyes, full lips, smooth skin. Put him in a toga and he'd look like a Roman god, she thought. He stood up to take his BlackBerry out of his pocket and she caught a whiff of his aftershave. Nils had never worn aftershave; it gave him hives. Bill placed the BlackBerry on his knee.

'My apologies,' he said, nodding at the telephone. 'Theoretically I'm on call at all hours. It's the malaise of the modern world, I'm afraid. A culture of instant communication.'

She smiled. He used sophisticated language. She doubted she would be clever enough for him.

As if reading her mind, he looked up at her. 'What did you do, Suzie, before you had a baby?'

Mercifully, the barista delivered their coffees.

'Enjoy,' he said, returning to the counter.

'It's tiny,' she said, squinting at the miniature glass before her.

'But short can be beautiful,' he replied, holding her gaze.

She reddened, daring to hope that he might be referring to her. Her stature had always bothered her; she'd been five foot three inches since she was fourteen. Throughout her teenage years, she'd kept waiting for a growth spurt that never came. People had often described her as 'curvy', which, as far as she was concerned, was a euphemism for plump. Even now, at twenty-eight, she still envied tall willowy types like Miranda, who looked elegant in anything.

'In answer to your question,' she said, eyeing the clothes rotating in a washing machine, 'I was a massage therapist before Freya came along.'

'Now there's a talent not to be sniffed at.'

She glanced up at him. 'I was studying naturopathy part-time by distance education. But after Freya, I had to defer. I still want to finish the course. I've always been interested in natural medicine. But the course is pretty expensive. And it's a full-time job looking after Freya at the moment.'

'Naturally.' He sat back on the stool, his arms folded, study-ing her. She felt as if his eyes might bore through her.

'I had a massage business at home,' she continued. 'But a few months after Freya was born, I had to move to a smaller place in Dee Why and . . . things got a bit difficult. Freya started waking up mid-session. In the end, I decided it was all too hard.'

'And you can't get any help at home?' he asked. 'To restart your business?'

She shook her head. 'My parents live in Brisbane. I'm from Queensland originally.' She smiled, thinking of her mother and father and their two-bedroom weatherboard home in Sunnybank. She missed them, and her younger sister Tanya too. When Nils had left, her parents had invited her to move back home, and to bring Freya with her. But Suzie knew what an imposition that would be. Tanya still lived in the bed-room that she and Suzie had shared growing up. Despite her mother's assurances that they'd manage, Suzie couldn't quite see how. So she'd decided to stay in Sydney, until she'd figured out her next step.

'I do have my mother-in-law nearby . . .' Suzie continued. 'Well, the mother of my ex-boyfriend. But it's complicated with her.' She stopped, conscious that she had been doing all the talking.

'What about you, Bill? What do *you* do for work?'

'I'm the executive general manager in the private client services division of Federation Bank.'

She nodded, impressed.

'It's all terribly mundane, I assure you. Massage therapy would be far more fun.' He winked at her. 'Perhaps I could become a client of yours. I don't mind if your daughter cries, I'm used to it with my nephews. I've got a lot of tension in my shoulders and neck at the moment. And if you're good, I might be able to put a few referrals your way.'

She wasn't sure if he was serious, or if she wanted him to be.

'Would you consider it?' He studied her face. 'It'd have to be after hours, though. Which might alleviate the crying baby problem. I'm just up the road from you, in Collaroy.'

'I . . .' She didn't know this man at all. But then again, when she'd first started her massage business, she'd placed a small advertisement in the classified pages of the *Manly Daily* and taken unknown clients. At least with Bill, she'd met him before.

'Can I take you to dinner first, to prove I'm not a psychopath?'

She laughed. 'Well, maybe.'

'Good,' he said, standing up at the table. 'Give me your number and I'll call you to organise it. How about next week, when I'm back from Melbourne? We'll go somewhere nice.' He picked up his BlackBerry and began pressing the buttons. 'Suzie Someone . . . what's your surname?'

'Raymond,' she replied.

'And your number?'

She recited it.

'Good.' He fished some coins and a set of keys out of his pocket. She noticed the shiny Lexus key ring. He placed eight dollars on the counter.

'What's *your* surname?' she asked.

'White,' he said. 'Common as mud. Did you like the doppio?'

'Not as much as the short macchiato.'

'Well, you're a fast learner. I'll call you. Bye-bye, little one,' he said, pinching Freya on the cheek.

'Freya,' she reminded him. 'Her name's Freya.'

'The Scandinavian goddess of love,' he said. 'My goodness, you're interesting.'

She sat, dumbfounded, as he strode out of the café.

Having dinner with Bill at the exclusive Saltfish restaurant was the stuff of Suzie's dreams. He reserved the premier table, with a waterfront view. They shared a seafood platter and expensive wine, while he recounted entertaining stories of the cities he frequented for work: Beijing, Shanghai, London, Mumbai. Suzie had never been overseas in her life. She sat riveted, hardly daring to interrupt. They held hands over dessert and Bill spooned chocolate mousse into her mouth, lingering playfully at her lips.

He dropped her back to her apartment in Dee Why and walked her to the door.

'Lovely Suzie,' he said, before leaning in and gently pressing his lips against hers.

The kiss left her wanting more.

'Can I book you for a massage in a couple of weeks, when I'm back from Tokyo?'

She didn't want to wait that long.

'Yes,' she said. 'I'd love to.'

It pained her to do it, but when the time came, she called on Monika. As she dialled the number, she consciously attempted to relax. *Breathe in, breathe out.*

'Hello?'

Even the sound of Monika's voice, the slightly caustic tone, made Suzie recoil. In better times, she and Nils had always laughed about Monika. How it had been a great cosmic joke that Monika—who was as uptight as a spring-loaded coil—had given birth to a son like Nils, so laidback and uninhibited.

'Hello, Monika, it's Suzie.'

The silence spoke volumes.

'How are you?' Suzie asked, adopting a bright tone.

'How's Freya?' asked Monika, ignoring the question.

'Fine, thanks. Great. That's why I'm calling, actually. I was hoping . . .'

'It's been so long,' interjected Monika. 'Weeks.'

'Yes, I know, I'm sorry,' Suzie said. 'I've been busy.'

Suzie resisted the urge to point out that Monika could have picked up the telephone and called *her*. It had always been like this, even before Freya came along. The onus had always been on Nils and Suzie to get in touch with Monika, never the other way around. And if they left it too long, Monika invariably let them know how slighted she felt.

'Monika, I wondered if you might be able to help me.' She grimaced as she said the words. 'I want to start up my massage business again. It's hard surviving on government benefits.'

She wasn't lying. The paltry sum offered to single parents hardly covered her living expenses. With Nils now conveniently embracing agrarian socialism at the commune, he claimed he had no money to contribute for Freya's upkeep. Desperate, she'd sought some advice from the local legal aid centre. The supposedly mandatory child support payments didn't apply in his case, and couldn't be enforced.

'Anyway . . .' She interpreted Monika's silence as licence to proceed. 'I was hoping to start practising two nights a week, not too much. Now that Freya's sleeping through. I wondered if you might have her overnight on Tuesdays and Thursdays?'

Monika made a snorting noise. An expression of surprise or outrage, Suzie couldn't be sure.

'Of course,' said Monika.

Suzie blinked, awaiting the caveat. Monika said nothing.

'Well, thanks, Monika. I don't suppose we could start next Tuesday?'

She held her breath.

'Of course,' Monika repeated.

Suzie couldn't believe her luck.

'Okay. I'll pack everything in advance. Some frozen breast milk just in case, a change of clothes, the port-a-cot and sheets. I'll drop her over at six o'clock, after she's had her bath and dinner. She shouldn't give you any trouble. And I can pick her up in the morning before you go to work.' Monika was a driving instructor. It was something else that Suzie and Nils had laughed about privately, imagining her haranguing hapless teens behind the wheel.

'Good. That will be . . . nice. Thank you, Suzie.'

Suzie was floored. 'Well, thank *you*, Monika. See you then.'

She put down the phone and shook her head. Getting Monika to say yes to something had never been so easy.

The following Tuesday at six o'clock, she dropped Freya off at Monika's home, fighting the urge to linger. Everything will be alright, she reminded herself; Monika thinks of everything. But just the act of passing Freya into Monika's arms, knowing she wouldn't see her daughter again for twelve hours, was disconcerting. It was the first time she'd ever left Freya with anyone else overnight. And with *Monika* of all people—a woman she'd never warmed to, even when everything had been working out with Nils. If only her own parents didn't live a thousand kilometres away.

Bill had better be worth it, she thought.

When she opened the door at eight o'clock, she knew instantly that he was. He leaned casually in the doorframe, a bottle of wine in one hand and a bunch of pink roses in the other. He held out both.

'Your other clients didn't come bearing gifts, I hope.'

She smiled. He smelled freshly washed, his aftershave a heady combination of musk and sandalwood. He clearly hadn't come straight from work, as he'd said he would.

'I stopped off for a gym session,' he explained. 'A boxing class.' It was easy to imagine him pummelling a speedball.

'No wonder you have neck and shoulder tension,' she admonished.

He looked her up and down. 'You're beautiful.'

Her stomach churned with delicious anxiety.

After dropping Freya at Monika's, she'd hurried home to soak in a lemongrass bath. Then she'd rubbed almond oil all over her body before donning a figure-hugging purple dress. She'd left her face makeup-free, brushing a touch of gloss on her lips and letting her blonde curls tumble across her shoulders.

'Thank you,' she said. 'Come in.'

She'd prepared meticulously for this moment. The massage bed was positioned in the centre of the darkened lounge room, where the coffee table usually stood. It had taken some effort to heave the coffee table into Freya's room without any help, but she'd managed it. If nothing else, single motherhood had taught her self-sufficiency. Three towels were strung across a large oil heater. On a small table next to the massage bed, tea lights floated in a glass bowl filled with frangipanis she'd collected from the next-door neighbour's front yard. The aroma of ylang ylang and orange blossom hung in the air, complementing a recording of Indian sitar playing at low volume. A large bottle of avocado oil stood in a flask of hot water.

'Welcome,' she said.

Without a word, he began to unbutton his shirt. She turned towards the kitchen; protocol would deem she leave the room.

'Don't go.'

She stood, transfixed, as he stripped down to a pair of black boxer shorts. She instantly imagined wrapping her legs around him.

He smiled at her in the half-light, shadows flickering across his bare chest. 'Face up, or face down?'

'Down,' she said, swallowing hard.

I'm going to have sex tonight, she thought.

It had been more than nine months since she'd had sex and more than a year since she'd enjoyed it. In the final few months of her relationship with Nils, sex had become laborious. In fact, sex had always been disappointing with Nils. It had all seemed so promising in the beginning; he was an attractive yoga instructor with an interest in tantra. But in his dogged pursuit of cosmic sexual power—*kundalini*, he called it—Nils couldn't even get the basics right. He'd touched her like a housewife following a recipe; methodically, reading aloud, always double-checking the ingredients. His endless questioning during lovemaking left her cold. She didn't want to have to explain what she wanted, or direct his fingers to the right place. For someone so in touch with his feminine side, Nils had roundly neglected hers. By contrast, Bill oozed a primitive sexual confidence. He was the archetypal alpha male.

He lowered himself face down onto the massage bed. She pressed a warm towel along the length of his back, brushing over his buttocks and applying another towel along his legs. She held the soles of his feet in her palms for a moment, steadying her breathing. She attempted to centre herself in the way she usually did before giving a massage, imagining a beam of white light spearing down from the sky, cleansing her body and spirit. Then she visualised a long, thick rope tied around her waist, plunging down into the centre of the earth, anchoring her to its hot core. Warmth spread through her body. She opened her eyes and looked at Bill, lying prone before her.

She was ready.

Afterwards, she lay on the couch with her back against him, her body pulsating. Behind her, she felt him prop himself up on one elbow and snake his other arm around her waist.

'Here,' he said. His hand hovered in front of her lips, thumb and forefinger pinched together.

'What?'

'Gotta have a smoke after sex.' He drew his fingers to his lips and puffed on an imaginary cigarette. 'You try it.' He thrust his hand towards her.

She smiled. 'Um, okay.'

She pretended to take it from his fingers, then sucked noisily. 'Wow, great shit.'

He laughed aloud then rolled onto her, pinning her shoulders to the couch. His face hung centimetres above hers.

'That was a princely fuck. I feel like a king.'

She giggled. No one had ever spoken to her like that. It felt good. She remembered how sex with Nils had usually ended: with the noisy groaning of his premature ejaculation, followed by an interrogation as to whether she'd had an orgasm. Or not.

Bill didn't need to ask. Her climax had been volcanic—both of them.

He sat up and swung his legs to the floor. 'That was a good massage, too. I'll recommend you to my friends. On the proviso that you don't fuck any of them. I want you all to myself.'

He pulled on his boxers and zipped up his trousers. As he buckled his belt, his BlackBerry fell out of his pocket. He picked it up and glanced at the screen.

'Damn,' he said. 'We'll have to leave dinner for another time. I've got some work to do.'

'At nine thirty at night?' She'd prepared a green bean and papaya salad before he'd arrived.

'Yes, it's standard for me. Access all hours.'

He buttoned his shirt at the wrists and raked his fingers through his hair. He fished around in his back pocket and pulled out his car keys and wallet. Opening it, he counted out six fifty-dollar notes and placed them on the massage bed.

'Thanks for the massage, my shoulders feel much better.'

She stared at the notes; three hundred dollars was three times what she would ordinarily charge.

'I'm not a prostitute.'

'What?'

She looked away.

'What do you take me for, Suzie?' he demanded. 'Come here.'

She edged towards him, slightly fearful of his tone.

He reached over and pulled her to stand in front of him, grasping her shoulders with his enormous hands. 'Don't *ever* say that again.' His anger made him seem taller. 'You are a beautiful woman, and an excellent masseuse. I am paying you for that massage.'

He picked up the notes and folded them into her right hand, then ran his hands down both sides of her face. 'So beautiful,' he said. 'I'm a lucky man.'

He leaned forward and kissed her, his tongue probing hers. 'Repeat after me: the fuck was free.'

'Yes,' she breathed. 'It was.'

As she drove over to collect Freya the next morning, she could hardly focus on the road ahead. She hummed to herself, basking in the sensual wonder of the night before. Bill had worshipped at the temple of her body, his lips and hands prising open its secrets. She'd never felt so feminine.

Monika opened the door with a flourish, before Suzie had even knocked.

'Hello, Suzie!' She was uncharacteristically exuberant.

The image of Bill evaporated.

'Hi, Monika. How's Freya?'

'Good, good.' Monika's tone was businesslike. 'She's just watching a *Play School* DVD.'

'Oh.' Suzie took a deep breath. How many times had she told Monika that she didn't believe in exposing children under the age of three to television? And how many times had Monika nodded, as if she understood?

She followed Monika down the hallway.

'She only woke up twice in the night for a feed,' said Monika.

Only twice? For a *feed*? Suzie said nothing. For more than a month, Freya had been sleeping through until five-thirty in the morning. She'd only packed the frozen breast milk as an emergency measure.

She entered the lounge room. Freya was propped up on a large cushion in front of the television. The curtains were drawn and the light from the screen flickered across her face.

Suzie walked to the window and threw open the curtains. Sunlight streamed into the room.

'Hello, sweetie, how are you?'

She walked over to the television and turned it off, then crouched down next to Freya.

'Oh my God.'

She lifted Freya up, staring at her head, then rounded on Monika.

'You cut her hair.'

'Just a little.'

'Just a *little*?' Suzie's voice trembled.

'It was flopping in her eyes.'

Suzie scooped Freya off the cushion. 'I didn't *want* her hair cut,' she said. 'It wasn't that long. And it's *my* job to do it.'

She began to stride from room to room, gathering up Freya's things. When Nils had walked out, Suzie had resigned herself to the fact that Freya would be the only child she'd ever have. She didn't need Monika robbing her of precious first experiences that couldn't be repeated.

In the kitchen, she retrieved the empty bottle and teat from the sink. As she stuffed them into a plastic bag, she noticed a tin of infant formula on the bench top. She stared at it, then wrenched opened the freezer door. Her two sachets of carefully expressed breast milk were still frozen, sitting upright next to the fish fingers.

'They were too hard to defrost in the middle of the night,' explained Monika.

Suzie turned, enraged.

'And you just keep a tin of infant formula handy, do you?'

Monika knew how opposed Suzie was to complementary feeding; she'd sworn that no formula would ever pass Freya's lips.

Suzie stormed to the front door, Freya on one hip and several bags slung across her shoulder.

'I'll help you to the car,' offered Monika.

'No, thank you.'

She slammed the front door behind her.

The next week at the mothers' group, she told them the whole story. It was a bright summer's morning in December, and the babies seemed fractious in the heat.

'Monika *cut Freya's hair* without asking you first?' Cara repeated, incredulous.

'*And* fed her formula,' said Suzie, 'when I'd specifically given her bags of expressed breast milk.'

'God, that *is* a bit of a problem,' said Cara. She waved at the barista behind the counter. 'Another round of drinks, girls?'

The barista nodded at them. After so many mothers' group meetings at Beachcombers, he practically knew their order by heart.

Suzie dabbed at her eyes with a tissue. Cara put an arm around her shoulder.

'I shouldn't be so upset,' said Suzie. 'It's not like it's totally out of character. This is the sort of stuff Monika does all the time, so I shouldn't be surprised.' She blew her nose. 'I guess I was just hoping that things would be fine. Now I never want to leave Freya at her place again.'

'Don't worry, I can totally relate, Suze,' said Miranda. 'Willem's mum keeps her distance *most* of the time. But when she visits, it's hell on earth. She actually goes around sliding her finger along the tops of doorframes and showing me how dusty they are. And Willem's no help, he just tells me to ignore it. Men *always* side with their mothers.'

'Oh, Jesus,' laughed Ginie. 'What I wonder is, didn't any of these women have mothers-in-law *themselves*?'

'They're not *always* so bad, Gin,' said Cara. 'My mother-in-law is quite nice, really, but we don't get to see her very often. She's too busy looking after Richard's dad.'

'He's got Alzheimer's, hasn't he?' said Miranda.

Cara nodded. 'It doesn't leave much room for grandchildren, unfortunately. My dad's got it too. That's how Richard and I met, actually—our mums both go to the same support group. Not the most romantic of first meetings, unlike Suzie here.' Cara turned to her. 'How's it all going with Bill, anyway?'

Suzie tried to suppress her smile. She didn't want to seem smug. 'It's great. We have a real connection.'

'That's good.' Ginie laughed. 'Because you'll need it when you meet *his* mother.'

Suzie hadn't even thought of it. Bill hadn't mentioned his parents or any other extended family, apart from a sister with two sons. The idea that she might end up with *two* mothers-in-law was appalling, considering Monika's track record.

Made cleared her throat. 'My younger sister in Bali, her name Komang. She marry husband last month, now she live with mother of husband.'

Everybody groaned.

'You've *got* to be kidding,' said Ginie. 'How old's your sister, anyway?'

'She seventeen now.'

'And that's *legal*?'

Made nodded. 'In Bali, this is normal. Our culture say woman after marry must move in with husband family. Mother of husband help to raise children. Everyone in family compound help. Aunty, uncle, cousins.' She tickled Wayan's feet; he cackled his throaty, infectious giggle. 'My sister Komang, she have less freedom now. Husband mother tell her what to do. She cook, she clean, she do many other thing for husband mother. In Australia, women very lucky.'

Suzie reddened, a little embarrassed by the comparison. Perhaps she'd overreacted to Monika's behaviour.

'It's like that in other countries, too,' added Cara. 'I had an Indian friend at university whose sister was burned to death by her mother-in-law in a dowry murder.'

'Christ,' said Ginie, shaking her head. 'What the hell are *we* bitching about, then?'

'I really don't know,' snapped Pippa, out of the blue. Her eyes flashed. 'There's not much that *any* of you should be complaining about, as far as I can see. Healthy babies, working husbands, in-laws that help out. What more could you ask for?' The bitterness in her voice was palpable.

No one spoke. Eyes darted from face to face, seeking direction from others.

Pippa's cheeks were burning. Her hand shook as she stirred her coffee. Then suddenly she dropped the teaspoon into the saucer with a clatter. Tears began to slide down her face, dripping onto her shirt, the table, even Heidi. She pulled Heidi closer to her chest and buried her face in her hair.

Suzie looked around the table, alarmed. Everyone was shocked, that was clear, but still no one moved. If it had been anyone else in the group, Suzie might have reached out. But she could sense the anger seething beneath Pippa's tears.

After what felt like an eternity, Cara leaned across the table and laid a gentle hand over Pippa's.

Suzie exhaled. Thank God for Cara.

'Is everything okay?' Cara asked quietly.

Pippa shook her head. Her shoulders were rounded, defeated.

'I have to go into hospital in a fortnight's time,' she said finally. 'I'll be in for about a week and I don't know how Robert will cope. I've never left him with Heidi for longer than two hours.' She looked up, the tears starting anew. 'I wish I had some in-laws, anyone, to call on.'

'But *we'll* help, of course,' said Cara immediately. 'Are you alright?'

Pippa blushed a deeper red.

'I will be,' she replied. 'I have to have an operation . . . to repair the damage done when Heidi was born.' She closed her eyes. 'I had a bad tear. It made me incontinent.'

'Oh, no,' said Cara. She glanced around the group, as if looking for support. 'I mean, I'm not the same down there either—Astrid stretched everything—but not to the point of incontinence. That must be awful.'

Pippa stared out at the playground. Heat haze rose from the sandpit.

'I might as well tell you everything,' she said. 'I mean, why hide it anymore?' Pippa pushed her oily hair behind her ears. 'I've been incontinent since Heidi was born. I haven't been able to control my bladder. Or my bowels.'

Suzie clapped a hand over her mouth. She'd heard that some women had pelvic floor issues after birth, but she'd just assumed that, like her, most bounced back unscathed.

'I let it go too long,' Pippa continued. 'I kept thinking it was going to get better.' She covered her face with her hands. 'The doctors say it's one of the reasons I got . . . post-natal depression.'

'Oh.' Suzie made the sound involuntarily. She'd never imagined that behind her thorny armour, Pippa was hiding *this*.

Pippa looked up at the sound. 'Yes.' She nodded at Suzie. 'I've had trouble bonding with Heidi. It's not been fair on her. But it's hard to feel positive when you're worried about changing your own nappy, let alone your baby's.' Pippa's cheeks were scarlet, her eyes haunted.

Suzie felt terrible. She'd ignored the signs of Pippa's distress; it had been too hard to connect with her. What would *she* do, she wondered, with a pelvic floor in tatters? She certainly wouldn't be going out with Bill. The idea brought tears to her eyes.

No one said anything for a moment.

'Oh God,' said Cara. She put her arm around Pippa. 'You poor, poor thing. Why didn't you *tell* us?'

Pippa leaned into her for a moment, then shrugged. 'You were all enjoying your babies. I didn't want to drag you down.' She sniffed, then straightened up, pulling away from Cara. 'I'm getting the right help now, anyway. I'm on medication for the PND and the operation will help with . . .' She looked suddenly embarrassed. 'Look, I'm sorry for dumping all that on you. Any help you can give while I'm in hospital would be great.'

Pippa's face was resuming its usual expressionless mask. Suzie leaned towards her, proffering a plate of biscuits. It was a feeble gesture, she knew, but what else could she say or do?

Pippa shook her head. 'I should go. I have a doctor's appointment in thirty minutes.' She stood up and buckled Heidi into her stroller. 'See you next week.'

The group watched her leave, pushing the stroller over the grassy slope and into the car park.

A moment later, Ginie coughed. 'Well, that explains a lot, doesn't it?'

'Yes,' said Miranda. 'I wish I'd known about it earlier. I might have tried to help.'

'She's been pretty hard to help,' said Ginie.

'Still,' sighed Cara. 'I suspected something was wrong from the beginning, but I never actually *did* anything about it.'

'Me too,' admitted Suzie. 'It was obvious something was wrong.'

'We still can help, I think?' said Made.

Suzie nodded. She knew what it was like to be alone, without family support. 'You're right, Made,' she said. 'It's not too late.'

Within a week, Suzie had devised a plan. She sent an email around the mothers' group entitled *Project Pippa*, calling for volunteers. Much to her delight, everyone agreed on jobs they would do to help support Pippa while she was in hospital. Ginie volunteered her nanny's services in the kitchen, preparing a week's worth of frozen dinners for Robert. Miranda offered to mind Heidi in the afternoons, so that Robert could visit Pippa. Suzie decided to postpone her morning coffees with Bill, popping by Pippa's house instead to help with Heidi's breakfast routine. By the time Pippa was admitted to hospital in January, every day of her absence had been accounted for.

Three days after Pippa's surgery, Suzie and Cara walked over to the hospital together. It was a cloudless summer's day and miraculously, both Freya and Astrid were asleep in their prams by the time they arrived. Suzie bought a huge bunch of sunflowers from an expensive florist on the ground floor, while Cara found out which room Pippa was in.

They knocked on the door.

'Come in.'

Suzie peeked through the small rectangular window. Pippa looked tiny, almost childlike, against the bleached expanse of hospital sheets enveloping her. She waved them in.

'These are from the mothers' group.' Suzie pushed the sunflowers into Pippa's hands. 'Although I see Made's already been.' She nodded at a woven basket on the tray table, its wide green leaves decorated with fresh flowers, rice, and a small cake.

'Yes, it was there when I woke up from the anaesthetic,' Pippa said. 'The sunflowers are beautiful, thank you. Robert's told me all about the meals, the coffees, the play dates . . . I just don't know what I would have done without you all.'

Cara pointed at Suzie. 'She organised it. We're just her slaves.'

Suzie laughed and sat down on the edge of the bed. 'There's this as well.' She passed Pippa a pink envelope. 'How are you feeling today?'

Pippa smiled. 'Well, they bring me my meals, a morning newspaper, I get to sleep whenever I want . . . I've had more straight sleep in the last seventy-two hours than I've had in the past eight months. If it wasn't for the pain, I'd consider it a holiday.'

Cara laughed. 'Are you in much pain?'

'Not when I'm lying down. It hurts a bit when I move. They'll take the catheter out this morning.'

'Open the envelope,' Suzie urged.

Pippa lifted the flap and removed a card with the words *Get Well Soon!* emblazoned across it in fluorescent pink letters. A voucher dropped into her lap. She turned it over and gasped; it was a three-hundred-dollar voucher for a gourmet meal delivery service.

'Oh!' She looked stunned.

'We thought you wouldn't feel like cooking when you get home,' explained Suzie. 'That should help out for about a month. And you know . . .' She paused. 'I'm sorry for not seeing how hard things were for you. If anything awful ever happens again . . . I hope you'll tell us.' She looked at Pippa. 'I mean, you won't always *want* to tell us. We're all pretty different in the mothers' group. If it wasn't for our babies, we mightn't be friends. But we have to look after each other.'

She glanced at the floor, wondering if she'd said too much.

When she looked up again, Pippa's eyes were filled with tears. She reached for Suzie's hand. 'Thank you.' Her voice was shaking. 'That's so kind.' They held hands in silence for a moment. Suzie marvelled at how natural it felt.

There was a brusque knock and the door swung open. Suzie turned to see a tall, dark-skinned doctor with a stethoscope slung around his neck.

'Good morning, Mrs Thompson,' he said. 'I'm one of the surgeons.'

Suzie couldn't pick his accent.

'Oh, you have visitors.' The doctor nodded at Suzie and Cara. 'I'll come back . . .' He stopped and stared at Cara. Suzie watched, confused, as the doctor's earnest expression morphed into a neon smile.

'Cara?' he asked. 'Is that you?'

Cara stood up from her chair. 'Ravi?'

The doctor glanced at Pippa. 'I'm sorry,' he said. 'Cara and I are old . . . friends.'

'Oh,' said Pippa. An awkward silence ensued.

'Um, would you two like to talk outside?' Suzie suggested.

Cara turned to her. 'Oh,' she said, her tone flustered. 'Sorry. Yes, good idea.'

The doctor held the door open and Cara stepped past him.

More than five minutes passed before the door opened again and Cara returned.

'An old *friend*?' asked Suzie, pulling a face.

Cara blushed. 'We were at university together. We were never really, well, *together*.' She looked towards the door, her eyes alight. 'We'd better go now. Ravi is waiting to see Pippa.' She reached for her handbag.

Pippa nodded. 'Well, thanks so much for coming, both of you.'

'Let us know if there's anything else we can do,' said Suzie. 'I'll come again tomorrow.'

Pippa smiled. 'I can't thank you enough.'

They opened the door and the doctor stepped back into the room. He flashed a grin at Cara as they passed.

'Mrs Thompson.' He was the picture of professionalism again. 'I'm Dr Nadkarni. I helped Dr Sturgess with your procedure . . .'

The door shut behind them.

The following Friday, when Suzie returned home from mothers' group, she found a large bunch of orange gerberas lying on the doormat. Bill was so thoughtful. She tore open the envelope and read the card: *I'm sorry. Sometimes I overstep the mark. Monika.*

She shoved the card into her back pocket. She hadn't spoken to Monika since the incident with the haircut. It had been easy to avoid her over the Christmas and New Year period, when Suzie had visited her parents in Queensland. Freya's first Christmas had been cheerful and chaotic in her parents' hot weatherboard home. By the end of their three-week stay in Sunnybank, Suzie was loath to leave her family, but the prospect of seeing Bill was incentive enough. Returning to Sydney in early January, Suzie had been disappointed to discover that Bill had already been called overseas. But he was due to return in a week, and Suzie was counting the days.

Suzie scooped Freya out of the pram and parked it under the internal stairs leading to the second-floor apartments. As she did, she heard footsteps in the stairwell.

'Lovely flowers for a lovely lassie,' called old Mr Keogh from unit five. 'Not from that rogue who left you, I hope.'

She turned and looked up the stairs. 'Hello, Mr Keogh.' He was leaning heavily against the banister, a plastic bag of rubbish in one hand and a walking stick in the other.

News that she'd been abandoned had spread rapidly through the apartment block. Mr Keogh was vociferous in his objections, taking every opportunity to pass comment on Nils's behaviour. He meant well, of course, but it grated after a while. It was time to give him something else to talk about.

'Actually, they're from my new boyfriend,' she said. 'He treats me like a queen.'

Mr Keogh's eyes lit up. 'Well, now.'

She picked up the gerberas and pushed her key into the door. 'Time for Freya's nap. See you later, Mr Keogh.'

'Good for you,' he called after her.

She sat Freya on the rug and jangled a rattle next to her. Freya rolled onto her side, legs kicking furiously, then hoisted herself up onto all fours. Suzie smiled and egged her on, waving the rattle just out of reach. 'Come on, honey, grab it.'

Freya swiped the rattle from Suzie's hand, then rolled over onto her back.

'Good girl!' Suzie clapped.

Freya mimicked her, dropping the rattle and clapping back at Suzie, grinning. Eight teeth poked out from pink gums; Freya had been the first among the babies to cut a tooth.

'You're hardly a baby anymore, are you?'

Suzie could remember a time, not so long ago, when Freya couldn't even sit up. Now she was almost nine months old, and time was passing more quickly than ever before. When she'd first had Freya, strangers had stopped her in the street, peered into the pram, and gushed: *Enjoy it while you can, it goes so quickly.* And they'd been right, she reflected. Her little girl was growing up.

Suzie stood up and walked to the telephone. Taking a deep breath, she dialled Monika's number. She would reconcile with Monika, for Bill.

Suzie opened the door in her bathrobe.

'Hi,' she said.

Water dripped down the back of her neck from her wet hair. When she'd dropped Freya at Monika's, Freya had been unsettled. Suzie had been forced to stay longer than she'd planned, helping Monika to distract Freya before slipping out the front door. She'd got home with just fifteen minutes to spare before Bill's arrival. Nothing was ready in the kitchen, she wasn't as organised as usual. It had been that sort of day.

He caught her hand in his. 'You weren't at the café this morning.' His tone was accusing.

'I had an early appointment at the doctor's,' she said. 'I told you about it, remember? The blood tests, so we can stop using . . .'

He caught her other hand and pushed her back over the threshold. His grip was firmer than necessary.

'It's rude to keep people waiting. I was late for an important meeting.'

She looked up into his face. She'd told him about the blood tests a week ago; he'd promised to have his done too. And she'd reminded him by SMS the day before.

'I'll have to discipline you. Down on the floor.'

She raised an eyebrow. 'Oh. Okay.' She slipped her bathrobe off her shoulders. It fell onto the mat at her feet.

'On all fours.'

The first time it had happened, she'd been a little afraid. But now she knew what to expect.

'Now.' He pushed her onto the mat.

'Ouch,' she complained, rubbing her wrists.

'Shut up.'

For a moment, she considered standing up and backing away. Telling him to wait until they'd had dinner, or at least a drink. They'd been seeing each other for three months, with regular morning coffees and rendezvous at her apartment. In the early weeks of their relationship, he'd taken her out for dinner at several swanky restaurants. A month later, just before Christmas, they'd gone to the movies, leaning into each other in the back row of the theatre. But now, he was more inclined to stay in her apartment than go anywhere else. He was an expert in bed, never failing to please her, but she wanted more. She wanted foreplay of the cerebral variety. She'd tried to suggest some outdoor activities on weekends, a picnic in the park or a walk by the ocean. But when he wasn't travelling with work, the last thing he felt like doing was going out. I just want to enjoy you, he'd say, all to myself.

She heard his trousers fall to the floor behind her, the sound of his belt sliding out of its loopholes.

She screwed her eyes shut.

Suzie winced as she shifted on the timber seat. Yet again, Bill's discipline had been excessive. The mothers' group was gathered at Beachcombers as usual, but today was quieter: it was late February, the school holidays were over and the summer masses were starting to disappear. The babies were all crawling and rolling on tartan picnic rugs that Cara had laid out on a grassy patch nearby; it was almost impossible to constrain them to highchairs and prams now.

With Ginie receiving a steady stream of phone calls at the table, the conversation had turned to work. Ginie was stressed, juggling multiple clients; Cara was enjoying some freelance writing projects; Miranda was considering her options for April, when her maternity leave was over; Made was a stay-at-home mum and, as far as Suzie could tell, was quite content without any form of employment. *I'm* so lucky, Suzie thought, with Bill's financial support. His generous massage payments meant she didn't have to look for retail work, which was all she was really qualified to do. She'd hate to be in Ginie's position, she'd often thought, with a pressure cooker of a life. Bill's support gave her choices.

'I'm thinking of going back to work soon too, now I've had the operation,' said Pippa, after Ginie concluded her call. 'I mean, things aren't totally right for me physically, but they're so much better. And we could really do with the income.' She looked at Ginie.

'Um, Ginie, I was thinking about employing a nanny when I go back to work, rather than using day care. Can you give me the number of the agency you used?'

Ginie glanced up from her iPhone. 'Sure.'

'Thanks.' Pippa seemed to hesitate. 'And I'm right in thinking that you haven't had any problems with Nicole?'

Ginie shrugged. 'She's the best decision I've ever made.'

Pippa stirred her coffee. 'You've never felt a bit worried about having another woman in the house? You know, with your husband?'

Ginie looked baffled. 'Why?'

Pippa began to redden. 'That he might . . . I don't know . . . be attracted to her or something. You read about husbands falling in love with nannies.'

Ginie snorted. 'If she was a Brazilian goddess, maybe. But Nicole's an Irish frump.'

Pippa nodded slowly. Rather doubtfully, Suzie thought.

'I don't think infidelity's got much to do with looks,' ventured Suzie. 'If men are going to stray, they'll stray.' She remembered the woman who Nils had followed to the commune. She'd been nothing to look at, but that hadn't stopped him. Infidelity had been a symptom of a broader problem in their relationship.

'So I guess you've just got to trust them, then?' Pippa looked uneasy.

'Maybe,' said Ginie with a wry smile. 'But trust is a difficult commodity to come by. Hiring an *ugly* nanny has got to be a deterrent.'

Suzie laughed politely. Her stomach felt queasy. Bill claimed he loved nothing more than spending time with her, but she wasn't sure she believed him anymore. They had blistering sex, but not much else. He was full of promises of outings together that never seemed to eventuate. If trustworthiness was in such short supply, perhaps it was time to force the issue with Bill.

She badgered Bill for a fortnight without success. He was reluctant to commit to an outing, he argued, for fear of disappointing her when his work inevitably disrupted their plans. She rejected his reasoning with stony silence.

Then one Sunday morning in early March, the day that Freya was ten months old, he turned up unannounced.

She'd dressed Freya for their usual visit to the Manly farmers' markets and was just about to strap her into the pram when she sensed someone behind her. She wheeled around and there he was, carrying a large cane basket in one hand and a picnic rug in the other.

'I thought you were in Perth,' she said.

'My Monday morning meeting was cancelled, so I flew back last night,' Bill replied. 'I thought we could go for a picnic at Shelly Beach.'

Suzie beamed.

'Via the markets, of course,' he added. 'Hello, little one.' He bent down and kissed Freya, rubbing his nose against hers.

'Sounds perfect.'

They caught the bus to Manly, but this time, the journey was transformed by Bill's presence. Instead of whining and squirming, today Freya stood on Bill's knee, her face pressed to the window, squealing as he pointed out the passing sights. Once in Manly, they strolled to the farmers' markets via The Corso, the paved thoroughfare connecting the harbour and ocean beaches. They took turns at pushing the pram, weaving their way through the weekend crowd. Suzie linked an arm through Bill's and smiled. March was her favourite month: the unpleasant heat of summer was finally over, yet there was no hint of autumn in the air. And today, the moment she'd dreamed of since she'd first met Bill had finally arrived. They were going out as a family. Monika wasn't babysitting, Bill didn't have to work. They were a normal couple enjoying the weekend. Her heart sang.

At the market, they bought delicacies she'd never purchased before: dried fruits and expensive cheeses, cured meats and cream-filled pastries. They scoured the stalls for fresh juice but found none, settling instead for a tetra pack of orange juice bought from a 7-Eleven nearby. Then they wedged their basket onto the pram and walked to Shelly Beach, Freya riding on Bill's shoulders.

It was ten o'clock and the flat sandy expanse of Shelly Beach was already beginning to fill up with families. They chose a sunny patch beneath the boughs of an old fig tree, shaking out the picnic rug across the leaf litter. She sat Freya on the rug, an assortment of toys next to her. Suzie lifted her floating white kaftan over her head, revealing a red bikini underneath.

'Va-va-voom,' said Bill, his eyes lingering on her chest. She lay down in the sun next to Freya, arching her back for effect.

'Now that's just not fair,' he said. He bent towards her and whispered, 'I'd fuck you now if it wasn't so family-friendly here.'

A group of Indians was playing a lively game of cricket on the grass nearby, slanging each other in Hindi. Suzie smiled at their strident arguing. Bill began unpacking their purchases, arranging them neatly on disposable plates. He opened the orange juice and poured it into two plastic glasses.

'But wait.' He grinned. 'It won't taste the same without this.' He removed a wine cooler from his backpack and unzipped it.

'Wow,' said Suzie as he produced a bottle of French champagne. 'That's expensive.'

'Only the best for you.' He popped the cork with a flourish. 'We're celebrating two things this morning. One, Freya is ten months old.'

Suzie smiled. 'You remembered.'

'And it was exactly four months ago that we met.'

He topped up their glasses with champagne.

'You're one hell of a woman, Suzie. Here's to you.'

She blushed. 'Thank you.'

Freya reached for a croissant. 'Not for you, little one,' said Bill.

'I've got some oatmeal for her,' said Suzie. She found Freya's food bag in the bottom of the stroller.

'I'll give it to her,' said Bill. 'You relax.'

'Really?'

'I know what to do.' He laughed. 'It's not rocket science.'

He pulled Freya onto his lap and looped the bib around her neck. With the spoon clenched between his teeth, he unscrewed a tub of organic baby porridge and settled Freya into the crook of his arm. She gazed at him, blue eyes wide with interest, as he spooned the porridge into her mouth. He smacked his lips and made exaggerated 'mmm' sounds every time she swallowed. Freya threw her hands up into the air and giggled, revelling in the attention.

'You've not had breakfast this way before, have you?' laughed Suzie. 'I think you'll have to do this more often, Bill.'

'Bi bi bi bi,' Freya babbled, smiling up at him.

'She's saying your name, Bill!' Suzie's voice caught in her throat. 'She's not said anyone else's name, apart from mine.'

All the other milestones—first smile, first tooth, first night without waking—had been solitary moments of joy. But shared with Bill, the joy was multiplied.

Bill smiled. 'She's such a happy baby, isn't she?'

Suzie nodded. 'She's always been pretty easy, but I've got

nothing to compare her with, except the other babies in my mothers' group.'

'My sister belongs to a group like that,' Bill said. 'She's always out with them. Do you get along with the other women?'

She nodded. 'I do now. But in the beginning, it was a bit hard. I was the only one without a husband.'

She remembered her embarrassment at their first meeting, when she'd cried about Nils. After that, she'd never felt entirely comfortable in the mothers' group. She'd resented their endless chatter about forgetful or careless husbands. Ginie was particularly grating, constantly detailing Daniel's inadequacies. *Try not having a husband at all*, Suzie had wanted to scream, *then you might think differently*. The urge to do so had receded lately, now that Bill was in her life.

'Now it's really good,' she continued. 'We catch up at a café every week, and go to each other's houses too. They're some of my best friends now.'

Freya started to grizzle.

'Had enough, have you?' Bill wiped her mouth with the bib. 'Why don't we leave Mummy to relax, and we can go and look at that puppy?' He pointed at a Great Dane tied by its leash to a bench nearby.

'You're spoiling me,' said Suzie.

He picked up Freya. 'Let's go, little one.'

Suzie lay on her back on the picnic rug, staring up at the massive branches above her. She couldn't remember feeling this happy, ever. She rolled onto her stomach and looked around. We are part of this Sunday morning scene, she thought, our little family.

A sudden movement caught her eye. A woman was waving at her. A man carrying a child trailed behind her. Suzie smiled and waved back.

'I thought it was you,' called Cara, picking her way across the grass.

'Fancy seeing you here.'

'It's a family tradition for us, every Sunday morning at Shelly Beach,' Cara replied. 'You've met Richard, haven't you?' Cara beckoned to the man behind her.

Richard waved at Suzie. 'Yes—hi, Suzie. We met at the Fathers and Partners session. Back when our babies were actually babies.' He laughed and let Astrid, who was straining in his arms, slide down onto the grass. She rocked on her feet before taking several unsteady steps forward.

'Oh my goodness!' said Suzie. 'She's walking! That's early isn't it?'

'Well, she is the oldest in our group,' said Cara. 'An April baby, remember? But you know what she's like, always into everything.'

'Yes, it's only started happening in the last few days,' added Richard. 'Luckily, she doesn't get very far.' He picked her up again.

'Let me introduce you both to Bill,' said Suzie. 'My boyfriend,' she added, for Richard's benefit.

'Oh, so this is *the* Bill,' said Cara. 'I can't wait to meet him.'

Suzie stood up. 'Come on over.'

They walked towards the bench where Bill was crouched

with Freya, just out of reach of the Great Dane. The dog was tugging at its leash with excitement, but Suzie was relieved to see that Bill was not attempting to pat it. You could never truly trust a dog with children, as far as she was concerned.

'Bill,' she called. He didn't look up.

'Bill,' she repeated, louder this time.

He turned and smiled, Freya in his arms.

'Bill, this is Cara, from my mothers' group. We were just talking about the mothers' group, weren't we? And this is Cara's husband, Richard, and baby Astrid.'

'Pleased to meet you,' said Bill, shaking Richard's hand. 'Nice day for it, isn't it?'

'Beautiful,' said Richard. 'Do you live in Freshwater too?'

Bill shook his head. 'No, a bit further up the Peninsula.'

'You look very familiar,' said Cara. 'Where have I seen you before?'

'A lot of people say that,' he said, smiling. 'I must have one of those faces.' He turned towards the picnic rug. 'I think Freya's nappy needs changing.'

'Oh, thanks,' said Suzie, delighted he'd noticed. They watched Bill carry Freya back to the picnic blanket.

'Wow, he's hands-on,' said Cara.

Astrid wriggled in Richard's arms. 'Want to get down again?' Richard placed her on the grass and she tottered away, swaying like a drunkard. 'I think she wants to go and see Freya.'

'She's really moving now,' said Suzie.

Cara nodded. 'Yes, I can't believe it. Freya won't be far behind. They'll all be turning one soon and we'll be having our first Mother's Day. The year has just flown, hasn't it?'

Suzie watched Bill from a distance, digging around in the base of the pram.

'I'd better go and help him with the nappy change,' she said.

'Sure, we'll let you get back to it,' said Cara. 'Bye, Bill.'

Bill sat back on his heels and waved.

'He seems really nice,' said Cara. 'See you Friday.'

Suzie waved them off before turning towards the picnic rug. Bill had answered his mobile phone and was crouched next to Freya. Suzie reached the rug and Bill looked up at her, telephone to his ear, a curious expression on his face. Surely there couldn't be a work issue today? She bent down to pick up Freya, who was shredding a disposable wipe between her fingers. Suzie heard the distorted sound of the caller's voice. It was a woman, she could tell, and she didn't sound pleased.

She carried Freya over to the fig tree and lay her down on the grass. As she pinned a clean cloth nappy around her bottom, she glanced back at Bill. He sat motionless on the picnic rug, his jaw set with displeasure.

He stood up and thrust his BlackBerry back into his pocket.

'I'm sorry,' he called, walking towards her. 'That was my assistant. Something's come up at work. I have to go.'

They cleared the rug in silence.

For a moment she considered confronting him.

Just tell me now, Bill—is she your girlfriend, or your wife?

'Hey, I'm *so* sorry,' he said, catching hold of her hands. 'I'll make it up to you, I promise.' His tone was gentle, contrite.

He ran his hands down her cheeks, as he always did.

'Forget it,' she mumbled.

Then she snatched her kaftan from the grass and pulled it over her head. She couldn't bear him looking at her any longer.

The following week she confided in Cara.

It was an overcast Friday morning, the air crisp with autumn, and the group had gathered at Pippa's house for fear of rain. The babies were playing on the lounge room floor, crawling and shrieking and rolling over toys. Astrid was toddling around with greater confidence, keen to explore other parts of the house. Cara laughed as she ran after her. 'No, my little escapee,' she'd say, moving her back onto the rug. On one occasion Astrid made it as far as the kitchen and, when Cara stood up to find her, Suzie followed her in.

'Can we chat for a moment?' Suzie whispered, glancing back towards the lounge room.

'Sure,' said Cara. She plucked Astrid from under the breakfast bar.

'I don't know who else to talk to.' Suzie's eyes filled with tears.

'Oh, Suze.' Cara put a hand on her shoulder. 'Are you alright?'

Suzie shook her head. 'I think Bill is lying to me.'

Cara frowned. 'Why?'

'After we saw you at Shelly Beach last Sunday, he got a phone call. From a woman. I couldn't hear what she was saying, but she sounded really pissed off. Like a girlfriend.'

Cara looked at her. 'But it could have been anyone.'

'No,' said Suzie. 'It didn't feel right.' She pushed her hair behind her ears. 'I mean, we've been going out for more than four months and I've *never* been to his house, not once. And he's always travelling, working odd hours. I'm starting to think I've been really stupid.'

I *sound* stupid, she thought. She'd never allowed herself to dwell on the negative, she didn't want to be a naysayer like Ginie. But now, confessing her suspicions to Cara, she felt her uncertainty grow. It all sounded so ludicrous. *Why* had she waited this long?

'I don't know what to do,' she whispered. 'What would *you* do?'

Cara hesitated. 'I'm no expert in this department. But I don't think you're stupid, Suze.' Astrid squirmed in her arms and Cara let her down onto the kitchen floor again.

'I just don't want to get hurt again. Not after Nils.'

'I can imagine.' Cara put an arm around her. 'You really don't need this, do you? You've got enough to deal with already.'

New tears sprang to Suzie's eyes. Cara understood; she always did.

After a moment's silence, Cara looked at her. 'Have you gone through Bill's pockets to see if you can find anything?'

Suzie shook her head.

Cara shrugged. 'I know, it's a silly idea. Straight out of the movies.' She patted Suzie's shoulder again. 'I guess if it doesn't feel right anymore, Suze, you've got to follow your gut instinct. Maybe take a break from Bill?'

Suzie nodded.

'Hey,' called Ginie from the lounge room, 'what are you two conspirators whispering about in there?'

Suzie stiffened.

Without pausing, Cara called back to her, 'Some ideas for the babies' first birthday. It's not that far away, you know.' She walked over to the door and leaned against it, blocking Ginie's view of the kitchen.

'God, *you're* organised,' said Ginie.

'We were thinking about a group birthday party, rather than all of us having separate parties,' Cara continued. 'Maybe at Manly Dam where there's a barbecue area and space for kids to run around. We can invite partners, extended family, that sort of thing. What do you think?'

'Sounds great,' said Ginie.

'Any excuse to have some champers together.' Miranda laughed.

'Maybe we could have it on Mother's Day,' suggested Pippa. 'You know, make it a double celebration. Their first year as babies, our first year as mothers.'

'That's the second Sunday in May, right?' Ginie was scrolling through her iPhone calendar. 'Yep, I'm available.'

'I'll try to make sure that Willem isn't interstate,' said Miranda. 'Eight weeks' notice should be enough.'

Made wrote down the date in her brown batik notebook. She smiled. 'It good for our babies to have birthday together. First birthday, it very important in Bali culture.'

'Yes, and that's a fabulous idea, Pippa,' said Cara. 'I can't think of a nicer way to spend Mother's Day than with the most inspiring mums I know. Now, let's work out who's bringing what, shall we?' She glanced over her shoulder at Suzie.

Suzie smiled back, grateful.

Then she wiped her eyes with a tissue and moved towards the doorway.

'Maybe we could hire a clown, or a face-painter or something,' she said.

They joined the others in the lounge room.

'Got to go, sexy. Early morning meeting.'

She glanced at her watch in the darkness. It was only six thirty. She thought of Freya, asleep at Monika's.

He reached for his wallet on the bedside table, withdrawing six fifty-dollar notes in a fat wad. He held them out to her.

'Get yourself something nice. You deserve it.'

'Thanks.'

He placed the notes on the bedside table.

Bill's generosity had allowed her to buy things for Freya she never could have afforded herself. She'd relished shopping for new clothes and toys rather than rummaging through the racks and shelves of the Salvation Army store. When Cara had invited the group to Taronga Zoo one weekend, she'd been able to accept, despite the steep entry fee. When a children's pantomime was playing at the Opera House, she didn't hesitate to buy tickets. Bill's regular contribution had been so helpful she'd conveniently dismissed the niggling doubts she had about him.

She watched him as he stood up and walked naked to the bathroom, waiting for the familiar squeal of water straining through copper pipes. Light was just beginning to creep between the slats of her venetian blinds; the mornings were getting darker as winter approached. She remembered their morning tea on Shelly Beach. How Freya had crawled to Bill and he'd tossed her up in the air, as a father might. How wonderful it had felt to be a threesome, a family on a picnic rug drinking cheap juice and French champagne. Before the phone call, and the woman's voice.

She looked again at Bill's wallet on the bedside table. Then, glancing in the direction of the bathroom, she leaned across and opened it. She dug about for his driver's licence, anything that might tell her where he lived. Nothing. Her breath quickened as she pulled out a wad of materials concealed behind the notes compartment. A gym membership, a car insurance tag, a card announcing *I am a Blood Donor.* And then, a pink note tucked behind it. She unfolded it, even as she heard Bill turn the shower off. A gift voucher for a massage. Feminine cursive writing, penned in silver ink, on the note: *Happy birthday. Love, M. xx*

She refolded the note and replaced the wallet as she'd found it, then lay down again and covered herself with a sheet.

Bill walked out of the bathroom, a towel wrapped around his waist. She rolled over onto her stomach and closed her eyes. She listened to the sound of him dressing: boxer shorts, shirt, trousers, cufflinks, belt, tie, socks, shoes, jacket.

Finally, he sat down on the edge of the bed next to her. Peeling the sheet back, he leaned down and pressed his lips along her spine. Then he ran his fingers across her bruised buttocks.

'Fuck, you turn me on.'

She felt sick to the stomach.

He stood up. 'See you on Thursday at the café. Give Freya a kiss from me.'

She grunted, as though half asleep.

'Bye, sexy.' She heard the door close behind him.

She opened her eyes and began to cry.

After she'd put Freya to bed, she spent an hour at the kitchen table, composing the text message. She knew he was in Melbourne tonight, or so he'd said. There was part of her that wanted to telephone, to demand to know more, to understand what the other woman meant to him. To call him names and feel the cathartic rush of righteousness. But she was afraid of him, on some level. He was used to winning, always getting his own way. She'd never said no to him for fear of how he might react. She hadn't really known him at all, she reflected. She rested her head in her hands, ashamed. He'd as good as paid her for sex. 'M' might well be his wife, she thought. She just wanted it to be over.

She settled on two simple sentences: *I know about 'M', the other woman in your life. I don't want to see you anymore.*

She sat alone at the kitchen bench until after midnight, half hoping for, and half dreading, a response. She fell asleep with her head on her arms.

The next morning, she checked her mobile.

M is my mother.

She stared at the message, wanting to believe him. But instinct told her he was lying. That he'd lied about everything, right from the beginning. She shook her head and texted him back.

Bill, it's over.

Her telephone rang in the darkness. She sat bolt upright on the couch and looked around, wide-eyed. She couldn't tell what time it was, or how long she'd been asleep. The television was still on, the volume muted. She checked the caller ID. It was Monika.

'Hello?' she croaked.

'Suzie, did I wake you?'

'I was asleep on the couch.'

Monika paused. 'Are you alright, Suzie? I'm worried about you.'

She leaned back onto a cushion and pressed her hand into her eyes, hard.

Monika hardly ever asked her how she was. Suzie's lips began to tremble.

'I'm . . . not the best,' she admitted.

'Anything I can do? I could take Freya another night this week if you'd like, to give you a bit of a break?'

'Thanks.' For the first time ever, she didn't feel aggravated by the offer. Monika meant well, she knew. In fact, apart from the women in her mothers' group, Monika was one of the very few people who actually gave a damn about her. And she was the only person in the world who would drop everything if Freya needed it.

'Are you still there, Suzie?'

'Yes.' Suzie sighed. 'Monika, listen. I was wondering if . . .

if you might come around and keep me company one night this week. We could watch a DVD or something.'

Being by herself at night again was hard for Suzie.

'Oh.' She could hear the surprise in Monika's voice. 'Well, I'd like that. I could bring some dinner over on Friday if you like. Say, after six thirty?'

'Good,' said Suzie. 'We'll talk more then.'

She replaced the handset.

Monika's just like me, she thought. A woman alone in the world.

Without the extra income that Bill had provided, Suzie dropped all the activities she'd only just taken up. The swimming lessons, Gymbaroo, the music classes. Instead, she started taking a weekly train trip to Chatswood; it was cheap entertainment for Freya. They caught a ferry from Manly first, then a city loop train that took them to Wynyard. From there, it was only seven stops to Chatswood. They brought homemade sandwiches and met Monika on her lunch break in a park near the driving school. The outing cost less than ten dollars and they were always home in time for Freya's nap.

Suzie wasn't sure which was more enjoyable—the picnics in the park with Monika, or the train journey to Chatswood. Freya would watch the train approaching, clapping her hands as it pulled into the platform. Then she would make low humming and hissing sounds, mimicking the engine and the sliding doors. They would always sit in the easy-access carriage, best for managing Freya's stroller, and watch the world flying past the windows. Even the most mundane objects captivated Freya: a bright blue plastic bag blowing beneath a seat, a tartan shopping trolley, a cheesy advertisement for chewing gum.

Once at Chatswood, they would walk the short distance to the park and wait for Monika. Suzie would lay out the picnic rug and follow Freya as she toddled after pigeons or played in the autumn leaves. Monika would join them at midday, always bringing with her some small treat for Freya: a heart-shaped sticker, a lift-the-flap book, a stuffed toy.

One Thursday in April, as they sat on the picnic rug eating their sandwiches, Monika pulled a lollipop from a brown paper bag and thrust it at her. Suzie turned it over in her hands, inspecting the label.

'It's called a Nature-Pop. I bought it at a health-food store,' Monika explained. 'No artificial colours or preservatives. Apparently manuka honey has medicinal properties too. Is it okay for Freya to have one, after her sandwich?'

Suzie flushed, pleased to be asked. Monika had gone to considerable trouble to choose just the sort of edible treat she might buy herself. Months ago, Monika never would have been this considerate. How far she's come, Suzie mused. How far *we've* come.

'Of course,' she said. 'That's really nice of you.'

Monika dismissed the praise with a shrug. 'These sandwiches are a bit . . . chewy,' she said. 'What's on them?'

'Tahini.'

'Never heard of it.'

Suzie said nothing. Some things about Monika would

never change. But *she* could change, she'd learned, over the lonely weeks since Bill's departure. Monika wasn't perfect, but neither was she. And Monika had lived thirty more years of life than Suzie, and she had to respect that. She'd had her own life, her own challenges, and she loved Freya as any grandmother would.

Watching them interact, Suzie wished her own parents lived closer than Brisbane. With Bill gone, Freya had no male role model in her life, not even a grandfather. The mothers' group had become even more important to Suzie, offering rare social opportunities that *both* of them needed. Suzie hoped that, in time, there would be more group activities involving husbands and grandfathers. Gatherings like the combined first birthday party and Mother's Day celebration, which Suzie was helping to organise with Pippa. With more events like that, Freya could have at least *some* contact with adult males.

On a cold night in late April, the mothers' group finally held the book club session they'd been delaying for months. At Suzie's invitation, they'd gathered at her flat in Dee Why.

Cara, Miranda and Ginie squeezed themselves onto the sagging two-person sofa, Made sat cross-legged on the shag pile rug, Pippa was seated in a fold-out chair she'd brought from home and Suzie sank into her brown patchwork beanbag.

Without the babies present, and with the benefit of several bottles of wine between them, the conversation was intense— or perhaps it was the book, Suzie wasn't sure. She'd finished *We Need to Talk About Kevin* the night before, appalled to the very end. She'd found a scene close to the end of the book, in which a teenage sociopath went on a killing spree at school, deeply disturbing. The mothers' group had been talking in circles for more than an hour and the debate was getting heated.

'Well, I found it a bit far-fetched,' Suzie objected, passing a plate of cheese and crackers in Made's direction. 'The book made out that Kevin was a killer from the beginning. It painted him as some kind of child monster, even when he was in nappies. But I didn't believe that Kevin *was* as evil as his mother made him out to be. Okay, he was really a nasty kid. But the more I read, the more I thought the *mother* had problems of her own. Serious ones, like when she physically abused Kevin.'

'Oh, no, Suze,' groaned Ginie. 'It wasn't abuse, it was a once-off. And Kevin deserved it. I'm not saying it was right, but I totally understood why she belted him.'

'Well, if it's acceptable for a mother to model *violence*,' Suzie retorted, 'why wouldn't Kevin turn out the way he did?' She could hear the shrillness in her own voice, but she couldn't moderate it. 'As his mother, *she* was partly responsible for the massacre.'

Ginie shook her head. 'I disagree. Not every hideous act of a child can be linked to poor parenting. Kids make choices too.'

'But parenting is what moulds kids, Ginie,' Suzie countered. 'A lot of bad parents find it much easier, more *convenient*, to blame something external—you know, genetics, the government, their demanding job—than take responsibility for *their* role in their child's behaviour.'

Suzie wondered if Ginie detected the barb. For months she'd wondered why Ginie was so willing to outsource Rose's upbringing to a nanny, when so little was known of the longer-term consequences on children.

Cara intervened. 'I know what you mean, Suze. That scene where Eva broke Kevin's arm, it was horrible. But at the same time, like you, Ginie, I understood why she did it . . . and I felt terrible for sympathising with her! Then I thought maybe this is part of what the author is trying to do. Maybe it's a device to make readers—mothers like us—question traditional views about what mothers are *supposed* to think and feel.'

Suzie sipped at her glass of wine, considering Cara's words. It was all a bit abstract for her. She glanced around the room, waiting for someone else to respond. She'd positioned six large candles on the bookcase and turned off the main lamp. The candlelight flickering across the ceiling, while not unpleasant, was distracting. The soft scent of citrus hung in the air. The aroma, coupled with the shadowy light, brought Bill to mind. She squeezed her eyes shut against the mental image.

'What did *you* think of the book, Miranda?' prompted Cara, breaking the silence.

Miranda had been quiet the whole evening.

'More vino?' asked Ginie, tipping the bottle towards Miranda.

Miranda nodded, then hung her nose over the glass and inhaled. She and Willem were connoisseurs of wine and food, Suzie had learned. Miranda and Ginie were always swapping restaurant reviews.

'I think . . .' Miranda paused. 'Well, so many of you have already said what *I* was planning to say.'

'That won't wash,' objected Ginie. 'Get on with it.'

'Okay, okay.' Miranda quaffed a mouthful of wine and reached for her Evian bottle. She straightened her back against the sinking sofa.

'Well, I know everyone's been focused on the role of Eva, the mother, and how *she* contributed to Kevin's problems,' Miranda started. 'But I was more interested in the role of the father. So many things seemed to go unsaid between Eva and Franklin. Kevin would do something awful, and Franklin would just do nothing. After a while I thought, he's an intelligent guy, why is he so blindsided by Kevin? But Eva didn't try very hard to help him understand the extent of the problem, either. Maybe she didn't want to let Franklin down, I don't know. I just kept thinking that the pair of them could have stopped the tragedy *together* if they'd sat down and talked honestly. The title of the book was interesting, because it's the one thing they never did.'

'Wow,' said Suzie, impressed. 'Did you study literature at university?' The title of the book had seemed strange to her, but she *never* could have thought of that.

Miranda ignored the compliment. 'Fine arts, actually.'

Suzie turned to Made, wanting to be inclusive. 'What did you think of it, Made?'

'I only finish first chapter,' Made replied, apologetic. 'Even with more time. I sorry.' The group had extended the deadline on several occasions. Despite this, many of them had struggled to plough through it.

'But I wonder one thing,' Made said. 'From first chapter.'

The group waited.

'I wonder why author make main character from Armenia? Her name is . . .' She opened her book at the first page. 'Khatch-a-dour-ian?' She enunciated each syllable slowly. She looked around the group. 'This book about America, yes? American problem with guns, American families, society there. So why this mother is not American?'

Suzie shifted her weight on the beanbag. It was a good point, she thought.

'That's really interesting,' said Cara. 'I mean, whenever you see media coverage of high school massacres in the US, the perpetrators are usually white, Anglo-Saxon, middle-class males.' She paused and drained her glass. 'You know what, Made? I think you might have made the best point of the night, even without reading the whole book.'

Made smiled shyly, as if embarrassed.

'No, really,' continued Cara. 'We've spent all our time ana-lysing whether Kevin's mother and father were to blame for his actions. But maybe the book's saying something about the way humans look for *cultural* scapegoats. You know, the per-petrator of a crime always comes from somewhere else, never your own backyard.'

Made nodded, her expression thoughtful. 'This book sad for me, because it about blame. In Bali, many people look after child. Parents yes, but others too. If child do something bad, many in village sad, not just parents. *Many* feel responsible.'

'Yes,' said Cara, her face animated. 'Maybe *We Need to Talk About Kevin* is not about individual responsibility at all.

Maybe it's actually pointing to the failure of modern Western societies to give parents the kind of support you're familiar with in Bali. You know, the idea that it takes a village to raise a child.'

'Well, for me,' said Pippa suddenly, her eyes serious, 'all of you are *my* village. I couldn't have made it through the last eleven months without you. Seriously. I've got no other support, apart from Robert.' She looked around the room. 'I remember when I was a teenager, thinking that one day I'd get married and have kids and that it would be this *natural* sort of process.' She swallowed a mouthful of wine. 'But it didn't happen that way at all. I had no idea what motherhood *really* involved. The way my body's changed, how it's affected my relationship with Robert . . . I mean, I love Heidi of course, but I had no idea how *depleted* I'd feel.'

'It's funny, isn't it?' said Miranda. 'All those things no one ever tells you about motherhood. It's like secret mothers' business. Lots of my friends had babies before me, but not one of them *ever* told me it would be this hard. Now I ask them about it and they say, "Oh yes, but you can't tell a pregnant woman the negatives." It's like a code of silence.'

'So much for the sisterhood,' agreed Pippa. 'My specialist told me that one-third of women have serious pelvic floor problems after birth. But most of them are too ashamed to ask for help, so they end up having prolapse operations in their sixties.' She reddened. 'This past year there have been times I've felt like I couldn't go on. It was only this mothers' group that got me through, really.'

Made leaned forward. 'Yes, for me like that too.' She

smiled. 'Gordon is good husband, but moving to Australia very hard. Easier for me now with friends like you.'

Ginie cleared her throat. 'Well, I admit I was a bit of a sceptic about mothers' groups at the beginning.' She drained her glass. 'But now I tell people it's like having my own board of directors for babies.'

Everyone laughed.

'And given how different we are,' added Suzie, smiling in Ginie's direction, 'it's so nice that we've been able to give each other support. I've really needed it, with Nils leaving and everything. And now with Bill gone . . .' She bit down on the inside of her mouth, willing herself not to cry. She was the only one in the group who seemed to do so, at the drop of a hat. 'It's really good to have your friendship.'

Cara stood up. 'Well, given the negative content of tonight's book, it's great to end on a high note. I think we've agreed that it takes a village to raise a child, and that we trust each other with that task. And I say, bottoms up to that.' She raised her glass to the group.

Everyone clinked their glasses together.

Miranda

Miranda squinted at the alarm clock in the semi-darkness. I should be thankful, she reasoned. At least it isn't 3.57 am. Willem had left for the airport half an hour earlier, creeping across the floorboards in Egyptian cotton socks, gathering his things as quietly as he could. His efforts were futile, of course. She was so attuned to waking at the slightest sound. The muffled zipping of his suitcase jolted her out of sleep and she'd lain on her back, listening to him shower and shave. Preparing himself for that liberating moment when he could close the front door on family life, straighten his tie, climb into a taxi and enter an easier world.

There was no sound from Rory's room, for a change. Most days, he would wake before dawn and coo softly in his cot until she tiptoed in with a bottle of milk. The silence was unusual, but she resisted the urge to check on him. Digby, however, had stirred and called out just as soon as Willem had closed the front door. She'd crept into his room and, in a forceful whisper, told him it was still time for sleeping. Miraculously, he'd rolled over and slipped his thumb back into his mouth, nuzzling his ragged blue comforter. She'd pulled the blanket up over his shoulders and stooped to kiss his cheek, warm with sleep. As her lips brushed his skin, she'd felt a sudden bolt of tenderness. But as she closed his door behind her, she felt relieved, more than anything else.

Is this what a battle-fatigued soldier feels like? she wondered.

She shook her head, chastising herself for the analogy. I've never known true adversity, she thought. And Digby is not the enemy.

She climbed back into bed and retreated under the blankets, cocooning herself against the dawn.

And then Digby called out again, more insistent this time.

She glanced at the clock.

5.13 am

She always found it difficult to manufacture chirpiness this early. She pushed back the blankets and sat up in bed. Why couldn't he sleep just a little longer? Her head throbbed and the aftertaste of last night's ravioli seemed to linger in her mouth. She'd laboured for hours over the recipe, rolling out sheets of homemade pasta and carefully shaping delicate parcels of spinach and feta. But Willem had winced when he'd sampled one, setting his fork aside.

'What's wrong?' she'd asked.

'You used feta, not ricotta.' He'd wrinkled his nose. 'No Italian would ever make it that way. Too salty.'

Willem was fond of referring to his Italian ancestry, when he wasn't dropping names in Dutch. His father, Marco, the Australian-born son of Italian migrants, had met his mother, Hendrika, a stunning KLM flight attendant, on a flight from Rome to Amsterdam. After their engagement, Hendrika willingly made her home in Australia, but they named their first son, Willem, after her father. For all of Hendrika's Dutch blonde beauty, Willem had inherited his grandfather's Latino looks.

Miranda opened the top drawer of her bedside table and groped around for the packet of aspirin she kept under a jumble of socks, art journals and half-completed lists. She tore three tablets free of the foil and dropped them into the glass of water that stood on the bedside table. She listened to the comforting fizzing sound as the tablets dissolved.

'Mum. Mum. Mum. *Muuuuuum. Muuuuuum.*' Digby's usual refrain was gaining momentum.

Her body had become used to the numbing fatigue, but her mind continued to rebel. Before children, she'd been a devotee of yoga and meditation retreats, where she'd often sat straight-backed on hard wooden floors at ungodly hours of the morning. It had all seemed so virtuous at the time; she'd applauded herself for her mental and physical fortitude. Now, she could only fantasise about such solitude, the pleasure of cold floorboards pressed against her backside. Just one blissful hour of contemplation followed by a bowl of unpalatable gruel for breakfast. To be alone again, focused exclusively on the evolution of her soul. What bliss.

'*Muuuuuum. Muuuuuum.*'

She pushed her feet into her Birkenstocks and walked into the ensuite. She sank onto the toilet, her head in her hands. Her urine stank; it was acrid and yellow. I really must remember to drink more water today, she thought. It was a daily resolution that she never seemed to accomplish. She stood up from the toilet and held her hands under the cold water, staring into the mirror. At 33, her face had changed. Her skin was dull, her eyes bloodshot, and faint lines were beginning to crease her forehead. Not that long ago, Willem had called her beautiful.

'*Muuuuuum.*'

Digby's voice had disturbed Rory; she could hear him stirring in the next room.

She opened Digby's bedroom door.

'Good morning,' she whispered. 'Please can we use our quiet inside voices while baby Rory is still asleep?'

'Noooooo!' he shrieked.

She said nothing. According to the parenting manuals she'd devoured, the twin pillars of toddler behaviour management were, first, ignoring negative behaviours and, second, the art of distraction. She opted for the latter.

'I wonder what the weather is like this morning, Dig. Shall we see?'

She began to open the curtains.

'I do it,' shouted Digby, launching himself from under the covers. He grabbed a fistful of curtain and began yanking it towards the floor.

'That's not how we open curtains, Digby. Please let it go.'

'No!' he shrieked again.

'Let me show you how to do it so we don't break anything. Then you can try.'

'*Noooooo!*'

'Digby, honey,' she said, her tone firm, 'I'm going to count to three and then I'd like you to let go of the curtain, or Mummy will have to ask you to start the day again. Let's not pull the curtain until it breaks. Please, Digby, I'm starting to count now. One . . . two . . .'

Digby looked at her, expectant.

'Three,' she said. 'Right, lie down.' She prised his hands from the curtain. 'We need to start the day again.'

Digby began to snivel. 'But I don't *want* to start the day again.'

'It's not discussion time, Digby. I asked you nicely to stop pulling the curtain, and I told you what would happen if you didn't. Now, lie down.' It was utterly predictable: misbehaviour, warning, repeated misbehaviour, action. Consistency in consequences was the key, so the manuals said.

She tried to pull him down onto the bed.

'*Noooooo.*' He slid off his bed and ran towards the train table, diving underneath and rolling towards the wall.

'Nyah nyah nyah-nyah-nyah, can't catch me,' he sang.

She got down on her hands and knees.

'Digby, I have to give Rory his bottle now. When you're ready to start the day again, you just let me know.' She stood up and walked towards the door.

'I hate you, Mum,' he bellowed.

I'm *not* your mother, she thought, closing the door behind her.

5.26 am.

Rory was lying on his back, gazing at the rainbow mobile suspended above his cot.

'Hi, sweetie.'

He turned towards her voice and smiled, as always. At eleven months old, he had only just learned to crawl. The other babies in the mothers' group had all developed that skill much earlier. Some, like Astrid, had started commando crawling at just six months, pulling themselves up flights of stairs, onto chairs and into cupboards. But Rory had seemed reluctant to join the world of the upright, and Miranda hadn't been too concerned by it. She'd wanted to savour Rory's infancy for as long as possible, to linger in his babyhood. She loved everything about him: his mischievous smile, his lively eyes, his placid temperament and calm acceptance of the world as he knew it, so unfairly monopolised by the hyperactive Digby.

'How did you sleep?' she asked, leaning over and tickling the folds under his chin.

'Ma-ma-ma-ma.' Rory smiled up at her with a lopsided, toothy grin. She loved hearing him say her name.

She scooped him out of his cot and onto the change table. It was immediately obvious that he'd soiled his nappy.

'Oh, that's a smell only a mother can love. Let me change that.'

He kicked his feet in the air and giggled.

'*Muuuuuum*, I'm ready to start the day again,' Digby called from his bedroom. Miranda sighed. She'd hoped Digby might stay in his room and sulk just a little longer, so that she could enjoy Rory in the interim.

'Okay, Dig,' she called back.

She picked up Rory and gave him a squeeze. 'Let's get Digby.'

She turned the doorknob to Digby's room and stepped back, allowing him to race past her.

'You be the backhoe loader, I'll be the bulldozer,' he yelled on his way to the lounge room.

She rolled her eyes. 'I'm just changing Rory's nappy, Dig. I'll come and play in a moment.'

Since he'd turned three, Digby's favourite activity was what the parenting books called 'imaginative play'. This inevitably involved some kind of role-play in which Miranda found herself acting the part of an inanimate object. She'd spent hours conducting mind-numbing conversations with Digby as a backhoe loader, a steamboat, a lampshade. Sometimes Digby would choose household objects ('You be the dustpan, I'll be the brush') or gardening equipment ('You be the rake, I'll be the broom'). One rainy afternoon, he'd looked up from a drawing activity and thrust a crayon her way. 'You be the red crayon, I'll be the blue crayon,' he'd said, grinning. She'd almost cried with frustration. I *used* to be someone, she'd thought. Important people asked me for my opinion. Her life before children, as an art curator and gallery manager, had never felt so remote.

As she lowered Rory onto the change table once more, Digby appeared in the doorway. 'Has Rory done a big poo?'

'I'm not sure, Dig. I'm about to find out.'

She wanted him out of the bedroom. 'Do *you* need to go to the toilet?' she prompted, hoping he would take her cue and head to the bathroom.

'Nah.' He sauntered over to the change table and began to scale its side.

'Digby, please don't climb up.' She threw the soiled nappy into a flip-top bin.

'But I want to give Rory a kiss.'

She looked at him, doubtful. 'Okay.'

With his feet balanced on the shelf below, Digby pursed his lips and leaned forward. Rory smiled at him with the trusting adoration of a younger sibling. As Digby pressed his mouth against Rory's face, Rory screamed. The shock and indignation in his cry was palpable. She pulled Digby away and gasped at the teeth marks on Rory's cheek.

'Digby.' Her voice trembled. 'Go to your room now.'

'Nah.'

Her rage exploded out of her. 'How dare you!' She whisked Rory off the change table and onto the floor. Then she seized Digby by the shoulders, marching him into his bedroom and pushing him onto the bed.

'You will stay here until you learn how to behave properly!' she shouted.

Instantly he bounced off the bed and ran towards the door. She caught hold of his pyjamas and rammed him back onto the bed, shaking him as he rebounded on the mattress.

'*Muuuuuummmy!*' he screamed. 'Mummy, let go of me.'

The panic in his voice registered. She stopped, appalled by her own behaviour. I'm the adult here, she reminded herself.

She took a deep breath. 'I'm sorry, Digby. That was wrong of Mummy.'

She reached out to touch his face. He recoiled as if she'd

brandished a weapon. Rory's whimpering was audible in the next room. He was still on the floor, without a nappy on. She hoped he wouldn't wee on the carpet.

'I'm sorry,' she repeated. 'I was just so upset that you made Rory sad by biting him.' She looked at Digby, cowering on his bed. He didn't care why it happened, he didn't want to hear her reasons. All he knew was that his mother had manhandled him. She felt terrible.

'We use our mouths for speaking and smiling, Digby,' she continued. 'Not biting.'

Digby's lower lip protruded. He began to cry.

The sound competed with Rory's wailing in the next room. It was at times like this, with both children crying, that she felt like locking herself in the broom cupboard.

'I have to go and help Rory,' she said. 'His cheek will need some ice. Stay here, please, and think about what happened.'

'Noooooo,' Digby objected. 'I want a cuddle.'

Rory's cries were escalating. 'I can't do that right now, Dig. I have to help Rory. But we can have a cuddle later. I'd like that.' She didn't believe her own propaganda. By the look of Digby, neither did he.

'I hate you,' he yelled. 'I really, really hate you.'

She pulled the door closed behind her.

The antique clock in the hallway chimed six o'clock.

She sat with Rory on the expensive leather chaise longue that Willem had insisted on buying. There was nothing she liked about this house, nor the furniture in it. Willem prided himself on his aesthetic sensibility and, when she'd accepted his marriage proposal, he'd declared his intention to buy her a dream home. True to his word, he'd done that—except it was *his* dream home. His passion for interior design hadn't surprised her. But his desire to stamp his mark on every minor finish—from taps to toilet seats—had been disconcerting. It's like being engaged to my mother, she'd giggled to a girlfriend at the time; no detail in décor spared.

She dabbed at the edges of Rory's mouth with a soft cloth, careful that no drips strayed from the bottle. She'd learned from experience how unpleasant it could be if Willem discovered a mark on the leather. He valued order and elegance in his home, and things were always better between them when she respected that. While it was challenging to contain the walking disaster that was Digby, Rory was more predictable.

'*Muuuuuum*,' called Digby.

Rory had only drained half the bottle. Digby would just have to wait.

She smiled at Rory as he sucked at the teat, his small hands roving over hers. People often commented on how much he looked like Willem, with a prominent forehead, striking eyes and a square chin. It was true, she knew, but she liked to think that he had inherited some of *her* personality traits. He was amiable and relaxed, which was a miracle given that Digby was always shadowing him, like a vulture circling its quarry.

She closed her eyes. I need to be more positive about Digby, she thought.

It was another daily resolution that she always seemed to fail to meet.

*

Willem had been upfront about Digby, the son of his first wife, from the beginning. Digby was barely a year old when they'd met and only eighteen months when they married. For some reason, she'd thought that Digby's infancy might make it easier for her to slip into the role of stepmother. She'd certainly never imagined it would be as hard as this, not in a million years. But even if someone had told her how difficult it might be—and God knows, her mother had tried, in her own quiet way—she'd lost all capacity to reason. Back then, she'd been thoroughly seduced by Willem, and the lifestyle he represented.

He was articulate, well-travelled and charismatic. Not to mention his broad physique and disarming smile. A walking cliché—tall, dark and handsome—but with a mind that roved over a thousand topics at once. His capacity to digest and distil financial information had led to such outlandish investment success, she'd often wondered if he had savant-like talents.

He'd thoroughly charmed her, right from the beginning. When he bowled into the gallery one rainy afternoon, looking for an artwork for his sister, she couldn't believe her luck.

'She's a stay-at-home mother,' he explained. 'She keeps telling me how she's going mad, climbing the walls. So I thought I'd hang something decent on them for her.'

She laughed aloud.

They walked around the gallery for more than an hour. He drilled her on questions of form, texture and composition. She tried hard to demonstrate her intimate knowledge of the artists and their works, an eclectic curatorial selection of acrylics, mixed media and oils.

In the end, he chose two of her favourite Estelle Umbria pieces: oil, graphite and wax on linen.

'One for her, one for me,' he said. 'Can I have them delivered?'

She'd taken down his address, a prestigious street in the seaside suburb of Manly.

'Put them on that,' he said, passing her a platinum credit card. 'Art catapults us out of drudgery. That warrants the investment.'

She smiled, glancing at the name on his card as she processed the payment. *Willem J. Bianco.*

'Thank you, Mr Bianco.' She was careful to pronounce his surname with a slight Italian accent; she'd studied the language at high school.

'Willem's the name.' He signed the receipt with a flourish, using a silver fountain pen he pulled from the inside pocket of his Ralph Lauren sports jacket. His signature was bold, purposeful. 'May I ask yours?'

'Miranda Bailey.' She felt her face flush. 'I'm the manager here.'

'I can tell.' He held her gaze slightly longer than was comfortable.

'Well, Miranda, the pleasure was *all* mine.' He pulled his coat over his shoulders and stepped onto the wet street. 'Goodbye.'

She watched him stride away, sidestepping puddles as he went.

But of course it wasn't goodbye. He telephoned within two hours of making his purchase.

'Miranda,' he said, his voice smooth and low. 'It's Willem.'

She liked how he used their names together, so casual and familiar.

'I'm standing in my lounge room,' he continued, 'all at sea about where I should hang *The Predator*. Can you help me?'

'Certainly,' she replied. 'We offer a professional placement and installation service.' She checked the diary. 'The earliest I can have someone there is four o'clock on Friday. That's with Bruno, our most experienced installer.'

'I see.'

She could sense his dissatisfaction. 'There's no charge involved,' she assured him. 'It's a free service.'

'But what if I'd like *you* to do it, not Bruno?'

She flushed. 'Oh ... well, of course. I'm not as skilled as Bruno, but I'd be happy to help.'

'Good. You have my address. Four o'clock on Friday then?'

'I don't finish until four thirty.' She was afraid of displeasing him. 'Is five thirty too late?'

'All the better,' he'd said.

Willem opened the door holding a baby boy in his arms.

Miranda was speechless with disappointment.

'This is Digby,' he said. 'Say hello to Miranda, Digby.'

He picked up one of the baby's limp arms and waved it at her. The boy stared at her, his face impassive.

'He's a little shy around strangers. But he's only thirteen months old. I was probably shy at that age too.'

The boy began to whimper.

'Yasmin!' Willem called over his shoulder.

A stunning brunette appeared, barefoot on the buff-coloured carpet. She smiled at Miranda before whisking Digby out of Willem's arms and sashaying away.

'Yasmin's been with us full-time since Digby's mother died.' Willem watched her as she walked away. 'She's remarkable with the dinner and bath routine, which can get quite ugly, I'm afraid.'

Miranda's mind reeled as she processed this information.

'I'm sorry.' She was unsure what else to say.

'So am I, but life goes on. Come in.' He gestured towards the lounge area beyond. 'Welcome to my home, for now. I'm about to put it on the market.'

'Oh.' She wondered why he needed an art-hanging service, if he was planning to sell. She followed him beyond the vestibule and tried not to stare. It was a split-level monument to glass, wood and light, overlooking the ocean at Fairy Bower. A minimalist palette of ivory and grey offered a neutral canvas for the stunning artworks strung across the walls. Miranda took in the Brett Whiteley and the Albert Tucker as if she saw them hanging in private collections every day. But she couldn't contain her excitement at the Emily Kngwarreye.

'That's not what I think it is, is it?' She gaped at the large striped canvas.

'I suspect so. I picked it up at Sotheby's ten years ago for a ridiculously low sum. If I auctioned it now, I'd get twenty times the price I paid for it.'

She shook her head in wonder.

'I've decanted a bottle of Mount Mary Quintet,' he

announced. 'Can I offer you a glass while we consider where to hang *The Predator*?'

He held up a crystal Bordeaux glass and twirled it between his thumb and forefinger.

She smiled. 'Thank you.'

She wouldn't normally drink on the job, but she was in no hurry to return to her one-bedroom apartment above a Vietnamese bakery in Darlinghurst.

And as it happened, she never really did.

It was almost six thirty when she opened Digby's door again. He pushed past her with his usual gusto, seemingly unaffected by the time-out imposed. It took all of her resolve to call him back. She didn't want to wage another battle of the wills, but she couldn't let him get away without an apology. Of all the principles she attempted to enshrine at home, consistency was fundamental.

'Digby,' she called after him. 'Please come back here.'

He dragged his feet across the floor.

'Have you thought about why it wasn't okay to bite Rory?'

He nodded, eyes downcast.

'Why?'

'Because Rory is not a biscuit.' His eyes crinkled at his own joke. For a moment, she was tempted to laugh too. But then she remembered Rory's tears as she applied an ice pack to his cheek. Digby needed to apologise.

'Digby.' She lowered her voice. 'Big boys, three-year-olds like you, know what's right and wrong. What do you say to Rory, please?'

'Poo to you, Mr Moo. Poo poo poooooo.'

It was at times like this that she wished she could call on someone in the mothers' group for moral or practical support. Most of her friends lived on the other side of the Harbour Bridge, and it was hard to coordinate catch-ups. Despite their proximity, no one in her mothers' group truly understood what it was like with *two* children. Some of them tried, offering to babysit for an hour here or there. But it was never enough; the battle in which she was engaged was unremitting. Sometimes, when the other mothers complained of how tired they were, it took all of her willpower to remain silent, not to scream: *At least* you *get to lie down during the day, you only have* one *child to deal with.* They all made noises of admiration, telling her how strong she was, what a good job she did. But they were hollow words, as far as she was concerned.

'Digby.' She bent down on one knee, so that her face was close to his. She'd read somewhere that toddlers felt respected by adults who conversed at their level. 'How about that cuddle you wanted earlier?'

He wrinkled his nose. She could see he was considering it.

'Come on, Dig.'

Suddenly he leaned into her, wrapping his arms around her shoulders.

'Oh,' she said, squeezing him. His frame felt fragile in her arms. 'That's a lovely cuddle.'

He pulled away from her.

'Rory's on the mat in the play room,' she said. 'He'd love to play with his big brother. But you need to say something to him first. You need to apologise for biting him. It made him feel sad.'

Digby looked at her, his face deadpan. Then he turned on his heel and marched into the lounge room.

He crouched down next to Rory, too close for her liking. She resisted the urge to insist that he move away. He leaned into Rory's face.

'Sooooorry for biting you,' he said in a singsong voice.

She sighed, weary. She had nowhere to go now. It would be useless to insist that he apologise again, but this time with heart. She decided to let it go. Pick your battles, the experts said.

Digby 1, Mummy 0.

'Let's read a book before breakfast,' she suggested.

'*Green Eggs and Ham*!' yelled Digby.

'Can't we choose another one?' she pleaded, even as he thrust it into her hand.

She propped Rory up onto her lap and wound an arm around Digby. 'Okay,' she said. '*Green Eggs and Ham*, by Doctor Seuss.'

She could practically recite it in her sleep. Digby giggled in all the usual places. He never seemed to tire of it.

6.48 am

As she prepared breakfast, she thought of Willem, en route to Perth. Right about now he'd be somewhere over the Great Australian Fuck-All, or 'GAFA' as he called it, accepting second-grade coffee from a surly Qantas steward in business class. As co-founder and Chief Investment Officer of Stanford

Investments, a boutique investment firm, he worked in a world that she didn't really understand. What she did know frightened her: namely, that he was responsible for over $850 million of other people's money. It was a burden that appalled her with every market fluctuation, but Willem seemed to thrive on it, managing a small team of analysts and traders with almost evangelical zeal. He spent much of his time travelling around Australia and the world 'kicking tyres', as he termed it, trying to understand every facet of the businesses in which he invested. These site visits consumed at least two weeks a month, and he was good at it. The firm's success—driven entirely by Willem and his co-founder, Adam Tran, a friend from university—had enabled him, over a ten-year period, to count himself among Australia's high net worth community.

In the year they'd met, the annus horribilis of 2008, the market correction Willem had been predicting for years finally occurred. When the market plunged the clients of Stanford Investments survived the downturn and Willem was amply rewarded. Not long afterwards, he'd presented Miranda with a four-carat diamond engagement ring and a new home on the southern cliffs of Freshwater Beach.

She stirred the oatmeal and removed it from the stovetop. Digby liked his porridge lukewarm, drizzled with honey. She began to peel a pear, mashing it with a soft banana for Rory. Digby appeared in the kitchen doorway.

'Is breakfast ready?'

'Not quite, Dig. Almost there.'

He scuffed at the doorframe with his slipper.

'But there's nothing to do,' he whined. 'I'm bored.'

She smiled. 'It'll be ready in three minutes. Why don't you take your building blocks and build the tallest tower in the world?'

He scowled at her. 'I don't *want* to build a tower. You're silly.'

'Please don't speak to me like that.'

'Sorry, sorry, sorry!' he yelled, scampering away. He didn't mean that apology either. She just didn't know what to do with him.

Her mother had predicted this, she recalled.

She continued to mash the fruit.

Poor Mum. Her eyes filled with tears. She'd predicted a lot of things.

It was almost a year since she'd died, exactly one month before Rory was born, succumbing to the breast cancer that had metastasised into her brain, liver and lungs. She remembered that day, the moment when she realised her mother was dead. The nurse's platitudes about how she was free of pain now, that she'd gone to a better place, how peaceful her death had been. That it was a rare blessing to die at home. Miranda had wanted to strike her. All she knew was that her lifelong confidante, the one person who understood her better than she understood herself, was gone. And since that day, everything around her had felt like a cheap counterfeit of another, more authentic world in which she had once lived.

When Willem had walked into her life, her mother had been newly diagnosed. As their romance progressed, her mother had become brittle, short-tempered and humourless.

It was hard for Miranda to determine whether her mother's opposition to Willem was the chemotherapy talking. In the week before she'd died, Miranda had sat by her mother's bedside in her childhood home. The leafy streets of Strathfield always seemed a world away from Miranda's inner city life. But its memories were comforting: hot Christmas dinners and lopsided party hats, Easter eggs hidden in buffalo grass, territorial magpies swooping from majestic jacaranda trees. And on this particular day, for reasons she couldn't understand, Miranda had laid down next to her mother and held her tightly. Then she'd taken her mother's frail hand and pressed it against her pregnant belly.

'Can you feel the baby kicking?' she'd asked.

The corners of her mother's mouth had turned upwards.

'Don't let Digby bully the baby,' she'd murmured.

'What?'

'You heard me.' Her mother's voice was no more than a whisper. 'Toddlers are selfish. I want you to enjoy being a mother for the first time. Ask Willem for help. Don't let him shirk his responsibilities.'

Miranda had nodded, trying to conceal her anxiety.

Three days later, when Miranda's maternity leave had officially commenced, Willem had terminated the nanny's contract without consultation. When Miranda had ventured to ask why, he'd waved a dismissive hand at her. 'Well, you won't be working for at least a year after the baby is born,' he'd said. 'It'd be overkill to have you *and* Yasmin looking after the children.'

One week later, her mother was gone too.

7.08 am

'*Muuuuuum.*' Digby bolted into the kitchen. 'Rory's eating one of my toys.'

She ignored him. 'Time for breakfast now, Dig. Sit up, please.'

She ushered him towards the dining room and went to retrieve Rory from his playpen.

As she leaned over the wooden rail, it was immediately obvious that Rory had something wedged in his mouth. His cheek bulged and a string of drool stretched to the floor. She turned him onto his stomach and prised open his lips, causing him to gag. With a wheeze, he spat out a small wooden peg, one of eight from Digby's miniature tool set.

'Oh, honey, that's not for eating,' she said, lifting him up. As she walked towards the dining room, she tried to quell her anger. She'd packed away the tool set the night before, just as she did every night—lining up the eight wooden nails in the toolbox alongside the hammer and the screwdriver. Only Digby could have opened the toolbox. He knew that Rory wasn't allowed to play with it, as its pieces were too small, an obvious choking hazard. But he'd gone ahead anyway, presumably feeding a nail through the playpen's bars to a captive Rory. Most of the time Digby was just an irritating toddler, but actions like this felt premeditated.

She ignored him as she strapped Rory into his highchair.

'Where's my porridge?' Digby demanded.

'How do you ask nicely?'

'Where's my porridge . . . poo-lease?' Digby giggled.

She had an overwhelming urge to dump it over his head.

'Yuck,' he said, as she placed it in front of him.

'Excuse me.'

'Yuck, yuck, yuckety-yuck,' he sang.

She removed the bowl from his placemat and put it next to hers. Then she began to spoon mashed banana and pear into Rory's mouth.

'Would you like to try some of Digby's porridge, Rory? Digby doesn't want it ... Here we are, Rory ... oooh, yum yum.' She scooped up a large lump of porridge. Rory leaned forward towards the spoon.

'But it's *mine*,' yelled Digby.

She looked at him. 'Well, Digby, if you would like your porridge back, I suggest you think of some different words to use at the breakfast table.'

Digby pouted.

'Like, "Thank you, Mum", for example.' She slid the bowl back in front of him.

He seized it with both hands and, with a swift jerk, hurled it across the table. It smashed against the wall behind her. Porridge oozed down the edge of one of Willem's Namatjiras. Rory began to cry.

She stood up and yanked Digby out of his highchair. As he flailed in her arms, kicking his legs into hers, she tried to brace against his weight. Her stomach muscles were not what they used to be and, since she'd had Rory, there had been little time to focus on rebuilding her core. The daily physical exertion of tackling Digby, now a strapping eighteen kilograms, was aggravating her already sensitive lower back.

She hurled Digby onto his bed with as much force as she could muster.

'Food is not for throwing,' she hissed. 'And wooden nails are not for feeding to babies. Think about it.'

She drew the curtains, turned off the light and slammed the door shut.

'*Muuuuuum*,' Digby wailed. 'It's dark.'

She stomped back to the dining room and sat down. Her legs were trembling, her hands too. She closed her eyes and tried to steady her breathing. Digby's pitiful wailing made her wince; she knew he was afraid of the dark. But how else would he learn about consequences?

She opened her eyes and forced a smile as she looked at Rory. 'Now,' she said, picking up his plastic spoon, 'let's finish breakfast.'

7.32 am

Digby had gone quiet in his bedroom, hiding under the doona, she presumed. Rory crawled around in his playpen, swiping at the surfeit of toys that jangled, buzzed and spun on demand. She stood at the kitchen bench, dicing the potatoes for dinner that evening. Her day was a never-ending cycle of menu planning, meal preparation and washing up, punctuated by altercations with Digby over food. He hated this, he hated that. This was too hot, that was too cold. That tasted slimy, this looked yucky. He wanted only fruit, or no fruit at all. Willem couldn't understand why it wore her down so much. But that was unsurprising: *he* was never home for three meals a day, seven days a week.

She wondered how her mother would have dealt with Digby. She'd had two children in quick succession. And yet she'd never known what it was to be a stepmother, Miranda mused. Surely that was different? One thing was for certain: if her mother had recovered from the cancer, things might have been different for everyone. For her father, who lived alone in Strathfield now, hardly ever leaving the house. For her brother who, without the gentle guidance of their mother, had simply drifted away from the family. And certainly for Miranda.

She picked the potato peelings out of the sink and tipped them into the garbage bin, turning her attention to the carrots. Willem had no idea how hard she worked at home. In fact, he often contrasted his own frenetic working life with the apparent simplicity of her home-based tasks. He'd offended her the night before while protesting about his impending week of travel.

'What I wouldn't give to stop travelling for a week and just spend it with the kids,' he'd said over dinner, leaning back in his chair and draining his glass of pinot. 'It's fucking chaos out there in the real world, you know.'

She'd bristled. 'You can have the kids for a week anytime you like,' she replied coolly. 'Personally I'd love a week in an office. Or on a plane.'

He looked hurt. 'Miranda, I know it's hard for you.'

'Do you?'

He pushed his chair back and stalked into the kitchen. She could hear him uncorking another bottle of wine. He returned with the bottle and two fresh glasses, poured her a glass of shiraz and pushed it into her hand.

'How do you think we can afford all the things you enjoy?'
he asked.

She blinked, stung by the inference.

'I didn't realise my patterns of consumption were so
excessive.'

'Come on, Miranda. You know what I mean. I don't work
as hard as I do just for me.'

She doubted that. She saw the fervour in his eyes when
he talked about his next big investment target, the exquisite
thrill of chasing a 'hundred bagger'. It was almost a form of
white-collar gambling, she'd often thought, a socially acceptable addiction to making money.

He was waiting for her to speak, but she said nothing.

The truth was, she couldn't wait for him to go away again
in the morning. At the beginning of their relationship, she'd
anxiously awaited his return from business trips. She'd pre-
pare in advance, visiting the hair salon, the beautician, the
pedicurist. Waiting for that delicious moment when he would
pin her to the bed and make love to her. He'd been as confident and skilled in bed as he was in every other part of his life.
Experimental in a way she'd never been, with a penchant for
sex toys and role-plays. She'd been hesitant at the beginning,
feeling a little ridiculous in costume. But once she'd got over
her awkwardness, she'd been surprised by her own audacity.

As soon as she'd fallen pregnant, however, within two
months of their marriage, things had changed. Despite what
the magazines said about the rewards of sexual intimacy
during pregnancy, she just couldn't stomach it. Willem had
started travelling more, trying to stay ahead of the global

financial crisis. And so Miranda had grown to know Yasmin far better than she cared to, up until the day when Willem dismissed her. After that, her fairytale life had started fraying at the edges.

Miranda winced. She'd caught the edge of her finger on the potato peeler's blade. Blood smeared across the tip of a carrot. She held her finger under the running water in the sink and watched the blood disperse. Involuntarily, she thought of Sandra, his first wife. Willem had experienced a level of tragedy she'd never known, she reminded herself. She ought to cut him some slack.

7.50 am

She finished the carrots and submerged them in a saucepan of cold water. The effect of the aspirin and her second cup of coffee had kicked in, and she felt human enough to be generous to Digby once more. She bundled Rory into the stroller and opened Digby's door.

'Let's go out,' she announced. Digby had pushed his train table beneath the window and was standing with his head under the curtains, nose pressed against the glass, whimpering. She wondered how long he'd been there, the picture of vulnerability in his pyjamas, and how many passers-by had seen him.

'Dig, let's go to the park,' she said. 'You can have a packet of sultanas on the way, if you put your clothes on nicely.'

She hated resorting to bribery, but it was usually the only strategy that worked.

He slid down from the train table. 'Okay.'

They walked to the park most days, even when it was raining. She'd discovered soon after Yasmin's departure that if Digby wasn't exercised in the morning, he wouldn't sleep in the afternoon. By dinner time, he'd be pacing the house like an angry lion.

As they walked their familiar route to the park, an elderly man sitting at a bus stop hailed Digby. 'Hello there, son,' he said.

Digby immediately hid his face behind her legs.

'Say hello to the gentleman, please, Digby.'

Digby clung to her leg, refusing to look at the man.

'I'm sorry,' she said. 'It's still a bit early for him.'

Excuses, excuses. She was always making them for Digby, explaining away his behaviour.

To a casual observer like the old man, they appeared a picture-perfect family: mother holding hands with the toddler, pushing baby in the pram. Singing and clapping, stopping to peer at flowers, birds and stones. No one was privy to her impatience, her resentment. She didn't want to go to the park, she didn't enjoy walking at a glacial pace. Her days were filled with activities she'd rather avoid, if given a choice. But choices were a thing of the past, an indulgent feature of her life pre-children.

At the park, she went through the usual motions: monitoring Digby on the climbing frame, high-fiving him as he slid down the slippery dip, pushing him on the swing. Sometimes she'd pass the time of day with the other women in the park, as they shepherded their children from one piece of equipment to another. Behind their dark sunglasses and fixed, tight smiles, did any of them feel the way she did?

Since Rory had started crawling, the park had become more challenging—she now had to keep a close eye on both of them. She could never wholly trust Digby to respond to verbal commands, so she had to be in constant reach of both. Sometimes, when Digby was in a reasonable mood, she would permit Rory to sit on his lap on the slippery dip.

'How about you and Rory play trains on the slide together?' she suggested.

Digby kicked at the pine bark beneath the swing set. 'Okay.'

'Thank you, Dig,' she said.

He climbed to the top of the slide and waited while she positioned Rory on his lap.

'One-two-three . . . Choo, choo!' yelled Digby, wrapping his arms around Rory's waist.

Rory squealed as they slid down together. They landed at the bottom, arms and legs entangled, Rory cackling with a glee he reserved for Digby alone. Miranda laughed too, and reached for her phone, capturing a picture of their delight.

After an hour in the park, she checked her watch.

9.30 am
'Coffee time,' she announced.

They retraced their route, stopping off at her favourite café at Freshwater Village.

'*Ciao, bella*,' said Alberto, the ageing Italian barista.

She smiled, even though she didn't feel remotely *bella*.

As he frothed the milk for her cappuccino, she fished around in the stroller pocket for coins. Predictably, Digby began to whine.

'I want a marshmallow.'

She ignored him, until he attempted to climb the counter. She guided him back down.

'I'm sorry, Dig, that's a treat. We don't eat marshmallows every day.'

'But I WANT a marshmallow,' he bellowed.

Alberto clipped a lid over her coffee and she pushed four dollars towards him. He ducked under the counter for a moment, emerging with a jar of marshmallows.

'Here we are, *bambino*,' he said, unscrewing the lid.

Digby thrust his hand into the jar, fingers moving over the pink and white puffs.

'Just one, Dig,' she admonished. He pulled out three and began licking them.

'Can I pay you for them?' she asked, embarrassed.

'No, no.' He smiled. 'My pleasure.'

She turned to Digby. 'What do you say to Alberto, Digby?'

The corners of Digby's mouth turned upwards and a slyness crept into his eyes. He took a step forward. *Please say it, please say it, go on, Dig.*

'Poo to you, Mr Moo.'

She jerked him backwards, away from the counter, reefing his arm towards her. His feet slipped with the sudden movement and he landed on his knees, hard, on the tiled floor below.

Digby howled in outrage. People turned and stared.

'Oh no, no, *Signora*, no . . .' Alberto waved his hands. 'He only small . . .'

She flushed, humiliated by Digby's behaviour, her own

loss of control in public, and Alberto's obvious objection. It wasn't the European way, she knew. Hendrika and Marco were *always* indulging Digby.

She pulled Digby away by the hand.

'Thanks, Alberto,' she muttered.

9.45 am

She pushed the pram so quickly that Digby struggled to keep up. She could hear his small sneakers padding against the pavement several steps behind her, his little grunts of effort. She knew it was infantile, but she wanted to punish him. She couldn't possibly return to the café. Not tomorrow, not ever. It was just another part of her life that Digby had spoiled.

As they approached a bus stop, she noticed a woman leaning into a minivan parked illegally in a loading zone. The van's hazard lights were blinking and a shrill squealing sound was audible over the intermittent noise of passing traffic. Another mother with a baby, Miranda thought.

As she neared the open door of the minivan, Miranda saw the object of the woman's attention. A young man in a wheelchair, his arms and legs twisted with spasticity, was shrieking with indignation as he strained to reach the straw cup the woman proffered.

'Here it is, honey,' Miranda heard the woman say.

From behind, Miranda could see that the woman's hair was greying and the backs of her hands were peppered with age spots. She couldn't be younger than fifty. But the patient tone of her voice, the gentle hand on the young man's jaw, the tilt of her head, all were maternal. It was, Miranda recognised, an intensely private moment between mother and son.

She lowered her gaze and pushed Rory beyond the minivan.

'Come on, Dig,' she said, turning and reaching for his hand.

Tears blurred her vision.

I'm so lucky, she thought, I'm so lucky. I *have* to remember that.

She stopped and kneeled in front of the stroller, pulling Digby onto her lap. Rory grabbed two fistfuls of Miranda's hair and yanked them. Digby laughed and batted at Rory's hands.

'Let go of Mummy's hair,' he giggled.

Gently, Miranda prised Rory's hands away, drew them to her lips and kissed them.

'I love you both,' she whispered, cuddling Digby to her chest. 'More than anything in this world.'

Digby leaned into her.

Then she stood up, brushed the tears from beneath her sunglasses, and resumed pushing the stroller home.

10 am

Still too early, she thought.

She switched on the television and called out to Digby. All her best intentions about limiting television had been abandoned. It was the only way she could get some peace and quiet.

'*Play School*'s on,' she called, piling some cushions in front of the television. 'You and Rory can watch it, if you like.'

'Yay!' Digby was never quite as thrilled by any of her other suggestions.

She propped Rory on a cushion next to Digby. They sat transfixed, their eyes following the movement and colour. It was only thirty minutes, she reasoned. She returned to the kitchen and scanned the to-do list stuck to the fridge door.

She picked up the telephone and dialled Computerworld. Her laptop had crashed a week ago, just after Digby had knocked it off the coffee table. All her photos and movies were stored on that laptop, along with her art archives, contact lists and important documents. Stupidly, she'd never backed up any of it.

'Chris,' she said, 'it's Miranda Bianco. Any news on the laptop?'

'Not good, Miranda.'

Computerworld had been recommended by Ginie. It was another benefit of belonging to the mothers' group: whenever anyone needed a referral, someone always had a suggestion. Over the past year, Miranda had sourced a plumber, a cleaner and a landscape gardener in exactly the same way. So when she couldn't restart her computer, she'd sent a brief text message to the mothers' group: *Computer's died. Anyone know someone who can help me get my life back?* Within three minutes, Ginie had responded, sending her Chris Moran's mobile number and the message: *Chris is Daniel's best mate. Been in IT for years. Expert at data recovery. Good luck.*

'The hard disk has a serious internal hardware fault,' said Chris. 'The hard disk heads are damaged or malfunctioning. We might be able to recover some of your data, but it's the worst possible scenario, I'm afraid. It will cost at least three thousand for my senior engineer to go in and try, and he may not be successful. We'll need a thousand-dollar deposit to start the work, then the remaining two thousand on completion.'

'Oh.' Miranda had hoped for better news.

'Do you want some time to think about it?' asked Chris.

'I guess I need to talk to my husband. Three thousand dollars . . . I could buy a new laptop with that.'

'I know,' he said. 'It reflects the complexity of the task, I'm afraid. I've given you my best price, seeing as you're Ginie's friend. I'd normally charge four thousand. I guess it's a matter of whether you've got mission-critical data on that disk.'

She sighed. Most of her photos of her mother were on that hard drive: three thousand dollars was a small sum to pay to retrieve them. She didn't need to talk to Willem.

'Look, start the job, Chris,' she said. 'I'll give you my credit card number for the deposit.'

Willem was due to return on Friday; she'd tell him about it then.

10.30 am

'The Wiggles are on now,' yelled Digby from the lounge room.

She considered her options: turn off the television and resume combat with Digby, or be granted a further thirty minutes of peace. It was a no-brainer.

'Okay, Dig,' she called back. 'Is Rory still happy?'

'Yep.'

She walked to the kitchen door and looked into the lounge room to verify this. Rory was transfixed, his eyes lowered in lazy half-slits. In thirty minutes, he'd be ready for a nap. It couldn't hurt him to chill out a little longer.

She walked back to the kitchen and sank onto a stool. The kettle had not long boiled. She arranged the plunger, spooning in four tablespoons of ground beans before adding hot water. As the coffee brewed, she flicked through the *Manly Daily*, scanning the job advertisements. Accounts payable, telemarketers, early childhood intern, baker's assistant. She poured the coffee into a giant mug and grimaced at its bitterness.

It pained her to be financially dependent. Willem claimed that he held nothing over her, that it was simply his turn to shoulder the responsibility of work while she looked after the children. But she'd always had her own income prior to Willem and her altered circumstances grated. She hated having to ask him for money. Each month he combed the credit card statements with forensic interest, interrogating her about every unfamiliar item. 'What's CG Express, Narrabeen?' 'Ninety-one dollars at Ho Vanh—is that a clothes store?' 'What did you get at Rebel Sports?'

She resented being answerable for every petty expenditure, especially given the fact that they could afford it. She wanted to lash out at him, to call him a miser. Mostly she stayed silent, but recently he'd detected her frustration.

'I don't know why you've become so sensitive about this,' he'd said, a puzzled expression on his face. 'I'm just tracking our expenses. If you can't measure it, you can't manage it. You know that.'

She'd nodded, the compliant wife, while she inwardly seethed. If only *she* could make enough money somehow, she thought. She could have her own credit card, spend whatever she wanted and be answerable to no one.

Sometimes she fantasised about ways to do that. She'd considered going back to the gallery when Rory turned one, but the manager's position was full-time. She'd been angling for a part-time or job-share arrangement, but the owner was reluctant. He'd made it clear that the position of manager was being held open for her while she was on maternity leave, but that it would only be offered on its previous terms—five days a week, eight hours a day. But she didn't want to leave Rory in full-time care, and travelling from Freshwater to Paddington would be onerous. She had changed, it seemed, but the world had not.

She'd worked hard to attain the position of gallery manager. After completing a masters in Visual Arts, she'd spent four years in the UK and Europe before returning to Australia, buoyed by her exposure to the world's finest galleries and museums. Back in Sydney, a series of contract roles at the Australia Council led to her dream job as the manager of a contemporary gallery for emerging Australian artists. She'd only been in the role for two years when she'd met Willem and fallen pregnant. It was hard to believe that fifteen years of study and professional development would now be wasted.

11 am

An irritating, mechanical melody sounded the show's conclusion. Digby rushed into the kitchen.

'Where's my sandwich?' he demanded.

'Just a moment, Dig. I'll get Rory.'

They sat at the stainless-steel island bench, Rory in his highchair and Digby balanced on a bar stool next to her. Rory rubbed his eyes and ignored his egg sandwich. Digby ploughed into his, having worked up an appetite at the park.

'Can I have Rory's sandwich too?' he asked, swallowing the last hunk of bread.

'Okay, Dig. I don't think Rory's eating his.' She passed the plate to Digby. 'I'm going to put Rory to bed now, okay? Here's a drink of water for you.'

Digby guzzled the water from the plastic cup she gave him.

Rory's eyes were drooping as she slipped him into his sleeping bag.

'Shhh, shhh, shhh,' she whispered, although he needed no settling. He'd already turned his head to one side, his usual sleeping posture, as she closed the door behind her. What an angel, she thought.

1.30 pm

She looked at her watch, fuming. It had been over an hour since she'd put Digby to bed, and yet he still wasn't asleep. She could hear him ranging around his room, knocking over books and toys, clicking his bedside lamp on and off, sliding the wardrobe door open and shut. He'd demonstrated all the usual tired signs but, as was often the case now, he had simply willed himself *not* to sleep. Why couldn't he just have a rest at least, lying down quietly with his picture books? Rory was due to wake up soon.

She rested her head in her hands on the island bench. She

was exhausted. Apparently it would get better, so her sister-in-law said, when the children were about eight years old. The prospect of waiting another five years was demoralising. She'd be almost forty by then. And she suspected that any notion of a 'break' was pure fantasy; surely children were challenging in different ways at different stages. She might as well write off the next twenty years.

The telephone rang. It was her mother-in-law, Hendrika. The best part of forty years in Australia hadn't softened her Dutch accent.

'Are the children asleep?'

'Not quite,' Miranda said. 'They're in their bedrooms, but . . .'

'Well, they're as good as asleep then.'

Miranda said nothing. Her mother-in-law had a habit of finishing her sentences.

'Does Digby still have a cold?'

Hendrika pronounced Digby as 'Dickby', which irritated Miranda no end.

'No, he's much better now, thanks.' Digby often had a runny nose, which Hendrika attributed to him not wearing enough clothes. There was no arguing the point with her.

'It's Willem's birthday on Sunday.'

As if Miranda didn't know. She'd already given him a gift voucher for a massage, more than a month in advance of his birthday, in an effort to make him use it. Even so, he was so busy with work, she doubted he'd find the time. He just never prioritised relaxation.

'I thought you might like to go out to celebrate on Sunday,' continued Hendrika. 'Just the two of you. I could take Digby and Rory, or at the very least Digby.'

'Oh,' said Miranda. 'Well, that's very nice of you, thank you.' She felt guilty for being so negative about Hendrika. She was obviously trying to be helpful.

'But only in the morning,' continued Hendrika. 'We have golf in the afternoon, you know.'

Of course. Miranda closed her eyes. Convincing Willem to get out of bed for anything other than work on a Sunday morning was likely to be difficult.

'Thanks, Hendrika. I'll check with Willem. He flies home this Friday. He might be working again by Sunday. You know how it is.'

'Yes, he works so hard, doesn't he? Not everyone's as dedicated.' There was maternal pride in her voice.

'I'll call to confirm on Saturday morning,' Miranda said. 'Thanks again, Hendrika.'

She replaced the handset and stared at the bench. Rory was calling out from his cot, and Digby was mimicking him from his bedroom.

No rest for her this afternoon.

She opened the fridge and removed the Evian bottle. She despised the 'afternoon shift', as the mothers' group called it. The long, downward spiral of escalating tension between two and seven o'clock that inevitably led to tantrum-throwing and tears. She drained the last of the water in the bottle, then placed it on the kitchen bench. She checked her watch again: ten past two. Close enough to two thirty, she reasoned.

She pulled open the freezer and removed the bottle of

vodka that Willem kept in the door. He hadn't noticed how many times she'd replaced it, as he usually preferred wine to spirits. It was easy to fly under his radar: whenever she shopped online for groceries, she simply included a bottle of vodka in the order. There was no telltale line item on the credit card statement. Willem simply accepted her expenditure at supermarkets, assuming she was buying household necessities. He'd never scrutinised a receipt, nor did he see the delivery's arrival, which she always arranged to occur while he was at work. She stored an unopened bottle in the pantry at all times, secreted in a large tupperware container of cake-decorating equipment.

She unscrewed the lid and, using a plastic funnel, decanted the vodka into the Evian bottle. She put the vodka back in its place and shut the freezer door. She stood momentarily with her back pressed against the refrigerator, her heart thudding in her chest. Even now, after so many months, she felt like a thief. She drew the Evian bottle to her lips and listened to Rory's and Digby's calls. Neither of them was particularly upset. She held the liquid in her mouth and closed her eyes, inhaling the familiar fire in her nostrils. As she swallowed, the warmth caught in her throat and then spread to her chest. She sighed with relief, opening her eyes.

4 pm

Her body felt free, her joints and ligaments pliant. Her mood was buoyant, irrepressible.

'Okay, buckaroo,' she called in her best American accent. 'Give us your best shot.' Rory was strapped to her back in the baby carrier, giggling with excitement. Digby was the picture of concentration, lining up the soccer ball between the two ancient lemon trees in their backyard. Miranda stood in front of them, pretending to be goalie. Digby took several steps backwards before running at the ball, booting it with a little grunt. Miranda feigned an attempt at stopping it before letting it roll past her legs and shouting, 'Goal!'

Digby clapped his hands and stamped his feet. 'Goal! Goal! Goal!'

Rory laughed in her ear.

Miranda stooped behind the lemon tree and retrieved the ball, rolling it back to Digby. He began to set up his next shot, the twenty-seventh since Miranda began counting. Other than that, her mind was pleasantly empty. She felt simultaneously present and absent; present enough to participate, but absent enough not to care. Digby had thrown himself on the ground several times, in a funk about something or other, but she'd maintained her equilibrium.

She gave Digby the thumbs-up sign. 'Ready, buckaroo?'

He nodded. 'You're the best, Mum.'

'Oh, Dig.' The unexpected compliment made her eyes water. 'That's nice of you to say it.'

He loved her, she knew, in his own contrary way. Surely she would find a better way of handling him, some day.

'Alrighty, Diggy-Dog, give us your best shot.'

She felt impenetrable, untouchable. Bullet-proof.

7.50 pm

She lay on the couch, drained, her limbs heavy. Was this the definition of legless? She giggled to herself. After the nightly circus of dinner, bath and books, she'd herded the children into bed. The kitchen was a disaster zone, but there would be time enough to wash up tomorrow. When at home, Willem would never countenance dirty dishes left in the sink overnight. He wouldn't have approved of dinner either: an emergency packet of fish fingers after she'd burned the home-made shepherd's pie. Much to Digby's delight, she'd served the fish fingers with great dollops of tomato sauce and suggested they eat them with their hands.

She rolled over on the couch, turning her back to the heater. Her clothes were still damp from bath time, which was always a maelstrom of arms and legs, sponges and flannels, plastic cups and bath animals that Digby addressed by name. As usual, Rory had sat in his bath seat, transfixed by Digby. And as usual, she'd had to play the role of two fat rubber duckies, whom Digby had christened Yellow and Diver, while Digby played the role of Captain Crabclaw. She found it difficult to conjure up new and exciting bath time adventures for Yellow and Diver on a nightly basis, but Digby simply wouldn't pull the plug without one.

'Fuck those rubber duckies,' she said aloud, giggling again.

Her mobile phone buzzed next to her. Probably Willem, she thought, wanting to tell her about his day. She fished the phone out from under the cushion and read the message: *Delayed in Mumbai. They've made us sit on the tarmac for three fucking hours!*

She considered her reply, irritation flooding her.

Delayed, permanently. Did the same jigsaw today with Digby for three fucking hours!

Instead, she deleted his message without replying, and closed her eyes.

I've got so much to do, she thought.

10.30 pm

She stumbled up from the couch and into Digby's room. She stopped, confused, at his bedside. Hadn't he called out for her?

He lay on his back, his blue comforter twisted around his hand. She reached out and brushed away a wisp of dark hair that had fallen across his eyes. He looked almost angelic in his sleep.

She tiptoed backwards out the door, closing it behind her.

Her head throbbed. She went to the kitchen and stood at the sink, gulping down several glasses of water. She filled up the Evian bottle with water and took it to her room, along with a fresh glass for tomorrow morning's aspirin.

She lay down on the bed and thought of Willem, of where he might be flying tonight. She'd stopped asking for itineraries months ago.

Tomorrow is a new day, she thought. I won't open the freezer tomorrow.

She closed her eyes, tired of resolutions.

By the time Willem returned on Saturday afternoon—not Friday evening as he'd promised—it was too late to line up Hendrika for babysitting.

'I'm so sorry, honey,' he said, looking over his wine glass at dinner. 'I have to go into the office tomorrow morning. Can we try for next weekend instead?'

She stiffened. 'Can't you even have Sunday off? For your birthday? I thought we could have a picnic, something simple.' She pushed her slow-roasted lamb shank, one of Willem's favourites, around the plate. She'd spent much of the afternoon preparing it, when she could have just as easily settled for a bowl of muesli.

'Sounds nice,' he said. 'But I told Adam I'd be in tomorrow. We're going through the strategic plan before the annual general meeting. It's the only chance we'll get to finish it off.'

She shrugged. She didn't really care why he was unavailable.

'What about next weekend?' he persisted.

'Okay.' She avoided his gaze.

He stood up from the table and walked around the back of her chair, draping an arm around her shoulders.

'Thanks for looking after Digby and Rory. You do it so well.'

She felt his breath on her neck and wrinkled her nose. *Don't you even think about sex tonight.*

'That's okay,' she replied. 'I'm tired.'

She was stating the obvious, she knew. But what else could she say? *I'm bored. I'm frustrated. I love Rory, but sometimes I feel like I could kill Digby.*

She searched for the right words, the honest ones.

'Being a mother is the hardest thing I've done in my life,' she said, staring at her hands. Her nails were shorter than they'd ever been, just like her hair. It came with the territory of motherhood: pragmatism was king. She'd even stopped wearing her engagement ring lately; it had a habit of connecting with Digby's flailing limbs.

Willem pulled away and looked at her. 'Sure, it's tough at times,' he said. 'But there's more pleasure than pain involved, isn't there?'

How would you know? she thought. Your experience of parenting is always mediated by me.

'Mmmm,' she murmured.

He poured himself another glass of wine, topping hers up too.

'I checked the credit card statement today,' he said suddenly. 'What's Computerworld?'

'Oh, I was going to tell you about that. It's a data recovery place.'

'And it's costing us a thousand dollars to get your hard disk back?'

His tone said it all.

She steeled herself.

'Actually, that's just the deposit. It's going to cost three thousand. I can email you the diagnostic report, the hard disk is . . .'

'I don't need to see the fucking diagnostics,' he snapped. 'You've been taken for a ride.'

She sat back in her chair, chastened. She loathed it when he swore.

'No, I haven't.' Her voice was calm. 'The guy who's doing it is a friend of Ginie's.'

Willem pursed his lips. 'So I should feel better about being ripped off, should I, if someone from your mothers' group is involved?'

She stood up. Her legs were shaking.

'Well, thanks *so* much for your understanding. Half my

life's on that computer, which *your* son's done a good job of destroying, in his usual fashion.'

Willem's eyes narrowed. 'What's that supposed to mean?'

'Tell me,' she said. 'How much did you spend on your last Armani suit? More than three thousand dollars, I'm sure. But I wouldn't know the exact price, would I, because I don't watch your expenditure like a fucking hawk.'

She slammed her wine glass down on the table so hard the base cracked.

Willem slept in the guest room that night.

Is it really only eleven o'clock?

She'd been up with Rory since the ungodly hour of quarter to five. He'd woken up crying and she'd been unable to resettle him. Willem had walked past her at seven thirty, on his way to work. He'd ignored her and hadn't even said goodbye to the children. She'd smiled brightly at Digby, pretending nothing was wrong.

She went to the pantry and removed the bread, the peanut butter and the Vegemite. She'd learned the hard way that more sophisticated ingredients—avocado, alfalfa, hummus or grated carrot—would only be ignored or, worse still, flung across the table or floor.

'Time for sandwiches,' she called.

Digby bounded into the kitchen. 'Peanut butter, peanut butter, peanut butter!'

'Okay, sit down, Dig, I'll just get Rory.'

She walked into the lounge room, bent over the playpen and lifted Rory into the air.

'Hi, sweetie,' she said, bouncing him above her head. Rory cackled with delight. If only she had more one-on-one time with him, perhaps life wouldn't feel like so much drudgery.

She walked back into the kitchen and stopped dead. Digby had scaled the bench and was now balanced on the edge of the kitchen sink, waving a long-handled knife in his right hand.

'Digby,' she gasped. 'Put that down, it's dangerous.'

'Ya ya ya!' he laughed, swinging it above his head.

She placed Rory in his highchair and approached Digby cautiously, as a zookeeper might approach a cobra. How had he scaled the bench in a matter of seconds?

'Dig, I don't want you to fall and cut yourself,' she warned.

'Fuck fuck.'

'What did you say?'

'Fuck fuck,' he repeated.

She was aghast.

'Where did you learn that?'

'Daddy,' he said. 'Daddy says it on the telephone. Fuck fuck.'

Her hands fell to her sides. She'd never heard Willem use the word in Digby's presence.

'Well,' she said quietly, 'I don't care what Daddy says. It's not nice. Now put the knife down and I'll help you to climb off the bench.'

'No.'

She took a step towards him.

It happened as if in slow motion. Digby raised his arm and threw the knife, with all the expertise of a trained ninja. It whizzed past her ear and speared into Rory's tray table, landing within centimetres of Rory's fingers. Unaware of the danger, Rory watched with interest as the knife quivered before him, like an arrow in a bull's-eye. She swooped down on it, pulling it free and out of his reach.

She turned to Digby and, without a word, lifted him off the bench. She carried him into his room and sat him on the bed. Adrenaline was coursing through her; she'd broken a sweat and she was breathing heavily.

'Digby,' she said, 'I'm calling Daddy right now. He needs to know what's happened. We never, ever throw knives. And we don't use rude words like that. Please lie down in your bed for a nap. When you wake up, Daddy will be here to talk to you.'

She backed towards the door.

'*Noooooo. Nooooo.* I want a peanut butter sandwich!' Light blue veins bulged at his temples.

'There's no lunch today,' she said firmly. 'Lie down and have a rest, please.'

She closed the door, ignoring his cries. She walked back to the kitchen and prepared Rory's sandwich, her hands trembling as she cut off the crusts. She placed four neat squares on Rory's tray table.

'There you are, honey,' she said calmly. 'Mummy's just going to call Daddy now.'

She lifted the handset.

When Willem answered, she fell to pieces.

'I don't care how important your work is,' she screamed into the telephone. 'You need to come home *right now*.'

It was only after she'd slammed down the handset that she paused for a moment.

She could have sworn she'd heard children in the background.

By the day of the babies' first birthday party in May, things had settled down between them.

After the knife-throwing incident, Miranda had been more assertive with Willem than ever before.

'Can't you see what Digby needs?' she'd demanded, her voice shrill. 'More of his father, less of his stepmother. Either you step up, Willem, or I step out.'

It was tantamount to an ultimatum. Willem had been subdued and irritable at first, resentful almost. But after several weeks, when she'd refused to succumb to his sexual advances, he started making a concerted effort to spend more time at home. Now, two months on, she was impressed by just how much he'd managed to pare back his work.

In return, she'd allowed him to touch her, almost as a sign of goodwill. But there was an urgency to it, a roughness, that left her uneasy. Two bodies bumping in the dark. At least this morning he'd gone to the trouble of bringing her breakfast afterwards, on a tray, for Mother's Day. Digby and Rory had perched on the end of the bed, lunging at the croissants.

'Stop it, boys, they're for Mummy,' Willem had objected, before finally relinquishing the tray to them.

It would take some adjustment for Willem, she knew, to prioritise family life in a way he'd never had to previously. But she could see that he was trying, and it reassured her.

2.50 pm

She checked her watch.

'Almost time to go to Rory's birthday party now, Dig,' she called out the back door.

Willem was kicking the soccer ball between the lemon trees with Digby.

Keeping an eye on both of them, she opened the freezer and removed the vodka. Some of it sloshed onto the bench top as she refilled the Evian bottle. She stuffed it into her handbag, alongside a small tin of mints she always carried with her. The smell of vodka was relatively easy to smother. Teamed with the mints, she smelled as though she'd just gargled with mouthwash.

'Come on,' she called. 'We don't want to be late. You can carry the fairy bread, Digby.'

Digby kicked the ball into the garden and galloped inside. 'Yay! Fairy bread!'

Willem followed, rather reluctantly.

'It's only from three to five,' she reminded him. 'It could be fun. You can meet some of the other dads.'

He nodded unenthusiastically. He'd never taken any interest in the mothers' group. She suspected he saw it as some sort of social club for bored housewives.

She picked up Rory. 'You look special in your birthday clothes, handsome. Doesn't he?'

Neither Willem nor Digby answered.

They arrived at Manly Dam almost twenty minutes late. It was one of the most popular spots for picnicking on the peninsula. Before Rory was born, Miranda had enjoyed weekly walks in the bushland surrounding the dam. It was like a rural island in a sea of suburbia, a haven for those who loved swimming, fishing and mountain biking.

Pippa was the first to greet them at the picnic area they'd reserved, not far from the children's playground.

'Well, happy Mother's Day,' she called, waving an enormous bunch of pink helium balloons at them. 'And happy birthday, Rory.' She smiled at Willem. 'You must be Willem. I'm Pippa. It's nice to meet you after all this time! I'm glad you're here, we need someone tall.' She looked at Digby. 'How are you going, Dig?'

As usual, Digby said nothing. Then suddenly he poked his tongue out at Pippa.

'Blurgh!' he spat.

'Come on, Dig, be polite, please,' Miranda urged.

Digby darted away, with Willem in pursuit. Miranda shrugged apologetically at Pippa. Despite Willem's increased presence at home, Digby's behaviour had a long way to go. At their recent book club session on *We Need to Talk About Kevin*, it had taken all of Miranda's power not to divulge her predicament. *I have a Kevin*, she'd wanted to say. *He's calculating, he's divisive, possibly a sociopath. I live with him, but he's not related to me. And the cult of motherhood says I'm supposed to love him.*

Willem dragged Digby back in front of Miranda.

'Apologise to your mother, please,' he commanded. Digby pulled a face and scuffed at the dirt. Willem had a lot to learn about effective discipline.

Pippa squatted down in front of Digby. 'I've got a very important job for you and your dad,' she said. 'Do you think you could hang these balloons up?' She nodded at the wooden pergola covering several tables alongside the barbecue.

'Okay,' said Digby, taking the balloons from Pippa. 'Come on, Dad.' He raced towards the pergola.

Willem smiled at Pippa. 'You've done that before.'

Always charming in public, Miranda thought.

Pippa turned to Miranda. 'Robert's just cooking the sausages.' She gestured towards the barbecue. 'And Suzie's gone to get some extra chairs from her car. I might get Willem to help her with them, if that's okay, once he's finished the balloons?'

Miranda nodded. 'You and Suzie have done a great job of organising this, Pippa. And my God, you look fantastic.' She stared at the bright blue leggings under Pippa's navy shift dress, teamed with ballet-style slip-ons. Since her operation, Pippa had gained weight and lost her trademark paleness.

Pippa beamed. 'Thanks, I've got a long way to go, but I'm feeling so much better.'

At least that's one of us, Miranda thought.

She felt for her Evian bottle. There was quite a crowd gathered, most of whom she didn't know. Older children chased each other around, laughing and throwing streamers. Grandparents sat smiling in fold-out chairs, picking over paper plates of crustless sandwiches. A face-painter had spread out her kit on a picnic table and was busy transforming Wayan into a bumblebee. Made crouched at his side, dressed in brightly coloured Balinese garb, while Gordon moved about taking photographs.

Ginie and Daniel loitered near the drinks esky, chatting with a group of people whom Miranda assumed must be Ginie's parents and extended family. The children ducked and weaved among the group, chasing each other and yelling, 'Tip!' Picnic rugs were laid out like patchwork squares across the grass, and a number of the babies were toddling across them, pursued by adoring relatives. Aunts, uncles, cousins and godparents, all gathered to celebrate the first birthday of first children.

Miranda felt envious; she'd had hardly anyone to invite. Her father had declined, as she knew he would, and her brother simply hadn't responded. Her sister-in-law was holi-daying in the Seychelles. Willem's parents had made it clear how inconvenient Sunday afternoon was for them, as though she had deliberately scheduled the party to clash with their regular golfing commitment. She still wasn't sure whether they planned to attend. If her own mother had been alive, Miranda couldn't have kept her away.

She swallowed several mouthfuls from her Evian bottle and replaced the lid tightly.

Rory grunted and pulled at his five-point harness.

'There you are,' she said, releasing him from the stroller. 'Look at these.' She removed several colourful plastic balls she'd packed and rolled them across the grass. Rory immedi-ately pursued a green ball with plastic spikes protruding from it. Astrid toddled after a spotted red ball, before stopping and pointing at a flock of ducks paddling at the dam's edge in the distance.

'Da-da-da!' Astrid stared with wonder at the birds.

Cara followed at her heels. 'That's right, Astrid, they're ducks. Clever girl.' She smiled at Miranda. 'Hi there,' she said. 'Great afternoon for our first Mother's Day, isn't it?'

'Beautiful,' said Miranda. 'Where's Richard?'

'Gone to pick up his parents. He dropped mine here first.' She nodded towards a man sitting in a wheelchair near a sandy bank at the water's edge, a tartan scarf wrapped around his neck. A woman was standing next to him, tucking a blanket under his legs. 'I think you've met them before, haven't you?'

Miranda nodded. 'When we went to the zoo that time. How's your dad?'

'His dementia's worse. He's almost immobile now.'

Miranda squinted at the old man in the wheelchair. Even at a distance, she could see the telltale slackness of his jaw, the unnatural absence of movement. Cara's mother fussed about, adjusting his cap and smoothing the lapels of his jacket.

'It's so sad,' sighed Cara. 'Uh-oh, there goes Little Miss Trouble again.' She moved off after Astrid, who was tottering towards the barbecue area.

Miranda was glad Rory wasn't walking yet. She knew it was going to be a lot of hard work.

She gazed out across the picnic area. It was a glorious autumn afternoon. A light breeze carried the earthy, native scents of banksias, gum, grevillea. Ducks moved in languid circles across the shining surface of the dam. The distant sound of children laughing in the playground was muffled by their lazy, low-pitched calls. She tilted her face to the sun and closed her eyes. Briefly, she was carried back to the spontaneous optimism she'd felt as a teenager at the beginning of the summer holidays. All those seemingly endless possibilities, the empty weeks stretching out forever.

When Miranda opened her eyes, she saw Suzie in the car park, carrying Freya on one hip and several chairs in the other. She clearly needed some help.

She glanced over at the pergola, where Willem was balanced on a milk crate, fixing the last of the balloons. Digby was standing next to him, holding a ball of string.

'Willem,' she called. 'Can you go over there and help?' She nodded towards Suzie, who'd set down the chairs in the car park. Miranda picked up Rory and moved closer to Willem.

'She doesn't have anyone else to help her,' she explained, lowering her voice. 'She's a single mother. I'll watch Digby.'

'Right,' said Willem. 'Hold these.' He passed her a packet of thumbtacks he'd been using to pin the balloons, and began walking in the direction of Suzie.

Miranda exchanged pleasantries with Robert while trying to keep Digby away from the barbecue.

'They're almost done, mate,' said Robert, smiling at Digby.

'But I want a sausage *now*.'

'I'll give you the first one when they're ready,' said Robert. 'I promise.'

'Come on, Dig, let's play ball with Rory,' she offered, attempting to distract him. She pulled Digby by the hand towards the picnic rugs. She could feel her lower back objecting to the strain.

As she set Rory down on one of the rugs and rolled a

soccer ball at Digby, Cara appeared at her side. She seemed a little breathless, as though she'd been running.

'Miranda, can you watch Astrid for a moment?' she asked. She placed Astrid on the rug and passed her a yellow ball. 'A friend of mine's just popped by to say hello, but he can't stay for very long.' Miranda glanced in the direction that Cara was looking. A tall, dark figure was standing near the children's playground.

'Sure.'

'Thanks a million.' Cara headed over to the man, her walk quickly becoming a jog.

Miranda scanned the other side of the picnic area for Willem. She'd sent him off to the car park to help Suzie ages ago. What could possibly be taking him so long?

She pulled the Evian bottle from her handbag and took another mouthful.

Astrid and Rory began scrambling across the picnic rug together, in pursuit of the yellow ball. Digby was scaling an enormous rock nearby, puffing as he pulled himself up to its flat top. 'I'm the king of the castle and you're the dirty rascal, nyah nyah nyah!'

She pretended to be interested, smiling and waving at him.

Then she saw them. Suzie and Willem, standing off to one side, beyond the car park, near the public toilets. They appeared to be talking intently. Willem's back was to her, but she could sense from his body language that something was wrong. Even at this distance, it was clear that Suzie was upset. What was going on? Had Willem said something inappropriate? He could often be blunt, and Suzie was oversensitive at the best of times.

'Sausage sandwich?' asked Robert, sliding a platter under her nose.

'No thanks.' Her stomach somersaulted.

'What, after I've worked so hard to cook them?'

'Oh, okay.'

He passed her a serviette and waved a set of tongs over the platter.

'Which one?'

'Any will do.'

She looked back towards Suzie and Willem. There was something intimate in their stance, in the way their eyes were trained on each other. Suzie was gesticulating and Willem turned away from her, glancing over his shoulder in Miranda's direction. It was a furtive, fearful gesture.

'Here we are,' said Robert, passing her a sausage on a long white roll. 'Sauce? I've got tomato, barbecue or sweet chilli.'

She shook her head and waved him away.

Her vision began to darken around the periphery as she watched the pair of them. Suzie and Willem. Everything else seemed to fall away. The taste of bile erupted in her mouth.

Willem turned again, and this time his eyes met hers.

And she knew, immediately. Suzie. Willem. *Bill.*

'Mum, watch me!' called Digby, leaping off the rock and landing with a thud on the grass below. 'Ouch,' he moaned, holding his right knee.

She struggled to breathe.

The sausage sandwich slid out of her hand. She fell to her knees and vomited. Vodka and bile spurted out of her mouth and nose.

'God, are you alright?' Pippa bent down next to her.

'Water . . .' She needed to flush out the foul taste. Pippa passed her the Evian bottle. She pushed it away.

Small fingers grasped her shoulder. She looked up, dazed.

'Mummy?' Digby's face was pale and fearful. His knee was bleeding.

Rory began crawling towards her, over the picnic rug.

She vomited again.

Several people she didn't know were standing nearby, watching her with curiosity.

She hauled herself up, embarrassed. 'I must have eaten something . . .'

'Here, you poor thing,' said Pippa, passing her some baby wipes. 'You're not pregnant again, are you?'

Miranda shook her head. She looked in the direction of the toilet block. Willem and Suzie had disappeared. Where? Had they gone somewhere together? How was she supposed to handle this?

She dabbed at her mouth, her hands shaking. Digby began to cry.

'It's okay, Dig,' she said, sitting back on her heels. 'Mummy's just feeling a bit sick.' She reached out and touched his knee. 'We'll put a band-aid on that.' The words, the actions, emerging automatically from somewhere within her.

'I've got a first-aid kit,' Pippa said. She walked towards a picnic table.

Willem suddenly appeared from the direction of the toilet block. Digby recovered immediately, dropping Miranda's hand and running towards him like an excited puppy.

'Watch me, Dad!' he called, climbing onto the rock and leaping off it again.

'Great, mate,' said Willem. He sauntered over to Miranda.

'Hey,' he said, lifting Rory off the picnic rug. 'What's wrong? You look a bit sick.'

She tugged Rory out of his arms and glanced around. No one else was within earshot.

She took a step closer to him, her face almost touching his. 'It's a shock to discover your husband has a whore. And that she's one of your friends from mothers' group.'

His mouth opened, but no sound came out.

'Don't bother,' she hissed. 'All those work trips of yours.' Her voice was low, inaudible to anyone else. 'What a fucking halfwit I am.'

'Miranda, I had no idea Suzie was . . .'

'Shut the fuck up.'

She couldn't bear to be near him.

'Look!' yelled Digby. 'A clown!' A crowd had gathered near the pergola where a clown, his outlandish red smile painted up to his ears, balanced on a set of wooden stilts. He removed his shiny black top hat and, miming surprise, pulled a live white rabbit out of it. The crowd gasped and clapped in appreciation.

Miranda saw that Suzie was now among the group, holding Freya up to see the show. A moment later, their eyes locked. Suzie flushed red, her expression a mixture of fear and shame.

Miranda held her gaze, even as Suzie squirmed.

You can have Willem, she thought, and Digby too. Make yourself an instant fucking family.

Suddenly Cara was at Miranda's side again, pink-cheeked and smiling.

'Where's Astrid?' she panted.

Miranda glanced at the picnic rug. 'She was right here.'

Cara's face fell.

'I . . . I was just watching her,' said Miranda. 'She can't have gone far.'

'Astrid?' Cara called, looking from group to group. 'Who's got Astrid?'

Miranda started looking in the opposite direction, turning once to Willem. 'Make yourself useful,' she spat.

Others joined them. Pippa searched behind the barbecue and under chairs. Ginie went further, scouting behind bushes and trees. Made bolted off towards the eastern edge of the picnic area, flagging down a man in a green uniform. A ranger or gardener, perhaps. After a minute of searching, Cara turned to Miranda, her face ashen.

'Where *is* she?'

'I . . .' Miranda looked from side to side, towards the bushland and then the dam. A toddler couldn't possibly walk that far.

'Is she with your husband?' asked Daniel, who was standing nearby holding Rose.

'My husband's not here yet.' Cara's voice was shrill. Her eyes darted around in every direction, scanning the picnic area.

'I saw a dark fellow hanging around here earlier,' said an older woman holding Freya. 'He was Pakistani or something. He kept looking over our way.'

Daniel nodded. 'I saw him too.'

'No, no,' said Cara, her voice shaking. 'That was my friend, Ravi. I was just with him . . .' She brought her hands to her mouth.

A group began to congregate around them.

Gordon laid a hand on Cara's arm. 'How long since you've seen her?'

Cara's eyes swivelled about in a confused way.

'I don't know, maybe ten minutes . . . I left her playing in the group.' She looked in Miranda's direction. 'With Miranda.'

Miranda's heart thudded in her ears. She felt as if the earth might swallow her.

Gordon turned to her. 'And what happened, Miranda? Did you see anyone with Astrid?'

Miranda's mind reeled. One minute Astrid was there, playing happily next to Rory. The next she was gone. How was *she* supposed to know what happened? It wasn't her fault. It was Suzie's. And Willem's. And Cara's. And everyone else who hadn't bothered to watch Astrid, while Miranda was on her knees puking.

'She was right here . . .' she pleaded, her voice hoarse. Miranda's legs buckled beneath her and she sank to the ground. No one offered to help her up.

Cara made a strange, guttural sound and began to weave across the picnic area.

'I'll call the police.' Gordon pressed the three digits on his mobile.

Made approached, accompanied by the ranger. Some of

the women began to cry. Others began to talk loudly, cutting across the top of each other. Miranda wanted to clap her hands over her ears and silence them all.

Miranda pulled Rory onto her lap and buried her face in his sweet-smelling hair.

She closed her eyes and wished herself away, far away.

If only she could start the day again.

Pippa

Pippa winced at the sound of the siren's wail. She'd been trying to comfort Cara, but her efforts were futile. She scanned the picnic area again, desperate for some sign of Astrid. A sudden relieved cry: *She's here!* But all was silent, bar Cara's rasping sobs.

'Take a breath, Cara,' she urged, as two young police officers climbed out of a car and made their way towards the group. 'Here, have some water.' She held out Miranda's Evian bottle, but Cara turned away.

Pippa lifted the water bottle to her own lips instead.

A fiery liquid filled her mouth. She spat it onto the ground, coughing.

She studied the bottle, then held it under her nose. Gin or vodka, she couldn't be sure. She screwed the lid back on and stared at Miranda, who was huddled over Rory on a picnic rug.

Who drinks alcohol neat from an Evian bottle?

'When did she go missing?'

Pippa looked up at a man in a green uniform, standing with Made.

He removed his hat and mopped the sweat from his forehead. 'I'm a council ranger here.'

Pippa motioned him to one side. 'We're not really sure,' she replied, her voice low. 'Maybe ten or fifteen minutes ago.'

The man nodded, watching as Gordon led the police officers over to Cara. Their words were punctuated by Cara's weeping. After several minutes, one of the officers strode back to the police car and began talking into his radio.

Returning from the car once more, the officer addressed his colleague. 'Shift sergeant's coming down. Search and rescue team mobilising, detectives called. Ambulance is en route for Mum.'

His colleague nodded and stood up.

'Right, everyone,' he said. 'A child is missing and we need to get names and addresses of everyone here. There are more officers coming down to help, but we need all of you to stay in the area.' He looked around the circle. 'Has anyone seen any of your party leaving?'

Several people shook their heads.

My God, they're treating this as a crime scene.

'*I* saw someone leave,' volunteered Monika, Suzie's mother-in-law. She jiggled Freya in her arms. 'A dark fellow. He was only here for a little while. Seemed like he was in a bit of a hurry.' She stepped towards the police officers. 'And he knew Astrid, too.'

'Do you know his name, ma'am?' One of the officers

opened a black notebook and began scribbling across the page.

'His name,' said Cara suddenly, 'is Dr Ravi Nadkarni.'

Pippa started. That was the doctor who'd assisted with her surgery four months ago.

'He's a friend from university,' Cara continued. 'How many times do I have to tell you?' Her face was mottled and her chest heaved, as if she was hyperventilating. 'Ravi didn't touch Astrid. He didn't even *see* her. He only saw me. He gave me a present for her . . . for her birthday.' She collapsed into tears. Made held Cara as she wept, gently stroking her hair.

The officer nodded, his face a mask of neutrality.

'Right,' he said, looking up. 'Let's get the details of everyone here. We'll start with you.' He nodded at Monika, who seemed to stand taller when he addressed her.

'Has anyone checked the dam?' It was the ranger's voice, urgent in Pippa's ear.

She turned and stared at him. 'She couldn't have got that far,' she said. 'She's only one.'

The sound of a siren drew closer: the ambulance, presumably, for Cara.

'I'll check, anyway.' He was already striding across the grass leading down to the dam, his green shirt damp across his back.

Pippa followed him. She glanced back at Robert, sitting with Heidi at the edge of the barbecue area. Thank God *she's* alright, she thought, before rebuking herself for selfishness. *My friend's child is missing.*

They passed Mrs Bainbridge, Cara's mother, pushing her husband in his wheelchair towards the group.

'What's happened up there?' she asked.

Oh my God, she doesn't know. And she's the grandmother.

Pippa placed a hand on her arm. 'Look, no one really knows yet. But Astrid is . . . missing.'

The old woman's hands flew to her mouth.

'The police are here and they've got it all under control,' Pippa lied. 'Would you mind calling Richard? Cara is very upset.'

Mrs Bainbridge began fumbling in her handbag. 'He's just picking up his parents,' she stammered.

'I know.' Pippa broke into a run after the ranger. Her ballet slippers rubbed painfully at her heels, her hair flopped in her eyes. She'd carefully washed and blow-dried it that morning, never imagining she might find herself running as she was now. She caught up to the ranger where a sandy strip of beach gave way to rocks and then, around a grassy mound, to an area overgrown with reeds. Waterlilies floated like cups and saucers across the dam's murky depths.

There were dozens of ducks congregated nearby, squabbling and sunning themselves on a grassy embankment that sloped into the dam.

Pippa squinted at the broad expanse of water, shielding her eyes with one hand. The sun's glare bounced off the dam's surface and she lowered her gaze.

And then she saw her, face-down in a blanket of frothy scum, behind a tuft of reeds. Her arms were outstretched, star-like, and her dress ballooned around her.

The ranger heard her gasp and swung around.

He plunged into the knee-deep water.

'Dear Jesus,' he said, grunting with exertion.

He wrenched her from the water and stumbled backwards. As he did, one of her shoes fell away, pink sequins glittering as it sank into the water. He stood before Pippa, dripping and heaving, holding Astrid to his chest. Her eyes were closed, her lips parted, her skin pale.

Pippa watched the ranger's mouth move in the silent vacuum that surrounded them. His lips formed shapes, a white fleck of spittle appeared at the corner of his mouth, his head bobbed up and down. It was senseless, like watching the television without volume.

Then, suddenly, a thousand noises assaulted her brain. Sirens and car engines, a thudding bass beat in the distance, the incoherent murmuring of a crowd, the insane screeching of the ducks. A wild, high-pitched wail. She turned to see Cara, running down the slope towards them. *Don't let her die, don't let her die.*

Pippa could hear the ranger yelling at her to run for help, but her legs refused to move. She watched, transfixed, as he lay Astrid out on the cold grass. Her wet baby curls stuck across her neck, the pink dye of her party dress leaching out onto pallid legs. He began pumping her tiny chest with meaty fingers.

Cara fell to the ground and held Astrid's head in her hands. *Oh, dear Jesus, don't let her die.*

Then Pippa began to run, faster than she'd ever run before, around the embankment and up the long slope to the barbecue area. She hardly noticed the sensation of urine running down her legs as she did.

Later, Pippa couldn't recall what she'd said to the people huddled there, but the ambulance officers immediately rushed to Astrid's side. Minutes later, they carried her tiny body on a vast stretcher towards the ambulance. An unnatural quiet fell across the group, broken only by Cara's howling as she lunged into the ambulance after Astrid. Then the doors slammed shut and the ambulance sped away.

As the siren faded, everyone began talking at once.

Someone said, 'That bastard drowned her. Did he interfere with her too?' An elderly man shook his fist at the police. 'Why'd you start taking names before having a decent look around, you bloody idiots?' he bellowed. A woman Pippa didn't recognise was doubled over on the ground, keening. *Why, why, why.* Pippa stood motionless in the chaos, searching the picnic area for Heidi and Robert. When finally she found them, over near the barbecue, she rushed at Heidi and hugged her to her chest. 'Thank God you're alright,' she whispered. '*Thank God.*'

Four more police cars arrived, bearing uniformed police and detectives in plain clothes. A State Emergency Services van appeared, bringing kind-faced people in fluorescent orange vests. They made cups of tea from portable urns, and comforted the grief-stricken. A forensic team cordoned off the picnic area with lengths of blue and white tape. Richard and his parents, haggard and weeping, were bundled into a police car to follow Cara to the hospital. They'd arrived late, expecting a birthday party in full swing. Instead, Richard had been given the dreadful news. He'd fallen to his knees and howled, even as others tried to comfort him. Pippa had never heard a grown man make such a wild, terrible sound.

Hours of police interviews followed. The afternoon's shadows lengthened as guests made their statements. As the sky darkened, those already interviewed began to disperse, trudging to their cars with slumped shoulders and swollen eyes. Ginie and Daniel and their entourage went first, then Made and Gordon with Wayan, Suzie, Freya and Monika, the ranger, the face-painter and the clown.

The police finally took Pippa's statement just before sunset. The detective identified himself as Detective Constable Warren Harrison and, wearily, opened his large black folio. She strained to hear him above the mechanical drone of a news helicopter, circling low over the dam. He took down Pippa's name, address and date of birth.

'Tell me what you saw happen today, Mrs Thompson.'

Pippa wept as she told him of her discovery at the dam's edge. 'I don't know how she walked that far,' she said.

'So what made you go down to the dam to look for Astrid in the first place, Mrs Thompson?'

'The ranger,' she said. 'He suggested it. I saw him working up near the bushwalking tracks when we arrived. Made brought him over to help. I guess we were focused on who might have . . . taken Astrid. It all happened so quickly.' She blinked away tears. 'I mean, we were *right* here. There were so many people around . . .'

The police officer studied her for a moment. 'Accidents happen in seconds.' He cleared his throat and referred to his folio again. 'And who *was* with Astrid, Mrs Thompson, to your knowledge, immediately prior to her disappearance?'

Pippa swallowed. 'As far as I know, it was Miranda ... Miranda Bianco. One of the women from my mothers' group.' Her eyes darted involuntarily to the figure of Miranda, still hunched over on the picnic blanket. She hadn't moved for hours. Willem had taken Digby and Rory home.

'How do you know Miranda was with her?'

'Because I heard Cara ask Miranda to keep an eye on Astrid while she went and talked to a friend of hers. And then I saw Miranda with her son Rory and Astrid on the picnic rug over there.' She nodded at the rug on which Miranda now sat.

'And then what happened?'

'I don't really know.' Pippa's eyes flooded with new tears. 'A clown was doing tricks near the barbecue and I got distracted. A lot of us did, I guess.'

The detective's black pen scratched across the page.

'And did you see anything unusual at all today, Mrs Thompson?'

Pippa hesitated. 'I don't know whether this is relevant or not ...' she began. 'I saw Miranda vomiting so I went over to help her. I thought maybe she was pregnant.' She paused. 'I offered her some water from her own bottle.' She held up the Evian bottle. 'But when I took a sip myself I found out it's not water in there. It's alcohol.'

The detective studied her. 'Do you think she might not have been in a fit state to look after a child?'

Pippa shrugged. 'I don't know ... We'd all had a couple of

champagnes. It was a birthday party, a Mother's Day celebration.' Her voice broke.

The detective produced a zip-lock evidence bag from his pocket, opened it, and placed the bottle inside.

'Was there anything else about Mrs Bianco's behaviour that suggested to you she might not be in a sound physical or mental state?'

Pippa shook her head. 'Just the vomiting,' she said. 'Honestly, she didn't seem drunk.'

'Thank you very much, Mrs Thompson. That will be all for now. We may need to come back to you with further enquiries as our investigation progresses.'

She nodded.

The detective motioned to a colleague.

Pippa began gathering up her things, suddenly conscious of the television cameras in the car park. She spotted Robert on a wooden bench on the southern side of the dam. He appeared to be spoon-feeding Heidi in her stroller. She glanced at her watch. It was well beyond Heidi's usual dinner time. Then she brought her hands to her mouth, physically struck by the thought of Cara and Richard at the hospital, cradling Astrid in their arms.

Two detectives approached Miranda. One of them touched her on the shoulder. She hardly raised her head.

'Mrs Bianco,' Pippa heard him say. 'We need to talk to you about what happened today, and we'd like to do that down at police headquarters. Can you come with us to the station for an interview?'

Miranda looked stunned. 'Am I under arrest?'

'No,' he replied. 'And you're under no obligation to come down to the station, either. But given today's events, we'd like to do the interview formally.'

Miranda looked from one to the other. 'Can . . . can I call my husband first?'

'Of course.'

She found her mobile phone and began dialling the number. Then she stopped suddenly, and slipped the phone back into her pocket.

'I'll come with you now,' she said.

The detectives helped her up.

As she watched Miranda in the semi-darkness, Pippa had an overwhelming urge to reach out to her.

'Miranda,' she called. 'If you need anything, let me know.'

But Miranda just stared at her blankly, as if she wasn't there.

Robert's hand clasped hers as they sat on the lounge, awaiting the late news. It was the second item of the night, following a story on destructive floods that had killed more than three hundred people in Brazil. A smiling picture of Astrid hovered beneath the caption *Mother's Day Tragedy*. A fresh-faced reporter with a blonde bob and distracting lipstick stood in the car park in front of Manly Dam. The picnic area was illuminated by large halogen lamps, under which a forensic team continued to work.

'Forensic investigators are working into the night following the tragic death of one-year-old Astrid Jenkins at a popular recreational area for families on Sydney's northern beaches,' she announced. 'Police are unable to confirm whether a criminal investigation will proceed, but it is understood that Astrid was in the care of family and friends when she was found face down in shallow water. Ambulance officers were unable to revive the child, who was pronounced dead on arrival at North Shore Hospital. Witnesses at the scene claim an unidentified man may have lured the child away from her first birthday party. Police are unable to confirm these allegations.'

The camera cut to a balding, middle-aged policeman identified as Detective Chief Inspector Russell Bale, Superintendent of Manly Local Area Command. 'A tragedy has occurred today and we won't be speculating about what happened,' he said. 'The case will be referred to the coroner and investigations are continuing.'

The blonde journalist stared into the camera lens. 'Bystanders observed that the dam in which the child was found was unfenced.' She paused. 'Jocelyn Farrell, Channel Nine News.'

Pippa turned off the television and they sat in silence for several minutes.

'Do you want to talk about it?' Robert asked.

She shook her head.

'We should go to bed,' he said. 'It's been a long day.'

She imagined Cara and Richard in the silent rooms of their comfortable home. What were they doing now? she wondered. What *could* you do, when your child was dead?

'Well, I'm turning in,' said Robert. He cupped a hand under her chin. 'Don't stay up too long thinking. It's terrible, but you need to get some rest.' He gestured in the direction of Heidi's room.

He's right, she thought. There's another life entirely reliant on me.

So much life, so much death. A world so arbitrary and heartbreaking.

She couldn't possibly sleep tonight.

'Hey.'

A patch of wetness had pooled at the corner of her mouth and her right arm was numb.

'Hey.'

She opened her eyes. Robert, in his work gear and boots, crouched next to her in the early morning light.

'It's six o'clock,' he said. 'You slept out here all night.'

She'd lain awake on the lounge for most of it, reliving the day before. Had she been remiss in some way? Could she have done something to prevent Astrid's death? She'd heard Cara's conversation with Miranda: why hadn't she watched Astrid too? It wasn't until she heard birds welcoming the dawn that finally, weary of her thoughts, Pippa surrendered to sleep.

'I've got to go to work now.' He took her hand. 'Will you be okay?'

She nodded.

'Are you sure?'

She nodded again.

'Can you . . . I don't know, call your psychiatrist or something? Tell her about what happened yesterday. I mean, you were there when they pulled Astrid out.'

One of the SES workers had made a similar suggestion.

'I'll be alright.'

Robert hovered in front of her.

'Things were just, you know, starting to get a little bit better with your mood and everything. I wouldn't want this to . . .'

She stared at him in disbelief. 'What, ruin our lives?' She shook her head. 'I don't think we should be worrying too much about how Astrid's death might affect us, Robert. Think of Cara and Richard. Their lives are never, *ever* going to be the same.' Tears began to leak from the corners of her eyes.

'I just . . .'

She cut him off. 'Has it even *registered* with you that a child is dead? My *friend's* child?'

Robert looked hurt. 'Of course it has,' he said quietly. 'I was there too.' He scuffed his boots. 'We all deal with these things differently, you know.'

She exhaled, her anger dissipating. She looked at Robert's tired eyes and reached out to touch his face.

'I'm sorry,' she said. 'You're right.'

'I've got to go,' he said, kissing her hand. 'But when I get home, I want you to tell me you've made an appointment with the psychiatrist. It's important, Pip. Promise me?'

'I promise.'

He'd come a long way, this high school sweetheart of hers, to develop such emotional intelligence. He'd always been a physical person, a champion athlete in high school who'd pushed his body to its limits. He'd attended a Catholic boys' school in Manly and she'd been at the sister school. They'd met in Year 12 at a regional cross-country competition. They'd been attracted to each other's physicality and, in the early years, their relationship had been defined by their feats of endurance together. Trekking the Kokoda Trail, kayaking the Murrumbidgee River, cycling across the Nullarbor Plain. He'd proposed at the peak of Mount Kosciuszko on the eve of their fifth anniversary, when they were twenty-three years old. At the time, he'd just completed his building apprenticeship, while she was in her final year of a degree in organisational psychology.

'All airy-fairy,' Robert had joked about her studies. 'Give me something I can touch and feel any day.'

Their families had been thrilled by their marriage. He was the youngest of seven children from a working-class family in Narrabeen. His father was a fitter and turner, his mother a shop assistant. When the family's dwindling finances threatened to disrupt his education, he'd been fortunate enough to receive a bursary to fund the final two years of his schooling.

By contrast, as the only child of middle-class parents in Fairlight, Pippa had never wanted for much at all. She'd been a miraculous surprise late in life for her parents. Her father was close to retirement at the time she was born, and her mother was an 'ancient forty-five', as she termed it. Now in their seventies and nineties, her parents lived in a two-bedroom flat in Fairlight, with a Persian cat, a budgerigar and a patio of African violets. Although they telephoned Pippa every week, a range of infirmities prevented them from visiting. They were more like grandparents to Pippa now, she sometimes reflected.

Pippa and Robert had started trying for a baby just as soon as they were married, after a three-year engagement. Robert was far more observant of Catholic teachings than she was; her draconian schooling had all but bludgeoned the life out of her faith. Robert, on the other hand, went to Mass every Friday and Sunday and was opposed to abortion, euthanasia and contraception. She didn't object. At twenty-six, she was ready for a baby. She didn't want to leave it too long and end up like her own parents: too old to truly enjoy her children.

But things didn't go according to plan. Much to Robert's surprise and increasing consternation, their bodies combined bore no physical fruit. After three years, they consulted a specialist. A raft of tests revealed that Pippa suffered from uterine fibroids, the same condition as her mother. 'Only these days,' the specialist assured her, 'we can do something about it.'

It had taken one operation and nine expensive IVF cycles before finally they were blessed with a pregnancy.

Perhaps it was the struggle and effort involved in conceiving their first child. Perhaps it was their reckless sense of relief when, finally, the pregnancy reached full-term. Whatever the reason, neither of them was prepared for what occurred after Heidi was born.

It had all happened so quickly. When she was six centimetres dilated, the urge to push was overwhelming.

'Don't push!' the midwife scolded, peering between her legs. 'You need to wait longer. You're not ready yet.'

But Pippa couldn't wait. She'd pushed twice, as hard as possible. The baby had shot out of her and into the midwife's hands.

She hadn't felt the tear, or the repair work completed by the obstetric registrar under local anaesthetic. She was too elated to care. With Robert lying next to her in the birthing suite, she'd cradled their baby and cried with joy. The daughter she'd always hoped for.

'Heidi,' she'd whispered, kissing the baby's slippery cheek.

Three days later, she'd been released from hospital. A midwife had given her a fact sheet entitled 'Caring for Vaginal Tears' and a starter pack of absorbent pads.

'You'll have some vaginal bleeding and incontinence for a while,' the midwife advised. 'The stitches will dissolve over the next six weeks. Any questions at all, just call.'

In the initial weeks, she'd been too deliriously happy and too focused on Heidi's needs to pay much attention to her own. The bleeding stopped within three weeks, but her perineum stayed swollen like a tennis ball. Urine and faeces continued to trickle onto the incontinence pads. The volume surprised her, the smell was repulsive.

When Heidi was six weeks old, she'd telephoned the birthing suite and described her symptoms. The midwife had retrieved her file and counselled her to wait.

'You had a big baby—a nine-pounder,' said the midwife. 'So your symptoms aren't all that surprising. It can take quite a while for everything to heal. Has the leaking got worse?'

'No, it's been fairly constant,' Pippa replied.

'Well, I'd recommend waiting longer. Having a baby is a big thing for your body to go through, especially when it's your first time. It can take up to six months for everything to return to normal.'

And so incontinence pads had become a staple of Pippa's weekly shopping list. After three months, sick of bleaching her underwear, she found a website that stocked incontinence aids. She upgraded from sanitary-style pads to pull-on adult nappies, which allowed her to leave the house for short stints without having to take a stash of pads with her. Ordering on the internet alleviated the embarrassment of standing at the supermarket checkout, handing over items with jarring names like 'Confidence', 'Assure' or 'Depend'.

'It's just for a little while,' she'd explained to Robert, the first time he'd caught sight of her stepping out of her skirt with a nappy on. 'Heidi was so big, the midwife at the hospital said it can take six months for everything to get back to normal.'

Robert nodded, a strange expression on his face. Pippa recognised it instantly for what it was: revulsion.

As Heidi grew, so did the distance between her and Robert. They'd always had a good sex life, but making love was now fraught. She was too embarrassed to talk to him about it, and she could understand his abhorrence. After all, she was repulsed by the incontinence too.

She started to reduce the amount she ate, especially in public. Robert had railed against this initially, as eating out had always been something they'd enjoyed together.

'For God's sake, Pippa,' he'd said, four months after Heidi was born. 'We can't avoid the outside world forever.'

'I can't control what comes out of me,' she'd snapped. 'But I *can* control when it goes in.'

His face softened. 'I'm sorry . . . I guess I don't really understand.'

It didn't surprise her. He couldn't understand why she refused to go jogging either, an activity they'd both relished prior to her pregnancy. But her pelvic floor just wasn't up to it now. As it was, lifting the washing basket or walking up a flight of stairs could cause an alarming surge between her legs.

He began to take on more work, as they were missing her income. They had a mortgage to pay, a car loan, a credit card. But how could she return to work in her condition? As a human resources officer for a small firm specialising in 'career transition'—a euphemism for redundancies and restructures—she spent her working days in close proximity to others. Conducting one-on-one interviews, breaking difficult news, comforting the crestfallen. They'd originally planned for her to re-enter the workforce when Heidi was four months old, but her medical problems now forced her to extend her maternity leave for up to twelve months.

To compensate, Robert slotted in extra jobs at the beginning and end of his working day, as well as on weekends. There was always a steady stream of work for a reliable builder on the northern beaches. There were plenty of young families renovating homes, as well as house-proud retirees who needed a handyman. Most days he left the house by six am and didn't return until after eight pm. He was tired, and it showed.

She tried to be the best homemaker she could be; it only seemed fair. Once Heidi was asleep for the night, she would reassemble the ruins of the day in preparation for Robert's return. Warming his meal in the oven, cleaning the kitchen, tidying the lounge room, wiping over the bathroom basin and turning down the sheets. Trying not to resent the many domestic chores that had somehow naturally become her lot in life. The endless cycle of washing, drying, folding and ironing. I'm not a maid, she would sometimes think as she pegged Heidi's tiny jumpsuits, singlets and socks in neat lines. Often she would stop under the washing line and stare up at the night sky, watching clouds skidding past the moon. How can those clouds be moving so fast, she would wonder, when my life is moving so slowly?

Despite her fatigue, she had trouble sleeping at night. She would lie next to Robert, listening to his breathing, until long after he'd fallen asleep. As she felt the leakage creep up towards her hips, she would remember their former life. The hiking, the cycling, the lovemaking. Where had it all gone? She had turned into someone she never imagined she would become, with a cornucopia of minutiae tumbling out of pockets and bags. Nappies, wipes, rash cream, teething rings, soft toys, cloth books. Endless piles of clutter, a baby marketer's dream, crammed into the voids of her existence.

When Heidi awoke in the night, as she inevitably did, Pippa would curl her fists into tight balls and press them into the mattress so hard that her fingernails bit into her flesh. Eventually she would sit up and make her way to Heidi's room, feeling the weight of her nappy wedged between her legs. Hating herself. Despising her life.

Robert slept on. He always did.

And so he never saw her stand at the foot of the cot and watch, immobilised, as Heidi screamed and screamed. He never knew how hard she sometimes held Heidi to her body, trembling with the desire to shake her. He never heard her spit obscenities at Heidi as she changed, fed, settled and resettled her. But the words she spoke in those dark, small hours always returned to accuse her in the morning. How could she treat this tiny, defenceless human—the baby they had longed for—so badly?

The guilt was annihilating.

She'd attended the mothers' group at Robert's urging.

'We don't have much family support,' he'd said, stating the obvious. 'And you're not seeing as much of your friends.'

He was right about that. The incontinence had made her antisocial.

'A mothers' group might come in handy,' he said. 'Just go along for a few months and if it's not for you, drop out.'

She'd gone along to appease him, despite her debilitating anxiety. Was she leaking? Was it staining the seat? Could her nappy be seen under her skirt? At the first session of the mothers' group, she'd deliberately suggested an outdoor venue for future meetings, in the hope that none of the other women would *smell* her. She'd resented having to worry about it at all.

No one else in the group had a similar problem, as far as she could tell. Everyone else was *normal*.

Apart from the mothers' group, she had few social outlets. Her own parents extended little help from their flat in Fairlight, through no fault of their own. Whenever Pippa visited them, they would sing to Heidi, or bounce her on their laps, but they offered no other practical support. They were getting older, and always asking Pippa for some kind of help themselves: to change a light bulb, go to the shops, or reprogram the television channels. Pippa didn't begrudge these requests, but she needed a place of respite. With her own problems to contend with, she started avoiding her parents. She felt bad about it, but what else could she do?

Instead, she paced the hallway of her home with Heidi crying in her pram, or did hundreds of circuits of the small square of concrete that Robert called a backyard. Eventually she ventured further afield, spending whole days walking Heidi to nowhere in particular. One week, she summoned the courage to visit Warringah Mall, doing loop after loop of its air-conditioned levels. But then a humiliating incident in a bookstore sent her home again quickly: she'd passed wind, loudly, while buying *Eat, Pray, Love*. Her body had betrayed her, she loathed its imperfection. And so she resolved to walk without rest, staying ahead of the repugnant odour that she imagined trailing behind her. She walked from Freshwater to Curl Curl, Dee Why or Manly. Every day, irrespective of the weather. Her jeans became loose, her face haggard. She just couldn't keep the weight on.

*

'You're going to the beautician tomorrow,' Robert announced one evening, when Heidi was six months old. 'A facial at ten o'clock. I've paid for it already, and I'm taking the day off to look after Heidi. All you have to do is turn up.'

Pippa sat up on the sofa, taken aback. She'd never known him to have a day off work.

'You need a break,' he said. 'Look at you, thin as a rake. You're so busy looking after Heidi, you've forgotten about yourself.'

She looked at him as though for the first time. This *was* Robert, the man who bought practical birthday gifts—socks, underwear, sports equipment—if he actually remembered her birthday at all. They'd been together for sixteen years and he'd never once surprised her with a spontaneous gift.

I really must have let myself go.

Her eyes filled with tears. They hadn't had sex for more than six months, a prospect neither one of them would have believed before Heidi's birth. Every time she considered it, Pippa recoiled. *If we have sex, I might split into pieces or leak all over you.* Without their usual physical intimacy, an awkwardness had developed between them, an unspoken rift that neither one of them knew how to breach. Robert's generosity was overwhelming.

Tears began to stream down her face.

'What?' asked Robert, his expression confused. 'Don't you want a facial?'

She struggled for composure.

'Thank you,' she whispered. 'It means a lot.'

*

It was the first time she'd left Heidi, ever. As she slid into the car and turned the key in the ignition, she fought the urge to run back into the house, wrest Heidi from Robert's arms and retreat to the lounge room. Robert waved at her through the bedroom window, jiggling Heidi on his hip as she reversed down the driveway. She glanced over her shoulder one more time as she steered the car onto the road. She'll be fine, she thought. It's just two hours.

Before she reached the end of the street, her telephone beeped receipt of an SMS.

We'll be fine. Enjoy yourself.

She laughed aloud.

Driving the car was a different experience without Heidi in the baby seat. She turned off the *Baby Meets Mozart* CD and found an FM radio station, catching the end of the ten o'clock news. It had been months since she'd caught up on current affairs. The world had continued rotating on its axis and yet *she* had radically changed: irrevocably altered by the heady intoxication and utter devastation that having Heidi had entailed. Even the weather forecast sounded different.

The news ended and a familiar tune began, an anthem from her youth. She turned up the volume, bobbing her head in time with the beat. She could remember crooning 'Forever Young' into a hairbrush with school friends in her lounge room, dancing about in fluorescent socks and 'Choose Life' T-shirts. That was twenty-five years ago, she thought, with a jolt of shock. She wound down the window and, abandoning her usual caution, belted out the lyrics.

Pulling up at a red light, she glanced at the vehicle in the next lane. A tradesman winked at her from the open window of his ute. Embarrassed, she stopped singing. The tradesman pulled a face, as if disappointed.

Her eyes widened. *Oh my God, he's* flirting *with me.*

She gripped the steering wheel, repressing a smile.

The traffic lights turned green and the tradesman accelerated away, tyres squealing.

She smiled all the way to the beautician's.

She checked her telephone three times before the facial.

'Sorry,' she said, activating the mute setting. 'I've just never left my daughter alone with my husband before.'

The beautician laughed. 'Oh, don't worry, I know how you feel. I always check on my husband when he's babysitting our kids. It's hard to relax, isn't it? But you've got to have a bit of me-time too.'

Pippa lay back on the recliner, considering the beautician's words.

When he's babysitting our kids . . .

Yes, she thought, that's exactly how it is. When a woman looks after her children, she's parenting. When her husband looks after them, he's babysitting.

The beautician smoothed a headband across the top of Pippa's forehead, then pressed a hot towel over her face. Despite her anxieties—*Will the pad last the distance? Can the beautician smell me?*—Pippa could feel herself floating beneath the beautician's hands.

Why haven't I done this earlier? she wondered.

She awoke with a start to the beautician lightly tapping her shoulder.

Pippa smiled up at her. She felt as though she'd been asleep for a week.

'We're done now, Pippa. Take your time getting up.'

The beautician began to tidy the room, screwing caps back onto bottles and squeezing out sponges.

'Uh, I don't want to worry you,' she added, 'but your husband rang the salon earlier.'

Pippa sat bolt upright. 'Why? What's wrong?'

The beautician put a steadying hand on her arm. 'He was just checking what time the facial finished.'

Pippa frowned. But why would he call, if nothing was wrong?

She scrambled off the table.

'Thank you,' she said. 'That was lovely.' She dug around in her handbag for her mobile. Four missed calls, all from Robert. Her stomach dropped.

As soon as she was outside the salon, she telephoned Robert. He didn't answer. She ran to the car and accelerated out of her parking spot. In the seven minutes it took to drive home, a hundred terrifying scenarios raced through her mind.

The instant she opened the front door, she heard Heidi crying, an unusual, low-pitched moan. She ran down the hall, panic overwhelming her. Robert was standing at the kitchen bench, peeling potatoes. Pippa stopped, confused. Heidi was nowhere to be seen.

'Where's Heidi?' she asked.

Robert put down the potato peeler.

'In her room,' he said. 'She had a bit of a . . . bump. She cried a bit, then started rubbing her eyes, so I put her to bed. She's been in there about ten minutes now. She hasn't gone to sleep, so I thought she might be hungry.' He gestured towards the potatoes.

Pippa stared at him, speechless. Then she turned on her heel and started down the hall.

Robert followed her. 'She's fine, don't worry. How was your facial?'

Pippa didn't reply. She opened Heidi's door and gasped.

Heidi was lying in her cot, red-faced, saliva streaming from her mouth. A large, egg-shaped lump bulged above her right eye.

'Oh my God.' She scooped Heidi out of her cot and lay her on the change table, then bent over her to study the lump. Burst blood vessels streaked purple across its surface.

She turned to Robert, hovering in the door.

'How did this happen?'

'She was on the lounge,' Robert started.

'What?' Pippa couldn't believe he would put Heidi anywhere except the floor.

'I was right there,' he said. 'But my phone rang and she just sort of slipped off. I'm sorry.'

'She *slipped off*?' Pippa stared at him, uncomprehending. 'How did that happen exactly, if you were right there?'

Robert looked weary.

'Look, it was an accident. A work call came in, I had one hand on Heidi, then I picked up the phone and she slipped . . .'

Pippa put Heidi back into her cot and turned to face Robert. White-hot rage, unlike anything she'd felt before, surged through her. As she walked towards him, she felt as though she was wading through quicksand: the indignity of her incontinence, the humiliation of Robert's revulsion, every long, lonely walk she'd ever taken with Heidi in her stroller. Had she endured all of that, as well as three undignified years of IVF treatment, for Robert to *drop* their precious baby, like a carton of eggs, on the floor?

She slapped him with a force that stunned them both.

'I'm taking Heidi to the hospital,' she said. 'She could have concussion.'

Robert held a hand over his cheek, staring at her like a beaten dog.

'Now,' she said, pushing past him.

She collected the nappy bag, her wallet, the car keys. She carried Heidi on her hip and pulled the pram out the front door, slamming it behind her.

She didn't have to wait long in Accident and Emergency. Both Heidi and Pippa had been sufficiently distressed for the triage nurse to prioritise them. Within ten minutes, they were ushered into a consultation room by a young registrar.

'Hello,' he said, smiling at Heidi. 'I'm Dr Lee. Now, what happened to Heidi?'

Pippa took a deep breath. 'She slipped off the couch and knocked her head. My husband was looking after her, it happened about an hour ago.'

Dr Lee jotted some notes on his clipboard. 'Okay, let's have a good look at her. You can keep her on your knee for the time being.'

Dr Lee ran his hands over Heidi's head and neck, palpated her limbs, tapped her reflexes with a tendon hammer, then checked her blood pressure. As he peered into her eyes, Heidi reached for the ophthalmoscope. Dr Lee smiled and nudged her in the chest with it. Heidi giggled.

'Well, she seems fine,' said Dr Lee at last. 'She's had a bump and a bit of a shock, but that's about all. I'll give her a dose of baby paracetamol for comfort. And we'll need to keep you here for the next four hours for observation. That's standard practice when a child presents with a head injury.'

Pippa nodded. 'Okay.'

'You said your husband was looking after Heidi at the time of her injury.' Dr Lee paused. 'Is this the first time that's happened?'

'Yes, I feel so bad. It's the first time I've ever left Heidi with anyone else.'

Heidi began to squirm on her lap, gnawing at a teething ring. Pippa shifted her weight on the chair. Amid all the drama, she'd forgotten to change her incontinence pad. The wetness was becoming uncomfortable.

Dr Lee looked up from his clipboard. 'Is there any violence in the home?'

Pippa was shocked. 'You mean my husband?'

Dr Lee nodded.

'No, of course not.'

Pippa's cheeks flushed as Dr Lee continued to look at her.

'Certainly *not* my husband.'

Dr Lee raised an eyebrow.

'What I mean is . . .' She was stammering. 'Today, when my husband let Heidi slip, I was so angry with him I could have killed him.' She pushed her hair behind her ears. 'I slapped him across the face. I was completely out of control. I've never hit anyone in my life.' She could feel the tears welling in her eyes.

She stared into her lap, embarrassed. She wished she'd said nothing at all. Dr Lee passed her a box of tissues. She removed one and dabbed at the corners of her eyes.

'And how have you been coping generally?' Dr Lee set aside his clipboard. 'The transition to motherhood can be difficult. How have you found it?'

She leaned back in her chair, considering him. He couldn't be more than twenty-six, this clean-shaven doctor. Barely out of university. Yet he'd posed a question that no one else had ever bothered to ask. Not Pat at the baby health centre, not the women in her mothers' group, not even her husband. Since Heidi's arrival, no one had asked whether she was, in fact, coping.

She exhaled. 'I'm not coping very well. Today showed me that.' The wetness was seeping onto her skirt, she could feel it. 'I need an incontinence pad,' she blurted. 'Is there a spare one here?'

Dr Lee cocked his head.

'I'm still leaking from the birth,' Pippa explained. 'Heidi was a big baby. I had a nasty tear.'

Dr Lee picked up his clipboard again. 'But that was . . .

more than six months ago. Those symptoms should have resolved by now.' He jotted more notes. 'No wonder you're having trouble coping. Do you often feel sad or anxious?'

Almost permanently, she thought.

'Well, I'm not very happy a lot of the time.'

'That's understandable, given your symptoms,' he said. 'Who's your obstetrician?'

'I don't have one. Heidi was delivered in the birthing suite downstairs.' Pippa could hardly remember that night at all. 'The midwives told me to wait six months for my body to recover fully.'

Dr Lee nodded. 'Look, I'm an emergency room doctor,' he said. 'Today's consult is for Heidi. But I think you should get a second opinion on what's causing your incontinence. And a mental health assessment. It's not uncommon for women in your situation to have post-natal depression. I can give you some referrals now to specialists at this hospital. Would you like that?'

Pippa stared at him, digesting his words. A second opinion on her incontinence couldn't hurt. But post-natal depression? It had never occurred to her that what she'd been experiencing might have a label like that.

'Okay.'

As he wrote out the referrals, Pippa hugged Heidi to her chest. She thought about Robert and the look on his face as she struck him. How would she ever make it better?

'There,' said Dr Lee, passing her the paperwork. 'Now, I'll be back to check on Heidi in two hours, and then again two hours after that. I'll ask the nursing staff to bring you some pads, and a few more toys for Heidi. There's tea and coffee in the corridor.' He waved a hand towards the door. 'There's also a telephone out there, if you need to call anyone.'

'Thank you,' she said.

Dr Lee stood up. 'See you shortly.' He left, closing the door behind him.

Pippa reached into her bag for her mobile phone and dialled Robert's number.

When the specialist told her she had a grade-four tear that could only be fixed by surgery, Pippa wept with quiet relief.

'We'll book you in for the procedure as soon as possible,' Dr Sturgess said. 'It should have been done much earlier than this. But once you've had the surgery, you should notice a difference immediately.'

Robert squeezed her hand.

Pippa imagined returning home, gathering up all the incontinence aids in the house—the pads, the mattress protector, the adult nappies—then burning them in the backyard.

'What does the operation involve?'

Dr Sturgess passed her several fact sheets.

'Read these at home,' he said. 'We'll repair the muscles and ligaments in the area. It's not always apparent what's actually needed until the patient is on the operating table, but in your case, I think it'll be a combination of bladder and rectum reinforcement. There'll be myself, a senior surgical colleague, an anaesthetist and a nurse in the theatre.'

'What kind of recovery period is involved?' Robert wanted to know.

'Ah, husbands are *always* worried about that.' The specialist smiled. 'You should be back on your feet within a week, and we do a follow-up at six weeks. Would you like to book in with my secretary?'

'Yes, please.' She didn't need to discuss it with Robert. She didn't care how much it cost.

'Any questions?'

Pippa shook her head. 'Thank you, Dr Sturgess.'

On her first night home from hospital she eased herself into bed, wincing with the pain. Robert appeared to be asleep already; his six days as Heidi's primary carer had clearly exhausted him. She'd arrived home that afternoon, buoyed by the support of the mothers' group and the raft of kindnesses they'd shown her. Meals prepared and coffees delivered to Robert, play dates for Heidi, visits and flowers and gift vouchers for Pippa.

But how quickly things revert to the status quo, she mused. It was as though she'd never left home. A stack of unwashed dishes lay in the sink, at least four loads of washing were piled in the laundry, and the pantry needed restocking. There was no soap in the soap dispenser, no paper on the toilet-roll holder, no milk in the fridge.

She reached out to turn off the bedside lamp, but Robert suddenly rolled over and wrapped his arms around her. His breath was warm on her face, their bodies closer than they'd been in months.

'I never appreciated how tough it is,' he said, his face earnest. 'With Heidi, I mean.'

She looked at him in the lamplight.

'I mean, I knew you worked hard with her,' he continued. 'But it wasn't until you were in hospital that I learned *how* hard. And it wasn't as if I was doing it on my own. The women in your mothers' group were amazing. I didn't have to make any meals for myself, or for Heidi. You normally do all *that* as well.'

He stroked her cheek.

'I'm really sorry, Pippa. You've had no help at all, even when you were sick. I didn't know how to handle the . . . the injuries after the birth. I just thought they'd go away somehow. And I thought that if I was around at weekends, that'd be enough. I took you for granted, and I'm sorry for that.'

Tears slid down her face. For the first time in months, she felt understood.

She thought about the day of the facial, how she'd slapped him. They hadn't spoken about it since. 'I'm sorry too,' she whispered. 'I never should have hit you. I'll never *ever* do that again. I don't know what came over me.'

'I do,' said Robert. 'You were protecting your daughter. I stuffed up, she was hurt, and you reacted. You've been under a lot of pressure these past eight months.'

She nodded. 'But I could've handled it better. I'll get out of this rut, Robert, I promise.'

He smiled at her, his eyes gentle.

'*We'll* get out of this rut. We'll do it together.'

And, slowly, they had. It was as though the surgery knitted together not only her physical injuries, but the deeper wounds of her heart.

She started seeing a psychiatrist specialising in post-natal depression. He prescribed antidepressants and suggested she attend a weekly PND support group. At first she felt self-conscious, but when the other women spoke of their darkest hours, she understood them perfectly. She needed to hear their stories, and to tell hers too.

The surgery wasn't a miracle cure. It fixed the worst of her symptoms, but her bladder was still weak. On the specialist's advice, she began seeing a pelvic floor physiotherapist and, eight weeks later, she and Robert finally had sex again. She was nervous and awkward and she felt next to nothing, yet she cried with relief afterwards. There *is* hope, she thought, as Robert held her in his arms in the dark. I have survived.

When she finally told the mothers' group of her problems, a fortnight before the surgery, she felt relieved of her secret burden. She started to get to know them in a way she hadn't allowed herself to previously. And she hoped that, in time, she would be able to repay them the generosity they had shown her while she was in hospital.

One Wednesday morning, when Heidi was nine months old, one such opportunity presented itself. Pippa's mobile phone rang and she sat up from the play mat to take the call. 'Hello?'

'Pippa, it's Ginie.' The background noise was distracting, as though Ginie was at an airport.

'Hi,' she said. 'Aren't you in Melbourne?'

'Yes, I've just arrived.' Ginie's tone was urgent. 'Can I ask for your help?'

'Sure.'

'I wouldn't normally trouble you with this, but since you live around the corner . . .'

'Go ahead,' said Pippa.

'Well, Rose has an appointment today for her six-month immunisations. They're overdue by three months, but I've just been so busy . . .' The line crackled. 'Sorry, I'm at a taxi rank. Look, the appointment's at eleven o'clock. I reminded Daniel about it on Monday, but I'm sure he's forgotten. I've tried his mobile six or seven times, but he's not answering. The nanny's gone shopping in the city, so she's no help.' Ginie paused and spoke in a muffled voice to a cab driver.

'Anyway,' she continued. 'I really don't want Rose to miss the appointment. We're going overseas in a fortnight.'

At the previous week's mothers' group meeting, Ginie had mentioned their upcoming family holiday to Tahiti, with the nanny in tow. Pippa had been quietly envious at the thought of lying on a beach while someone else looked after Heidi.

'Would it be too much to ask for you to go over to my house and just bang on the door and remind Daniel about the appointment?' asked Ginie. 'He's probably got his hands full of Rose and can't find his phone. Men can't multi-task.'

Pippa laughed. 'Sure. I'll pop over now.'

Ginie's house was less than two kilometres from hers, a pleasant walk along a tree-lined street that barrelled towards the coast. Pippa parked the stroller on the grass near the letterbox and lifted Heidi out. Carrying the baby on her hip, she bypassed the front door in favour of the side gate. She'd been to enough mothers' groups at Ginie's house to know her way

around. If she knocked at the front door, Daniel was unlikely
to hear. The best way to attract his attention would be via the
backyard, where an enormous kitchen and living area spilled
out onto a large patio overlooking the ocean. The family
spent most of their time out the back, reserving the front of
the house for more formal occasions.

As she walked along the hedge bordering the backyard,
she heard someone giggle. She knew the voice; it was the
infectious laughter of Nicole, Ginie's nanny. She must be back
early from her shopping trip, Pippa thought.

She rounded the hedge at the southernmost corner of the
yard and stopped dead. In the living area beyond the patio,
Nicole was seated on a lounge, wearing a figure-hugging dress
that plunged at the neckline. Her eyes were closed and Daniel
stood in front of her, board shorts slung low on his hips,
squinting through a long-lens camera. Pippa could hear the
camera's shutter clicking as he moved around her. He leaned
forward and said something to her in a low voice, prompting
her to giggle again. Rose was nowhere in sight.

Pippa immediately stepped back behind the hedge, her
heart hammering. Startled by the sudden movement, Heidi
arched her back and wailed. Pippa tried to stifle the sound
by pressing the baby against her chest, which only aggravated
her further. She could hear their panicked whispering on the
other side of the hedge. She hesitated, unsure what to do. Her
natural inclination was to bolt straight back down the side
path. But how would she explain that to Ginie? She made a
split-second decision.

'Hello?' she called out, as loud as she could. She paused,

stalling for time. Then she rounded the hedge once more, rocking Heidi on her hip. As she walked across the lawn, she focused on Heidi, making a deliberate fuss of her.

'Goodness,' she said, apologetic, as she stopped in front of the living area. 'What a racket we're making.'

Daniel stood in front of the couch, his arms folded across his bare chest, regarding her suspiciously.

'Hi Daniel,' said Pippa, endeavouring to sound relaxed. 'I'm Pippa, one of Ginie's friends from mothers' group. We met at the Fathers and Partners session last September.'

He looked confused. 'Oh yes.'

He glanced over his shoulder, towards the couch. Was Nicole hiding behind it? Pippa wondered. She desperately wanted to leave.

'Um, I had a call from Ginie this morning. She couldn't reach you on your phone.' Her eyes moved involuntarily to Daniel's chest. 'You must have been . . . in the shower.' She cleared her throat. 'She wanted me to remind you about Rose's appointment at eleven o'clock.'

Daniel looked at her blankly.

'For her immunisations,' Pippa continued. 'Ginie didn't want you to miss them, with your overseas trip and everything . . .'

'Oh.' Daniel's jaw slackened. 'I was just doing some work.' He glanced at his watch. 'Well, I guess I'd better take Rose now. Thanks for letting me know.'

'That's okay.' She smiled and edged back towards the hedge. 'I hope it's not too distressing for Rose. When Heidi had her immunisations, it wasn't much fun. Was it, madam?' She tickled Heidi in the ribs, making her squirm. She couldn't believe her powers of small talk under duress. 'Bye, then.'

She didn't wait for Daniel's response. She clasped Heidi to her chest and fled down the side path.

Later that night, Robert sat in silence as she described what she had seen.

'I don't know what to do,' she concluded. 'How do you tell a friend that her husband is cheating on her?'

Robert quaffed the last of his beer then set the bottle down. 'You don't.'

Pippa frowned. 'What, I'm just supposed to pretend I never saw it?'

'That's about right.'

'But if I was in her position,' she objected, 'I'd want to know that my husband was having sex with the nanny.'

'Well, you're *not* in her position. And you've got no idea what's going on in their relationship, Pip. Even if you did see something . . .'

Pippa gaped at him. 'What, do you think I just made it all up? That I'm some stupid housewife with nothing better to do than concoct stories about other people's husbands?'

'No, that's not what I said. It just mightn't have been quite what you *think* it was.'

Pippa snorted. 'What? With her cavorting around, pouting and giggling? Him whispering sweet nothings? I can't imagine what else it might have been.'

'He *is* a photographer. Maybe it was a legitimate shoot.'

'Oh, please.'

Robert pushed his dinner plate away. 'Look, Pippa, you've just got to be very careful about sticking your nose into other people's business.'

'I don't *want* to be involved,' she snapped. 'I didn't go over there looking for trouble. I went over to help Ginie. But I saw what I saw. They're going away next week. The bloody nanny's going with them. He'll be screwing the pair of them on holiday. How would it be acceptable for me to keep that to myself?'

He stood up. 'Look, you asked me for advice. I've told you what I think. But don't listen to me, I'm just your husband.' His eyes flashed. 'You don't want my opinion, Pippa. You want confirmation of your own. If you decide to tell Ginie, don't come crying to me when it causes a shit-fight.'

He picked up his mobile phone and car keys from the bench.

'Where are you going?'

'Out.' He slammed the front door behind him.

Pippa slumped onto the dining room table.

The longer she considered what she had seen, the less confident she became. Eyewitness accounts are notoriously unreliable, she reminded herself; a degree in psychology had taught her that. Had she just stumbled across a harmless photo shoot after all? No harm done, as Robert suggested.

But no, she would protest. It couldn't possibly have been harmless. There was too much in their body language, their proximity, their laughter. The fact that Ginie thought

Nicole had gone shopping for the day was, in itself, suspicious. But whenever Pippa concluded that she'd caught Daniel in a brazen act of infidelity, she began to fret about *how* to deliver the news to Ginie. After all, even after eight months of mothers' group meetings, she didn't feel close to her. There was an air of arrogance about Ginie that Pippa found off-putting. She was opinionated and self-confident— everything Pippa wasn't. And the truth was, Ginie frightened her a little. So Pippa procrastinated, waiting for the ideal moment to speak up.

No time was ever right, however; there were always too many others within earshot. Ginie never lingered after mothers' group, always barging off somewhere immediately after. And it was impossible to organise one-on-one catch-ups, because Ginie worked practically full-time. Indeed, she often missed mothers' group on Fridays because of work demands. And Pippa couldn't stomach just telephoning her—what exactly would she say? *Hello, Ginie, it's Pippa. I'm ringing to tell you that Daniel is doing the nanny.*

Days dragged into weeks: the more she imagined telling Ginie what she'd seen that day, the more she started to relish the fantasy. Watching Ginie's horrified face as she broke the news. *How's your perfect life looking now, Ginie?* Pippa was ashamed and appalled by herself for even *thinking* like that. It must be the PND, she told herself. The doctor said it would take at least six months to see the full effect of the medication.

Once, she'd tried casually to gauge whether Ginie had an inkling of an affair between Daniel and Nicole. She'd made up some fanciful story about considering a nanny herself, but pretending to be worried about the possibility of an attraction between Robert and the hired help. Ginie had dismissed the possibility unreservedly. Eventually, Pippa grew tired of carrying around the mental burden of it all. Crippled by uncertainty, she decided to follow Robert's advice and say nothing at all. It was better for everyone, she reasoned. At the very least, Robert would feel that she'd followed his counsel for once.

Robert. She opened her eyes, certain she'd heard the familiar sound of his ute pulling into the driveway. But that was impossible: it was only eleven o'clock in the morning. She must have fallen asleep again when she'd put Heidi down for her morning nap. She sat up on the sofa, remembering how she'd promised to call her psychiatrist. For Robert, as much as for herself.

She stood up from the couch and walked along the hallway to the front door. On his way out, Robert had slid a copy of the local paper under it. She collected it from the mat and padded back to the kitchen, glancing at the loaf of bread next to the toaster. She was eating normally again, but she didn't feel like breakfast today. She perched on a stool and turned the newspaper over.

BABY'S TRAGIC DEATH A MYSTERY declared the unusually large headline, followed by a bold sub-heading—MOTHER TURNS HER BACK, CHILD DISAPPEARS. Pippa gasped at a photograph of a smiling Astrid on Cara's knee, taken at Beachcombers. The caption read: *Cara and Astrid Jenkins in happier times.*

The article had been compiled by a junior reporter, who cited unnamed witnesses at the scene. Pippa's eyes widened as the article speculated about the possible molestation and drowning of Astrid by one of the party guests. Worse, it quoted a 'personal friend of Cara's from her mothers' group' as saying, 'I don't know why she left Astrid alone in the first place. It's very out of character.'

Pippa stared at the newspaper, her hands shaking. Had someone from the mothers' group actually *spoken* to a journalist? She wouldn't have believed it, if not for the photograph.

She slumped down onto her forearms. *Oh God, poor Cara.*

Heidi began to whimper in her cot. The day beckoned, with all its trivial permutations. How could she go through the motions of changing Heidi's nappy, spoon-feeding her porridge, reading her nursery rhymes and putting her to bed when Astrid was *dead*? And yet, she had no choice. The rhythms of Heidi's life continued, irrespective of her own needs. The world was utterly insensitive to those it had abandoned. Life goes on, ready or not.

During the day Pippa snatched every spare moment to follow the media coverage of Astrid's death. While Heidi napped at three o'clock, Pippa listened to a popular talkback radio program. She grimaced at the announcer's opening comments: '*We don't know the full details, listeners, and police investigations are continuing, but we do know that the child's mother wasn't present at the barbecue when she went missing. What are we to make of that, listeners? Nothing is more important than watching your child. Your comments, please.*'

His lines were jammed with callers for the next hour, mostly women with children themselves, expressing their deepest sympathy but . . . *'How could a mother turn her back on her child? No one could be that selfish, or that stupid. Some women just aren't fit to be mothers.'*

Pippa listened until she felt sick, then switched the radio off. *It's Cara you're talking about*, she wanted to scream. *Sweet, generous, kind-hearted Cara. She couldn't hurt a fly if she tried.*

Later in the day, she checked the internet and was shocked by the number of comments in online articles and blogs covering Astrid's death. Someone had even set up a Facebook page dedicated to the incident. There were vitriolic comments deploring Cara's neglect of Astrid, others condemning the local council for the lack of fencing around Manly Dam, and postings from people who were convinced of paedophile involvement because *'How could all those people at a party just let a child wander away?'* Pippa wept as she scrolled through dozens of posts.

Over dinner, she flicked between television channels as she guided sausages and peas into Heidi's mouth. All the commercial channels had covered the ongoing police investigation, despite the absence of any new information.

She went to bed before Robert arrived home, but lay awake, reliving the day's media coverage. When she finally heard Robert creep into the room after nine o'clock, she feigned sleep. To her relief, he simply climbed into bed and turned off the light. She couldn't bear sharing it all over again.

*

Three days later, her fingers hovered over the buttons of her mobile phone, as they had a hundred times since Sunday.

A text to Cara would be useless, she knew. What could she possibly say? How could she roll the universe into a hundred-character text message? She couldn't intrude on her grief so soon. A text to Miranda? After all, Pippa had left her with the police on Sunday night, alone. It was now Thursday and she'd heard nothing from her. God knows what had happened at the police station, or what had become of the Evian bottle. And did Miranda know that *she* had dobbed her in?

She recalled all the help the mothers' group had given her during her own time of crisis. Surely they could all pull through this together? She needed to talk to them, to share what she'd seen, to find out how they were coping. Her fingers moved over the keypad of her telephone. *Anyone welcome at my house after 10 am tomorrow*, she typed. Beachcombers just didn't seem right anymore. *I'm so sad*, she continued. Then she deleted it.

She sent the one-sentence invitation to everyone except Cara. She had no idea who might accept.

Made was the first to arrive, stepping forward to embrace Pippa on the doorstep.

'Oh.' The sound escaped from Pippa's mouth like air from a blow-up mattress. She leaned into Made's tiny frame, bowing her head. 'It's just so unfair.'

Made nodded, patting her back. 'No words,' she said. 'No words.'

Eventually, Pippa raised her head and motioned Made into the lounge room.

'Tea?' she asked, wiping her eyes.

'Thank you,' Made replied, lifting Wayan out of his stroller and onto the floor. Heidi and Wayan began to play with their usual enthusiasm, unaware that one of their number was gone forever.

Suzie arrived next, carrying Freya on her hip. Her eyes were swollen.

'Is Miranda coming?' she asked, placing Freya on the floor.

Pippa shrugged. 'I don't know.' Unsure of what else to do, she patted Suzie awkwardly on the shoulder. Everyone's fragile, she thought. Maybe this wasn't such a good idea.

Suzie slumped onto the sofa and covered her eyes with her hands.

'I'm making tea . . .' started Pippa.

'No thanks,' said Suzie. 'I can't keep anything down.'

Just then, Ginie walked through the door. She was carrying Rose, who waved at the other children.

'Oh, I thought you'd be . . .'

'Working? No.' Ginie looked at Pippa, her voice unsteady. 'I've taken the week off. I need to be near Rose. I can't let her out of my sight.'

Pippa nodded, understanding. She felt the same about Heidi.

Ginie sat down on the sofa next to Suzie. Rose immediately crawled off her knee and onto the floor in pursuit of a green plastic caterpillar.

'I didn't ask Cara, obviously,' said Pippa. 'I just didn't think . . .'

'No, it would be too hard for her,' sighed Suzie, waving a hand towards the children. 'But we should . . . I don't know, try to do something for her.' She stifled a sob.

'But what *can* we do?' asked Ginie. 'Nothing's going to bring Astrid back.'

Pippa frowned. 'I don't know, we should stand with Cara somehow. Let her know she's not to blame . . . that she's not alone.' Pippa remembered how isolated she'd felt from the mothers' group once, trapped in her own private hell.

'But she *is* to blame, there's no way around that.' Ginie's voice was low and controlled. 'Cara should never have left Astrid for that long.'

Suzie gasped. 'How can you *say* that, Ginie? The only thing Cara did was leave Astrid in our care, her mothers' group. We've all done that before. If she's to blame, we're *all* to blame.'

'Oh come *on*,' snapped Ginie. 'It's not like we're registered child carers. None of us had any formal responsibility in relation to Astrid. Look, Cara's a nice person, don't get me wrong. But unless some paedophile came along and kidnapped Astrid, there's only one culprit here and that's Cara, whether we like it or not.'

Pippa's hand flew to her mouth. The conversation was spiralling out of control. 'Look, we're all upset. I . . . I think we should all take a breath.' Her mouth went dry. 'Astrid died last Sunday. We don't know exactly what happened. We should let the police investigate before we . . .'

Her phone beeped receipt of an SMS. She glanced down. The message was from Miranda. Pippa read it several times over before saying quietly, 'It's Miranda. She's in a drug and alcohol clinic.'

'What?' Ginie sounded incredulous.

Suzie made a small sound, and her mouth dropped open.

Pippa read the text aloud. '*Won't be there today. Admitted to Delamere Clinic D&A unit yesterday. It's okay to tell the others. Willem is here. Hendrika is looking after the boys. I'm so sorry for everything.*'

'What the fuck is going on?'

Pippa hesitated, considering how much she should reveal. 'I don't know for sure,' she said, 'but I think Miranda might be an alcoholic.'

'No,' objected Ginie. 'I don't believe it.' Her eyes narrowed. 'What makes you say that?'

'You know that Evian bottle she carries everywhere? It's not water in there.' Pippa felt her cheeks redden under Ginie's gaze. 'I happened to taste some of it last Sunday.'

'Oh?'

'There was neat alcohol in it. Vodka or gin.'

'So what?' Ginie demanded. 'We all had a few drinks, didn't we?' She looked around the room. 'It doesn't mean we're alcoholics. That's a big assumption to make.'

Pippa sighed. 'Look, this is what I know. There was neat alcohol in Miranda's water bottle at the birthday party last weekend. And I heard Cara ask her to watch Astrid. The police took Miranda down to the station for a formal interview on Sunday night.'

'What?' Ginie exploded. 'Did she have any legal representation?'

Pippa shrugged, suddenly weary. 'I don't think so. She went willingly.'

'And did *you* tell the police about the alcohol?'

Pippa felt as if she was being cross-examined. She nodded.

'God almighty, Pippa, what were you *thinking*?' Ginie's eyes flashed. 'You realise that this might lead to a manslaughter charge against Miranda?'

Pippa's stomach clenched with fear. She'd had no idea it might come to that. 'I . . . I just thought it was the right thing to do,' she stammered. 'To tell the police everything.'

'Oh, *please*.' Ginie shook her head. 'I don't care how drunk Miranda was, or anyone else for that matter. Mothers are only asked to do one thing in life, and that's to look after their children. It's pretty simple stuff. If your *mother* doesn't look out for you in this world, who will?' A single tear streaked down Ginie's face; she swiped it away angrily. 'Last weekend, it was *Cara* who walked away from Astrid. Sad as it is, *she's* the one to blame. But congratulations, Pippa, you may well have ruined Miranda's life too.'

Suzie began to cry, weeping into her hands. Made sat statue-like on the floor, her head tilted to one side, as if listening to a barely audible sound.

Pippa's heart thudded in her chest; she could almost hear the rush of blood between its chambers. No one had ever spoken to her like that.

'I . . . I just told the police everything I saw,' she faltered.

'My parents brought me up to tell the truth.' She'd always known that Ginie didn't suffer fools gladly, but the last time she'd felt like this, she'd been on the wrong side of the school bully.

'You know what I think, Ginie?' she ventured. 'What happened on Sunday to Cara, it could have happened to *anyone*. It could have been me, it could have been you. But maybe you left all human empathy behind at law school.'

Pippa couldn't believe she'd said the words, or how good it felt.

Ginie stared at her a moment. 'It could have been *you*, for sure.' Her tone was cool. 'But not me. I'd never have left Rose exposed like that. No sensible mother would.'

Pippa bristled. 'So says the woman with a full-time nanny. *You* leave Rose in someone else's care all the time. Nicole sees more of Rose than you do.'

'That's a low blow.'

'Stop it,' cried Suzie. 'Just stop it now, both of you.'

Made reached across and patted Suzie's hand.

But Pippa wasn't finished. She'd put up with a year of Ginie's comments, her self-righteous assertions. This attack on Cara was too much. Pippa stood up and plucked Heidi from behind the sofa. 'Things aren't always totally in your control, Ginie,' she said. 'Sometimes life gets away from you. Things happen that you can't predict. Maybe you *think* you've got it all worked out, but you don't.'

Ginie snorted. 'Risk management is my living. People pay thousands of dollars for my expertise. What would *I* know?'

Pippa's fury erupted. 'Well, if you need *evidence* that you haven't got everything under control, go home and ask Daniel what he's been doing with the nanny.'

Ginie's iPhone clattered to the floor.

'What did you say?'

Pippa met her gaze. 'You heard me. That day I went around to your house, when you were in Melbourne and Rose needed her immunisations? I saw them together.'

Ginie's face was ashen. 'No,' she said. 'Daniel's got a lot of faults, but he isn't a cheat.'

Pippa shrugged. 'I saw what I saw.'

Ginie stood staring at Pippa, her lips moving almost imperceptibly.

Then she began to walk around the room, retrieving her belongings: Rose's shoes, the nappy bag, her car keys.

'I don't know what you *think* you saw,' said Ginie eventually. 'But let's not forget you've been diagnosed with a *mental illness*.'

Their eyes locked.

Ginie picked up Rose and strode across the rug. When she reached the door she turned. 'I feel sorry for you, Pippa,' she said. 'I know the depression's been hard on you. But I don't need to put up with that sort of bullshit.'

And then she was gone.

Pippa sat shell-shocked on the sofa. A great wave of relief had flooded through her as soon as she'd uttered the words. She'd felt euphoric, triumphant, a messenger of truth. But now, staring after Ginie, she felt nothing at all. Like an empty vessel, drained of life.

Suzie sat on the floor, wide-eyed. Made sat next to her, head bowed. Looking at them both, Pippa was painfully struck by the realisation of what she'd just done. Not only to Ginie, but to the mothers' group itself. How had it got so out of hand? What should have been a moment of shared grief and understanding had somehow descended into venom and vitriol. And *she* was responsible.

A moment later, she was weeping, hiccuping into her hands. Made moved to the lounge and put an arm around her.

'I'm sorry, I'm sorry,' Pippa repeated. 'I shouldn't have said any of it.'

Suzie offered her a tissue. 'Don't be. We're all human. It was bound to happen with Ginie. It's been coming for a long time.'

Made looked thoughtful. 'Death hard for people,' she said. 'People say wrong things, because too hard at first. But time passes, things get better. Maybe Ginie come back, some time.'

Pippa simply couldn't imagine it.

One month later, on the psychiatrist's recommendation, Pippa increased the dosage of her antidepressants.

'It's just a stop-gap measure,' he assured her. 'You won't be on them forever. You've been through a significant trauma. Your husband's right: you need some extra support right now. You were making some excellent progress before Astrid's death. But now you need to let yourself grieve *safely*.' The psychiatrist paused, studying her. 'You have to give your-self permission to grieve, Pippa. Part of the reason you got post-natal depression was that your old life, the life you loved before Heidi arrived, disappeared when she was born. And you didn't *allow* yourself to grieve its passing. This time, go with it. Think about how you're going to *recognise* your grief, how you're going to honour it. Because it's only when we've honoured our grief that we can learn to let it go.'

When Robert returned home from work later that day, Pippa sat at the kitchen table opposite him, dreading a disagreement.

'I don't want to go back to work next month,' she announced, staring at the tablecloth. She'd taken a full year of maternity leave, and a further eight weeks of accrued annual leave.

Robert's mouth opened in surprise. 'But . . . you haven't got any more paid leave. And you're better now. I thought you wanted your old life back.'

'I do. I mean, I did.' She sighed. 'It's complicated.'

With the help of her psychiatrist, medication, and the PND support group, she was feeling a lot better about life, about mothering. It was as if she'd been given a second chance, and that was precisely the issue. Now that she'd been given her life back, she didn't want to spend it at work.

'Rob, I feel like I'm only starting to be a proper mum now,' she began. 'I'm actually starting to *enjoy* Heidi. I don't want to rush back to work and miss out on her first years.' She looked out the kitchen window, at the vegetable patch they'd just planted. 'Heidi's only young once. Who knows what the future will bring? We only get one chance. Astrid's shown me that. I don't want to have any regrets.' Pippa stared at the kitchen table. 'I know it's not what we agreed. I know we're treading water financially. I'll go back to work if you say so.' The possibility brought tears to her eyes.

'We'll make ends meet,' he said, reaching across the table for her hand. 'Call your work tomorrow. Explain the situation. Tell them about the surgery, about Astrid. They don't know any of it, do they?'

She shook her head.

'Ask them if they'll extend your leave again. If they say no, we'll find a way around it.' He squeezed her hand. 'You deserve a second crack at motherhood.'

Against all odds, her work agreed to a further six months of unpaid leave.

Life felt new again, as though blinding scales had been sloughed from her eyes. Suddenly she saw it all. The incredible beauty of Heidi asleep, translucent lids twitching as she dreamed. The intense physicality of Heidi awake, striving to master her own body and the world around her. The breathtaking power of her smile, the beauty of her tiny fingers exploring tinier spaces. The crushing pain of separation from Heidi, outstripped only by the pleasure of reunion. She could smell Heidi, taste her, feel her embedded within her being. Only death could separate them, and that prospect was unbearable.

She remembered the early months of Heidi's life, when every aspect of her own life seemed barren, when nothing had felt right or normal. Now, it felt entirely natural that she should seek the best for Heidi. Pippa wasn't religious, but she suddenly recalled the biblical message she'd had drummed into her at school all those years before: *For God so loved the world that he gave his one and only Son, that whoever believes in him shall not perish but have eternal life.* It was only now, as a mother, that the concept held any potency. If there was in fact a God, she mused, it seemed entirely befitting that He was a parent. What else could divine love be, if not parental? A love so fierce, so willingly sacrificial, so self-abasing and abiding? The love between adults, siblings or friends all paled into insignificance compared to parental love. She'd do anything to prevent pain in Heidi's life. Only a superhuman force could allow their child to suffer for the benefit of others.

When she looked at Heidi now, she felt as if she'd discovered life's true meaning. She shuddered to think of the hell she'd once experienced, standing alone next to Heidi's cot, listening to her scream. She didn't know how, she didn't know why, but somehow she had been delivered from that dark place. By grace, it seemed, for it wasn't of her own doing. By Astrid, perhaps. And she wanted to acknowledge that somehow.

She gravitated towards Made, seeking out her company on Friday mornings, in place of their usual mothers' group meetings. Suzie sometimes came, Ginie never did. More than two months after Astrid's death, she finally asked the question that had been lingering in her mind.

'Made, when you visited me in hospital, you brought some flowers in a woven container,' she began.

Made nodded.

'It had incense and other things in it. What was it?'

Made looked apologetic. 'I hope you not mind,' she began. 'It is Hindu offering for healing. You not like?'

'No, no,' said Pippa. 'It was beautiful, I still have it. In fact, I wondered if you might be able to help me.' She blushed. 'I'm not a Hindu, but . . . I'd like to give thanks for my healing, for Heidi. And to pray for Astrid and Cara. Could I ask you to help me do that?' She wasn't entirely sure what she was asking.

Made smiled. 'You come next week to my house. We make prayers together.'

And so it was that Pippa found herself in Made's backyard, a batik sarong wrapped around her waist, holding an offering in her hands. She followed Made's directions and placed the basket on the shrine. Incense billowed around her as she gazed up at the parasol, its tassels dangling in the breeze.

Made rang a small silver bell three times and brought her hands together in the prayer position. The chiming petered into silence and, suddenly, there was no sound at all. Not a breath of wind rustling in the leaves, no birds twittering in branches, no distant hum of suburban traffic. Pippa closed her eyes, submitting herself to the emptiness.

An image of Astrid and Cara emerged from the darkness. Goosebumps crept across the backs of her arms. A small white bird darted across the canvas of her mind and ferried Astrid up, up, into an endless blue sky. The image of Cara remained, her face twisted in anguish. A warm orb of light descended from the same sky, hovering over Cara, nursing her gently in her grief.

Pippa couldn't tell how long she spent in that place. Eventually, the image of Cara faded. As Pippa breathed in and out, she felt every part of her being release. All the despair of the past year seemed to drain from her body. Her heart felt light and warm. She was grateful beyond words.

Heidi gave a sudden shriek. Pippa opened her eyes with a start. The moment was broken, but perfect nonetheless. Heidi was waving her pudgy fists in the air and grinning.

Pippa grinned back.

Made rang her silver bell three times again, then opened her eyes and stood up. She brushed a stray gum leaf from her sarong.

'We visit Cara,' she said. 'The ancestors tell me.'

Pippa nodded. 'It felt like that for me too. Cara and Astrid were right there in front of me. Thank you, Made, for praying with me.'

Made shook her head. 'No, you no understand. We make visit to Cara soon. It right thing to do, ancestors say.'

Pippa swallowed. The idea of seeing Cara was too painful for words, but looking into Made's face, she knew it was the right thing to do.

Cara

Cara awoke with a start to the sound of crying. Her own, or Astrid's? She couldn't be sure. Disoriented, she pulled at the cord dangling above her head. The blind whizzed upwards with a speed that jarred. Light filtered through the heavy green vines that grew along the trellis beyond their bedroom window. Dust motes swirled in patches of pale winter sunlight. It was early afternoon, she guessed.

A bunch of lilies, delivered the day before, were arranged in a vase on her bedside table. Bulbous crimson stamens jutted from yellow throats. Their pungent, musky odour was almost sexual. She'd disposed of the card just as soon as she'd read it, but she couldn't remember why. She sat up in bed and listened for noises from Astrid's room, but heard nothing.

And then it hit her. The crushing awareness, storming through the tranquillising fog of her prescription sedatives. No sounds of crying or laughter from Astrid's bedroom now. No use for the jumpsuits and tiny dresses still neatly folded in drawers, untouched. No wayward hairclips in the bathtub, stuffed toys in the car, dolls' houses or finger puppets. The one she loved most in the world, her shining star, was dead.

She lay back on the pillow and stared at the ceiling. The medication had done something to her tears. It was August; Astrid had only been gone three months and yet she couldn't cry as much. But the desolate feeling was still there; it always would be. The creeping, agonising consciousness of Astrid's lonely death in a dirty dam and her own flippant ignorance as it happened. The endless imaginings of Astrid's final moments: the struggle for air where there was only water; arms reaching for an outstretched hand; confusion, per-haps—then nothing.

Cara's only respite was the numb haze of sedated sleep.

Her eyes wandered to the lilies again. Those flowers are from Ravi, she thought suddenly. Yes, Ravi had sent her flowers every week for the last three months, ever since it hap-pened. Richard had said nothing, dutifully delivering them to her bedside. Hoping, perhaps, that she would stand up from her bed to accept them. Watching silently as she tore the card into tiny pieces.

Richard was racked with grief himself, that was clear. His eyes were dull, his face lined, his shoulders stooped. And yet he never failed to bring her three meals a day, leave a newspa-per at the foot of her bed, or ask her how she was feeling. Every morning, he would climb the stairs to the bedroom they used to share, open the door and arrange his face into a smile.

'Nice day,' he'd say, or some other banality.

Ignoring her silence, he would potter about the room.

Opening blinds and windows, removing the previous night's dinner dishes, laying out a fresh change of clothes.

'Well, I'm off to work,' he'd announce, when there was nothing else to say. Then he would bend down and kiss her cheek. The mild scent of his aftershave reminded her of her grandfather.

Despite her silence, he'd turn at the door. 'Call me if you need me, Cara.'

And she would nod, though they both knew she never would.

He was a gentleman, Richard, even in tragedy. Why had she failed to recognise this before her world imploded? Why had she harboured useless fantasies of a life without him? It was something she would never truly understand, or forgive, of herself.

She'd thought she'd finished with Ravi on his wedding day.

The foyer of the university's Great Hall was filled with familiar-looking people she couldn't quite place. One even greeted her like an old friend.

'Cara!' the woman gushed, thrusting an order of service into her hand. 'You look fantastic! My God, how long's it been?'

Cara searched the wide blue eyes for some relic of her student past.

'Too long,' she replied. 'You look lovely yourself.' She peered into the chapel. 'Which side's the groom's?'

'Oh, you know Ravi,' said the woman affectionately. 'There *are* no sides. Sit wherever you'd like.'

'Right,' Cara replied. 'We'll catch up later then?'

But the woman was already ushering other guests over the timber threshold and into the hall's darkened interior.

You know Ravi.

Cara was conscious of the clicking of her heels over the black and white marble. Guests sat on wooden benches arranged in rows, like church pews, talking in hushed voices. A large table was positioned on the far side of the hall, draped in purple bunting. Four solid white candles, each festooned with braided marigolds, rested on top. An Indian touch, at odds with the Westminster-style pipe organ that towered above them.

Clutching her handbag, Cara walked along the red carpeted aisle, glancing around for a seat. For a moment she imagined, in spite of herself, traversing its length as Ravi's bride. She turned into a row and squeezed past several other guests.

'Excuse me,' she whispered, careful to catch no one's eye.

She sat down heavily. Sweat was beginning to trickle from her armpits, staining the delicate fabric of her dress. She closed her eyes, concentrating on her breathing. *It's just like any other wedding.*

The murmuring of guests subsided as the opening bars of Pachelbel's Canon echoed around the hall. Cara turned to see a string quartet tucked in a corner near the door. How very traditional; how unlike Ravi. A lot must have changed in a year.

Several figures had emerged at the front of the hall and were loitering beyond the reaches of the candlelight. She strained to see the tallest figure. It was Ravi; his profile was unmistakable. He appeared to be talking to a man in long robes, an officiating celebrant of some description. Then suddenly Ravi stepped into the light, flashing an exuberant smile. Cara's stomach somersaulted, as it always had, at the sight of that smile. Flawless white teeth against soft olive skin, hazel eyes laughing at some private joke. He held himself with the same air of quiet confidence she'd always admired, a combination of heritage, humility and sheer hard work. After all this time, he was still her Ravi.

Her heart sank as the music grew louder and a spear of daylight illuminated the carpeted aisle. *Here comes the bride.* The guests rose from their seats with a collective shuffle. Cara craned her neck to see the object of Ravi's devotion.

She was graceful, that was for sure. Fine-featured, diminutive, like a ballet dancer. Her lace gown clung naturally to her, like lichen on a slender tree. Her hair was caramel-coloured, not unlike Cara's, pinned in a classic French twist. Cara held her breath as she passed, unable to fault her. The sighs of admiration were nauseating.

The service was surprisingly old school: a marriage liturgy adapted from the Book of Common Prayer, interspersed with several poetry readings and a token reference to the Hindu Upanishads. A bland instrumental piece marked the signing of the register before the celebrant turned to offer his final, formulaic pronouncement.

'Friends, I proudly pronounce Ravi and Tess . . . man and wife.'

Spontaneous applause rippled through the crowd. The

couple smiled at one another and moved together for a long, lingering kiss. Cara winced as someone behind her wolf-whistled.

And then they were walking down the aisle together, hands swinging like happy children.

The reception was held in one of the university's original buildings, a two-storey sandstone edifice with gabled windows and a manicured rose garden. The garden was off-limits to students, accessible only by a staircase descending from a marble balcony on the second floor. But Cara could remember scaling that six-foot hedge with Ravi one evening after a trivia competition, several months after they'd first met. They'd tumbled down the other side, breaking a bottle of cheap champagne they'd intended to drink among the roses. Covered in sticky pink alcohol, they'd cackled in the darkness until a surly security officer shone a torch in their faces and told them to bugger off. Later that same night, they came dangerously close to kissing at Redfern station. Ravi leaned towards her, his breath warm with alcohol and a faint hint of spice.

'Cara, you're beautiful,' he whispered, his lips centimetres from hers.

'Ravi, you're drunk,' she replied.

And then her train arrived, a wall of air billowing from the tunnel at the platform's end. Brakes squealed, automatic doors hissed open and shut. She sat in an empty carriage, smiling out at Ravi through the window. He stood on the platform as the train lurched forward, a curious expression on his face.

It was the same expression he would wear years later, when gazing at his new bride.

They'd met in a cultural studies class called 'Women, Madness and Medicine'. Cara was in the first semester of a graduate diploma in media studies, full of zeal to change the world. Ravi was in his second year of a Masters of Public Health, on a federal government scholarship for talented postgraduates from emerging economies.

It was the third week of first semester, and Cara was delivering a stinging critique of psychiatry's intervention in the lives of female patients.

'And in conclusion,' she declared to the tutorial group, 'biological psychiatry is a totalising epistemological paradigm that offers one-pill solutions for women, failing to recognise the systemic social issues that inform female mental health.'

She shuffled her papers, self-conscious, while her fellow students offered up a polite round of applause. Glancing around the room, she noticed an exotic-looking male at the rear, clapping with gusto. She looked away, but her eyes were drawn back to him. As her gaze met his, he did an outrageous thing: he *winked* at her. She lifted her chin and avoided further eye contact.

The tutor, a mousy-looking postgraduate, stood to address the class.

'Wonderful presentation, Cara,' she said. 'Questions, anyone?'

She nodded towards the rear of the room. Cara knew exactly where it would lead.

Mr Exotic smiled. 'It was a magnificent presentation,' he said, with a delicious British Indian accent. 'The parallels between patriarchy and psychiatry are interesting. But, Cara, do you honestly believe that there is *no* biological basis for mental health issues like schizophrenia in females? That these conditions are exclusively a product of women's societal context?'

Cara reddened. Her name had rolled off his tongue so naturally. His accent was distracting.

'Well, no, I don't agree. I mean, not entirely,' she fumbled. 'But I'm no expert on schizophrenia.' She thumbed her tutorial paper. 'Are you?'

'No expert at all.' He smiled. 'But my medical studies suggest that most mental illnesses have a biological component. Not every sickness of the mind is sociological.' He paused. 'But, then, perhaps I am complicit in a patriarchal medical system that sees the normal human being as male.'

Several students sniggered. Cara couldn't tell if he was ridiculing her. She stared at the back wall, wishing the tutorial would end.

Eventually, it did. Students streamed out the door, chatting and laughing. As Cara slid her presentation back into its plastic sheath, she sensed his presence. She looked up only when he cleared his throat.

'The way you constructed your arguments was impressive,' he said. 'I'd like to hear more of your thoughts on the medical system.' His formality was disarming.

'Oh?' She wanted him to flounder.

'But only if you are prepared to share them,' he added. 'I

think doctors can learn a lot from the humanities and social sciences.'

'I'm sure that's true.' She zipped up her satchel and walked towards the door.

'Wait.' He jogged to catch up with her. 'I'm Ravi.' He thrust a hand towards her. 'I was captivated by your paper, Cara. We surgeons are notorious for our bluntness.'

Cara stopped. He'd used her name again, in the same sentence as the word 'captivated'. And had he just said he was a surgeon? She turned to face him and couldn't help but smile. She wasn't good at pretending.

'Do you drink coffee?' he asked.

'No,' she replied. 'I mean, I don't like the taste. But I drink other things. Chai, tea, you know . . .' She blushed, fearing she sounded desperate.

'Do you want to go to Holme?' The building had a café and was within easy walking distance.

'Great,' she said. 'But my next class starts in thirty minutes.'

'Don't worry,' he assured her. 'This won't take long.'

And he was right. It hadn't taken more than half an hour for Cara to begin to fall for Ravi.

Over their first cup of chai, she'd learned something of his background. At twenty-eight, he had already completed a medical degree and surgical training in India. Intending to return to his home village to practise, he'd been surprised by the offer of a postgraduate scholarship in Australia.

'Fortune smiled on me that day,' he said.

Cara doubted it had anything to do with luck. 'Don't you miss your family?'

He nodded. 'Yes. But my mother and sister are very strong women, Cara. My country is not like Australia. Have you ever been to India?'

She shook her head. 'I'd like to.'

'It's very basic in Gudda, my village. It's unusual for someone like me to end up here. They were all amazed when I went to university in Delhi. They didn't think Australia would be next.' He laughed aloud. 'My family is very proud.'

She couldn't imagine how hard he must have worked to find himself here, drinking chai in a student café at the University of Sydney. By comparison, she was impossibly mediocre. From an average middle-class family, with two white Anglo-Saxon parents and a wayward younger brother. She'd grown up in the white-picket-fence suburb of Seaforth and attended an Anglican private school. And her world might have been limited to that, had she not won a Rotary scholarship in Year Eleven that took her to Papua New Guinea. That six-month stay had changed her forever. She'd been shocked by the poverty, the lack of education, the level of preventable disease. And she'd returned from the experience determined to help improve the standard of living in the world's poorest nations. After school, she'd completed an honours degree in international development. Then she'd started on a graduate diploma of media studies, in the hope of becoming a social justice journalist.

'Journalism is a noble calling,' said Ravi when she shared her ambition. 'The free press is the only true basis for civil society.'

Encouraged by his interest, she asked if she might interview him about his experience as a 'new arrival' in Australia for *Honi Soit*, the campus newspaper. They'd swapped telephone numbers—he shared a flat in Glebe with an engineering student—and arranged to meet again after the following week's cultural studies class.

Cara hadn't known it at the time, but that first cup of chai was the beginning of a ten-year friendship.

'Good evening, all.' A disembodied voice came over the PA system. 'My name is Michael Hughes. Not only am I the lovely bride's brother, but it's my great pleasure to be your master of ceremonies this evening.'

Cara shifted in her seat, straining to see the source of the voice. A thirty-something man was standing behind a rostrum near the bridal table. He had the same waif-like quality as Tess, but it wasn't nearly as attractive in a man.

She leaned back in her chair, steeling herself for the predictable catalogue of announcements and speeches to follow. What was I thinking, she wondered, attending this reception at all? The ladies' room beckoned. She pushed back her chair and struggled upright.

'Excuse me,' she muttered to no one in particular.

It felt as though two hundred pairs of eyes were trained upon her as she picked her way between the tables in the semi-darkness. The MC was waxing lyrical about the bride and groom. Suddenly a waiter serving entrees veered into her path, balancing a stack of plates.

'*Sheeet*,' he muttered, trying to dodge her. His evasive action was too late; the plates slid from his grip and crashed to the floor, splintering into tiny pieces.

'*Sheeeeeeet*,' the waiter groaned again, glaring at Cara.

The MC stopped mid-sentence, and the bridal party turned to stare. Cara dropped to the floor and began to pick at the shards, desperately hoping Ravi hadn't seen her.

'Don't,' said a voice nearby. A smooth white hand reached across hers. Cara looked up into kind eyes. 'Don't,' he repeated. 'I'm sure he can clean it up himself. Here . . .' He passed her a napkin. 'You've got some sauce down your front.' She looked down and gasped. A giant streak of brown was smeared across her cleavage, dripping onto her dress.

'Oh God.' She sponged desperately at the mark.

The pale eyes smiled at her. She began to back away.

'Um . . . sorry. And, thank you,' she said, obscuring her chest with her handbag.

She bolted back to the table and sank into her chair. Grateful for the darkness, she joined the crowd in applauding the matron of honour, who proceeded to regale the crowd with tales of Tess's schoolgirl antics on the hockey field. It all sounded very banal.

Then suddenly Ravi was at the microphone, adjusting its position to accommodate his height. He pulled a sheaf of speaking notes from his pocket and grinned at the audience with trademark casualness.

'The first time I met Tess . . .' he began.

The room seemed to contract around Cara. The walls leaned inwards, threatening to collapse. The audible thud of her heart overrode Ravi's words. She could hear voices gibbering in the distance, but couldn't decipher them.

*

After their exchange on the railway platform, her friendship with Ravi had deepened amid tutorials, trivia nights and work on the campus newspaper. But they'd remained friends and no more. Cara had replayed that night over and over in her mind, recalling Ravi's declaration. Had she offended him by her dismissal? Whatever the reason, Ravi had never again strayed into romantic territory, and they spoke no further about it.

All that changed, however, on the night of Ravi's graduation.

They'd been friends for nine months and Ravi had surprised her with an invitation to his graduation ceremony.

'My flatmate's coming along, but I wondered . . .' He paused. Cara thought she detected a flush of pink creeping across his olive cheeks. 'Would you do me the honour of attending my graduation ceremony?'

'I'd love to.'

On the afternoon of Ravi's graduation, she paid special attention to her appearance. 'He's got no family in Australia,' she reasoned, applying an extra coat of mascara. 'There's no one else to invite.'

The Masters in Public Health was a relatively new course and Ravi was one of just twenty students to graduate. Cara had sat proudly in the third row of the Great Hall, amid parents, siblings and spouses, her camera poised. As he'd tipped his mortarboard at the vice-chancellor and turned to leave the stage, his gaze had zeroed in on Cara. Flustered, she failed to take a photograph at all and, instead, rose to her feet and clapped. She sat down almost as quickly as she'd stood up, embarrassed.

'He looks lovely,' whispered a matronly woman seated to her right. 'You must be very proud.'

'Yes, I am,' she said, blushing. It was only then, talking about Ravi to a complete stranger, that she realised she was in love with him.

The graduation was followed by refreshments in the quadrangle under a billowing white marquee. Cara nibbled at a chicken sandwich, but only managed a few mouthfuls. As she sipped her second glass of champagne, Ravi waved at her from the other side of the marquee.

'Cara,' Ravi called. He gestured towards a dishevelled-looking young man at his side. 'This is my flatmate, Paul.'

'Hello,' said Cara.

'Hi,' Paul replied.

Ravi nodded towards the lawn. 'There's my photo call. I won't be a moment.'

Paul was a subdued character and conversation was a challenge. Her attempts at polite chit-chat were met with monosyllabic responses, but she persisted out of courtesy. Eventually, when Paul went to the bar, Cara drifted over to the other side of the marquee where the graduates were posing for photographs. Some threw their caps in the air, some kissed their lovers, others linked arms with friends and cheered at the camera.

'Hello,' said a soft voice in her ear.

She turned and smiled at Ravi. 'Congratulations, Doctor.'

'Do you want to get going?'

'Yes, please.'

He took her hand and they waved goodbye to Paul, who was still loitering near the bar.

'He's not a very forthcoming person,' Ravi said, apologetically. 'But he's been a good flatmate.'

They'd walked quickly to Ravi's terrace on Glebe Point Road. Inside, a gloomy hallway led to a set of creaking stairs. At the top, Ravi turned and, with a hint of self-consciousness in his voice, asked, 'Um, would you like a cup of chai?'

'No thanks,' she said quickly.

He opened his bedroom door and turned on a bedside lamp. He clearly hadn't planned a seduction. The bed was unmade, clothes were stacked in uneven piles along one wall and medical textbooks were strewn across the floor. A balcony lay beyond the window, several towels strung across its cast-iron balustrade.

'Sorry for the mess,' he said.

Cara shrugged. The state of his room was inconsequential.

And then suddenly he was in front of her, their faces almost touching.

'You *are* beautiful, Cara.'

She stared at him, speechless. It had been nine months since that moment on the station platform.

He lifted her hand to his cheek.

They kissed first with curiosity, then with increasing intensity. He pulled her onto the unmade bed and lowered himself next to her. They writhed fully clothed until, finally, Cara sat up and unbuttoned her shirt.

Sometime later they were startled by a knock at the door. Cara pulled a sheet over her chest and Ravi leaped from the bed.

'Who is it?'

'It's Paul, mate. Sorry.'

Cara frowned. Paul must have been downstairs for a while. Cara hadn't heard anything except Ravi's breathing.

'Your mum's on the phone from India,' he called through the door. 'She's rung twice and I put her off. I knew you were . . . busy. But she sounds a bit pissed off. She's still on the line.'

Ravi sighed. 'I'll be down in a moment.'

Cara listened to Paul's retreating footsteps. Did Ravi *really* have to take the call from his mother?

'My mother rarely rings,' he explained, sensing her disquiet.

'Okay.' She leaned across the bed and began groping about for her underwear, holding the sheet to her chest.

'A passion killer,' he said, with a wry smile.

'A little, but that's okay.' She pulled on her blouse. 'I'll go. Thank you for a lovely night.' She stood up from the bed, feeling rather foolish.

'Cara.'

Ravi stood shirtless in front of her. He put a smooth hand under her chin, forcing her to look into his eyes. 'It's been the night of my life.'

She smiled, relieved. 'I'll show myself out.'

She floated all the way to the railway station, her heart full of Ravi.

The next day, an ordinary Saturday in November, Cara's world looked completely different. Colours seemed brighter, the weekend papers more entertaining, a phone call from her brother—as usual, asking for money—more tolerable. Everything, from the junk mail in her letterbox to the unopened television guide, seemed full of promise. Ravi didn't telephone, but he would call on Sunday afternoon, she was sure.

By Sunday night, there'd still been no call from Ravi. She settled in front of the television with a bowl of macaroni cheese. He was probably just giving her a respectable amount of space, she reasoned. She drank half a bottle of red wine, watched a war documentary, then went to bed.

He didn't ring on Monday, or Tuesday. She couldn't make any sense of it. Didn't he feel the same way she did? Had she put him off somehow, without even knowing it? He didn't attend their usual Wednesday night trivia session at Manning Bar and no one in the group knew where he was. By Friday afternoon, her confusion had been replaced by anger. *What sort of bastard is he, not calling for a week?*

On Saturday morning, she picked up the telephone. Paul answered within three rings.

'Hi Paul, it's Cara. Is Ravi there?'

'No,' said Paul, monosyllabic as ever.

'Do you know when he'll be back?'

'No.'

'Well, tell him I rang, will you?' She put down the telephone.

Another week passed without Ravi returning her call. Cara's anger began to dissipate, replaced by gnawing regret. How had she misjudged the situation between them so badly? And if he didn't want a relationship, why couldn't he tell her to her face?

The following weekend, Cara tried telephoning again. She dialled Ravi's number, a cold pit in her stomach.

'Paul,' she said quietly, when Ravi's flatmate picked up the phone, 'it's Cara. I'm having trouble getting in touch with Ravi. Is he there?'

'No.'

'Paul,' she urged, 'please, can you help me?'

Paul was silent for a moment. 'He's disappeared. And he's left me to cover the rent.'

'What do you mean?'

'He just packed up his things and bloody nicked off, that's what I mean.'

'When?'

'The morning after his graduation. I got up and saw the taxi drive off.'

Cara was stunned. 'Why?'

'No idea—you tell me. You were the last person to see him.'

Cara attempted to digest Paul's words. Her mind reeled. Gone? Without saying where or why? It made no sense.

'I can't imagine what's happened,' she said. Tears sprang to her eyes. 'I hope he's okay.'

Paul was silent.

'Um, well, if you hear from him, tell him that I'm trying to contact him, please?'

Paul grunted an acknowledgement.

Cara replaced the handset and stared into space. Was Ravi in some kind of trouble?

*

Three weeks later, the telephone rang. It was Paul.

'Have you heard from Ravi?' she asked, breathless.

'No,' said Paul. 'Nothing.'

'Oh.'

She bit her lip, fighting back tears.

'Do you want to see a movie?'

Cara paused. 'What for?'

'Because uni's finished,' he replied. '*Witching Hour* is supposed to be good.'

And then it dawned on her. Paul had called to ask her out on a *date*.

'No, thanks.' Her tone was curt. 'It's just that Ravi and me, we're . . . well, we were . . . Anyway, no, thanks.' She didn't need to explain herself. 'Goodbye, Paul.' She put down the phone.

Weeks became months and, slowly, the first insult of loss began to loosen its grip. Cara called over to Ravi's house and, with Paul loitering behind her, looked over Ravi's room. There was nothing to suggest anything except an orderly departure. Most of his personal effects had been taken, with a few large items left behind, like the wardrobe and the bed. He'd even stripped the sheets. There had been no calls from India, Paul said, nothing to suggest that Ravi had been missed by his family. Cara nodded mechanically as Paul informed her that a new tenant would be moving into the room the following week.

'Do you want Ravi's bed?' he asked. 'Since you two were . . .'

She shook her head.

'Good. I'll sell it on eBay.'

She'd sent a dozen emails to Ravi, all of which went unanswered. In a last-ditch attempt to find him, Cara visited the university student centre and explained her situation to a grey-haired bureaucrat who peered over his spectacles with a disapproving air.

'I can't give out that sort of personal information about students unless you're next of kin,' he said. 'Privacy laws.'

Cara's lips began to tremble.

The bureaucrat looked uncomfortable. He pushed his spectacles over the bridge of his nose, then began tapping at his keyboard. After several minutes of silence, he squinted at his screen. Then he turned to Cara.

'All I can say,' he said, kinder now, 'is that if you're his friend, he'll find a way of contacting you.'

Cara felt like she'd been slapped.

She stumbled out of the student centre and down the sandstone steps, mute with disbelief. The university knew where Ravi was. She could only conclude that he was deliberately avoiding her.

She walked out of the university and did not return. She had satisfied all the requirements for her diploma. There was no need to linger in student life any longer.

As summer turned to autumn, she threw herself into the task of finding a job. Within three months, she'd landed an internship at a women's magazine. It was a coup for a recent graduate, and although the magazine's fashion focus was not

Cara's natural fit, the intensity of her working life prevented her from thinking too much.

Eight months after Ravi's disappearance, Cara began seeing a photographer, Jason. She'd met him on a shoot and, unlike many others in the fashion business, he was genuinely interested in the world beyond magazines. He was a dreamy, caring character, who showered her with quirky gifts. They laughed together and she was happy, if not in love. After four months of spending every weekend at his house, Jason asked her to move in with him. She'd never lived with a boyfriend before and, at twenty-five, she was ready to try. Within a fortnight, she'd packed up her things and moved into Jason's large, converted warehouse in Erskineville.

Five months later, more than a year after Ravi's disappearance, an email appeared in her inbox: *Cara, I am back in Australia. I only just received your emails. Can we meet? Ravi.*

She typed a long, vitriolic response. She called him names, asked why she should meet him, and then concluded the email with: *PS I am with someone else now.*

She never sent it.

Instead, she composed a short reply: *Ravi, I am surprised to hear from you. Meet me at Café Pronto, corner of Alfred Street, 11 am Monday. Cara.*

All of her intended aloofness dissolved the moment she saw him.

'Where in God's name have you been, Ravi?'

His eyes were wretched.

'I had to go to India,' he said. 'My mother rang me the

night we . . . after my graduation. I caught the first flight out. I left a note for you with Paul. My sister died in a kitchen fire.' His voice was flat.

'What?'

'Lina, my little sister. Dead.' Ravi shrugged.

Cara's stomach churned.

'But why?'

'You *know* why,' said Ravi, his tone terse. 'Because bride-burning happens all the time in India. Because men don't respect women. Because mothers-in-law can be evil. Because the rule of law doesn't always apply.' He raked his fingers through his hair. 'I'm sorry.' He swallowed. 'Lina married an older man, Anant, from my village—remember? A good match, everyone thought.'

Cara nodded. She recalled Ravi agonising about the fact that he couldn't afford to fly home for the nuptials. She had offered to lend him the money, but he'd refused.

'A month after the ceremony, Anant asked my parents to pay more dowry money, but my parents couldn't afford it. They'd already given him everything they could. So on the morning of my graduation, Anant's mother doused Lina in kerosene and set her alight.'

Cara gasped.

'She didn't die straight away. It took three months. She had internal injuries. I tried to do what I could. I got a burn specialist in from Delhi, but . . .' He shook his head, unable to speak.

Cara reached across the table.

'Oh, Ravi, I'm so sorry. I had no idea.'

He pulled his hand away. 'The note I left with Paul had my contact details in Rajasthan.' He looked at her accusingly. 'I was waiting for a phone call from you, a letter maybe. There is no internet in Gudda, but at least there are telephones. You didn't call. I thought you had forgotten me.' He looked wounded.

'But I spoke to Paul several times, Ravi,' she objected. 'I even went to your house. Paul didn't say anything about a note.'

'I left it on the kitchen bench,' he insisted. 'He couldn't have missed it.'

Cara searched his face; she could see he was telling the truth. Suddenly she remembered how Paul had called several weeks after Ravi's disappearance to ask her out. Surely he hadn't kept Ravi's note from her *deliberately*?

'This is awful, Ravi.' She didn't know what else to say.

His hands trembled as he brought the coffee cup to his lips.

'My father died a month after Lina,' he continued. 'A heart attack. Only my mother is left now.'

'Oh, Ravi.' Now she understood why he'd been away so long. 'Has a case been brought against the mother-in-law?'

'No, nothing can be proved. Most cases of bride-burning in India are not prosecuted. But that is my country. Such beauty, such barbarity.'

Cara didn't know what to say. 'How is your mother coping?' she asked after a minute or two.

'She moved to another village, where my aunt lives. She is a widow too. My mother cannot live in Gudda anymore.'

Cara nodded. 'But why didn't you . . .' She stopped short. She wanted to ask if Ravi had left Gudda in the year he'd been away, if he'd ever travelled to a larger centre to check his emails. And why he hadn't taken any action at all to contact *her*.

She looked at his face, thinner and older.

Ravi broke the silence. 'This is all new to you, I can see that. I thought you had changed your mind about me. It was a stupid assumption. You really didn't get my note?'

She shook her head, her eyes smarting.

'I should have found out why you hadn't contacted me. But I was alone in the village, helping my mother. I am sorry.'

They sat in silence, looking at each other.

'What will you do now?' she asked. 'Will you go home again?'

He shook his head. 'No. My mother wants me to succeed, now more than ever. I'll complete my advanced training here. Perhaps I can bring her to Australia one day.'

Cara reached over the table and clasped his hand.

'I admire you, Ravi. And I'm so sorry.' She blinked away tears. 'If I can help you in any way, please tell me how.'

One Sunday morning about a month later, Cara was doing the weekend crossword when the telephone rang.

'It's for you,' Jason called from the kitchen, waving the cordless phone at her with a quizzical look.

She took the handset. 'Hello?'

'It's Ravi.'

Cara's breath caught in her throat. 'Hello,' she said,

businesslike. She shrugged at Jason, then walked into the bedroom and shut the door.

'Cara, I am going to Western Australia. I've been offered a general surgery role in the Pilbara, at an Aboriginal health centre. It's a real chance to help the indigenous community.'

How typical of Ravi to want to help the disadvantaged, Cara thought.

'That's a courageous step.'

'Come with me, Cara.' His voice was quiet, urgent.

She swallowed. Her heart began to pound.

'Come with me,' he urged again. 'We got it wrong this past year. Let's make it right.'

Yes, Cara thought. *Yes.*

She closed her eyes.

'I can't,' she said finally. 'I have a good job now. And Jason. I can't just leave them both.'

Ravi waited.

'You were away too long.' The words rushed out of her mouth. 'You didn't even *try* to contact me. You could have at least tried. Things have changed, Ravi. *I* have changed.'

'I understand,' he replied. 'It was foolish of me to ask.'

'Ravi, I . . .' She was already regretting her words.

'Don't,' said Ravi. 'I understand. We will be friends. I will email you.'

And he had, every month for the next four years.

Over that time, Cara left both Jason and her job. When Jason asked her to marry him on their three-year anniversary, she refused, unable to articulate exactly why. Not long after moving out of his warehouse, she started as a junior copyeditor at the Sydney office of *Global Voice*. She could hardly believe her good fortune and emailed Ravi: *One day I might get posted somewhere exciting!*

It had happened more rapidly than she'd imagined. When Ravi returned to Sydney two years later, she was already based in Johannesburg. He wrote her a long email.

> *It's strange to be in Sydney without you, Cara. I passed my exams and am sharing rooms with Dr Robert Sturgess, a general and colorectal surgeon. He's close to retirement and winding back his practice. There's secretarial support, referrals, and access to patients. I get to assist with some of his operations, mostly bowel resections and colonoscopies, a bit of urology. Yes, it's quite predictable, but I need a break from remote living. The problems in the Pilbara are more than one surgeon can fix. I'm not sure how long I'll last in the city, though. Who knows, maybe I'll end up in Africa?*

It was a throwaway comment to which Cara held tightly. As the correspondent covering social justice issues in Africa, her working life was relentless. She travelled from one country to another, filing articles on epidemics and famines, tribal warfare and ethnic cleansing. The work took its toll, slowly eroding Cara's belief in the possibility of change, her faith in human goodness. She lost weight, and heart. She wasn't lonely—she had a wide circle of expatriate friends and the odd romantic liaison. But none of them ever progressed to permanency. Everything was transient in South Africa; people left as quickly as they'd arrived. The prospect of Ravi landing in Johannesburg and standing alongside her, amid the anarchy of Africa, was thrilling.

On the day of her thirtieth birthday, the telephone rang in her office.

'*Global Voice*, Johannesburg.'

'Happy birthday, Cara.'

For a moment, it didn't register.

'Ravi!' Her excitement was childlike. 'It's so good to hear from you.'

Was he ringing to tell her he was flying over?

They exchanged stories about their work. She talked up her experience of Africa.

'It's despots, dictators and disease, mostly,' she said, laughing. 'But someone's got to do it. You'd love it here, Ravi. People with your skills are in high demand, you know.'

'I'm sure,' he said. Then, suddenly, 'I've met someone.'

'Oh.' Cara attempted to sound nonchalant.

'Her name's Tess. She's the office administrator here at the consulting rooms.'

'Oh,' she said again.

'She's a really nice person.'

'I'm happy for you,' she lied.

'Thanks, Cara.'

She closed her eyes and leaned back in her chair. She couldn't continue exchanging polite chit-chat with him, not now. Not ever.

'Ravi, I have to go. I'm sorry. I have a meeting in five minutes.'

'Sure.' She thought she detected a note of disappointment in his voice. 'Let's keep in touch.'

She put down the telephone and wept into her hands.

Alone in her office in Johannesburg, a world away from the people she loved, Cara recognised a simple truth she'd been denying for some time. It was time to go home.

A month later, she touched down in Sydney. As the plane flew in to land, Cara pressed her face against the window and cried. The ferries carved their frothy paths across Sydney Harbour, the curved sails of the Sydney Opera House shone brilliant white. Two great grey bridges straddled the city she loved. All these familiar sights that she'd missed so much.

Her parents collected her at the airport. As she walked through the glass doors of customs, she could see her mother in the crowd, jiggling a heart-shaped helium balloon emblazoned with the words *Welcome back!* Her father stood alongside her, waving madly. By the time she reached them, weaving between the crowd with her oversized suitcase, they were all crying.

'I'm sorry,' she blubbered into her father's chest. 'I've missed you, Dad.'

She moved back into her parents' home at Seaforth and began the search for an apartment. Her editor at *Global Voice* willingly accepted her back into the Sydney office. The team had expanded and now covered Indonesia, Papua New Guinea, Micronesia and New Zealand.

Not long after her return, she telephoned Ravi at his consulting rooms. He wasn't hard to find in the telephone book.

'Hello, Ravi.' Her tone was consciously even. 'I'm back in Sydney. How are you?'

'Wow,' he said, with a hint of an Australian accent. 'Cara, I can't believe it. I'm great. How are you?'

'Well, you know what it's like when you've been away. It feels strange to come home.' She was grateful he couldn't see her face. She took a deep breath. 'Can we catch up, Ravi?' She wanted to ask, 'Are you still with Tess?' but stopped short.

'Of course, how about tomorrow night?' he said. 'I can meet you after work.'

And so they'd met again, at a café in Glebe. Cara had trouble finding a parking space and was ten minutes late. She hurried through the café's door and instantly spotted him seated in a rear booth. Now in his mid-thirties, Ravi looked even more appealing. He'd lost some of his lankiness, which wasn't a bad thing. Cara noticed the odd streak of grey through his thick, dark hair. He beamed at her, his face alight.

'Cara.' He rose to his feet and kissed her on the cheek. Cara wanted to stay in that moment forever. The soft brush of his lips brought back the night of his graduation, all those years ago. He even smelled the same, a trace of spice.

But it was impossible to span the breach of more than four years. And besides, it was immediately obvious that Tess was still in Ravi's life. His eyes softened when he spoke of her.

'You must meet her, Cara,' he'd said. 'You'd like her. We're having a housewarming next Saturday night. We bought a flat in Waverton. Will you come?'

Cara shook her head. 'Ah, no, I can't, sorry. I'm busy.'

Ravi's eyes met hers. He knew she was lying.

And that was the last time they'd seen each other for almost a year. They kept in touch by email, and the odd telephone call. Cara waited patiently, hoping against hope that one day Ravi would announce that he and Tess had split. In the interim, she immersed herself in her work, taking several overseas trips. She found an apartment in Annandale and began to reconnect with old friends. She had a few dates here and there, but none of them went further.

And then, one Tuesday evening, she arrived home to find a gold-embossed envelope in her letterbox, her name and address inscribed in flawless handwriting. She opened it to find a crisp white card cordially inviting her to the Marriage of Ravi Nadkarni and Tess Hughes. Gasping, she stumbled against the kitchen bench as if she'd been physically struck.

She stared at the invitation for hours, willing it to be a figment of her imagination. But the handwritten note on the back of the card, in Ravi's trademark doctor's scrawl, was undeniable: *I hope you can be there, Cara. It would mean the world to me.* In the end, it was this that persuaded her to RSVP to Mrs Hughes and inform her that yes, she would be attending. And no, she wouldn't be bringing a guest.

'Excuse me, would you like to dance?'

Cara looked up, startled. She was the only person left at the table.

A benign-looking man smiled at her, the same one who'd helped her when she'd collided with the waiter. Standing this close, she noticed he had ginger hair and freckles.

'I'm sorry,' she said. 'I was a world away.'

Her dessert lay untouched before her. How long had she been sitting there, contemplating the past?

'Is that a no?'

She smiled. 'I'm sorry, how rude of me.'

'My mother is a friend of your mother's,' the man said suddenly. 'She told me to look out for you.'

'Really?' Cara couldn't fathom a connection.

'Yes, they go to the same support group in Balgowlah. My dad's got Alzheimer's too.'

Cara stared at him. Her father's illness was not something she talked about with her closest friends, let alone a complete stranger. After her return from South Africa, her parents had waited three months before revealing the diagnosis.

'I'm Richard, anyway.' He shook Cara's hand. 'I'm Michael's best mate.'

She looked at him blankly.

'Michael. The MC,' he explained. 'We went to school together.'

'Oh.' She nodded politely.

'I've dropped your mum back to Seaforth a couple of times, after support group,' he continued. 'My parents don't live too far from yours, over in Clontarf.'

Cara looked at Richard more closely now. She knew her mother had been attending a carers' support group every Wednesday afternoon.

'You don't work on Wednesdays?' Cara asked.

'Technically, I do.' He smiled. 'But I've got my own business. Things are pretty difficult for Mum at the moment. She's Dad's full-time carer. I figure I can take two hours out of my day to give her a bit of support. My office is in Balgowlah, so it's pretty easy.'

'That's nice of you.' Cara felt rather negligent by comparison.

'Your mother and my mother have become quite good friends. I'm driving them to the Opera House tomorrow morning.'

'Oh.' It felt strange to be hearing this information second-hand. 'Well, Richard,' she said, 'I suppose we'd better dance, then.'

They walked towards the dance floor. In heels, she was slightly taller than him. She manoeuvred herself into the dance floor's crowded centre and began to rock awkwardly from side to side. She'd never been any good at dancing.

And then she saw them, Tess and Ravi, not two metres away. The DJ saw them too and the music changed to the introductory bars of a love theme from a Baz Luhrmann film. Well-wishers began to encircle the couple and the DJ bent towards his microphone. 'Ladies and gentlemen, the bridal waltz.'

Cara began to back away, bumping straight into Richard. 'Sorry.'

'Are you alright? You look a little unwell.'

'I need some fresh air.'

A wall of onlookers blocked her exit.

Ravi and Tess, moving as one, turned beneath the spotlight trained on them. Tess rested her cheek against Ravi's chest, arms wound tightly around his waist. As they swayed together in a slow circle, Ravi raised his head and opened his eyes. There was nowhere else for her to look.

She pushed her way through the crowd. Someone called

her name, but she didn't stop. She ran out the door, down the stairs, and out onto the darkened street. It wasn't until she was at her front door, breathless and aching, that she realised she'd left her handbag at the function centre. She couldn't face returning there tonight. Sliding her fingers under a pot plant, she found the spare set of keys.

The click of the lock echoed through her empty apartment. All was in darkness, bar the eerie light of the fish tank. She tossed her earrings onto the dining room table and unpinned her hair. In the bedroom, she drew the blinds. Her dress rustled to the floor like falling autumn leaves. She threw her high heels at the wardrobe and sank onto the bed.

Someone was at the door. She sat up with a start and squinted at the clock. Nine thirty. It was probably her neighbour, she thought, who had no sense of boundaries, even on weekends. Wasn't Sunday morning sacred?

Cara threw back the bedcovers and found her bathrobe. She marched to the door and flung it open.

Her mother and a woman she didn't recognise hovered on the doorstep, flanked by the man she'd met the night before—Rodney, wasn't it?

'Oh, you *are* home. I left a message an hour ago,' her mother said.

'It's Sunday morning.' Cara's tone was terse. 'Of course I'm home.'

'Yes, well, Richard here . . .' Her mother glanced sideways at him. 'He was a little concerned. He mentioned you didn't look well last night. And he collected your handbag, with your keys inside it. *And* your mobile phone. I can't imagine how you left them at the function centre. And since we were passing, I suggested we drop in . . .'

Cara looked from one to the other. *Passing?* Her apartment in Annandale was nowhere near her parents' home in Seaforth. Richard looked apologetic.

'I'm fine.' She pulled her robe tightly across her chest. 'Thank you anyway.'

Richard passed her the handbag.

'We're off to the symphony,' said her mother brightly.

Cara vaguely recalled Richard mentioning this last night. The woman standing next to him must be *his* mother.

'Right. Enjoy that.'

'Sorry to wake you,' said Richard. He looked embarrassed. 'I . . . May I call in on the way back?'

Cara was puzzled. *What on earth for?*

Her mother was nodding and smiling.

'I'm going to the markets later,' Cara replied. 'But, um . . . sure.'

Richard looked relieved.

'Alrighty then, darling,' her mother chirped. 'Bye bye.'

Warily, she watched them depart.

Richard knocked on the door an hour later. She opened it with less force this time.

'Sorry about earlier,' she said. 'I'm not a morning person.'

Richard produced a bunch of daisies from behind his back and pushed them into her hands.

'I'm the one who should be apologising. I shouldn't have

said anything to your mother. But you looked awful when you left. I wondered if you got home in one piece.'

'It wasn't my best night.' She buried her nose in the flowers. They were curiously free of scent. 'Thanks for these. You really shouldn't have.'

She looked at him, all awkward on the doorstep. 'Would you like a cup of tea? I'm about to make one.'

'That'd be nice.'

She ushered him into the lounge room and gestured towards the sofa. 'Make yourself comfortable.'

She moved around the kitchen, arranging a teapot, cups, saucers and a plate of biscuits on a tray.

'It was nice of you to drive my mother to the concert,' she said, passing him a mug. 'Milk and sugar?'

He nodded. 'It's no trouble, my mum needs the break too. We had a close call with Dad last week.' He paused. 'He almost burned the house down while Mum was out shopping. He started frying eggs, then just walked away from the stove.'

'Oh no,' said Cara.

Richard shook his head. 'So a neighbour's with Dad today. But there'll come a time when a babysitter isn't enough.'

Cara stared at the tea leaves floating in the pot. 'It's an awful disease.'

She wondered whether her own father could be trusted at home alone, before dismissing the thought. He wasn't that far gone, she told herself.

They talked a bit about their work. Richard managed his own accountancy practice, having spent ten years working in a large corporate firm. His specialty was taxation law. She nodded politely as he described his typical working day; but anything financial bored her.

Perhaps sensing her lack of interest, Richard abruptly changed the subject.

'I'm taking my dad to Taronga Zoo next weekend,' he announced. 'He was a vet before he retired. Mostly cats and dogs, a suburban practice. He hasn't been to the zoo in years. I thought it might give Mum a break.'

Cara nodded, touched by his compassion.

'I wondered if you'd like to come along,' he ventured. 'And maybe bring your dad? Peter, isn't it?'

'Oh . . . ' Cara wasn't expecting an invitation. 'Um, let me check my diary.'

She rummaged around in her handbag and retrieved a black leather-bound book. She pretended to scan a list of events. The coming weekend was depressingly empty.

As she stared at her calendar, she weighed up his offer. It was a nice idea, but she hardly knew Richard. The prospect of taking her father anywhere without the reassuring presence of her mother was daunting. She'd never done it before. What if things went wrong, and her dad became distressed? How would she cope?

She glanced up at Richard, waiting patiently on the sofa.

'Well, next Sunday looks okay at this stage,' she said. 'From about three o'clock?' It was a safe suggestion; their outing would be limited to no more than three hours.

'Great,' said Richard, beaming. 'I can pick you up from your parents' house, if you'd like?'

'Okay.'

He continued to smile at her and she wondered, briefly, if she'd made a terrible mistake.

'I don't mean to be rude,' she said, 'but I actually have to go and get a few things from the markets.'

It was Sunday, after all. Her day for going to the fish markets and then reading the newspaper in the park nearby. She glanced at her watch.

Richard stood up. 'Of course. Thank you for the tea.'

She collected the cups.

'Thanks for the daisies.' She nodded towards the door. 'I'll see you out.'

He walked to the door and fumbled with the latch until Cara reached around him to release the lock.

'Goodbye, Cara.' He stepped out on to the doormat and turned, as if on the verge of saying something.

'Goodbye,' she said, closing the door.

She walked back to the lounge room. Just thinking about her father had drained her. She glanced at the wicker basket perched on the table, her shopping list folded neatly on top. The markets could wait until next weekend.

She curled up on the sofa and closed her eyes.

Two years later, she was married to Richard.

He'd wooed her with his good nature, his patience, his persistence. Their first visit to the zoo had turned into a fortnightly event. They'd spent every second Sunday afternoon shepherding their fathers through wildlife exhibits, admiring anacondas and iguanas, before taking afternoon tea at the zoo's café. Over the course of a year, Cara had come to see that Richard was reliable, loyal and generous to a fault.

Then they'd progressed from zoo visits to the movies, cafés and weekends away. Richard was the quintessential gentleman, always opening doors and umbrellas for her, refusing to split bills, walking on the street side of the footpath. Sometimes he seemed like a man from a bygone era who had been parachuted into the modern world. While their sexual chemistry was mediocre, their friendship was warm and utterly relaxed. He made her laugh, he made her think, he made her breakfast. And, slowly, Ravi had receded in her consciousness, emerging only now and then in dreams as a shadowy figure with olive skin and a shining smile.

When Richard asked her to marry him, she wasn't surprised. He was the right person in so many ways, and she was thirty-three years old. She was either going to have a baby by thirty-five, or miss the boat altogether. Here was a man who was financially independent, with a mortgage on a house in Freshwater, close to her parents. As her mother had pointed out, she was unlikely to do any better. But more importantly for Cara, Richard had shown that he was prepared to prioritise her above everything else in his life. He was solicitous in his attentions, devout almost. Life with him would be more than comfortable. And it was futile, she reasoned, to yearn for things she couldn't have.

The ceremony was a low-key affair in a registry office, with only their families present. She'd shunned a larger event, avoiding anything that showcased their fathers' slow deterioration. As it was, her father had burst into tears halfway through the proceedings and had to be escorted outside.

Within three months of the ceremony, she was pregnant with Astrid.

In the first intense weeks of Astrid's life, Cara had never felt happier. She was intoxicated by this delicate, innocent creature, and she spent whole days staring at her, bathing her, lying bare-chested on the couch with her. Obsessing about her feeding, sleeping, burping and bowel movements. Richard was thoroughly supportive, just as he'd promised. In the early weeks, he'd taken himself up to the baby health centre and gathered up dozens of pamphlets on infant care. He'd even confirmed her place in a mothers' group, anxious to ensure she had a good support network before he returned to full-time work.

By the time Astrid was three months old, Cara couldn't remember how she'd filled her days before motherhood. She knew she'd been busy, but never *this* busy. Astrid simply ate time. Cara would start her day with a list of twelve things to do, and arrive at the end having achieved two or three. Wonderfully, she didn't really care. What's more, Richard was quite flexible with his work. He left for the office most mornings after nine o'clock, returning home well before six. Just in time for 'arsenic hour', as they called it, when Astrid was inevitably tetchy.

But Richard went further than that. He insisted that Cara sleep in every Saturday morning, entertaining the baby for as long as possible before, eventually, waking Cara to breastfeed

Astrid in bed. On Sundays, they headed to the Manly markets, buying pastries and takeaway chai lattes; Richard knew how much she missed the weekend markets of the inner west. And sometimes, when Cara was feeding Astrid in the middle of the night, Richard would appear and stand in the doorway, just watching. Then he would tiptoe across the room and, in a gesture of solidarity, massage her neck.

Richard was so supportive in those early months, it sometimes moved her to tears.

'Um, honey, that's not really . . .' She watched as Richard attempted to change Astrid's nappy. The change table was littered with wipes and a soiled nappy was balanced precariously on one edge.

Richard stopped. A muscle twitched under his right eye. 'Why are you watching me?' he asked. 'What am I doing wrong?'

'I'm sorry,' she said, her tone conciliatory. 'But you're supposed to wipe from front to back.' She showed him the correct action. 'If you don't, she might get a urinary tract infection.'

'Oh.' Richard looked deflated. Then, after a moment, he said, 'I was only trying to help.'

Cara nodded. 'Yes, honey. You couldn't have known that.'

'But how did *you* know?' he asked. 'I mean, the direction for wiping?'

'Oh, I just knew. Women's business.' She smiled. 'And someone reminded me about it last week at mothers' group.'

'And who needs a husband when you've got a mothers' group, right?'

Cara laughed. 'Yes, they're pretty amazing.'

She began dressing Astrid for their regular Friday morning outing. She loved attending the mothers' group, it was a fixture in her week. Despite having many other friends with children, none of them were exactly the same age as Astrid. And she was looking forward to this week's mothers' group in particular, as it was the inaugural session of their book club. When she'd first raised the idea, everyone had been enthusiastic. Cara had nominated *A Suitable Boy* by Vikram Seth, a book that had been sitting on her shelf for years. Ravi had given it to her as a birthday present at university, but its length had always daunted her. She needed the discipline of a book club to *make* her read it. For the first session, however, Suzie's suggestion prevailed. *Eat, Pray, Love* had been an easy read for Cara; she'd finished it in less than a week.

She lifted Astrid off the change table and turned to Richard. 'Would you mind dropping us at Beachcombers on your way to work?'

Richard shook his head. 'Sorry, I have a meeting in town. But I can take you to Lawrence Street if you'd like.' From there it was a short walk to Beachcombers, downhill all the way, but it was unlike Richard not to help. Work must be getting on top of him, she thought.

'Okay, thanks.'

'You're creatures of habit in that mothers' group, aren't you?' he said. 'You never meet anywhere except Beachcombers.'

'Well, it's just so convenient. Miranda has Digby, you know.' She shook her head. 'Just watching him exhausts me. I don't know how she does it. He's completely hyperactive, but

Miranda just seems to take it all in her stride. If *we* think a baby is hard work, just wait until Astrid's a toddler. But they say girls are different to boys.'

'Do they?'

She studied his face. 'Richard, is something wrong?'

'No.'

'You just seem a little . . .' She searched for the right word.

'Hen-pecked?'

She blinked. 'Pardon?' He'd never used that expression before.

'I just never seem to get it right with Astrid, Cara. I can't live up to your standards.'

She gaped at him. 'I don't . . . I'm not . . . You *know* how much I appreciate your help.'

He looked at her, his arms folded across his chest.

'Richard.' She put a hand on his arm, balancing Astrid on her hip. 'You're a *great* dad.'

'Maybe I should just stick to making the money, Cara. Sometimes I think you'd prefer it if I didn't help with Astrid at all.'

She reddened. 'Of course not.'

In reality, sometimes she *did* feel that Richard's efforts at 'helping' were more of a hindrance. He meant well, but when he didn't get it right, *she* was the one who was left to deal with the consequences—a screaming baby, out of routine.

'You're a fantastic help,' she said brightly, fearing he saw through her. 'Let's go.'

They travelled in silence all the way to Lawrence Street.

Cara looked out the window at the procession of life on the street. Dog walkers and joggers, school children on bicycles, people on mobile phones. There was something in their purposefulness that she envied. She could remember a time when each new day stretched before her, too, ripe with untapped possibility. A new story to be investigated, an unscheduled telephone call, an impulsive dinner with friends.

Nowadays, family life was more than good. She was thirty-four and she wanted for nothing, Richard made sure of that. Except, perhaps, spontaneity.

'Here we are.' Richard pulled over in the shoulder just beyond the intersection.

'Thanks.' Cara planted a kiss on his cheek. Then she reached around and unbuckled Astrid from her car seat, while Richard lifted the pram from the boot. He wrestled with it with the clumsiness of an infrequent user, then stood aside while she manoeuvred it into place. She secured Astrid in the harness, then pulled the shade cloth over the pram. It was time for Astrid's morning sleep.

'Have a good day,' he said.

'You too, honey.'

She waved as he drove off.

It should have been enough, family life. Even when Astrid had morphed from defenceless baby into active agent and they'd started disagreeing about parenting techniques. Even when the global financial crisis began affecting Richard's business and he'd become short-tempered. Even when both their fathers had deteriorated, spiralling towards institutionalisation.

They still could have made it, she reasoned—had it not been for Ravi.

It had been months, years even, since she'd thought of Ravi. And then, out of the blue, he'd waltzed into her life once again. One moment she'd been visiting Pippa in a spartan hospital room, the next, she'd found herself looking into Ravi's warm chocolate eyes.

She'd replayed the events in her mind over and over. If only she hadn't visited Pippa on that particular day, at that particular time, she never would have seen Ravi. She never would have agreed to meet him for a cup of chai the following month, for old time's sake. She never would have relished the news of his unhappy marriage and divorce, or started emailing him again. And she never would have entertained the hope of—what exactly?—that had led her to invite him, on the spur of the moment, to call in at Astrid's birthday party at precisely the time she knew Richard *wouldn't* be there.

She hated herself. Just one cup of chai with Ravi, and she'd been hijacked by dormant feelings that commonsense demanded she ignore. She'd been thrilled by his attention, intoxicated by the possibility of a relationship reignited. She would leave Richard, she'd fantasised, and start life anew. Astrid would come with her and, in time, she'd adjust to the new environment. Cara and Richard would be gracious in separation, with an orderly schedule of care and visitation for Astrid. She and Ravi would try for a baby and, together, they would build the life they'd been destined to live since their very first meeting.

Her folly had been frivolous and fatal.

Often now she would sit, twisting the lid on and off her prescription sedatives. She would relive the events at Manly Dam: the excitement of seeing Ravi, dark and striking, loitering on the periphery. Their brief, enticing meeting. Ravi had brought a gift for Astrid and, as he passed it to her, bent forward to kiss her, his lips brushing hers. Their unhurried conversation, all laughter and shining eyes, about nothing in particular. How she'd noticed the chest hairs protruding above his buttoned shirt and how, when she'd looked up, he'd smiled at her with that same knowing smile of their first and only night together. How he'd asked her to lunch the following Wednesday and she'd nodded, her heart pulsing in her ears. How she'd turned on her heels and, without another word, hurried back to the party.

And then, how the world as she knew it had collapsed around her.

Now, three months on, she couldn't remember how Astrid had looked when they pulled her from the dam. It was not uncommon, the psychiatrist had explained, for the human brain to erase the most damaging memories. But she could still recall the creeping fear, then the instant, indescribable horror. Followed by misery and shame without end.

In the first month after Astrid's death, she would often sit and pour all the pills from the bottle onto the bed. Then she would scoop the fat tablets into her palms and watch them slide between her fingers, like sand through a child's sieve. Once, Richard had found her like that.

'What are you doing?' he'd asked, hovering in the doorway.

She didn't reply. She hadn't spoken to him, to anyone, since Astrid's death.

'I'm going to take them away, Cara.' His eyes were red with fatigue. 'I'll give you what you need for the day, but no more.'

She stared at him, glad he was sleeping in the spare bedroom now. She couldn't bear the human contact.

Since then, he had doled out her medication. She would tip three of the four tablets into her mouth and swallow them with water, deftly concealing the fourth pill. When Richard left the room she would slip it into a pencil case she hid under the mattress. For two months she'd been doing that, waiting to see if something might change for her, if the feelings might shift, even slightly. But they hadn't. Every day was like the one before it: a shower, three meals, the expanse of white ceiling above her head. The dull, unrelenting pain of Astrid's absence. Richard's futile attempts to lure her beyond the bedroom before retreating, defeated, to his work.

She'd collected fifty-six tablets in two months, but she wanted to be sure. In two weeks, she would reach her target of seventy.

'There's someone here to see you.'

She stared at Richard as if he'd spoken a foreign language. Since the funeral, she'd refused all visitors, even her parents. Richard had been more than considerate, diverting phone calls, steering away concerned friends, vetting the post. In the early weeks, he'd taken delivery of the countless flower arrangements that had congregated in the empty spaces of their home. Such flowers were rare now that the crisis period had passed, with the exception of Ravi's regular bouquets. Most of her friends had respected her wish to be left alone. But the media interest had continued unabated and much to Cara's dismay, people she'd never met attempted to contact her. Many of the letters arrived at Richard's office, after a newspaper article cited the name of his accounting firm. According to Richard, most of the letters were well-meaning. Some contained offers of help or prayers. Others offered 'opinion', he said, which was code for judgement. She couldn't bring herself to read any of them.

'It's some of the women from your mothers' group,' Richard told her. 'Without their children.'

She shook her head.

'I knew you'd say that.' He stepped into the room and closed the door behind him.

'You've got to try, Cara.' He rubbed his hands over the ginger stubble on his jaw. 'I don't know what to do. I've tried to support you, but she was *my* daughter too.'

Tears ran down his face. He slumped to the floor, his head in his hands.

'I don't know how much longer I can do this, Cara. You're not helping me. I miss her too. I miss *you.*' He looked up, his eyes haggard. 'You can't closet yourself away up here. You can't stay silent forever.'

Earnest, dignified, kind-hearted Richard. Reduced to this.

'Never *once* have I blamed you.' His voice shook. 'If she'd died on my watch, how do you think you would've treated *me*?'

A noise escaped from the back of Cara's throat, a tiny

guttural cry. She stared at Richard. They both knew the answer to his question.

'Talk to me, Cara. If we try to get through this together, we might be okay. *Why* aren't you helping me?'

'I'm sorry,' she croaked. Her first words in three months.

He looked at her, a glimmer of hope in his eyes.

'But it's not okay, Richard,' she whispered. 'It will never be okay for us.'

Slowly, he stood up.

'Show them in,' she said. 'You don't have to protect me anymore.'

Richard paused for a moment in the doorway, then he nodded and closed the door behind him.

She made no attempt to smooth her hair or plump the pillows. Their footsteps on the stairs were deferential, like students visiting a war museum. She could sense them hovering, uncertain, in the purgatory outside her door.

'Come in,' she said.

The doorknob turned slowly and Made peered around the door.

'We no wake? Richard say okay.'

Cara shrugged.

They filed in. Made was first, wearing a bright blue sarong that trailed across the floor. Tiny silver studs were woven into the fabric, like stars dotting the night sky. Pippa was behind her, a different woman to the one she'd once been. Her skin was ruddy, tanned almost, and she wore slim cream pants and a navy singlet. She carried a large bunch of yellow roses, gripping them with both hands. Suzie followed Pippa, her long purple dress billowing at the ankles, an expression of acute discomfort on her face.

They hovered at the foot of her bed. She didn't invite them to sit down.

'Where are the children?' she asked.

Suzie's mouth dropped open.

'They're with Robert,' answered Pippa. 'And Monika's helping too.'

'That's good of them,' she said. 'The babies must be so big by now.'

'Oh, Cara.' Suzie covered her mouth. 'I'm so sorry.'

'I know.'

'How are you doing?' asked Pippa.

She didn't reply.

They stood in uncomfortable silence. She wanted them to leave.

'We go see Miranda next week,' said Made suddenly. 'Maybe Cara come? Next Thursday morning. She at Delamere Clinic.'

Cara had never heard of it.

'It's a private treatment centre,' explained Pippa. 'For people with alcohol and drug dependencies.'

Cara had been aware of the police interview with Miranda, who'd declared herself inebriated on the day of Astrid's death. But police investigations had delivered insufficient evidence of culpability on *anyone's* part, let alone Miranda's.

Despite the initial media frenzy surrounding possible kidnapping and paedophilia, the post-mortem report confirmed that Astrid had *not* been subjected to physical force or sexual interference of any kind. The cause of death, it submitted, was drowning.

The media had continued to trade in blame, however, scrutinising the roles of both Miranda and Cara in Astrid's death. Richard had stopped bringing her the newspaper in an attempt to shield her from public opinion. But for Cara, it was merely external verification of what she already knew: that her daughter had died that Sunday afternoon because Cara had failed her. No one else had been responsible, not even Miranda. Indeed, most days Cara lay in her bed anticipating a knock on the door, when the police would arrive and arrest *her,* the guilty party.

So it had come as a surprise, several months after Astrid's death, when the coroner had handed down his findings. She'd reread the letter from the lawyer a dozen times: *The coroner is satisfied that an inquest will not take this matter any further. No suspicious circumstances were identified and it has been determined that Astrid died of an accidental drowning death. The matter will not progress to an inquest and it is unlikely to be referred for further criminal investigation.*

'Cara.' Three figures hovered at the end of her bed.

Oh yes, she thought. They're still here.

'I just wanted to say we're here for you,' said Suzie.

Made moved towards the bed. Cara stared at her sarong, mesmerised by its glittering silver orbs.

'I bring this.' Made removed a small green basket from her bag. Plump rose petals, a sprig of passionfruit vine, a sweet biscuit and grains of rice were nestled within the wide green leaves lining the basket. She removed two incense sticks and a box of matches from the folds of her sarong.

'I leave you to light. If you want to bring gods into room.'

Cara looked at her.

'And this.' Made placed a scroll of white paper next to Cara's hand. 'If you feel like to read.'

Cara nodded. 'I'm tired now.'

They left quickly.

She lay staring at the ceiling as their footsteps retreated. Eventually, Richard tapped at the door.

'Your sleeping tablets.' He passed her the four pills and a tall glass of water.

She held her thumb over one, tipping the rest into her mouth.

'Was it okay, seeing the others?' He laid a hand over hers.

She stiffened, afraid he might discover the pill.

'They . . .' She cast about for something to distract him. 'They brought some nice things.' She nodded at the flowers.

'What's this?' Richard picked up the scroll.

She slid the tablet under her leg.

'I don't know.' She was irritable. 'Open it.'

He undid the gold ribbon and unfurled the paper. 'It's a letter,' he said. 'I'll leave it for you to read.' He stood up from the bed, then turned to face her. 'What you said this morning, about us . . . I don't agree. We can make it, Cara. We just need to get through it together, one day at a time.'

'Richard,' she whispered. 'Please.'

His shoulders sagged. He turned and left the room.

She felt for the tablet beneath her leg, then pulled the pencil case from its hiding place. She unzipped the case and dropped in the pill, exhaling with relief.

As she settled herself back against the pillows, her hand brushed the scroll. She picked it up and began to read.

Dear Cara,

This my first proper letter in English, so please forgive mistakes that definitely inside here.

When I was younger girl, my brother die from blood fever. He is my mother's joy. He the light in our family. After he die, my mother very changed. She still has the sadness, even he die long time ago. I think now, why my mother still sad, when brother unhappy if he know this? Then I answer to myself, mother has no chance to heal inside since he die. She never stop working, she never be still and let the gods help her.

I have some news. Gordon no longer have Australia job. This economy crisis bad for his company, they ask him to stop work. We go back to Bali now for a while. Cheaper in Bali to live. We stay there until Wayan is two or three years, then we come back to Sydney for his lip operation. We stay in my mountain village whole next year, maybe little more.

My family compound not big. But we have spare room for you. We have noisy roosters that wake up at sunrise, but life in village is good. Time to be still and have healing place.

I want to ask if you come with us, Cara?

I not very good friend for you, I know. Not many years together. But you friend in my heart, in the sadness. You stay long in the village, you stay short, it no matter. My family welcome you. Richard too, if that is the wish.

We leaving September 21.

You come with us, we happy. You no come with us, we no matter.

You call me if you liking.

Your friend,

Made

Cara laid down the letter and stared at the ceiling.

This isn't *Eat, Pray, Love*, she thought. There *is* no happy ending.

'What are you doing?' Richard watched her, stunned.

She turned from the vanity towards him. 'Putting on lipstick.'

His mouth worked silently for a moment. 'It's . . . nice to see.'

She began applying blush to the hollowed recesses of her cheeks. She'd lost far too much weight.

Who am I? She wondered, staring into the mirror. I don't look the same. I don't feel the same. I'm not me anymore.

She picked up her handbag. 'I'm going out,' she said. 'To the Delamere Clinic. Miranda's in there again. She's relapsed a few times since . . .' She still couldn't bring herself to say the words. 'Pippa's picking me up.'

Richard frowned. He laid a hand on her arm, preventing her from brushing past him. 'Are you sure you're ready for this?' he asked. 'You haven't been outside for months. And . . . do you really want to see *her*?'

'Yes,' she said simply.

Richard looked uncertain. 'Well, can I pick you up afterwards?'

'No, thanks,' she said. 'Pippa will drop me home.'

A horn tooted outside.

'There she is now.'

Climbing into Pippa's car, she tried to ignore the obvious signs of Heidi. The half-eaten crackers, the smell of stale milk, the soft toys dangling above the car seat.

'Hello,' she said, clipping her seatbelt into place.

'Hi,' said Pippa. 'How are you?'

Cara didn't know how to answer that truthfully. 'Oh, you know.'

'I'm pretty sure I don't,' said Pippa. 'No one can, I imagine.'

Cara leaned back in the seat and stared out the window. 'You're right.'

They drove the rest of the way in silence. Pippa didn't attempt to force the conversation, and Cara had nothing to say. She looked through the window at the world outside, spinning violently without end.

The Delamere Clinic was an unassuming cream and blue building on an ordinary suburban street. Just like any other block of units, Cara thought, bar the notice hanging in the foyer: Change is the first step in a lifelong recovery process. A middle-aged woman in a pink blouse sat behind a reception desk. She looked up from her paperwork and smiled at them.

'We're here to see Miranda Bianco,' said Pippa.

She nodded. 'Please sign in, then go through to the visitors' area at the rear. Follow this corridor, turn right at the cafeteria, then you'll see it. Visiting hours finish at eleven o'clock.'

Pippa glanced at her watch. 'Twenty minutes will be plenty.'

When they rounded the corner at the cafeteria, Cara

immediately spotted Miranda among the residents and visitors gathered in the courtyard. She was sitting on a long wooden bench, her head bowed. A slim book lay on the bench next to her, open at the centre. In profile, she was still striking. Cara waited for the anger to rise, tsunami-like, inside her. But looking at Miranda now, she felt nothing at all. Miranda looked fragile. As if, with a breath of wind, she might shatter into a thousand pieces.

As they walked across the courtyard, it became evident that Miranda was talking to someone. It was Suzie, crouched on the other side of the bench. Cara could see from her heaving shoulders that Suzie was crying. Miranda's eyes were closed and her forehead knotted with pain. Cara stopped, reluctant to move any closer. Pippa hovered next to her. Neither of them spoke.

Miranda's eyes flew open. She looked at Cara, her mouth opening slightly with alarm or shock.

Suzie followed Miranda's gaze.

'Oh.' Suzie sat back on her heels. 'I didn't hear you. It's nice to see you both.' She wiped her eyes. 'Miranda and I were just . . . Well, I had an apology to make.'

Cara looked from one to the other. Both of them looked like they'd been crying for some time.

'Don't we all?' said Miranda. She pushed herself off the bench with bony hands.

Cara watched her, a skeleton moving under skin. Human bodies are so feeble, she thought. Astrid had abandoned her little body so quickly, they couldn't call her back.

Miranda took several steps towards Cara.

'I've thought about this moment a thousand times,' she said. 'I didn't think I'd ever get the chance.' Her chest heaved. 'You trusted me. And I failed you.' Tears coursed down her cheeks. 'I wish I could give up my life for Astrid's.'

'You and me both,' whispered Cara.

'I won't ask your forgiveness,' Miranda said. 'I don't expect that, ever. But I want you to know, I will pay for Astrid's death every day for the rest of my life.'

'So will I.'

I wish we were both dead, Cara thought. *It was my mistake, but* you *let it happen.* She screwed her eyes shut against the anger. *It won't bring her back. Nothing will.*

When she opened her eyes again, Miranda was still hovering before her, like a pale apparition.

Cara shook her head.

Then, weary of everything, she extended her hand.

Miranda caught it between hers.

'Hello.' A familiar voice interrupted them. Made stood behind them, carrying two trays of takeaway coffees.

Miranda dropped Cara's hand.

'Sorry I late, I bring the coffee,' said Made.

'We need some,' said Miranda with a weak smile.

Made looked around the group. 'It good to see you all.' She placed a soft hand on Cara's arm. 'Especially Cara.'

Made's touch was tender. For all of Richard's attentiveness since Astrid's death, he hadn't been able to touch her. She hadn't wanted him to. But Made's hand on her arm now seemed to reach into her chest and gently hold the pieces of her heart. Tears obscured her vision.

A squawking sound made Cara start. She sank into a chair at the sight of Wayan, sitting in his stroller behind Made, grinning his warped, toothless smile. His limbs were much longer. Dark hair flopped over his ears and his hands strained at the harness that confined him.

'You want come down, Wayan?' Made unbuckled him. He slid deftly to the ground and proceeded to walk unassisted.

'Here, Cara, coffee.' Made passed her a cardboard cup. Cara sucked at the hole in the lid, her eyes trained on Wayan. His haemangioma was still prominent, a purple cleft across his lip. And yet he was perfect, Cara thought. Such exquisite beauty in his humanity. They watched him potter about the courtyard, examining chair legs and pot plants and cracks between the tiles.

'When do you fly out to Bali, Made?' Suzie asked suddenly.

'Wednesday next,' said Made. Her smile was electric. 'I see family soon.'

Suzie nodded. 'I know how you feel. I'm moving back to Queensland.'

The others made noises of surprise.

'I've made some mistakes.' Suzie glanced at Miranda. 'And the cost of living in Sydney is too high. It'll be sad to leave Monika, but . . .'

'You don't have to do that on my account,' said Miranda suddenly. 'It wasn't your fault.'

Of course it wasn't her fault, Cara thought. It was mine.

Suzie sighed. 'I just really want to go home.'

There was silence for a moment.

'So do I,' said Miranda. 'I've been in here three times in

four months.' She dabbed at the corners of her eyes. 'There's no quick fix for my problem, though I wish there was, for the kids' sake. They're doing okay at Hendrika's, but it's been very destabilising for them. As for Willem . . .' She sighed. 'Things aren't looking good for us.'

She picked up the black volume on the bench next to her. Cara wondered briefly if it was the Bible, if Astrid's death had prompted some kind of religious conversion. 'Ginie sent this to me,' said Miranda, looking up. 'It's Daniel's novel.'

She turned the book over in her hands, fingering the raised silver lettering on the plain black cover. *Blameless* by Daniel Hargreaves.

Cara nodded. She'd received the same gift from Ginie several weeks previously, but she hadn't even opened it. She couldn't possibly tolerate reading about the fictional lives of others with her own in such disarray.

'Yes, I saw a review of it, then Ginie sent me a copy,' said Suzie. 'It's dedicated to Ginie, you know.'

Pippa gave a little grunt of surprise.

'I haven't seen Ginie since . . .' Pippa reddened. 'Since I said some things to her I shouldn't have. I need to call her and apologise. She didn't tell us that Daniel was working on a novel.'

'I didn't think it would ever get published.' Cara turned to see Ginie, right there.

'Oh . . .' Pippa's face was flushed.

'Hello.' Ginie looked around the group. 'When Made told me you'd all be here today, I just had to come.'

She stepped forward and laid a hand on Miranda's shoulder. 'How are you?'

'I've been better,' said Miranda.

Ginie nodded. 'It must be hard.'

Then she turned to Cara. 'Are you . . . alright?'

Cara shrugged.

'Stupid question.' Ginie shook her head. 'I'm full of them.'

Ginie seemed different, Cara thought. Still tall and angular, but softer, somehow.

Ginie gestured to the book in Miranda's hands. 'I didn't take Daniel's work seriously. In fact, I didn't take *him* seriously.' She sat down on the bench next to Miranda. 'Daniel and I have been going to a relationship counsellor. You got us there, Pippa. Here's your copy.' Ginie riffled through her bag, then passed a book to Pippa.

Pippa flushed a deeper red. 'I'm really sorry about what I . . .'

'Don't be.' Ginie cut her off. 'You told me what you saw that day. That's fair enough.' She looked around the courtyard. 'The thing is, Daniel swore he wasn't unfaithful. He's admitted he got too intimate with Nicole, and I'm furious with both of them. I had to fire Nicole, and it's been a bloody disaster for my work.' She put her head in her hands. 'I've also had to tell Daniel that just because he didn't put his dick in, doesn't mean everything's okay between us.' She looked up. 'It's not as straightforward as it looks. Daniel should *never* have got that close to Nicole, but after Rose was born, I stopped making an effort with him. I wasn't affectionate, I couldn't be arsed. But it's hard when you've got a baby, isn't it?' She hesitated. 'Anyway, you mightn't understand, but I've had to recognise *my* role in this whole bloody shambles.'

Pippa moved closer to Ginie, laying a hand on hers. 'I think we *do* understand.'

Ginie's eyes filled with tears. 'I've got an apology to make, too,' she said. 'To all of you. But especially to you, Pippa. I've said and done some things in this mothers' group that I'm not proud of. I've done a lot of soul-searching and I want to say sorry for being so . . . judgemental.' She looked around the group. 'I've finally figured out that I'm not in control. No one is. Daniel tried to tell me that and so did you, Pippa. And you were right.'

The tears slid down her face. Suzie rummaged in her handbag, pulled out a tissue and dabbed at Ginie's cheeks.

'Thanks,' said Ginie. 'I'm giving Daniel another chance. I have no idea if we'll make it, but we have to try. I mean, apart from anything else, there's Rose to consider.'

No one said anything.

Miranda thumbed the book on her lap. 'Daniel writes really well.'

'Yes, I'll give him that,' said Ginie. 'And it explains a lot about what Daniel went through as a teenager. The main character causes a car accident that kills his parents.' Ginie shook her head. 'It's quite a dark book, but there's hope in there too.' She looked directly at Cara. 'The boy emerges from his guilt, eventually, a better person. Not perfect, but whole.'

Cara stared at Ginie a moment.

But books are like that, she thought, with their endings tied up in pink bows. Her own life was a wasteland. With Astrid gone, she would never be whole again.

Someone coughed behind her.

'I'm sorry,' said a grey-haired woman with a kind face. 'But visiting hours are almost over. It's group time now.' Residents and their visitors began moving indoors.

'Thank you, all of you, for coming,' said Miranda. 'Especially *you*, Cara.' She turned to Suzie. 'I'll call you when I'm home next week. Let's finish that conversation.'

Suzie nodded, her face weary.

They walked together back across the courtyard, through the administration building and towards the entrance. As they descended the stairs onto the street, Wayan tugged at Made's skirt and pointed to his nappy.

Made laughed and turned to Cara. 'Wayan growing so big now, *he* tells *me* when to change nappy.'

Cara smiled, tears running down her face.

'What are you doing *now*?' Richard leaned in the doorway, a haunted look about him.

'I'm going away for a while.' She placed the last of her clothes in a neat pile in the suitcase, next to her toiletry bag. She didn't need to take much. You could buy almost anything there, she'd heard.

'For how long?'

'I don't know.'

'Where?' His voice was shaking.

She plucked a photo frame from her bedside table and removed the image inside.

'Remember this?' She smiled, smoothing the crease in its centre.

'Of course I do.'

The three of them—Cara, Richard and Astrid—seated in their sturdy Toyota sedan, poised for their first ever journey together, home from hospital. Cara could remember how nervous they'd felt, strapping their newborn daughter into an oversized car capsule. Richard had driven so slowly that drivers behind them had honked their horns in frustration. They'd hoped against hope that nothing would go wrong: that Astrid wouldn't cry, need feeding or changing or, God forbid, that an accident might occur. At the time, the short drive home had seemed like a gratuitous risk. But they'd smiled at each other and driven home anyway, trusting that everything would be alright.

'Where are you going?' Richard's tone was curt.

'Bali.'

Richard began pacing the room, muttering under his breath. Then suddenly he was in front of her, seizing her by the shoulders and shaking her with a force that made the air rush out of her lungs.

'Richard!' she shrieked.

His hands fell to his sides. Then, with a howl of rage, he slammed both fists into the wall.

'What in God's name are you doing?' he yelled. 'What are you doing to *me*?'

Slowly, she edged over to the bed, crouched down and slid the pencil case from beneath the mattress. Then she opened the top drawer of her bedside table and found Made's letter.

'It was either this—' she pushed the letter towards him, 'or this.' She opened the pencil case and tipped the seventy sleeping tablets onto the bed.

Richard stared at the fat white pills scattered across their bedspread.

'I'm sorry, Richard,' she whispered. 'I don't expect you to understand. I don't expect you to be here when I get back. But I have to go away now, or I'll die.'

The taxi she'd ordered was idling outside. She felt for her passport in her handbag.

'I'll wait,' he said.

'You don't have to.'

He followed her downstairs.

She paused at the front door. 'I'm so sorry, Richard.'

He held it open for her.

She stepped around a delivery of flowers and turned to lift her suitcase over the doorstep. The aroma of tropical lilies assaulted her; the arrangement had been sitting in the sun all day. She hated those lilies, flowers of death. Good for nothing but covering the rank odour of rot. Ravi would stop sending them eventually.

She hauled her suitcase over the doorstep, knocking the arrangement sideways.

'Let me help,' said Richard.

He pulled the suitcase down the garden path. Weeds had sprouted in the cracks between the pavers, unattended since Astrid's death.

The cab driver met them at the gate and hoisted her suitcase into the boot. Then he opened the rear passenger door, ushering her into the dark anonymity of the back seat.

'Cara.'

Richard stood on the pavement, his eyes searching for hers behind the tinted glass.

She rolled down the window.

'We did our best.' His face was lined with pain.

'You certainly did yours, Richard.'

As the taxi pulled away from the kerb, Richard stood with one hand raised in a half-wave, the other dangling at his side. Like a wounded soldier saluting, faithful to the end.

She blinked back tears, watching the houses and streets of Freshwater disappear beneath the day's dying light. Such familiar territory, a life she'd thought she'd have forever, rendered utterly foreign now. The contours and comforts of suburban life altered irrevocably by a single, arbitrary afternoon. Lives cut loose by chaos, relationships fractured forever. Herself, what she understood as *me*, replaced by a person she didn't care to know.

She checked in at the airport, nodding woodenly at the steward who wished her a *bon voyage*. She was hurtling forward on an uncharted course, to an unknown destination. Towards a beginning or an end? She didn't know. Roll the dice and see what life delivers.

As she approached the opaque doors leading to immigration and the departure lounge, she felt as if her knees might buckle beneath her. Someone with white hair was waving at her. Gordon. And there was Made, carrying Wayan off in the direction of the parents' room.

'You came.' He smiled. 'I'm glad. We both are. You've been

through too much, you poor thing.' Gordon reached out and touched her on the shoulder. She didn't recoil.

'I lost my first wife and little girl twenty years ago,' he said softly. 'And it still hurts, every day.'

She nodded, unable to speak.

'Looks like we've got a farewell party,' he said, pointing behind her.

She turned. A group of people was approaching. There was Suzie and Monika, with Freya toddling between them, one small hand in each of theirs. Pippa and Miranda walked side by side, their arms linked as if propping each other up. Ginie followed next with Daniel, who was carrying Rose on his shoulders. Rose giggled with delight as he tilted her wildly from side to side. Cara's eyes smarted at the sound.

'Goodness,' said Gordon. 'We weren't expecting *all* of you.'

'We couldn't let you leave without saying goodbye,' said Suzie.

She turned to Cara. 'It's good to see you.' Suzie stepped forward and embraced her, pulling her tightly to her chest. Then Pippa joined them, sliding her arms around both of their shoulders. Cara closed her eyes and leaned her head against theirs.

'Come on, ladies.' Suzie beckoned to Miranda and Ginie.

Miranda laughed and nudged Ginie forward.

'Oh, God,' said Ginie. 'Only *you* could suggest a group hug, Suzie.'

They all laughed. Then they stood with their arms around one another, saying nothing at all. The commotion of the airport swirled about them but, for a moment, there was nothing beyond themselves. Their bodies leaned into one another, their breath warm against each others' faces.

Gordon stood at a respectful distance, talking quietly to Daniel and Rose, while Monika jiggled Freya on her hip.

'It's good to see all of you,' whispered Cara. 'Thank you for coming.'

And she meant it. She felt as if her heart might implode. These women had walked alongside her in motherhood, bearing witness to the life and death of her one and only Astrid. She might never see them again, but their presence in her life would endure.

An arm wound itself around her waist from behind. 'My friend,' said Made.

Cara turned and hugged her. 'Hello, Made.'

Behind her, Wayan clung to Made's knees and began to whimper. It was almost six o'clock, close to bedtime. Cara crouched down and touched a hand under his chin.

'Hello, young man,' she said, her voice unsteady.

'Huroo,' he replied.

Cara's mouth dropped open. 'He's *speaking*.'

'Yes, he try now,' said Made. 'But his lip make hard for him.'

Tears began to slide down Cara's cheeks, dripping onto the cold white tiles. Every new development in other people's children would always be a source of both grief and joy.

'We'd better get moving, Made,' said Gordon. 'They'll call our flight soon.'

Cara stood up. Small groups of people, just like them, were gathered outside the doors leading to immigration. Couples and families and friends, hugging and smiling and weeping. Countless last goodbyes as the doors slid open, revealing a sign with red letters advising *Passengers only beyond this point.*

'I have something for you,' said Ginie suddenly, pushing a small white box into Cara's hands. 'For everyone.' She pulled several more from her bag, passing one to each of them.

'Go on, open it.'

Cara eased the lid up and stared at the glittering object inside. A delicate gold pendant, fashioned in the shape of a bird, set with tiny purple amethysts.

'Oh,' she said, taken aback. 'It's beautiful.'

'It's a phoenix,' said Ginie. 'To remind us all that beautiful things can be reborn from ashes. It's hard to imagine that you can go through something terrible and come out the other side stronger. But it's got to be possible.' She looked around the group. 'We've all got things we're trying to leave behind, I guess. And things will be born again, too, whether we're ready for them or not. It's out of our control.' She touched her hand to her belly and, instantly, Cara knew.

'You're pregnant?' Suzie gasped.

Ginie nodded in Daniel's direction. 'I'm learning the art of compromise.'

Things had changed radically for Ginie, Cara thought. For everyone. The thought of a new life growing in Ginie's womb filled her with piercing sadness, and quiet hope. Will I ever have another child? she wondered, her heart aching. Not to replace Astrid. Never to fill the space she had vacated. But to love and to tend for its own sake, to walk alongside amid the capriciousness of life and, finally, to set it free.

Made turned the pendant over in her hand. 'This bird, it like bird in Bali called *garuda*. He is bird of strength. We see him in Bali soon. And tonight we fly Garuda airline to Denpasar.' Made glowed, as she always did when talking about her homeland.

'Well, how appropriate,' said Ginie. She leaned forward and kissed Cara on the cheek. 'Be kind to yourself,' she whispered.

'Thank you,' said Cara. New tears welled up in her eyes. She looked at them all, unsure what to do, what else to say, in this moment.

'Time to go, ladies.' Gordon picked up Wayan and placed a hand on Made's back. 'Ready, Cara?'

Cara nodded, then turned to look at the group one last time. 'Goodbye.'

Made clasped her hand as they moved through the sliding doors.

In the departure lounge, Cara looked out the vast window at the patchwork of runways beyond. Planes landing and taking off with routine monotony; thousands of bodies in motion, bound for foreign lands. This is life, she thought. Millions of arrivals and departures without end.

Beyond the airport, the neon lights of Sydney flickered like the luminous fairyland of storybooks. Cara stared at the sky stretched above them, a deep orange cathedral holding up the edges of the world. A splendour so eternal, yet so transient.

A white vapour trail scarred the otherwise perfect sunset.

Not perfect, but whole.

Acknowledgements

This book has been influenced by a bunch of marvellous people in my life, without whom I would be lonely and ignorant.

My husband, Stuart, has been an unflagging supporter of this novel from the get-go. I am grateful to him for his patience, enthusiasm and daily acts of kindness. He is the most generous person I know.

Virginia Lloyd, my friend and literary agent, has continued to believe in me and my writing, and has provided crucial guidance every step of the way.

I am indebted to the following people—specialists in their vocations—for their technical expertise and beyond-the-call-of-duty support: Dr Connie Diakos, Dr Lisa Brown, Senior Sergeant Danny Russell, Katie Firster and 'Professor Ibu Dokter' Jan Lingard.

Special thanks are also due to Jodie Thomson and Amanda Collins, whose input as both writers and mothers enabled me to craft an infinitely better work.

Thank you to the readers of early drafts—Melissa Attia, Debra Reed, Rachael McLennan and Suzanne Kent—for their feedback and friendship.

The fabulous members of my own mothers' group—Sarah Bramwell, Sarah Barrett, Gaile Pearce, Kim Healey, Michelle Taylor, Natasha Brain and Amanda Thomas—not only gave me helpful suggestions for the novel, but have been personally responsible for preserving my sanity since 2007. I couldn't have done it without you, girls.

I would like to acknowledge and thank the following people, all of whom have provided moral, practical or technical support somewhere along the journey to publication: Lesley Collins, Beverley and Richard Higgins, John Attia, Tim Haydon, Cate Campbell, Margie Bale, Genevieve Freeman, Don Norris, Louise Williams, Ian Thomas, Ellen Fanning, Peter Dredge, Peter Kerr, Simon Longstaff, Jane Porter, Timoer Nugroho, Veronica Abolins, John Fairfax, Mark Nelson, Duncan Trevor-Wilson and Alice Chen, Nathan and Kate Fabian, the late John van Geldermalsen, staff at Tresillian Family Care Centre Willoughby, and Anne Blackstone and all the staff at the Harbord Early Childhood Health Centre.

The team at Allen & Unwin, led by the brilliant Jane Palfreyman, have been nothing short of outstanding. I would like to thank Jo Lyons, Ali Lavau, Kate Butler, Siobhán Cantrill, Catherine Milne, Lisa White, Wenona Byrne, Andy Palmer and Karen Williams, as well as the wider Allen & Unwin team, for your professionalism and enthusiasm.

Finally, to little Oliver, Skye and Luke—all my love, always ... but with special thanks to Skye, my sleepless beauty, for keeping me up and writing.

Fiona Higgins lives in Sydney with her husband and three children. She is the author of *Love in the Age of Drought* and has worked in the philanthropic sector for the past ten years.

www.fionahiggins.com.au
www.facebook.com/fionahigginsauthor